Cassandra Brooke read English Literature at Oxford and embarked on a varied career as art historian, journalist, critic, lecturer and travel guide, broadcaster, scriptwriter for television and radio, historical novelist, Arts Council committee dragon, and as a campaigner for such causes as the preservation of tropical rain forests, the protection of endangered vultures, and women's membership of Lord's cricket ground.

She made her debut as a novelist with the bestselling *Dear Venus* and has gone on to further success with *With Much Love* and *All My Worldly Goods*.

Between these activities, Cassandra has lived in France, achieved two marriages, three children and a large house in south-west London. She is currently at work on another novel.

The Outfit

CASSANDRA BROOKE

POCKET
BOOKS

LONDON · SYDNEY · NEW YORK · TOKYO · SINGAPORE · TORONTO

First published in Great Britain by
Pocket Books, 1995
A Paramount Communications Company

Copyright © Cassandra Brooke, 1995

Simon & Schuster Ltd
West Garden Place
Kendal Street
London W2 2AQ

Simon & Schuster of Australia Pty Ltd
Sydney

A CIP catalogue record for this book is available from the British Library

ISBN 0-671-85255-8

Typeset in Perpetua 12/15pt by
Hewer Text Composition Services, Edinburgh
Printed and bound in Great Britain by
HarperCollins*Manufacturing*, Glasgow

For Anne

———————— o ————————

With Angela's ideas, Gail's know-how and Caroline's connections, how can The Outfit fail? Unless . .

1

Caroline

———————— o ————————

It was the unmistakable sound of autumn, and it carried across the tall Victorian houses lining the common, and only a little more faintly to those set less favourably in the quiet streets which ran down to the railway. Quite possibly even the people who lived beyond the railway-line may have heard it too, not to mention those commuters in the rush-hour blockade who weren't at that moment tuned into the traffic reports or using their car-phones to explain why they'd be late this morning as usual.

It was a sound which told us all that the quiet drift of a London August was finally over; that bruising family holidays in Marbella and Corfu could now be thankfully forgotten; that very soon it would be chestnuts by the fire, bonfire smoke, blackberrying in the old graveyard, and our children battering the trees for conkers and counting the days until Christmas. It was a familiar, comforting sound whose absence would be sorely missed, almost as much as if the September moon failed to rise, or the dawn chorus were never to be heard again.

In fact I'd already begun to think of it as a kind of dawn chorus. It had become part of my life. I opened the kitchen window to make sure I could hear it properly. And there it was – no mistake – perfectly distinct even at this distance and in spite of the wind blustering across the intervening gardens. It wasn't quite as melodious as a nightingale, perhaps, yet it had something of the same dying fall, the same tug on the heart-strings. More reassuring, though, was the fact that it was invariably the same, and its message could never possibly be misunderstood.

'Samantha, . . . will . . . you . . . move . . . your . . . arse . . . and . . . get . . . into . . . the . . . bloody . . . car!'

That was Caroline. I shared a school run with her, all other mothers around the common having by now abandoned the dreadful experience and made their own quieter arrangements. But I was a relative newcomer; I had no ready answer to the demand on the doorstep one day – 'Angela, you can do Monday, Wednesday and Friday; I'll do Tuesday and Thursday' – even though fairness didn't seem to be part of the deal.

Clearly there was something irresistible about Caroline. After a week or two I decided it must be her unshakable assumption that whatever she happened to want must be what everyone else wanted too, and if they protested then obviously they were ignorant or else intolerably selfish.

I managed to avoid either category by simply complying: it made life a lot easier. I was also quite a few years younger than she was. Everything I was learning she'd learnt long ago – and learnt better. She made that quite clear.

What was particularly shattering about the Caroline experience was that her earth-moving righteousness embraced an innocence that Wordsworth would have climbed mountains for. And it was innocence in the most deadly form: she was incapable of lying – she didn't see the point of it, or perhaps didn't even know what it was. Whatever Caroline felt, she let others feel; whatever she knew, she let others know. When applied to herself, this naked truthfulness could be shocking, or it could be wonderfully entertaining; when applied to those around her it could be the sweetest embrace, though more often it was gunshot. I'd already noticed how several houses along the common contained severely wounded occupants who might never recover; and my husband Ralph had taken to referring to the entire area as 'Little Bosnia'.

As for me, I was already nursing a few minor scars.

'Angela, the last woman I met with breasts like yours had a silicone implant. Have you?' (This was on the second occasion we'd met.)

'I rather like fellatio, don't you? But Patrick always

thinks I'll bite it off.' (This was over coffee a week later.)

'Don't be ridiculous; of course the Pope masturbates. Everyone does.' (This was at the first dinner party Ralph and I had been invited to, given by timid neighbours who, as it turned out, were Catholic converts.)

Because they were in awe of her, everyone talked about Caroline. It wasn't exactly gossip because there were no secrets to gossip about. It was more a matter of spreading the latest truth: how wasps had managed to nest above her gas-boiler, and how she'd understood quite correctly that paraffin was the answer, but then assumed that – paraffin being paraffin – you lit it; or how Caroline had gone to dinner at the Armstrongs', got drunk, fallen asleep, and finally woke up at midnight to thank everyone for coming and apologised for the food.

Life on the common, I very soon realised, was life either with or without Caroline. She was our malignant deity, our dark conscience. She presided. If you were someone she declined to talk to, you were dead. And if she did talk to you, you might be dead too.

Had she been a crashing snob it would have been possible to dismiss her, even to laugh at her. But her likes and hates were eccentrically democratic. The local bookmaker came to dinner: the Tory peer two doors down was never invited, and the local vicar absolutely never – she referred to him casually as 'the Rev. Arselick'. Aesthetically she understood the difference between the

4

row of splendid nineteenth-century mansions where she herself lived, and the utility neo-Georgian terrace jobs where we hung out and which flanked the common on either side. But it would never have occurred to her to look up or down on people for such piffling reasons. When Caroline looked down on anyone it was for quite other reasons, often bewildering, and invariably from a terrifying moral height.

It was through the school run that I began to know her. 'I quite like you,' Caroline announced rather severely one morning. She was standing by the car door waiting with unusual patience for my daughter Rachel. Her own daughter Samantha was already huddled on the back seat like an angry ferret. The car was stationed more or less in the middle of the road, together with an ever-increasing number of other cars which were trying to get past. She didn't seem to notice.

'Why don't I drop in for coffee on my way back?' she called out as she drove off at the head of a caravan of snarling commuters. She gave no time for an answer.

She returned around nine-thirty, leaving her car more or less where it had been before, and strode in. I'd never really looked at Caroline closely. She was a pretty woman when the scowl lifted: blonde, elegant, and around thirty-five, I imagined — in other words seven or eight years older than me. She was wearing a riding jacket buttoned over jeans which were tight enough to show she had extremely good legs. She didn't bother to smile.

I stood watching as Caroline's eyes took in our little

two-bedroom house with its pocket-handkerchief garden, and at that moment everything most likely to provoke disapproval seemed to stand out like beacons – the carriage-lantern, the posters, the cheap reproductions, the Axminster carpet. Outside the window the frightful birdbath with cupids which Ralph's mother had given us chose to be in full sunlight. A spider had spun a tightrope across the view of the dustbins.

Caroline's house by comparison was so effortlessly grand, so carelessly adorned with heirlooms, brownish paintings that were no doubt frightfully valuable, wheezing clocks of amazing age, ormolu this and that, and a hundred-and-one other mementoes of ancestral ease and privilege. There was nothing *nouveau* about Caroline's *richesse*: everything hinted at a family which had already enjoyed a famously long shelf-life. Among a number of sepia photographs framed on her mantelpiece was one of a Byronic gentleman in a uniform encrusted with gold braid. 'He was from Montenegro,' Caroline had explained casually when she saw me gazing at it. 'My great-great-grandfather.' Was he a general? I enquired. 'No!' she replied in the same lazy voice. 'He was king.'

All we had on our mantelpiece were a few unpaid bills and a holiday postcard from Guernsey. I thought she'd never stop gazing around her. My life was being fiercely inspected.

'It's quite small,' she said eventually. 'But then there's only the three of you, I suppose.' Caroline's

6

two elder children were at suitable boarding schools. Then she turned to me briskly. 'God, this is good coffee. Angela, how do you make it?'

Nonplussed, I explained that I poured hot water on to ground coffee-beans. Caroline looked disbelieving, and changed the subject.

'How do you keep a figure like that? I diet and all I get is a tyre round my middle.' And she lifted her blouse to demonstrate. It was a very small tyre. 'Disgusting! I hate it. And three children are death to the boobs. You wait.' Then, without waiting herself, she added, 'Is Ralph good in bed?'

I gulped and said yes, he was.

'You're lucky,' she went on. 'Patrick's terrible. If I had to rely on him I'd starve.' And suddenly she laughed. 'You know his father owns most of Rutland: it's no coincidence it's the smallest county in England. Where do you come from?'

'Ipswich,' I said.

Caroline looked surprised.

'Where's that?'

'Suffolk.'

She looked thoughtful.

'Ah!' she said, gazing out of the window. 'Suffolk! Yes! I think one of my ex-lovers owned much of that. Or was it Norfolk?'

A crescendo of hooting outside broke her train of thought.

'I must go,' she announced. 'I'm supposed to be

interviewing a new gardener at ten. I hope he understands about vines.'

The front door slammed. I could hear her swearing at the man who'd been trying to get his car out for the past quarter of an hour. Ralph came downstairs at that moment, looking haggard. He'd been learning his part for a play at the Royal Court. I smiled.

'Caroline asked if you were any good in bed.'

Ralph brightened.

'And what did you say?'

'That you were.'

'Thank God!'

'Apparently Patrick isn't.'

Ralph helped himself to coffee.

'Hardly surprising. It'd be like fucking a Rottweiler.'

One day I realised I'd got over being frightened of Caroline. I liked her because she was dreadful – and fun; whereas most of the people I'd met along the common were nice – and boring. The coffee sessions after the school run began to grow into a habit, either at our house or at Caroline's, depending on who'd been driving Samantha and Rachel to school, or more often depending on Caroline's whim. When it was warm enough we'd sit in the garden, either on my patch of grass between the dahlias, or under Caroline's vine trellis, which was pruned in such a way that she could be aristocratically topless if she chose – 'which I rarely do now gravity's taking its toll,' she exclaimed with a laugh. 'You're so young: I hate it,' she added. Ralph was nearly always out rehearsing now – thank God he was in work – and Patrick was doing his thing in the City, Caroline explained languidly. She didn't seem to know exactly what her husband did, and it was clear she didn't need the money he earned. We on the other hand needed every penny Ralph usually didn't earn.

I suppose one of the things that drew me to her was the absurd contrast in our lives and expectations. And maybe for Caroline I had a similar novelty value. Every now and then she'd drop a comment about her family. 'Navy. Generations and generations of them,' she explained in that familiar languid voice. 'Always at sea, the lot of them: only came on dry land to breed – like penguins. And even then they couldn't forget the navy. My father was an admiral; used to communicate with us through signals. He'd run them up a flag-pole in the garden. When I became Deb of the Year he signalled, "Am heading out to sea – Full Steam Astern." We never saw him again for six months.' And she laughed.

'But what about you?', she added suddenly. 'At the age when I was being Deb of the Year, what were you doing?'

I said I'd been working in a bank, with a clutch of five O Levels of the nondescript kind girls were supposed to achieve at my school.

'A bank!' Caroline looked taken aback. 'A merchant bank? Which one? Lazard's?'

It was my turn to laugh.

'No. Just a bank. In Ipswich.'

Caroline continued to look surprised. I realised she'd probably never met anyone who'd worked in a bank except through a grille.

'Goodness!' she said. 'And what were they like, the people in your bank?'

She made it sound like Alcatraz.

I explained that the girls were recruited because they were like me – with five O Levels. And the men were recruited because they were handy with figures; 'and they were certainly handy with mine,' I added. That pleased her a lot. I was gaining confidence with Caroline by this time: I wouldn't have dared say things like that a month or so earlier. I even told her about the assistant manager who'd called me into his office one day to ask me if I knew what it meant when a man had a large nose; and proceeded to show me what it did mean.

Caroline gave out a yelp of pleasure.

'I don't believe it. And what did you do?'

I told her that since I'd never seen a man's cock before I didn't have the faintest idea if it was large or not. In any case I hadn't liked the look of it much and left it well alone – and all others like it; which was how I'd kept my virginity intact, though not always my clothing.

Caroline's face was radiant.

'Goodness, I *do* like you. You're almost as vulgar as I am. Just think of it. I was being groped at the Queen Charlotte's Ball, and you were being groped in a bank.

How wonderful! What were you like then? I was a real bitch. I still am.'

I tried to recall what I was like at sixteen or seventeen. I had a cascade of dark hair, I said, and a figure that turned people's heads. Men gulped. Women spat. People used to treat me as though I reeked of sin. In fact, if I reeked of anything it was probably innocence and cheap perfume.

Caroline gave another snort of pleasure.

'I always wanted to reek of sin. But you've got to be silent for that, and I never stopped talking. So – go on! – what happened then?'

There was something about Caroline's bluntness which was infectious.

'My parents were killed in a car crash returning from a Rotary Club dance,' I said. 'That was when I realised I loved them.'

There was total silence. Caroline just looked at me. Then she put a hand on my arm, and squeezed it.

'God!' was all she said. Her face looked as though I'd slapped it, and unconsciously I suppose I had. I realised Caroline had probably never been on her own in her entire life – had never had nothing, had never had nobody. Whereas all I'd ever had was home, and suddenly home was alone.

She asked me where home had been. I told her it had been a semi-det. in Ipswich at the end of one of those meandering suburban roads which pretend to be country lanes. All the houses had looked precisely the same, and bore scented names – Rose Haven, Jasmine Lodge, The Lilacs, and so on. The one next-door was called Bougain-Villa, which I'd never understood. Ours had been christened Vine Cottage, which I didn't understand either since there was no vine; and in the days when I thought I hated my parents I used to refer to it as Vile Cottage. But once they were dead I suddenly loved it, just as I loved them. I suppose it was all of them I had left. It was family. Living there alone I relived what might have been, and fed on sadness. I was eighteen.

Caroline went on gazing at me incredulously.

'Well,' she said after a while. 'Think of it. At that age I was living in Wilton Crescent, skiing in Davos, riding to hounds and going to bed with rock stars.'

I smiled.

'But I did catch up,' I assured her. 'One day I decided to stop loving and grieving. I sold Vine Cottage, pocketed the money and left for London. I had my nest-egg, and knew that life was about to begin.'

'And how long did it take?'

'Oh, about a week.'

We both laughed.

We were walking on the open common. It was the morning of the first heavy frost. The long grass was crisp underfoot, and the leaves were falling like shattered glass. Caroline was wearing a long black cape with a hood: she looked like Lara in *Doctor Zhivago*.

'I bet it's a Bill Gibb,' I said.

I was beginning to learn how to tease Caroline. It wasn't something she was used to. She looked at me, surprised.

'How did you guess?'

'Because I used to have one too. A yellow one.'

What Caroline was thinking was: How the hell could someone like you ever afford a Bill Gibb cape? – and I wouldn't have put it past her to have announced as much. But for once Caroline's truthfulness deserted her; she merely said, 'Really! And what happened to it?' which was tame by her standards.

'I had to sell it?' I said.

Now I was the one being truthful.

I could see Caroline struggling to take all this in, fitting it into her picture of what I was – the ingenuous young wife of a none-too-successful actor living in a modest terrace-house and running an old Volkswagen Beetle.

'All right, it's my turn to guess,' she said. 'You married Ralph Merton when he was the hottest property in television. And then he wasn't any more.'

She looked pleased with herself, standing there in the frost and jabbing at a frozen tussock with her boot. She threw back the hood of her cape and gave me a quizzical look.

'So, how did you come to marry him? You of all people,' she added, perhaps not intending to be rude.

'I sneezed,' I said.

She raised her eyes to the heavens.

'Oh, for Christ's sake, Angela.'

'It's true. I sneezed all over him.'

It *was* true. Fresh from Ipswich, I'd got a job in a Chelsea boutique. And Ralph came in. Of course I recognised him: there'd been this romantic drama series on television which had been running for years. Ralph was the hero – incredibly handsome and dangerous-looking. He was the dream of every girl I'd ever met, and he was always in the tabloids attending one function or another with some half-naked bimbo on his arm. 'Good morning, Mr Merton,' I said. 'Can I help you?' All the other assistants were busy, but their eyes were throwing daggers at me. I was wearing something tight-fitting and I wondered if he noticed my stomach shaking, though I don't think it was my stomach he was particularly interested in. All sorts of wild creatures were flying around inside me. And then I sneezed. I couldn't find a Kleenex. I sneezed again, and again. It was terrible. My eyes were watering. I couldn't see anything. My mascara must have been running. I was a mess. Then suddenly this handkerchief appeared, thrust gently into my hand. I gurgled a kind of thanks, mopped up and tried to look composed. He was laughing. 'Keep it,' he said – 'for another time.' Then he added, as if it was the most natural thing in the world, 'Perhaps there could be another time. How about dinner?'

And that was it. I'd only been there a week – the fresh-faced girl from Ipswich. I stood there in the shop long after he'd gone, clutching his handkerchief in one hand and a piece of paper with the address of a restaurant in the other – *in his handwriting*! Wow! Then I wafted home to my bedsit saying to myself – 'I'm about to lose my virginity to the sexiest man in England.' And I wondered whether there'd be champagne and roses by the bed.

'Oh Jesus, how corny!' Caroline snorted. 'Pure soap!' Then in an irritated voice – 'Well, go on!'

She grew even more irritated when I said, 'Well, we went to bed, didn't we.'

She clicked her tongue.

'You're hopeless. What did he say to you?'

'He asked me wherever I'd got such a body from. And I was so confused I said "In Ipswich", which made him laugh. Well, I couldn't exactly say "At Marks & Spencer's", could I?'

Caroline was now grinning with pleasure.

'You're a hoot! I am glad I met you.'

So I told her how one of the assistants in the boutique had sworn there was absolutely no muscle in a man's prick; and I remembered lying there in Ralph's bed thinking, Christ, if this isn't muscle, what the hell is it? Then I explained how I'd walked home the next morning with such a smile on my face that people turned their heads, and all the summer seemed to shine on me – until I said to myself – 'Angela, you've just behaved like a sixties flower-child, and this is supposed to be the dark and dangerous eighties. Supposing you're pregnant. Supposing he's got VD. Or worse.' The thought wiped the smile off my face. Next time I'd be very careful: except of course there wouldn't be a next time. 'Ralph Merton,' I remembered saying, 'I hope you had a good one-night stand. Thank God I'm not in love with you.'

But there was a next time. And the next. And the next. In the evenings we used to go to restaurants where Ralph believed he wouldn't be recognised. At least this was what he claimed. He always *was* recognised, and usually the eye-meet was as blatant as the cleavage, though I had little difficulty winning that one. I couldn't help finding it all rather a turn-on, and we used to go home and make tremendous love.

Then I went to live with him. Soon I was everywhere – in all the tabloids – 'Ralph Merton's new love, beautiful nineteen-year-old Angela Blake'. Some were cruder – 'Busty boutique girl Angela captivates superstud Ralph', or 'Ralph Merton's Ipswich eyeful', and once simply 'Angela – Oh wow!' My statistics grew more vital with every story. I was photographed at first nights, at gala premières, at Goodwood, at Tramp, at the Gavroche, on film sets, on yachts, with Ferraris, with anyone who was anyone, everywhere. I was photographed wearing Bruce Oldfield, Mary Quant, the Emmanuelles, Caroline Charles, and on one occasion (courtesy the *paparazzi*) nothing at all. Designers threw their creations at me, model agencies their offers, and Ralph's former mistresses their insults.

It was all wonderful, bewildering, and unreal. I grew up in a dream.

'And then I married him,' I said.

'Where?' Caroline asked.

'Battersea Registry Office.'

She threw back her head and laughed.

'Brilliant! I got married in the chapel of the House of Lords.'

She never used to talk much about Patrick, except to be mildly rude about him – at least, mild for Caroline. He gambled too much. He drank too much. He went to bed ridiculously early, and then was too pissed to get it up, and even if he did you hardly noticed the difference. The only thing he ever did with the children was to take them to race meetings. He'd spend the weekends on the golf-course with his cronies. He was idle. He was a philistine. He was *boring*.

In fact I didn't find him boring at all, partly no doubt because he fancied me. He was funny, rather pretty in a vain and effeminate way, and entirely immune to Caroline's jibes, which if anything he provoked. His world was an old-Etonian club, and it had done him very well: somebody he'd been to school with could always be relied upon to oil the wheels when necessary, and his no doubt substantial salary appeared to come as effortlessly as turning on a tap. Just as effortless was his fund of scurrilous stories about the grand and great, which no doubt reached him on the same Etonian grape-vine as the directorships that came his way. He was, I suppose, in his mid-forties, though not a line of pain or strain marked his face, and his hair remained prettily curled. It was impossible to imagine the Hon Patrick Uppingham growing old; or even growing up, as Ralph unkindly remarked.

But a philistine he certainly was. Eton had done him no favours there, and nothing could have bothered him less. Caroline threw a dinner party which had a mildly intellectual flavour, and for some reason included us. The conversation eventually circled around recent novels we'd enjoyed or hated, until there seemed no way we'd ever be liberated to talk about anything else, and Ralph was being particularly intense about Márquez, when Patrick dropped a jewel into the muddied waters.

'I think I read a book once,' he announced wistfully.

Caroline had the presence of mind not to contradict him, and the evening was rescued.

I wondered if in fact they were devoted to one another. Their life was a double-act, and I imagined it was probably being rehearsed even as they'd stood by the altar rails of the chapel of the House of Lords. Perhaps it would see them through.

Ralph wasn't a man given to envy, yet he found it hard dealing with ease and wealth, having had both and lost both. He was twelve years older than me, and was already viewing the approach of his fortieth birthday with a stoic gloom. It wasn't just that he was no longer offered the sexy romantic parts to play on television: he was increasingly aware that he was just another middle-aged actor in a crowded marketplace

– more handsome than many others, certainly, but not conspicuously more gifted – and that the huge success he'd once enjoyed had probably been due to phenomenal luck rather than phenomenal talent.

It made him look tired. The eyes still crinkled, but they no longer crinkled wickedly, only with scepticism.

I often wondered if being faithful to me had taken the heat out of him. Ralph's passions were the slow burn of middle age.

'Are you happy with him?' Caroline asked.

We were in my house this time. It was snowing. We would have a White Christmas for once. School had broken up, and Rachel and Samantha were building a snowman on the common. There seemed to be some disagreement over where to put the carrot: I put that down to Caroline's influence. We could hear their shrieks, and catch the occasional glimpse of a blonde head and a dark head bobbing about between the trees.

'Yes,' I said. 'I am happy. Don't I look it?'

Caroline was in one of her probing moods.

'You look disgracefully sexy in black. Do you have affairs?'

I shook my head. It seemed more non-committal than saying no, even though no was true. It was also true that I'd sometimes thought about it, but only safely in the abstract: I couldn't imagine actually being unfaithful to Ralph, living with all those lies, all that pain, all that sense of betrayal. It was more the thought of only having had one man in my entire life: didn't human experience perhaps require more than this? Could I not please have my unlived youth back again without anyone noticing?

'Huh! Oh come all ye faithful, eh!' was Caroline's reaction. She would have liked not to believe me. 'Don't you ever get bored?'

I could feel Caroline was on the war-path, and needed to step out of the way.

'Never!' I said roundly.

She gave a deep sigh.

'Oh God! Why did I ever think you were interesting?'

There were times when I decided Caroline was dreadful – heartless and parasitic; that she was far too cocooned by privilege to understand how people sometimes have to cling to the need for survival, and cling together in order to do so, grow closer by fighting together. Dreams and longings take a back seat: trust is more important. My life with Ralph had been increasingly like that – after those few golden years.

She was in an altogether jollier mood the next time I saw her. It was a few days before Christmas, and she'd driven a bunch of children to a party on the far side of Richmond Park and, I suspect, had enjoyed the party spirit off-stage while Father Christmas was busy ho-ho-ho-ing it with the kids in the living room.

At any rate she returned at dusk to the accompaniment of two police cars and many raised voices. Rachel dashed in, her eyes bright as coals. Samantha's mum had crashed the park gates, she explained breathlessly. 'Twice!

They were just closing them, and she drove through. It was wonderful, Mum. Real cops and robbers. We were yelling, "Go on, go on, Mrs Uppingham! Faster!" And there was another police car at the far gate, and she crashed that one too. We hit eighty down Roehampton Lane, Mum.'

I could see that next term I'd be doing the school run Monday, Tuesday, Wednesday, Thursday and Friday. What was the penalty for breaking and entering a royal park? And how long did one lose one's licence for these days?

But I misjudged Caroline, as so often. I ventured cautiously into the street just in time to see the police sergeant tear up the charge-sheet.

'But don't do it again, Mrs Uppingham,' I heard him say. It was the voice of a man resigned to defeat. 'And next time a child is taken ill it might be better to call an ambulance.'

Caroline had one hand soulfully on the sergeant's wrist, while the other was wiping away a tear.

'Well, that was fun,' she said, throwing her coat down on the kitchen table. 'Such a nice man.'

I assumed the other children had been left to make their own way home in the dusk.

We opened a bottle of wine, and Caroline threw herself into a chair.

'Jesus!' she said. 'I'm a lousy mother.' There was a pause while she reflected on this, and sipped at her wine. 'Perhaps we all are. Except you, probably: I'm sure you're frightfully good at it. You would be.' She made it sound like a fault. Then she gave a dramatic sigh, usually the signal for a pronouncement to come. It came. 'Yes, we all are. If you're lower-class you clip them round the ear and turn them into delinquents, and if you're upper-class you banish them to boarding schools and turn them into delinquents. No wonder they grow up hating us.'

I said I thought all that was rubbish, and she looked quite pleased. Then, as always when challenged, she changed the subject.

'Don't you regret getting married so young?'

'In some ways,' I said cautiously.

'And never having had a lover. That amazes me.'

We were back to this again. I wished she wouldn't go on about it: I was beginning to feel a freak.

'And to think you could have anyone you liked. You're clever. You're stunning. You've got a body a man would die for. Patrick certainly would, as you know. I sometimes wish he would.' Caroline laughed, and poured herself some more wine. 'Mind you, I wouldn't recommend him: it's like making love to a betting slip, and you know the horse is going to lose.' Then she looked serious for a moment. 'Funny, isn't it, being married to a man called Uppingham? I've often thought it should be Halfwayuppingham. D'you think he'd change it by deed poll if I asked him nicely?'

I was used to these marital endearments by this time, and simply smiled. Caroline's eyes did a vague wander round the room. I saw them settle on a photograph of Ralph taken in his days as a television star.

'Christ, he was gorgeous,' she exclaimed. Then, with unusual tact, she added, 'He still is, I suppose. It's just that fame is so sexy, isn't it? Knowing a man's only got to click his fingers.'

Didn't I know! I used to fight them off.

Caroline was still gazing at the photograph.

'So what went wrong?' she asked suddenly.

I just laughed.

'Everything,' I said. 'They axed his series. That's what.'

Caroline looked puzzled. She couldn't see the connection. I realised that, for her, money was something you either had or didn't have; and if you had it you went on having it – it was salted away in shares, or houses, or land, or family trusts, or life insurances, where nothing short of a marxist revolution could do anything worse than nibble at it with taxes and death duties.

I tried to explain. I told her how I'd assumed at first that offers would pour in for Ralph: that it would be like Sean Connery after 007. But that it hadn't turned out that way. Ralph had pointed out ruefully that when you'd been associated for so long with a single role, you *were* that role. People saw you as that, and they didn't believe you if you tried to be something else. You got treated as though you'd died, until after a while people assumed you had.

Now, five or six years later, Ralph did the occasional

voice-over for TV commercials because he had a lovely voice. And recently he'd been offered smallish stage parts here and there: evidently he'd been dead long enough to be permitted a small resurrection.

'But ghosts don't get paid all that well,' I said. 'And they don't have a union.'

I didn't think Caroline knew about unions, except that they were apt to call inconvenient strikes.

'What about Hollywood?' she suggested vaguely.

Caroline made it sound like a hotel you could just check into, and never have to pay the bill. I explained that Hollywood called you, you didn't call it. And – well! – they hadn't. And by now they certainly wouldn't.

She invariably left me feeling troubled. It was rather like being taken to court for a crime you hadn't committed, only to realise in mid-session that maybe you had done it after all. It was those innocent leading questions that were so easy to answer until you tried to answer them, and then what you uttered suddenly didn't sound true any longer. Was I happy? Why didn't I have affairs? What went wrong?

Ralph's play was opening in the New Year. I'd see less and less of him. Evenings on my own. Much of the day on my own: just Rachel rushing in and out between friends. What was I doing? I could hear Caroline's voice – 'Christ, you're so young!' I was twenty-eight. It didn't feel young. I felt wasted.

When Caroline phoned it was always as though one ought

to have been there on the spot to save her the trouble. The voice was a summons.

'Angela!'

It was January. The snow had gone. London was enjoying one of its non-winters. There wasn't even a frost. Our jasmine was in full flower. There was even a snowdrop or two. And people walked around without coats.

'Angela, I'm having a garage sale.'

Why Caroline should choose to hold a garage sale in mid-January I didn't ask. She explained that she wanted to get rid of a whole lot of old clothes: she needed the cupboard space, and besides she was too fat to wear most of them. I didn't believe that: Caroline was always convinced she was becoming gross. I suspected this was one of those frenetic bursts of energy which would occasionally overtake her, and usually swamp anyone near her.

'Come round and help, could you?'

I'm not sure what I imagined 'a whole lot of old clothes' to be. I think I probably envisaged sweaters with holes in the elbow, frayed jeans and some of Patrick's discarded shirts. What I certainly hadn't expected were Gucci leather boots, Jean Muir dresses and Lanvin suits. There was a pile five feet high on a trestle-table by the time I arrived, and more to come. I made a rough calculation of the original cost, and gulped.

'Caroline, you're mad,' I said.

She ignored me.

'I can't be bothered to price them,' she said. 'Everything's ten pounds. What I want you to do is stick some notices up in a few stationers. For next Saturday morning. Oh, and pin a few on the trees around the common. Patrick's got a photocopier: it shouldn't take long.'

Then she was off to fetch another pile.

I eyed the Gucci boots. They were gorgeous – purple leather and suede, slim and soft. I put them on before Caroline returned.

'Do you think I could have these as my fee?' I enquired.

She glanced at me dismissively.

'Oh, take whatever you like.'

I added a rainbow-coloured Paul Costello jacket and an Yves Saint-Laurent silk scarf. I laughed to myself. It wasn't so very long ago that designers were throwing clothes like these at me for the honour of their creations being seen on 'Ralph Merton's Ipswich eyeful'. Now here they were being thrown at me again.

I made out the notices. I took them round various stationers. I pinned them to the trees. I earned my keep. And, as I might have known, I was expected to man the store for much of that Saturday morning, it being a little too chilly for Caroline, who in any case was nursing a slight hangover. And I wore her purple Gucci boots.

'Oh Christ, Angela, what on earth made me give those away?' she announced, emerging from the house

26

and staring fiercely at my legs. 'I must have been mad. They look glorious on you.'

She was right: they did. I decided that Caroline must have worn them at least twice.

By midday just about everything had gone, most of it to a wild-looking woman with a tumble of red hair who never said a word, but every now and then would add another dress, or suit, or pair of shoes, to the growing pile I was guarding for her. Finally she stood back, gave me a hard look, and produced a wad of twenty-pound notes.

'There you are, me darlin',' she said in a warm Irish brogue. 'You're a fool. They're worth much more than that. You should learn.'

And she handed me her card. On it was printed 'The Designers Emporium. Manager – Abigail O'Connor', with an address in Knightsbridge, and a phone number.

'Call in some time when you're clearing out the next lot,' she added. 'It might amuse you anyway. It's where you learn about life, I can tell you.' And she laughed, tossing her hair back from her face. 'Now, darlin', d'you think you could give me a hand with these?'

Caroline reappeared in time to see the contents of her wardrobe vanish into the back of a van. I showed her the woman's card, and Caroline gave a snort.

'You mean, I've just been ripped off by some shark in the rag trade!'

The Irish lady poked her head out of the back of the van. Her face told me instantly what she thought of Caroline.

'If you're such a bleedin' idiot as to sell stuff like that for nothing, you don't deserve any better, do you?'

She drove off. Caroline gave another snort.

'What an appalling woman!'

I laughed. Because I already had an idea. A wonderful idea.

2

Abigail

———————— ○ ————————

Ideas, whenever I had them, needed to pass the bath test. As I lay there deliciously soaking I would challenge them to survive; and it was no small challenge since the immediate effect of a bath was to fill my mind with wonderful and beguiling distractions.

The first distractions would be shamelessly narcissistic – I'd admire my body. I had long legs, slim hips, and breasts which rose proudly above the shampoo, though I imagined that one day they would begin to drift soggily around like sea anemones in the tide; but thank heavens not just yet. Then I'd begin to imagine other eyes admiring my body, and I have to say they weren't often eyes the Church of England would have approved of; but then one is promiscuous in daydreams, and there's something about the embrace of water which suggests the touch of unfamiliar hands. A bath is a sexy place to be.

From bodies my mind would float to higher things

– not very much higher perhaps, but at least more outward-looking: namely, my life. What was I doing with it? How was I making out? Where was it all leading? From the helplessness of being in a warm bath it was so easy to plan ventures which a mere foot set outside the front door would immediately discourage; and of course I knew this perfectly well. None the less, basking there, those plans invariably raced through my head. I would learn a language, qualify for the Bar, write a novel, become a cottage industry, engage myself in charitable works, read the great philosophers. And so on.

There being no coherent pattern to these thoughts, least of all any conviction, they tended to survive no longer than the bath water. I could almost hear them gurgle away. But this particular day was different. It was the evening after Caroline's sale. My Gucci boots stood there like a trophy – my fee. I dried myself and, pulling on a sweater and jeans, announced to the four walls of our bathroom – 'To be a wife and mother is *not* enough.'

The certainty with which I heard myself utter this convinced me of something else – something considerably more important. That my idea was right: absolutely right!

It had passed the bath test.

I gazed at the card. '*The Designers Emporium*', it said. '*Manager – Abigail O'Connor*'. I thought hard about what I was going to say to her. Perhaps the best course was simply to remind her of the invitation to visit the place, and then to play it by ear. It would be rash to assume anything: I might after all have made a terrible mistake.

So after dithering a while I rang. A man answered. A man of sorts, that is: his sibilants whistled down the phone like snakes. Oh Lord, it was that kind of place, I thought. But I persisted.

'Please might I speak to Mrs O'Connor?' (I assumed she was a Mrs.)

More sibilants followed.

'Who sshall I ssay it iss?'

I said she wouldn't know my name, but that I'd sold her a whole lot of clothes the other day.

'One minute pleasse.'

There was a long pause. Then a boisterous Irish voice came down the phone.

'So, have you cleared out another attic then?'

I laughed and said no I hadn't; in any case the clothes hadn't been mine; I'd been selling them for a friend.

'Ah yes! That'd be the rich bitch who turned up her nose at me. I remember. I meet plenty like her. All money and no manners.'

That seemed to sum up Caroline rather well, but I didn't say so. I explained that I'd very much like to take up her invitation to come to the shop and see what went on.

'Of course. Be a fly on the wall by all means,'

31

Abigail said cheerfully. 'You'll see some rare sights with any luck. But for the love of Jaysus don't laugh out loud, will you? Only I'm allowed to do that.'

There was an earthy chuckle. In the background I could hear the sibilants chatting up a customer. I suggested Wednesday, and we agreed on ten-thirty.

I decided to say nothing to Ralph, and certainly not to Caroline. Rachel was spending the last week of the school holiday with a friend, so I wouldn't have to hurry back. I was absurdly excited. I told myself that adventures didn't get much smaller than this; none the less it felt like a giant step for womankind – or at least for this woman.

I did one other thing. I rang the building society. For almost ten years my nest-egg had been sitting there – the money I'd got for Vine Cottage. I'd kept an occasional eye on it, watching it grow little by little, knowing one day I'd need it to hatch. Ralph had always refused to let me spend it on 'us', whether out of pride or generosity I never quite knew. It was entirely mine, he insisted, whenever I offered it at a time of crisis. He never said so, but I think he regarded it as my 'pension', knowing he might have very little to leave me if he died first. And so in the end I decided to keep it.

The manager told me what it was worth, and I wrote the sum in my diary. Then I took the bus into town, feeling a truant.

Abigail had told me I couldn't miss the place: it was 'opposite the carbuncle'. There was no problem seeing what she meant. A 'thirties' block of flats had been 'improved' by some Post-Modernist architect to the tune of a spiral staircase on the outside, rising six floors and entirely glazed-in so that it resembled a giant syringe. I had a vision of people being squirted up it; then the happier vision of some Highlander battling for six flights to keep the secret of what a Scotsman wears under his kilt. Caroline, who claimed she hated wearing knickers in summer, would have been in deep trouble.

And there, right opposite, it was. The Designers Emporium. I walked in. Abigail waved, and beckoned me over. She was just finishing with a customer who had 'Embassy Wife' written all over her, and had brought in something expensively horrible. Abigail shook the garment out and handed it to the young man I took to be the one with the sibilants, who received it between forefinger and thumb as though he were plucking a cherry from a cake. Abigail talked ceaselessly throughout the proceedings, hurrying here and there, grabbing a receipt book, searching for a pen, taking a swig of coffee; and all the time her storm of red hair was enjoying a life of its own. I sat unobtrusively to one side of the desk, and admired the performance.

At least an hour must have passed while I simply watched. Occasionally Abigail would lean over as she passed by and make some remark about a customer – who she was divorcing, whose mistress she was, who was involved in what financial scandal: she could have edited a gossip column from this place. Yet in appearance The Designers Emporium could have been just an up-market dry cleaners. Plain metal racks of clothes lined each wall, and fierce strip-lighting banished all shadows. 'Soft lights are fockin' useless,' Abigail explained. 'You've got to be able to spot the stains and the cigarette burns.'

It was only when you peered at the designer labels that you knew where you were. They were all there – Bruce Oldfield, Bill Gibb, the Emmanuelles, Caroline Charles, Jean Muir, Lanvin, Joseph, Chrissie Clyne, Chanel, Yves Saint-Laurent, Paul Costello, Umberto Ginochietti. It made me smile: so many of them were the same designers who used to will their creations on me in my salad days as Ralph Merton's wide-eyed new girlfriend. And here I was in my faded jeans.

The assistant I'd spoken to on the phone was called Timothy. He fluttered a lot, and was sweet to me as gays always are. Abigail treated him like a pet poodle. 'Go and serve that old cow, there's a good boy,' she whispered, giving him a pat on the bum which made him giggle. Then she beckoned me to the back of the shop where there was a coffee machine. 'No dragons today so far,' she declared, sounding disappointed. 'If Madeleine comes in, I'll give you a nudge. She's the worst. Her husband's just left her, and she's starving for another fight.'

It was a simple enough business, Abigail explained. There were so many rich bitches who bought designer clothes – 'like that friend of yours' – and naturally they couldn't be seen wearing the same outfit more than twice; so the problem was what the hell to do with the bloody things taking up so much room? It wasn't the money that mattered, it was space. 'So they bring them to me: if it's space they want, they can have it. Two months — sale or return. I take 20 per cent. Often they don't even bother to come back: probably in Hawaii by then, or divorced.'

Abigail laughed, throwing back her whirl of red hair while keeping a sharp eye on Timothy as he performed a pantomime round the 'old cow' who had tried on a Jean Muir number that would have flattered someone half her age.

So the prices were ridiculously low, Abigail went on. All the clients knew that: they could pick up a six-hundred-pound Joseph suit for eighty or ninety, worn a couple of times at most, and everyone believed their husbands were as rich as Croesus or they had a lover in the Mafia — or the Vatican.

'Vanity to vanity. That's what it's all about, darlin'. You can't lose.'

She laughed again, then put down her coffee-cup and sailed across the room to greet a gorgeous stick-insect, all eyes and legs, who'd half-opened the door and was standing there uncertainly holding a package. Abigail took it from her without a word, unwrapped it, then held up some floating creation in black silk.

'A wicked girl you are, to be sure,' I heard her

say. 'But leave it with me, darlin'. I know someone for that. About a hundred.'

The mirage of a girl floated away with a shy nod of the head. Abigail came back carrying the dress.

'You can't blame them, can you?' she said. And she placed a small label on the table in front of me. It bore the name of a leading young designer. 'They aren't supposed to sell them, of course, the models. But what are you supposed to do if you're sixteen and just beginning? You remove the label, don't you. In a couple of years that kid'll be good for half a million, and we shan't see her then, I promise you.'

The phone went, as it had infrequently all morning. Abigail put on a Knightsbridge voice – 'The Emporium' – and gave me a wink. Then her voice sharpened, and she made a grimace. 'No, not exactly,' I heard her say. 'Lady Fortescue's dead.' Abigail gazed up towards the ceiling. 'No, I don't know of any other . . . That could be embarrassing . . . Well, if you insist.'

She raised two fingers as she replaced the receiver.

'The fockin' boss. Am I supposed to manage this shop, or am I not?' Abigail looked thoroughly out of sorts, and gave her body a shake as if to restore her composure. 'Fock her!'

The 'old cow' had gone, without the Jean Muir. Timothy was preening in front of the mirror. It was nearly one o'clock, and time I came to the point.

'Abigail, could I take you to lunch?' I said.

She looked surprised.

'You don't need to.'

'But I'd like it.'

'All rightee,' she said after a moment. Then she called out to Timothy – 'Hold the fort for an hour, darlin'. And don't buy a fockin' thing. We'll be in Luigi's if Princess Di comes in with her wedding-dress.

'I musn't get too dronk,' she added quietly. 'Come on then.' And she handed me my coat.

It turned out to be a lot more than an hour, and Abigail did get drunk. So did I. But by the time we left the restaurant around three I'd learnt a great deal about her. More to the point, I'd found a friend. More to the point still, my idea had taken wing: it had become a project. A new life had suddenly rolled out in front of me.

'Call me Gail,' she insisted as the waiter showed us to a table by the far window. 'I'm Abigail to no one but the fockin' boss.'

She was a large woman, and like so many women with that Irish hair and complexion it was hard to guess her age, though I imagined her to be in her early forties. She had the look of someone who'd spent her life on a windswept farm, and the way she had of wrapping her clothes about her suggested that the wind was still blowing.

It wasn't true. She'd been born and brought up in Wicklow, she explained as she watched me pour out the Frascati. 'And what the fock was there to do in Wicklow, for heaven's sake?' So she'd drifted to Liverpool like everyone else, and got married to some stupid prick like everyone else, and got divorced like everyone else. But it was still Beatlemania time in Liverpool, and there were jobs going selling T-shirts, posters, song-sheets and stuff to all the idiots who came up to worship at the shrine and sniff the sweat of the Cavern.

'I used to fake Ringo's signature on photographs and flog them for twenty quid,' Gail said, scooping out the contents of a second avocado. 'The stories I made up – wicked it was! How I knew them all, been on gigs with them all. I didn't say I'd focked them all because I was Irish and still had a wedding-ring on, didn't I, and they mightn't have believed me. But I made a small packet all the same. Then I got married again. And this time it was for love, stupid bastard that I was.'

She was enjoying telling the story of her life, just as I was sure she'd enjoyed telling it a great many times before. Husband Number Two was a burglar, she said in a matter-of-fact voice; and not a very good burglar seeing as he was always getting caught and put away.

'I'm no good at being by meself,' Gail explained. 'That's the trouble, you see. I loved him and all that, but he was never there, was he? I kept telling him he should learn to do the job properly or get another one. But he wouldn't, stubborn idiot that he was. So in the end I left him. I think he's still there: he sends me Christmas cards from prison – always different prisons. I never knew there were so many of them. I keep telling him he should write a Good Prisons Guide.'

We were on to the *Ossobuco alla milanese* and Barolo before she told me about London and her present husband. From selling Beatles T-shirts she'd moved up-market to the lingerie department of Dickins and Jones in Oxford Street, and then into fashion, 'if you can call it that at Dickins and Jones'. She laughed and spilt Barolo down her blouse. The *Ossobuco alla milanese* had mostly disappeared.

'I loved fashion: Lord knows why with a figure like mine. The trouble is, I love food just as much. And wine.'

Gail looked hopeful as I poured out more Barolo.

'Then I met Rick. D'you know, that has to be a first – meeting your future husband in Dickins and Jones. God knows what he was doing there. Nicking things, most likely. I've always been attracted to thieves. Anyway, there he was, this little fellow, fingering the furs. I told him what he could do with his fingers, and he gave me a bit of lip. Real East-Ender is Rick. A wide boy. Clever – always inventing things. Done a bit of everything has Rick, and done a bit of time too. Oh, not another one, I thought. And younger than me – four years. He liked my hair, he said. "Good thing I don't like yours," I answered: "you've hardly got any." I didn't know then what else he'd got.'

She only drew breath in order to laugh.

Finally with the zabaglione she got on to the second-hand fashion business. It was eight or nine years ago, she said. Rick got her into it. Someone he knew; someone he 'did business with'. Gail grimaced, leaving the nature of the 'business' to my imagination.

'You see, there was this woman who had a shop and needed a manager.' Gail made a gesture with her head. 'Not this shop. Down in Fulham. A real flea-pit. But they had good stuff sometimes, and I learnt a lot. Then one day this other lady came in. All la-di-da and perfume. Asked how much I got paid, then offered me a lot more to go and work for her. And here I still am. Stuck.'

She paused to shovel up the last of the zabaglione.

'And a right bitch she is too, the boss.'

Gail burped.

'Christ, I'm pissed.' She wiped her lips with an air of finality and gazed at the dribble of Barolo in her glass. 'So now you've heard the life story of Abigail O'Connor,' she went on. 'My married name's Faith, by the way. I don't use it because I have no faith whatsoever.' She gave a fruity laugh. 'And neither does Rick, so I call him Ye of Little, which he doesn't like much because it suggests he's inadequate where it matters, which he isn't. Now tell me about you.'

It was half past two. We'd consumed two bottles of wine, and the coffee was unsteady in my hand. My plan had been waiting in my head for an hour and a half, and was now feeling soggy. I could see from the bill that I'd just spent £60 which I couldn't even begin to afford, and unless I could squeeze my brain a little drier I was about to have wasted that on listening to the life and loves of Abigail Faith, *née* O'Connor. And that would be that.

'I'm married, and I want to work,' I said.

That seemed about as pared-down as I could make it. Gail looked startled.

'Well, you and half the human race, me darlin', except you're more than a shade prettier than most. Go on.'

I felt inadequate and tongue-tied. How could I tell her that I'd only ever worked in a bank and a boutique – years ago – but that I'd always known since I was very young that one day I'd stumble on something unusual I really wanted to do: and now I'd found it – I wanted to set up a business buying and selling second-hand designer clothes?

Then I thought – Why can't I say exactly that? And I did.

Gail looked even more startled.

'Jaysus! A lady like you. Why?' she said.

I assured her I wasn't in the least a lady, and that I didn't really know why I wanted to do it, but I did. It had come to me quite suddenly at the weekend when I was setting out the garage stall, and Caroline was saying she couldn't be bothered to price anything – they were to be ten pounds each and that was that. There must be hundreds of women just like Caroline, I'd thought: spoilt and bored. Why not do something about it? And then Gail had come along and said, 'You're a fool. You should learn.' Well, I wanted to learn. I wanted to do something well. I wanted to feel the buzz of success. I wanted to have a real life outside our cosy little house on the common, where success had gone down with the sun a long time ago and didn't seem likely to rise again.

I said all that. I didn't feel tongue-tied any longer. In fact I felt a million dollars.

'And I asked you to lunch because I'd love it if you'd be willing to work with me,' I went on, calling the waiter for some more coffee and two brandies. Sod the bill! 'We could set up a place together as partners. You know everything there is to know about the business, and I've got enough money for a short lease,' I said. 'We share the profits. We share the risks. How about it?'

I amazed myself. Angela Merton, I thought, something's happened to you, and it's not just the wine.

Gail was now looking astonished.

'Well, I'll be damned,' she exclaimed.

She remained silent for a few moments, contemplating her brandy. She sipped it, swirled it round in the glass, and finally glanced up at me again. This time she had a mischievous look in her eye.

'Well, I'll truly be damned.'

And she went on swirling the brandy round the glass. Suddenly she tilted her head and swallowed the lot. She blinked, and gave out a loud 'Aaaah!' as if to extinguish the flames. And then she laughed.

'And why not?' she said. 'Indeed, why not? I like you.'

A muddle of powerful emotions swept me home that afternoon. I was a new person. Could one be born again at the age of twenty-eight? I kept thinking of the directions I'd taken in my life, and how all of them until now had been accidental or else willed upon me. First my parents had been willed upon me; then school; then the bank. And at the bank what had mostly been willed upon me were men's groping hands and an assistant manager at half-cock. Then there was my parents' sudden death, and the disposal of Vile Cottage. I could hardly count that as a positive decision on my part since there was no way an eighteen-year-old could be expected to live alone in a suburban Lego house at the far end of nowhere. After that it was London, and a similar pattern of chance events. I drifted into the boutique because it was raining. I drifted into sleeping with Ralph because what else does a nice girl do when Romeo beckons? I drifted into marrying him because he asked me and I was too flattered to say no. And I became pregnant because I was careless.

I'd scarcely been an advertisement for liberated womanhood, I decided.

But now! My new life was about to begin. To run a second-hand clothes shop might not sound the most glamorous of ambitions, but it was my own. And my life would be my own. I was in charge of it. I was boss.

It's true that I was more than a little pissed wandering through Knightsbridge on that soft winter afternoon, but the smile on my face had nothing to do with that. Or not much, anyway. I was on top of the world. To my surprise it made me feel outrageously sexy in an unfocused way, and I suppose this must have transmitted itself like semaphor since just about every man I passed gazed at me with eyes like hot coals. Angela Merton, I tried to say to myself, you're a wife and mother: behave! But I could only laugh, and the suave young man who'd just winked at me outside the tube station winked at me again. With a little more courage and a little less wisdom I might have taken him to bed there and then and we'd have fucked for hours: but I was safely on the train by the time I realised this. So I buried my gaze in the *Evening Standard* to blot out any further thoughts of this kind.

Nothing in the paper struck me as particularly interesting. There was a prison riot in Bristol. More huffing and puffing by the Chancellor. Yet another absurd statement from the Pope about women priests. An anorexic model photographed at Heathrow. Some chatter about the royal children. An avalanche in Chamonix. A greyhound was tipped to win something.

Then my eyes were steered to the property pages. There was a section headed 'Business premises – Lease-hold'. I skimmed down the column. Everything seemed entirely unsuitable – '25,000 sq ft of office space in Canary Wharf', 'Riverside warehouse in Bermondsey', 'Garage/showroom convenient M25'. All the prices were in millions o.n.o. I was on the point of turning the page and venting my irritation on the Pope when a sum of money printed in bold type caught my attention: it was precisely the figure which the building society had told me was mine that very morning. The coincidence was too great to ignore, so I read on. A shop in Pimlico Square, SW1, it said; with 21-ft ground-floor frontage, basement with rear exit. Seven-year lease. Available immediately. There followed the phone number of an estate agent I'd never heard of – Anstruther and Pratt: the name could have been invented by *Private Eye*. I folded the paper carefully and tucked it in my bag.

It was dusk as I walked back across the common. A low skein of mist was drifting up from the river. A few late dog-walkers glanced at me: in the summer, Caroline said, it was like a Kennel Club meeting out here, and everyone walked with their heads down trying to avoid the dog-shit. Caroline hated dogs almost as much as she hated dog-walkers; but then there weren't many things she didn't hate when she put her mind to it. She forgave me having a cat. I could see the lights of her house now, blazing through uncurtained windows and picking out the dark-blue Mercedes parked, I was fairly sure, as near the centre of the road as she could manage in a hurry.

There were no lights burning in our little house, but the cat leapt on to the fence as I approached and teetered along it with her tail raised like pampas-grass. She was indignant and hungry, and darted in ahead of me as I opened the front door, rubbing her back along the wall as she went. She was half-Persian, and at first Ralph wanted to call her Farah after the late Shah's wife whom he claimed to have been painfully in love with at fifteen. I said that seemed a pretty stupid reason for naming a cat after her, and if he insisted on a Persian name why not at least choose something appropriate: she showed every sign, after all, of being an unusually large cat. So we tried Fatima, but Ralph insisted that was Egyptian and not Persian. Finally we settled on Fatwa, which turned out to be monstrously apt since Fatwa very soon established a rule of koranic ruthlessness over all around her. In fact she dominated the neighbourhood almost as savagely as Caroline, which was perhaps why Caroline liked her; plus the fact that few dogs in the area had so far escaped her claws. Great Dane or chihuahua — they were all the same to Fatwa: she tore them to shreds. It didn't make her very popular, except with Caroline, though it did keep the local vet healthily in business, in recognition of which he rewarded us with a fine bottle of claret at Christmas.

Fatwa was now purring, imagining no doubt that her Whiskas was minced bloodhound.

There was a note from Ralph on the kitchen table drawing my attention to a review of his play at the Royal Court. It was ten lines and didn't mention him. I felt sad. In the first years I was with Ralph, when he was king of the small screen, he'd scoffed at critics: 'castrati' he used to call them, 'singing impotently for their supper'. Nowadays he dashed for the papers and tried not to look forlorn.

There was nothing else in his note at all, not even an 'x'. I didn't mind really — or did I? Actors, I'd come to realise, ride their profession like proud sea-captains when the wind is in their sails; but once the ship begins to sink they cling desperately to the rafts. Ralph never used to think about being an actor: he just did it, and praise and money and women flowed his way. Now he thought about it all the time, even to the exclusion of an 'x'. Yes, I did mind, but I understood.

The house was cold and empty. I lit a fire. Then I phoned Gail and read out the advertisement in the *Evening Standard*. What did she think?

'It's your money, darlin',' she said. 'Go and have a look at it. And thanks for the lunch.' She sounded abrupt, and I was disappointed. I wanted her to be bubbling over. I wanted my plan to be the most important thing in her life. And suddenly I felt frightened that it wouldn't work, and I'd lose everything. 'I must go,' she added. Then in a low voice, 'Sorry, but the fockin' boss is here. Ring me tomorrow: and good luck!'

That made me feel a lot better.

So I rang the estate agents, Anstruther and Pratt. I wondered which of the two I'd get on the phone, and whether Anstruther was in reality the prat and Pratt frightfully grand. But it was a woman who answered: she had a voice exactly like those eager robots who give out the weather reports on TV. 'Can I help *yeeooo*?' I explained that I was enquiring about the ad in the *Standard*. She hadn't heard of it. There followed a lot of 'One minute *pleeese*' while she answered numerous other calls; and finally, 'I can put you through now. What name *pleeese?*' By this time I no longer felt in a co-operative mood. 'Does it matter?' I said. There was a short pause; then, 'One minute *pleeese*' while she took yet another call, followed by, '*Sorreee*! What did you say your name was?' 'Mother Teresa,' I answered fiercely. 'One minute *pleeese*.' Another pause, then a man's drawl – 'Yes, can I help you, Mrs Teresa?'

At this point I ran out of humour and explained that I was interested in the property in Pimlico Square, and might I perhaps come and see it?

We made a businesslike arrangement to meet at his office in Ebury Street at ten o'clock the following morning. He would show me the full details, then take me to the shop in Pimlico Square – in person, he assured me. His voice was becoming warmer, closer to my ear. Telephonic seduction is an under-valued art. Clearly he enjoyed escorting ladies round properties, perhaps vicariously staking out little love-nests.

It was my turn to ask, 'May I know your name, please?'

'Anstruther. Keith Anstruther,' he answered.

The boss, eh! I thought. Well, that has to be a good start.

'By the way,' I added, 'the name's not Teresa. It's Angela Merton.'

'Then I look forward to meeting you, Miss Merton,' he said. He made it sound like an assignation.

'God, you're a flirt,' said Caroline. 'Just an estate agent on the telephone, and already he's wetting his knickers over you. I can't flirt. I don't know how to. I just ask for what I want. Then I either don't want it, or don't get it.'

I'd never intended to tell Caroline my plan, but after I'd spoken to Mr Anstruther I panicked. How did one set about this sort of thing, for God's sake? How did one know what to ask? What did one look for? Gail would know, of course, but she wouldn't be there tomorrow. Caroline was exactly the sort of person to take along. She was fearless. She'd recognise bullshit a mile off. And she'd probably terrify the poor man. She'd be my Rottweiler.

'Will you come?'

Caroline looked bemused.

'Why?'

'To hold my hand.'

Silence from Caroline invariably meant yes. Her tongue was better at negatives – it was an instrument sharpened to kill, rather like Fatwa's claws.

'What on earth do you want a *shop* for?' she asked.

The way she said 'shop' intrigued me: it established her own social position, and mine. People like Caroline didn't run shops, though they might hold shares in companies which owned them, built them, supplied them, or insured them. But people like me *did*, though clearly it was an unfortunate hangover from my upbringing, and I really should have grown out of it. However, since she didn't like to think of herself as a snob, and I was a friend, she preferred to put it down to eccentricity on my part; and eccentricity was something she valued. It spiced a dull life. Her most frequent complaint about the people who lived round here was their predictability. They all had the right kind of job, the right kind of children, the right kind of partner – or the wrong kind, which was even worse because then they complained stoically or else had guilt-ridden affairs which the neighbours gossiped about: it was all so half-hearted and tawdry. At least Patrick, when he'd had an affair, had done it properly and fallen in love, which had rather pleased Caroline at the time because she hadn't believed him capable of it. Their life had improved quite a bit since then.

(One day I would ask her whether she'd ever fallen in love herself, or had always dived in and out of passions too quickly to feel the heat of them.)

'So, why on earth *do* you want a shop?' she repeated. 'You mean you want to *sell* things over the counter?'

She sounded incredulous.

'I want to run my own business,' I said. 'I want to get out of the house. I don't want to sit around watching Rachel grow up, and waiting for Ralph to come back complaining that tonight's audience consisted of seventeen yobs munching Golden Wonders and that the play's closing next week.'

Caroline smiled.

'And what are you going to sell in your shop? Antiques?' She laughed. 'Or sweets?'

'Clothes,' I said. 'Second-hand clothes.'

'You mean like Oxfam?'

'No!' I explained. 'Designer clothes. Like the ones you threw out last week.'

She looked disapproving.

'And that dreadful Irish woman bought them.'

I nodded. I wasn't going to tell her Gail was about to be my partner.

Caroline gave a little shrug.

'Ah well!'

That meant she was bored by the subject, but happy to go along with my little eccentricity. She handed me a welcome glass of wine, then she went over to the phone and gave orders to a friend to come and feed Samantha tomorrow, take in the laundry and pay the cleaning lady.

She put the phone down and suddenly broke into a delightful laugh.

'Goodness, it could be rather fun really. Angela, would you let me come and serve in your shop some-times?'

I believe she actually meant it. She was Marie-Antoinette longing to play at being a milkmaid at Versailles. The thought doubled me up.

51

'Of course,' I said.

In the morning I was surprised to find her smartly dressed for the meeting with Mr Anstruther. Then she announced she was driving me in, and that we were having lunch in Chelsea afterwards – on her! But first she had one or two phone calls to make. I waited an hour. Finally we set off, making good speed along the bus lanes and ignoring several No Entry signs. Finally, as we approached Ebury Street she reached into the glove pocket and handed me a small card.

It said *Disabled Driver*.

'No! That's the wrong one.' And she snatched it back. 'This one'll be better.'

It said *Doctor on Call*.

'Stick it in the window,' she said calmly, parking several feet out from a double yellow line. She didn't bother to lock the car.

Until now I'd always imagined Caroline didn't know how to lie. Now I realised I was quite wrong. It was merely that she didn't lie in order to get out of things, as most people do. She lied positively, to make quite sure the battle of life went her way. And she did so with a vengeance.

We were only half an hour late.

Caroline proceeded to be ominously polite to Mr Anstruther, though not before she'd established that he wasn't related to the Anstruther who'd been at Eton with her husband Patrick. He produced the full details of the premises, and we looked at them carefully while

Mr Anstruther looked carefully at my breasts, and then at my wedding ring. I looked at his gut. He had large hairy hands and smelled of aftershave.

'And that's the asking price, is it?' Caroline said after a while.

The man nodded.

'Well, well!' she added.

At this point Mr Anstruther glanced at his watch and suggested we walk down to Pimlico Square. The owner of the place would be waiting, he explained. Caroline pulled the collar of her fur coat over her ears and marched ahead of us along the pavement as though she knew precisely where she was going. The white spire of the Pimlico church glistened in the winter light. We passed a house with a plaque announcing that Mozart had composed his first symphony there in 1764 – at the age of eight! But Caroline hadn't noticed: she was gazing in the opposite direction at a grand-looking grocery shop.

'You buy wonderful white truffles in there,' she announced loudly, as though I did so all the time.

Then another shop front caught her eye. 'Designer Dress Hire', it said. And in large letters above, the name of the place: 'One Night Stand'.

Caroline was laughing.

'I've always wanted one of those,' she called out over her shoulder. 'Haven't you, Mr Anstruther?' She waited for us to catch up while Mr Anstruther struggled with a cough. 'Well, Angela,' she went on, 'that's one name you won't be able to give to your place. A pity, don't you think so, Mr Anstruther?'

I could see that the Rottweiler was getting into training.

The owner was a small, sly-looking man with a few well-greased hairs that did a circuit of his pate before coming to rest above his brow. Anstruther introduced him as 'Mr Harben'. I could see Caroline sizing him up, rather like Fatwa crouching to attack a passing spaniel. The shop was grey and empty. But it was enough: I was already gazing about me, my mind excitedly filling it with racks of clothes just like the Emporium, as amazing creations kept floating in through the door, and out again. I knew by now what I was going to call it. The Outfit. Already I felt I owned the place. And Gail would be there bustling and chattering away, confident, businesslike, laughing, her red hair in a perpetual storm. I could hear her voice. 'We're doing well, Angela me darlin'. Fockin well!' I couldn't wait. Everything was going to be all right.

Caroline meanwhile was running a finger along the shelf below the window.

'Been empty a long time, Mr Harben,' she began quietly. 'Must be hard on people like you in a recession.'

Harben gave a dismissive laugh and began to explain rather pompously that the shop had been empty in order to carry out certain 'refurbishments' so that it could be offered 'in tip-top condition'.

Caroline looked at him blankly.

'Which would explain the graffiti of course,' she said in the same flat voice, her finger wiping dust from a pencilled scrawl by the window which read 'Bollocks'.

Anstruther was having further trouble with his cough.

Caroline's gaze continued to dissect the place. Then she stepped back to obtain a broader view, at the same time giving a firm stamp on one of the floorboards with her heel. It gave way. She seemed unperturbed.

'You'll be replacing all these, of course,' she said, not bothering to look at the owner.

Only Gucci boots, I thought, could have wreaked damage like that.

There was an uncomfortable silence.

'Yes, it could be very nice,' Caroline went on soothingly, 'once it's in tip-top condition. Perhaps we should come back when it is, Angela – in a month or so.' She turned an expressionless face towards Harben. 'Unless you'd rather we did it. Might be cheaper and quicker. Not more than five or six thousand, I should think. Just knock it off the price.'

She didn't wait for Harben to respond, but announced that she'd like to take a look at the basement and the rear exit. I continued my daydream with a smile while the two men took up glum positions at the top of the stairs.

They didn't have long to wait. Caroline re-emerged holding up a dead mouse in one hand and a used condom in the other. Without a word she handed them out, the mouse to Harben, the condom to Anstruther.

'Oh, there's a window broken, and the lock,' she said, carefully brushing her hands. 'People have been getting in, and I don't imagine it was the health authorities, do you, Mr Harben, or you'd have heard about it?'

Anstruther started to bluster something, but Caroline was already placing an arm on my shoulder and guiding me towards the door.

'Come on, my dear. The place is a tip. We can do much better than this, and we've got that other appointment in Chelsea.' She gave a final backward glance at the owner, and added — 'I suppose twenty grand off the price and it might just be worth it. On the other hand it's such a short lease.'

She kept walking. The two men followed. It had started to drizzle. The rain glistened on Mr Harben's pate. He hurried to join us, mumbling a sum that was ten thousand less than the asking price.

Caroline didn't appear to listen, but went on walking. By now we were passing the dress-hire shop called One Night Stand.

She glanced up at the sign.

'Now we know where they go for it, Mr Anstruther, don't we?' she said laughing. 'Do you still have your trophy?'

Mr Anstruther's cough was by now a serious complaint. He also seemed to have forgotten he was still holding the condom, and hastily dropped it in a litter-bin. I noticed that Harben had managed to dispose of the mouse. He was looking wet and flustered.

Caroline grasped my arm and we continued our brisk walk along the pavement. Behind us we could hear owner and agent exchanging hurried words. Then Anstruther hastened to catch us up and explained that Mr Harben would be prepared to take another five thousand off the price if we could manage to complete the deal within a fortnight.

Either Caroline didn't hear, or she chose not to. She was back on the subject of white truffles, which she said were now in season and really we ought to buy some: in a few weeks it would be too late. Then suddenly she turned towards the two men as if she'd forgotten something. Her voice was composed and charming.

'That's agreed then, is it, Mr Harben? Twenty thousand off the price – and it's probably better if we don't say anything to the health authorities: don't you agree? It would only delay things, and I don't imagine you want unnecessary trouble. It's so tiresome and expensive.'

She shook the two men's hands warmly, then swiftly turned away, glancing at her watch.

'We'd better hurry, Angela.'

And we walked on through the rain towards Caroline's car. I didn't have the nerve to look back. I was feeling slightly ashamed that I'd said absolutely nothing; but how could I have competed with a star performance like that? Caroline was making serious suggestions about lunch: 'our other appointment in Chelsea – remember?' she added with a laugh. From somewhere behind us I heard Mr Harben's voice.

'Ball-breaker!'

I think he meant it to be heard. Caroline only half turned.

'In your case, Mr Harben, that would be no great matter,' she said with a winning smile. 'We'll be in touch tomorrow, Mr Anstruther.'

She turned back to me.

'I liked that place quite a lot, didn't you, Angela?' she said in a quiet voice. 'D'you think you might want it?'

I said that at that price I most likely would.

It all happened unbelievably quickly. The following afternoon Gail went to see the place, approved of it (especially the price), and proceeded to take over. After the performance with Caroline, I was relieved not to be dealing with Mr Anstruther. In fact, as Gail reported on the phone that evening, it was now Mr Pratt who was responsible – and she said 'Pratt' as though she meant it.

Over the weeks that followed, all the rigmarole and red tape of acquiring a business lease seemed to be cut through effortlessly by Gail – with a little help from Rick, she explained with a meaningful smile. Rick was a born fixer: he knew all the ropes and the strings, which palms to grease, which tricks to pull. I chose not to ask too many questions, but provided the occasional bottle of whisky or box of cigars whenever Gail suggested such things might be appreciated: I didn't ask by whom.

Ralph was surprised and puzzled when I told him. I realised that he'd never given a thought to the possibility of my doing something with my life. It emerged that my shop was due to open the day after his play was due to close, and I found myself wondering if there might be some significance in this.

Rachel, on the other hand, was excited. Would I be able to bring home some dolls' clothes, she enquired. I promised I would.

And Caroline went on being Caroline. She cursed at having to find someone else to share the school run, and blamed me for letting her down. Now that the shop inconvenienced her, it had become a stupid idea. Then we managed to compromise. Ralph or I would do the morning run each day: she would do the afternoon. She looked aggrieved that a solution should be so easy.

'Huh!' she said.

But thanks to Caroline I now had money to spare from my nest-egg. I could afford to do the place up properly.

'We're in business, me darlin',' Gail announced, laying in front of me the names of all the Emporium's clients. 'There's nothing like beginning with a good theft,' she said cheerfully. 'I wasn't married to a burglar for nothing. Now we can start planning.'

But first she produced a bottle of vintage champagne.

'I never ask Rick where he gets things from,' she
said. 'Let's drink to The Outfit.'

3

The Warming

———————— ○ ————————

'We can't call it an opening, darlin'; we've got fock-all to put in the shop.'

Gail was leaning sturdily across the table half engulfed by invitations which had arrived from the printers that morning. She handed one of them to me.

'That's why I've called it a "shop-warming",' she went on. 'Like when you move house and you've got no furniture except a bed, but you want people to come and bring a bottle and say "Hello!".'

But what people? Gail had been briefing me about 'the clientele' for much of the past week as we polished the new floorboards, cleaned windows and sloshed white paint on the walls and ceiling. She was thoroughly enjoying being my tutor.

'The important thing to remember in this line of business,' she explained, gesticulating energetically with the paint-brush, 'is that the women who *sell* things and the women who *buy* things are mostly the same people;

so it stands to reason, doesn't it, that the more people you can persuade to bring stuff in, the more stuff you'll shift . . . and that means money and more champagne for us, me darlin', which is what it's all about.'

So what we needed was an introduction party, she said emphatically; with as many women as possible wearing clothes which the other women would admire and not be able to do without. And vice versa.

'That's when things start happening. "Designer incest", one of my customers called it. Another used to describe it as "sartorial rape".'

Gail nearly fell off the ladder laughing at that. And all the time she continued to wield her paint-brush like a conductor's baton, until by the evening her hair looked as though a flock of seagulls had spent the afternoon circling overhead.

It took the best part of two days writing out the invitations to all the clients she was intending to steal from the Emporium. It wasn't simply a matter of Gail writing the names and me doing the addresses; she insisted on adding the flourish of a personal note at the foot of each card. These would vary from 'I hope we may have the pleasure of a visit from your ladyship to our new establishment', to 'I've abandoned the old bitch at last; come and enjoy a noggin with myself and my lovely new partner'.

'And Jaysus Christ, if they all come we'll have to spill outside. Thank the good Lord there's a wine merchant's next door.'

Then there were those who were to be invited by word of mouth. Rick would bring some of his 'business' friends. Ralph was told to bring along a selection of TV glamour – preferably male, 'or at least pretending to be', to help balance the numbers and make people feel they were in famous company. I cautiously mentioned Caroline, who I explained was either related to everyone who mattered, or else had most probably slept with them at some time or another. Gail thought that sounded promising, and that she could probably tolerate Caroline in a crowd. And Patrick, of course, must be persuaded to trawl for affluent fish in the City.

I undertook to invite the wine merchant in the hope of a special deal on champagne: also the antique dealer on the other side of us who was a rude bugger, Gail said, but you didn't want to make enemies of your neighbours, did you, and maybe the sight of a few languorous models would soften his temper and harden his prick – if he had one, that is. I also suggested we invite the man who occupied the flat upstairs – 'for diplomatic reasons,' I said, 'also because he's a well-known photographer and could prove useful.' I didn't add the other reason – that I'd already been awarded a few scorching eye-meets, and that he looked dangerously interesting. In any case, this was going to be quite an ordeal, with me knowing almost nobody, and I wanted to ensure that there was at least one good-looking stranger I could flirt with.

Then there was Renato who owned the Trevi res-taurant across the square. He wasn't just good-looking;

he was magnificent. Gail and I had taken to wandering over there for a pasta at lunchtime, and he'd already adopted us. Gail, with her Catholic instincts, swore he'd be a hopeless lover because he'd only see a mirror of himself while he screwed you; besides, he was a widower, entirely besotted with his ethereal daughter who sometimes served us, and it was Gail's conviction that any Italian in love with virginity preferred an altar to a bed.

But whatever his predilections might be, Renato had undertaken to provide large quantities of pasta salad, salami, olives and the like. I was already 'Angela, my angel', and as far as I was concerned I was perfectly happy to be the Virgin Mary just so long as his Italian charms were directed my way. That made two men I could flirt with. Things were looking up.

I was becoming aware that my thoughts on this party weren't entirely businesslike; but then, life with a semi-employed husband hadn't offered much to lift the spirits in recent years, and as Caroline never ceased to point out, I was still 'horribly young, damn you!'

Besides, wasn't I paying for all this? The party was certain to mop up the very last of my money. I hoped Gail really knew what she was doing. Sometimes I woke in the night shivering with fear, and when I wrapped Rachel in my arms it was with a silent plea to forgive me should it turn out that I'd squandered our little security on a selfish whim.

'When can I come and see your shop, Mum?'

'Very soon, darling. Very soon.'

'Is it as big as Waitrose?'

'No, darling!'

'Will you sell Mars Bars ice-cream?'

'I'm afraid not, darling.'

It was Rachel's enthusiastic acceptance of what I was doing that did as much as anything to boost my courage. Somewhere inbred in me, I suppose, had always lurked the conviction that energies spent outside the home weakened the love and care I could give to my daughter. Now I knew this wasn't so: if anything it was the reverse.

Other things, too, were beginning to surprise me. I'd always imagined that whatever I might possess in the way of talents were largely physical; and flattering though it was that people envied my body, I'd often wished I could have a mind they envied too – especially since my body wasn't going to last, and before long I'd be left with nothing: I'd be a droopy moron.

Now suddenly I found myself wondering – was this merely a triumph of social programming? Had my body been deceiving me all this time, and was there perhaps something behind the curves after all? Might it be possible to have a bust *and* a brain?

It was Gail who first hinted at this possibility.

'Angela, where d'you get all these ideas from?'

I was puzzled and asked what she meant.

'Well, the shop to start with,' she said. 'Look at it.'

I realised it was true. The shop was acquiring a personality that I had to admit was to a large extent mine. Certainly I'd been responsible for the more unexpected additions. For instance, an artist I knew slightly had painted me a sign to hang outside, which surprised even Gail. It had been my idea. The sign swivelled like a weather-cock. On one side the name – The Outfit – was shown suspended like a wonderful necklace across the shoulders and torso of a young woman who was about to unzip a dress. On the other side she'd already unzipped it. I suppose it did look rather provocative. Certainly people kept stopping to stare at it, which seemed to prove its success. The only disquieting feature was that the artist had chosen to repay the compliment of my commission by depicting me.

'You don't think people will imagine it's a strip-show, do you, Gail?' I asked anxiously.

'Oh, it sometimes is, I can tell you,' she said, laughing. 'So, don't worry! They won't be able to get you under the Trade Descriptions Act.'

Then there was the lighting. I wasn't going to have the bare strip-lighting of The Emporium, even if we did miss a few cigarette burns. I wanted class, without having much idea what class was. But I'd noticed a place in Chelsea that sold reproduction Tiffany glass, which I fell for; and in a burst of self-confidence which astonished me I persuaded the owner to let me have a gorgeous set of wall-lights free in return for a notice acknowledging the gift.

'Jaysus, you're a cheeky one,' said Gail.

But my greatest triumph was the espresso coffee machine. We'd agreed that the social aspect of The Outfit was most important; and that during working hours social life tended to centre on drinking coffee – *real* coffee, naturally. If we stayed open late and decided to hit the alcohol, then that was quite another matter; but generally speaking a cup of espresso or cappuccino was what we would offer to any clients who wished, so that Gail could then convivially talk them into purchasing something far more expensive than they'd ever intended.

'A cup of cappuccino costs about 25p to make, and it's often worth a hundred quid, I can tell you,' Gail explained. 'Not a bad return for your money.'

That was all very well, but by this time I was down to my last fifty pounds without eating into the housekeeping, and espresso coffee machines cost almost as much as a new car, as I discovered.

Again I surprised myself. I'd already decided we'd have to settle for Cona, or one of those glass gadgets you squidge down until the hot coffee spurts straight in your eye, when I noticed that a café across the square was in the process of being gutted. I knew the story of it from Renato. The Italian café-owner had been fiddling his books for years, and had finally done a bunk rather than face an income tax tribunal. In any case, his lease had all but run out, and there wasn't much he needed to leave behind.

But what he had left was now out on the pavement waiting for the skip. And this was what caught my eye.

I glanced down as I walked past. And there it was! A vintage espresso coffee machine just lay there, gleaming gold and silver in the morning sunlight. It looked like the front end of a car that James Dean might have driven in *Rebel without a Cause*. It was superb. It was a masterpiece. But did it work? I ran down the street to the Trevi restaurant and called out for Renato.

He hurried towards me from the rear of the restaurant, anxiously wiping his hands.

'What is it, Angela, my angel? You are in trouble?'

'Please come quickly,' I said breathlessly, grabbing him by the arm.

I pointed to the espresso machine on the pavement.

'Renato. Expert advice, please! Will it work?'

He seemed perplexed for a moment, then looked at me and raised both hands in the air.

'But of course, my angel! For ever!'

That was enough. The two workmen clearing the shop had been watching us with blank expressions. I took out a ten-pound note, and at the sight of money they understood immediately.

'Where to, sweetheart?'

I pointed across the square. They heaved it on

to their shoulders and we processed through the mid-day traffic.

'There we are, Gail,' I announced triumphantly.

'Jaysus! Not again!' she said. 'That fockin' thing should be in the Science Museum.'

But Renato was right. With a little help from Rick it did work, and we drank our first cup of espresso the day before the shop-warming.

There was just one other personal triumph on the final morning. I was feeling sick with anxiety, and had taken a different route from the Underground station merely as a distraction. I wanted to run away. I wanted just to be a mother and housewife. I wanted to have cosy coffee-mornings with the other mums. I wanted to get a little dog and walk it on the common.

Suddenly there it was. *In* a skip this time. At first I could only see its arms sticking up among the packing-cases. Then the face. Then the torso. There seemed to be no damage on it: the stitching was all in place. And she really was rather beautiful.

I heaved her out and walked confidently down the street with my tailor's dummy.

'How about this lady for the window, Gail?' I announced, backing in through the door.

This time Gail said nothing, but just looked at me before giving a nod of defeat.

'We haven't got any clothes, so we can't dress her,' I said. 'But I do have a Butler and Wilson necklace – all hearts and cupids – and some terribly sexy Janet Reger knickers and bra Ralph gave me for my birthday. How about it?'

I think Gail knew she'd got a real partner.

Ralph was in surprisingly high spirits, and I wondered if I would have coped as well in his shoes. His play had closed the night before; he had no idea when or if the next job might come; and now he was dressing to go out and celebrate the launch of his wife's career. I might of course have got it quite wrong: perhaps he wasn't being stoic at all, but looking forward to an evening surrounded by glamorous women, some of whom no doubt would remember sighing over the dashing Ralph Merton and praying that one day they might catch his eye across a crowded room. Well, tonight they could. I felt an old spark of pride at the thought – even a spark of jealousy, remembering what it had been like in the days when Ralph's presence at any party had been like fly-paper, and I'd had to prise them off him – without, I have to say, a great deal of co-operation.

So perhaps he was happy because he was brushing up the old magic. He certainly looked disgracefully handsome in his dark-blue Armani suit and his white shirt open just deep enough to reveal the Greek medallion nestling in his chest hair. It acted as a sort of marker-buoy, assuring you that if you continued downwards through the invisible forest you would eventually reach his prick, which always used to excite me. Why did I say 'used to'? Did it still? I wasn't sure. It was almost exactly ten years since that first encounter in the Chelsea boutique, when I'd sneezed and sneezed while he gazed at me, laughing and knowing already that he'd take me to bed that night, because who ever said no to Ralph Merton?

I often used to wonder what I would have done if I'd met him now; and it worried me that once again I was unsure of the answer. I could almost hear Caroline's voice – 'However would you know? You've never had anyone else to compare him with.' Then she'd add, a little unkindly – 'Think what it must be like for him, having had every woman under the sun for all those years, and now only you.'

Rachel was watching me dress. Her face wore that look of curiosity of a young girl who is imagining herself to be grown up, and trying to feel what it must be like. Entirely absorbed in that act of dreaming, she seemed for a moment to become the adult she would one day be. Her whole appearance changed. I was quite shaken. My child had gone. Who was this beautiful creature whose eyes were suddenly so full of experience and wisdom? And then the illusion vanished.

'Urrghh! What's that muck you're putting on your face, Mum?'

I told her that if she wanted to watch she'd better shut up. So she sat quietly in the corner of the bedroom saying nothing until I wished I hadn't told her to shut up because I wanted to know what she was thinking. In a couple of hours she'd be giggling and comparing notes with Samantha, Caroline's au pair girl having long ago abandoned the fruitless task of getting them off to bed.

I'd thought carefully about this evening. What sort of person did I want to be? Sophisticated hostess? (I doubted I could be that.) The most beautiful woman in the room? (Not with all those glorious models around.) Stylishly mysterious – the woman in black? (That was more like it.) I always went for black whenever I was unsure of myself, and I was certainly that right now. Gail had presented me with her last little theft from the Emporium. 'Exactly right for you,' she'd said. It was a black Joseph suit with a short skirt, very tight, and a jacket with just a single button at the waist so that it billowed out at the bosom – 'which you do anyway,' she added, laughing. I chose a tiny black T-shirt to go underneath; then black tights, and suede shoes with heels.

From her expression I could see Rachel was beginning to approve. She was glancing down at her own legs to make sure they were going to be as good as mine. At seven she was learning the gentle art of vanity. I doubt if any teacher at school ever got this kind of attention.

Her concentration on becoming the next Lolita was broken by cries of agony from the street. Rachel looked alarmed for a moment, then shrugged her shoulders. She was familiar, as we all were, with Fatwa's safaris among the local dog population. I wondered who the much-loved victim was this time. But at least the vet would be happy.

Then Ralph put his head round the door: he was puzzled, as men always are, by how on earth women contrive to take quite so long getting dressed.

'You look lovely,' he managed to say; then spoilt it by adding – 'as always.'

I told him I had a long way to go yet, and he'd better go and fix himself a drink. He seemed to think that was a good idea, and closed the door.

I opted for dramatic eye make-up – a double layer of mascara. My eyes are very dark anyway, and with these tremendous eyelashes I decided I looked like Medea. So, if it was to be the dangerous look, then go for it, I thought. I looked out my brightest red lipstick – Cherry Bold, it called itself; then let my hair flow loose – black on black. Oh yes, Angela! Who shall I devour tonight?

Jewellery was more of a problem. I'd sold all my best stuff, and the Butler and Wilson necklace was promised to the tailor's dummy in the shop window. Then I remembered the Indian junk I'd picked up somewhere off the Tottenham Court Road. There were those silver earrings made up of lots and lots of tiny dangling bells. Exactly right! I'd tinkle like an oriental call to prayer every time I moved.

Finally – perfume. I had none! Caroline, I felt certain, would be awash in the most expensive Paloma Picasso available only in New York. There was no point trying to compete. India came to my rescue again. Musk!

Did that go with temple bells? Or with Medea? Probably not. Never mind: Indian musk it was going to be.

'Mum, you pong!' was Rachel's verdict.

She rose and left the bedroom, holding her nose.

I knew the gods were blessing us when, as we drove in, the clouds began to slide away into the evening, and in the square a late sun picked out tiny points of green on plane trees which until yesterday had been wintry and bare. London in April suddenly felt like June. So, if the room became too crowded, now we could spill outside at the back of the shop where there was an enclosed courtyard with seats and a small lawn which residents of the flats around us used as their communal garden. I crossed my fingers that they wouldn't mind. 'Sod them if they do,' had been Gail's view; 'it's as much ours as theirs.' And to stress the point she'd promptly rung Rick to see if he knew where we might borrow an open brazier for roasting chestnuts.

'It's not exactly the season for chestnuts, is it?' I ventured.

Gail had given me a patronising look.

'Precisely, darlin'. That's why Rick'll have little trouble getting hold of a brazier.'

'And the chestnuts?'

'Listen! Nothing's ever out of season for Rick. He'll find some.'

He did. And the fuel. And the tongs. And the little brown bags. I didn't ask questions. Rick even volunteered to be chef, claiming he'd done this many times outside London theatres as a boy, whenever the shoplifting season was a bit quiet. I'd grown to like Rick: he was the kind of gentle thief you'd always want on your side: like having a tame stoat around the place.

By the time Ralph and I arrived Gail had done virtually everything. Our desk was already covered with a white cloth and arrayed with champagne flutes all neatly ranked. Behind it a huge tin bath rattled with ice. A neighbouring table was laid out with the salads and salamis which Renato had faithfully delivered, promising to come back and join in the celebrations whenever things were slack in the restaurant.

It was nearly seven o'clock. Through the rear window I could see Rick busying himself with the chestnut brazier in the dusk. He'd brought along some lanterns, and by the light of them I noticed that he'd commandeered all the wooden benches from the communal garden and arranged them within warming distance of the fire.

'Here we go, then,' announced Gail, clapping her hands. 'I need a fockin' drink.'

And she opened the first bottle of champagne with a flourish.

'To us, and the fortune we're going to make,' she said, raising her glass. And as she did so the shawls of wondrous colours which she'd somehow wound together to make a dress rippled like the sunset on a rough sea.

Then the first people began to arrive.

For an hour or so it was simply a party I was paying for, and increasingly wishing I wasn't.

'This is Angela Merton, my partner.'

'This is Angela Merton, my partner.'

'This is Angela Merton, my partner.'

Then after a while the champagne began to get a grip on Gail's tongue.

'Meet Angela. She's not only lovely, she's clever.'

'Meet Angela. Tough on you, darlin', she's married.'

'Meet Angela. She's a great girl, but not for you, darlin'; she likes men.'

Gail knew everyone, embraced them all, introduced me to them all – plucking me from one to the other until I felt like a parcel being passed around as rapidly as possible in case the music stopped. One minute it was an ambassador's wife from Mexico; the next it was a Knightsbridge lady with a tribal mask of a face; then an Argentinian polo player escorting a soulful creature who wasn't his daughter; then a Lady Something-or-other who talked *at* me without ever moving her smile; then a model so perfect-looking I felt like a bag-lady.

And suddenly Caroline, so infuriatingly at home she might have *been* at home. She half turned to me from a group of guests.

'I didn't know you knew all these people, Angela,' she said, surprised, and promptly turned back to them.

She was wearing incredibly tight jeans with brown suede boots up to the knees, and a cream silk shirt tied into the waist. This counted as 'dressing down' for Caroline, except that round her neck was a gold choker set with a ruby that could probably have settled the National Debt.

'I *don't* know them,' I answered defensively. But she wasn't listening.

I'd lost Ralph, though every so often I caught a glimpse of him over the far side of the room with a woman old enough to remember how famous he was. I felt a bitch for thinking that.

And there was Patrick, whom Caroline had rapidly discarded. I could see a look of boyish astonishment and delight on his face as he chatted to some willowy model, every so often making a vain effort to tear his eyes away from how little she was wearing.

And Renato. He pushed his way through the crowd to give me an operatic kiss, only for Gail to seize him and hurry him away in a flurry of wild hair and rainbow shawls.

I kept reminding myself that this was 'business'; that this was supposed to be the launch of my career; that these people were only here because I'd had a bright idea. But then a surge of panic would overtake me as I looked around and saw the last of my little nest-egg vanishing down sixty or seventy throats with nothing to show for it except an ever-rising volume of noise.

I said to myself – 'I loathe parties.' I detached

myself from the crowd and stood by the window gazing absent-mindedly at the tailor's dummy I'd rescued from the skip, and which now wore my Janet Reger knickers and bra. Suddenly there was a quiet voice right behind me.

'Whose are they, I wonder?'

Startled, I spun round and caught sight of the photographer I'd invited from upstairs. He had an amused look on his face.

'They're mine,' I said.

He gazed at me for a second or two, his mouth puckering slightly at the corners. Then he looked back at the tailor's dummy, and again at me. The silence was brief and electric. As his eyes undressed the dummy they undressed me, and when he looked back at me I felt naked.

'I'm Josh Kelvin,' he said.

'And I'm Angela Merton.'

He nodded.

'I know. I've seen you.'

I found myself laughing, and as I did so the bells on my earrings tinkled.

'And now you've seen my underwear too,' I said.

Even as I said it I knew I probably shouldn't have. But it was a game he'd started, and at that moment I was happy to play it. I wasn't sure what the rules of the game were, how you won or lost, and whether it was perhaps fire I was really playing with. None the less, standing there in my Medea black, with my husband safely not too far away, I knew I was enjoying it – even if it was fire. I felt suddenly very, very alive. This evening, after all, was the beginning of my new life. And I was drinking champagne.

'Perhaps I could photograph you one of these days,' he was saying. 'With your earrings,' he added with a smile.

(Now – did I go on with this game, or not? And when he said 'with your earrings', did he mean 'with your earrings *only*'? My stomach did a little spin.)

'Maybe,' I said, knowing perfectly well my face had said, 'Yes!' and that he knew it.

He wasn't an obviously handsome man, but he had the kind of looks that made you not think in those terms. I imagined him to be about forty, though he had the sort of etched, craggy face that made him look older than he perhaps was. He had thick dark hair, and wore a loose black sweater with no shirt underneath. It revealed a long scar at the base of his neck, and as I noticed it I remembered reading about this photographer who'd been wounded by shrapnel in Beirut. That was probably when I'd first heard his name. From then onwards I seemed to hear it all the time. Or I'd see it somewhere. 'Photograph by Josh Kelvin.' 'Special feature by Josh Kelvin.' 'Josh Kelvin returns to the Falklands.' He seemed to do a bit of everything – even fashion occasionally. It was Caroline, when I told her who lived above our new shop, who reached for a magazine and said, 'That man doesn't give a damn about clothes; he just wants to get them off. You can tell.'

Yes, I could tell. The question right now was — did I want him to get mine off?

Angela, I told myself, you've had too much champagne.

And so, I realised, had quite a lot of people. Josh was being hauled away by some predatory witch, and there was no sign of Ralph. Many of the guests had moved out into the courtyard to eat hot chestnuts by the light of the lanterns, and I thought I'd join them. But the narrow staircase to the basement and the rear exit was jammed. People were laughing and cheering, and raising their glasses.

I was straining on tiptoe to see what could possibly be going on when suddenly there was Gail. She put her arm round me.

'I told you, darlin'. It's all happening,' she said loudly in my ear above the noise.

'What *is* happening?' I asked.

'The changing-room. It's packed. You can't move.'

It had all begun with one woman, Gail explained. 'An old customer — very vain, and a real lush.' She'd fixed her eyes on this other woman across the room, and made a bee-line for her — 'except that a bee flies a hell of a lot straighter than she could manage'. She then announced that she absolutely adored the suit this woman was wearing, and she was so envious it was entirely ruining her evening. The other woman had looked a bit startled at first; then she confessed she was thoroughly tired of it and infinitely preferred hers.

'So they agreed to swap – there and then. And now they're all at it. It's Vanity Fair, me darlin'. Take a look!'

I did. I couldn't believe it. There they were – society ladies, foreign diplomats' wives, actresses, fashion editors, costume designers, rich bitches of uncertain age, and God knows who else: and they were squeezing in and out of our tiny changing-room zipping and unzipping things, waving garments at one another, yelling their heads off, stumbling about trying to hold on to their champagne as well as their skirts. Some weren't even bothering to wait for space in the changing-room; they just stripped down to their underwear in the corridor or on the stairway. 'Try this, Chloe: I'm about your size.' 'No, I can't let you have this; I've got no bra on.' A few of them didn't even mind that: what could be exposed on a Riviera beach wasn't going to be shy in a Pimlico basement.

Christ, I said to myself; I start a respectable business and already it's a bacchanal.

The men couldn't believe their eyes, or their luck. Some of them joined in, smart enough to realise that quite a few garments are unisex, especially those closest to the skin. There was a healthy trade in vests. I caught sight of Patrick struggling to pull a minute T-shirt over his bare torso; next to him the model who'd given it to him was nonchalantly admiring her own torso before wrapping her nakedness in his magenta velvet jacket. Caroline's expression might have been engraved in stone: it was a jacket she'd given him for Christmas and had cost four hundred pounds, she'd told me. Next to her a taciturn figure I'd been introduced to as the ambassador from one of the sterner Gulf states was almost choking with astonishment. He'd been averting his eyes from the champagne all evening, Gail assured me, but he clearly wasn't going to avert his eyes from all this pulchritude. The Persian Gulf was never like this. Perhaps he imagined he'd stepped straight into the pages of *The Satanic Verses*. I wondered what his wife was doing. No doubt an urgent pilgrimage to Mecca was already on the agenda.

'Is this the way it always goes?' I asked Gail, feeling more than a little bewildered.

'Oh yes, if you're lucky,' she said through a mouthful of chestnuts. 'Clothes make people go wild. They forget themselves: become other people – as you can see.' She gave a laugh. 'And the champagne helps.'

By now we were standing at the open door leading on to the courtyard. Rick was still crouched over his brazier, silhouetted against the glow of the fire and handing out little bags of hot nuts to other silhouettes which – judging by their shapes – were in varying stages of undress.

Suddenly there was a flash. Then a second one. Gail gave another laugh.

'Ah well! 'Tis better to go down in history having a good time than not at all, don't you think?'

With that she grabbed a young man in a dapper suit who was making his way indoors with the man holding the flashlight camera.

'Angela, you'd better meet Conor. He's promised to make us famous, haven't you, me darlin'?'

Oh Christ! I thought. The press. That must account for the tape-recorder I'd noticed parked next to a glass of champagne while I'd been talking to Josh Kelvin. So we were going to hit the gossip columns. The evening was getting totally out of hand, and tomorrow God knows what horrors would leap out at me from the tabloids.

'We need them, darlin'. We need them,' Gail assured me once Conor had slipped away. 'It'll bring them in in droves.'

Then she'd gone, her red hair and rainbow shawls dancing through the light of the brazier as she swooped from guest to guest, a bottle of champagne in both hands and her laughter echoing round the lamplit courtyard. Even if I'd been able to remember who the guests were, I no longer could, so many of them now wore quite different clothes, or else hardly any at all. Patrick, having struggled into the minute T-shirt, had struggled out of it again and was searching for his velvet jacket. But the girl had gone. I could hear Caroline's voice through the hubbub: 'You stupid fucking idiot, Patrick! How am I supposed to get you home like that?' But the heir to the smallest county in England seemed entirely oblivious. He was holding the girl's T-shirt like a love-token, his eyes as far away from Rutland as from the board meeting he'd no doubt be missing in the morning.

I was so bemused by this whole transvestite panto-mime that the appearance of two policemen in uniform made no impression on me at all. It wasn't until I heard Caroline's voice once more that I realised they really were policemen.

'What d'you mean – an orgy?' she was saying indignantly. People were gathering around. 'I don't care who's complained. Can't you see we're collecting clothes for Oxfam? This is a perfectly respectable meeting, and we have permission from the Chief Commissioner of Police, who happens to be my father. Now, officer, in the interests of charity perhaps you and your colleague would join me in a glass of champagne. Angela, bring me two more glasses.'

The departure of two extremely cheerful police officers was the signal for other guests to start drifting away too, some of them still managing to wear the clothes they arrived in, others not. I never did identify the fundamentalist ambassador's wife, but I did momentarily catch sight of Josh as he passed from the courtyard into the light of the doorway. There was a young blonde with him, and as he paused to let her pass through the door, he steered her gently with one hand on the right buttock of her jeans. 'Such a gentleman,' I said to myself sourly. I saw his hand slide up on to the strip of naked waist; and then he'd gone.

I decided it was high time I went too. Gail said she

and Rick would lock up, and I'd see her in the morning – 'not too early,' she added. By now her rainbow shawls looked as though the rain had won the battle, though I guessed it was only champagne. Then I cast around for Ralph. Eventually I spotted him in a dark area of the courtyard. He saw me, though not quite in time to retrieve his hand from a loose-fitting blouse.

Ah well, I thought: that was quite an evening one way and another. Ralph chose not to say anything, and for not dissimilar reasons neither did I. As we drove back, fears of being breathalysed were dispelled by a sensation I'd never imagined it was possible to have – the sensation of feeling jealous *twice* at the same time. It was painful, absurd, and strangely erotic. We made love that night in the glow of an April moon, our bodies silver-blue and heavy-breathing. It was like I remembered it used to be, though I couldn't have sworn it was always Ralph I imagined to be deep inside me; and maybe it wasn't my body alone which aroused such wonderful lust in him.

We fell asleep together, and dreamt apart.

4

Pimlico Square

———————o———————

The morning greeted me with a thunderous truth; that apart from our housekeeping for the month and today's bus-fare I hadn't a penny in the world. Ralph was out of work. The car was threatening to do the same. The roof leaked, and the washing-machine was taking on a new lease of life as a shredder. What was more, Rachel's birthday was less than a month away, and already I was having my ear bashed with, 'Samantha's got a new necklace with lovely shiny things in it: could I have one too, Mum?'

And even as I counted these calamities I could hear the postman offering a whole heap more through the letterbox: bills, I'd come to recognise, make a special plop as they fall on the mat.

It was also raining.

I didn't want today to happen.

I nudged Ralph. He turned his head blearily and made unappealing noises. Fatwa leapt on to the bed and attacked his feet.

'Ouch! Bloody cat!'

I was on Fatwa's side.

'Serve you right for feeling up that woman last night. Who was she anyway?'

Ralph looked cornered as well as bleary.

'I don't know. I was pissed. I'm sorry,' he said.

That didn't improve my mood. I wished he'd been able to say something cavalier like, 'Poor woman, she'd dropped a chestnut down her blouse, and I was helping her find it'; and I would have slapped his face and laughed. That would have been the old Ralph, the Ralph I married.

I lay in bed feeling hypocritical. After all, whatever Ralph had been doing at the party last night was nothing compared to what I'd been contemplating doing with Josh Kelvin. That troubled me – not as much as it should have, admittedly, and certainly not as much as being entirely broke. This was *real* trouble, and it made me shiver. I'd blown everything on an extravagant whim, and now it was too late. Why, why, why had I done it?

It was not a good beginning to the day.

Gail had said 'not too early', and just as well. Ralph was in no condition to do the school run, and Samantha wasn't ready when I rang Caroline's doorbell. A flower-pot lay smashed in the front garden, surrounded by splinters of glass. I looked up and could see where it came from. Through the broken window pane violent sounds were emerging, accompanied after a moment or two by the T-shirt Patrick had exchanged for his velvet jacket. It settled over the mutilated geranium like a tiny shroud. More violent sounds followed. Hurricane Caroline showed no sign of abating.

I waited over half an hour before Samantha finally emerged.

'Mummy's in a bate,' she said cheerfully, enjoying the fact that for once it wasn't directed at her. 'Daddy's wounded,' she added.

It was ten o'clock before I clambered on to the bus, feeling that today was already fulfilling its worst promises.

But the rain had stopped by the time I reached Pimlico Square, and the young green of the plane trees looked polished and bright in the watery sunlight. Renato was waving to me from the door of the Trevi restaurant.

'An-gel! An-gel! Wonderful party. You were so beautiful.'

That made me feel better still. I waved back and blew him a kiss.

The square was unusually crowded. Traffic was blocked on both sides, and there was much hooting and swearing. Then I saw the reason. Ahead of me cars were doubled-parked, many of them with doors and hatchbacks open. A meter-lady with peroxide hair bulging under her cap was scribbling earnestly at her pad and slipping fines under windscreen-wipers, although not one of the drivers was taking the slightest notice;

they were all too busy unloading armfuls of whatever it was and making their way along the pavement.

Still I didn't realise. It wasn't until I caught sight of Gail standing by the open door of our shop that the truth struck me. They were all making for The Outfit. They were carrying clothes – most of them women, though there were a few men among them, including several uniformed chauffeurs. I began to recognise some of the guests from last night.

Gail saw me, and beamed. And as I approached she gave me a huge wink.

'The jackpot, darlin',' she whispered. 'It's been going on for more than an hour.'

Inside, the shop looked like a jumble sale. Clothes in precarious mountains rose everywhere I looked. Gail was hurrying to and fro among them, over them, through them, casting an eye on each garment as it arrived, rejecting one now and again, keeping up a volley of banter and chat, tearing off receipt slips and handing them out to each and all. It was bedlam. I stood there bewildered.

'Hang them up. Just hang them up – anywhere for now,' Gail was saying, her hair flying. 'Mary, mother of Jaysus, 'tis no way to treat a hangover.'

Finally at one o'clock she cleared a passage to the door and hung up a note – 'Closed for lunch till two.'

'I'm famished,' she announced. 'And it's too long since I had a drink. Renato beckons.'

'It'll have to be on the slate,' I said. 'I don't have a sou.'

'Then I'll treat you, darlin'. And by the way, you forgot your knickers and bra yesterday. Ten people wanted to buy them this morning.'

With that she swept down the road in a swirl of hair, singing something Irish. For a woman suffering from a hangover, I thought, she had the constitution of an ox. I trailed behind, still bemused by the events of the past hour. I hoped Gail would sit down quietly over her minestrone and tell me exactly what was going on.

I also wished Gail *had* sold my knickers and bra: at least then I'd have some money in my purse.

We sat at a small table by the window. Renato attended us – especially me – with that air of beautifully mannered flirtatiousness which he'd perfected in so many years of overcharging people he didn't like and undercharging those he did. Renato was a true Italian democrat: he was confident of his priorities, and attractive women were indisputably at the top. Right now, confused and penniless, I was extremely grateful.

Renato closed his fingers to his mouth as though he were eating a tiny strawberry, and blew me a kiss. '*Bella Angéla!*' Behind him at the cash-desk his ethereal daughter tossed her hair, and the faintest smile formed on her lips: it was a smile which acknowledged where her father's pure love lay. Renato, with his back to her, was smoothing the tablecloth and gazing first at Gail, then at me. 'Specially for you,' he went on, lightly touching my shoulder. 'Today I have . . .'

I chose a mushroom risotto and green salad. Gail tucked in rather more heavily.

Then, with some food inside her, she began to explain.

We'd got it exactly right, she assured me. She couldn't say precisely how and why we'd got it right, but after ten years or more in this business she could tell. It was always an excellent sign when clients came rushing in as they had this morning: it meant there was a buzz in the air; people were feeling restless, and restlessness was wonderfully good for trade. I needed to understand what a promiscuous world this was, Gail insisted. Most of these women were bored, not just with their husbands – although this was often true – but with themselves. They were longing for a change. Most of them couldn't afford to change their husbands, or didn't have the courage to; but they could change what they looked like, what they felt like, how they presented themselves to the world. You gave them a party like the one we had last night, and all those longings got stirred up. They'd wake up the next morning, gaze at their wardrobes, and couldn't wait to sweep everything away and begin again. New clothes were a kind of vicarious love affair.

'But there won't be many coming in this afternoon, you'll see,' Gail went on, eyeing the wine but deciding it would be unwise. 'They'll wait for *me* now.'

'Wait for you to do what?' I asked.

Gail's resolution was wavering. She poured herself another half-glass of wine, contemplated it sadly, and poured out the other half.

'To phone them, darlin'.' She raised the glass, swept her hair defiantly back from her face, and drained it. Then she looked at me over the rim. 'And tell them what they simply can't live without. Because I know them, you see. I know what they like. I know what they'd like to be.' She laughed. 'Which is why this afternoon we must go through everything most carefully – beginning now!'

Gail suddenly looked at her watch, and rose. She didn't wait for Renato, but strode over and passed a credit card to the ethereal daughter, who took it with a celestial smile.

Renato came up to me as I was waiting.

'That was your husband last night, I'm sure, An-gel,' he said confidentially. 'I could tell from the look in your eye.' I felt surprised and half pleased. 'Yes, I recognised him – a very fine photographer.'

I gulped, and murmured something non-committal. Gail was grabbing me by the arm.

'So, tomorrow's when we really begin,' she assured me as we crossed the square. 'I'll be on the phone all day, and much of the evening too. And then . . .'

She didn't finish. An ancient Rolls-Royce was parked right outside the shop.

'Jaysus!' she exclaimed. 'It's the fockin' duchess. I'm wrong, darlin': it's going to begin today.'

If that were so, I realised with profound relief,

I might actually be able to afford tomorrow's bus-fare without dipping into the housekeeping. And with that thought I experienced a deep gratitude that the world should contain duchesses who were poor enough – or perhaps simply mean enough – to purchase their designer dresses second-hand.

With my smile at the ready I followed Gail into the shop, raising an imaginary toast to the poverty of the English ruling classes.

We took twenty thousand pounds in that first week. With our 20 per cent commission this gave us a clear profit of four thousand. I could hardly believe it until I wrote myself a cheque for my half-share; and on Saturday morning I ran all the way to Barclays Bank in the High Street to pay it in quickly in case it should bounce, before realising that of course it couldn't. People in the queue saw me laughing and out of breath, and looked disapproving. One isn't supposed to laugh in banks. If there hadn't been a bulletproof screen between us I would have kissed the spotty clerk who served me.

On the way back I chose Rachel the necklace she longed for, and a summer shirt for Ralph which I hoped would brighten the gloom of his fortieth birthday.

Then I called in on Caroline. I shouldn't have done. I told her the news, and her face remained fixed.

'I suppose there can't be any *real* money in that sort of business,' she said dismissively.

I felt like replying – 'You spoilt bitch, you've never

earned a penny in your whole life.' Instead I bit my tongue and said rather feebly – 'Who can tell?'

Caroline was reclining on the sofa looking fierce, surrounded by the detritus of her Saturday morning reading. From the state of it she evidently hadn't enjoyed it much. I realised that whatever was on her mind was clearly going to burst out very soon, and it was merely a question of whether I wanted to be there when the explosion took place, or not. I'd just decided that I didn't when she reached down for a glossy magazine, killed it with a scowl and thrust it towards me.

'He's such a shit, Patrick: look at that!'

I did. There was a page of photographs under a rather leering headline, and Caroline's finger was tapping one of them. It was of our 'shop-warming', and it showed the winsome girl Patrick had been chatting up all evening: she'd been caught by the flashlight buttoning herself into Patrick's velvet jacket and looking like a piece of absurdly delicious confectionery.

'Was it you who invited the press?' Caroline shot at me. 'Or that dreadful Irish woman?'

But I wasn't really listening. Next to the offending picture was another. It was of Josh Kelvin with a girl who was giving him the benefit of everything she had, which was quite a lot. Even more naked was the look he was giving her: it was exactly the look he'd given me.

I felt stupid, childish, angry with myself, and ridiculously unhappy. Jesus, I was twenty-eight, married, and a mother! What on earth was I doing harbouring fantasies about a man I'd talked to once at a party, about whom I knew nothing whatsoever except that he obviously fucked everything in skirts he could lay his hands on. It was absurd. It was undignified. It must stop. *I love my husband*, I said to myself firmly.

Caroline reached over and took the magazine, giving it a final scowl. Then she peered more closely.

'Isn't that your photographer friend?'

I muttered something, and got up to leave.

'Rather ugly, isn't he!' she went on. 'But he's marvellous in bed, I gather. I seem to remember Amanda told me – or perhaps it was Harriet.'

Oh Caroline, what SAS unit did you train with? Do you know what you do?

'And how did *you* miss out?' I retorted sourly.

She gave me a sharp look. And I left.

I'd forgotten how well the day had started.

For several weeks I refused to admit to myself that The Outfit was doing incredibly well. It was a flash in the pan. It couldn't possibly go on like this. Soon people would possess all the designer clothes they could conceivably want, and a great emptiness would take over the place.

Perhaps I clung on to my pessimism because I needed Gail to go on telling me everything was all right. She seemed to understand this, and her tone was cheerful and patronising.

'You're an innocent,' she kept saying. 'You don't

understand. These women *never* have enough.' She gave a throaty laugh. 'Maybe that too in many cases, and frankly when you look at their husbands it's no big surprise. But the point is, darlin', they all have friends. They talk. Most of them have nothing else to do but talk. They compare notes about clothes just as they do about men. That's what makes their world go round. Believe me.'

Eventually I did believe her. It took a while, but I did.

And suddenly I was on air. I had money in the bank. It was wonderful, and I was happy. I got up early and sang. I cooked supper and sang. I even did the housework and sang. Ralph was surprised. Rachel was mystified. Caroline said it was obvious I had a lover, and about time too.

I refused to think about it in case it went away.

Life at The Outfit soon began to take on a regular pattern; and in the centre of that pattern was my wondrous espresso coffee machine, which now hissed and gurgled at the back of the shop for much of each day. In no time it had become an object of pilgrimage – a reliquary more than a relic, I decided; and if ever it went wrong Rick would miraculously appear, give it his stoat-like glare, then scuttle off for an hour before reappearing with the appropriate part. I always expected these forays to end with Rick being pursued into the shop by some irate café-owner and several policemen; but it never happened, and I never asked questions.

Rick would merely give me an old-fashioned look, and tip his cap to the back of his head.

'All right, chick?' he'd say. 'Gotta go now. Job to do.'

That was another question I never asked — what his 'job' was. And Gail, assuming she knew, guarded the secret immaculately.

She was less immaculate about other things, particularly our customers. Most of them, as it turned out, weren't at all the pampered morons she loved to describe. Gail herself, when I reproached her about this, put up no defence at all and cheerfully admitted she was a lot more fond of her own tongue than she was of the truth, and surely I must know that by now. Then she laughed endearingly.

Naturally most of our regulars were women; and they were as varied as the customers in any shop would be. There were solicitors' and doctors' wives; there were actresses, university lecturers, Harrods ladies, secretaries, shop girls, the wives of foreign diplomats, divorcees of all ages and descriptions, mistresses who either did or didn't use their lovers' credit cards; there were Sloane Rangers, fashion models, members of parliament, committee dragons, patrons of worthy causes, television presenters, society hostesses, air hostesses, artists, dancers, call-girls, girls who looked like men, girls who *were* men, and girls who hated men.

Then there were the real men. Many of these were locals — the wine merchant next door, the tailor opposite, a couple of antique dealers, an estate agent (neither Mr Anstruther nor Mr Pratt, thank the Lord!), as well as several occupants of the neighbouring flats who could smell the coffee through their open windows day after day and finally couldn't resist tracking down its source.

Besides the locals there were the men who chose to accompany their womenfolk. These were the ones most grateful for my coffee machine since it gave them something to do while the dedicated business of dressing and undressing was going on around them. Some of the men came because they loved their wives very much, and wanted to share their pleasure at discovering a glorious Lanvin suit, however *ill*-suited it might be to their lumpen forms.

Others came because they disliked their wives intensely, and were only here to make sure they didn't spend too much, which thanks to Gail they invariably did.

Then there were the men who were accompanying other people's wives. I could always pick these out because they were the only ones who'd refuse my offer of coffee, anxious I imagined not to be drawn into conversations which might reveal who they were and what the hell they were doing here.

But easily the keenest coffee drinkers were the managing directors being dragged along by their secretaries, researchers, bimbos or whatever gorgeous nymph happened to be tickling their libido and their bank balance at this moment. Again it was never hard to spot them. They tended to stroll in breezily as if they were on the golf-course, referring to their mistresses loudly in the third person like jolly uncles who have decided to take their pretty little nieces and god-daughters out of school for an afternoon treat. They were also the most chatty, subjecting Gail or me to a barrage of bonhomie and implausible lies while sipping their cappuccinos and pretending not to sneak lecherous glances in the direction of the changing-room.

When they paid, Gail would make a careful note of their names, then nudge me whenever their wives came into the shop. And sometimes they'd come in with other men – men whose wives were also customers.

'You see, it's a jolly litle merry-go-round, me darlin',' she declared. 'Swapping clothes, swapping part-ners. It all makes for good business: we have it both ways, just as they do.'

The most faithful of our regulars were the window-cleaners. They took more interest in my coffee than in our windows – with the single exception of the tiny window in the basement which just so happened to look into the changing-room, and apparently needed cleaning extremely often until Gail decided to replace it with opaque glass, after which it mysteriously hardly needed cleaning at all.

Then of course there were friends. Patrick appeared from time to time during extended City lunch-hours – on the first occasion ordered here by Caroline to track down his velvet jacket, which in his interpretation meant trying to track down the girl; and subsequently on his own initiative in order to gossip and flirt with me.

Renato came more regularly, bearing little presents, usually of some disgusting Italian cake which he swore was his mother's favourite. When I took it home, even our tame garden blackbird wouldn't touch it.

Rick also dropped in every so often bringing gifts – rings, trinkets, a watch or two, a silk scarf; though perhaps they weren't so much gifts as loans since they tended to disappear again after a few days. Gail without a word provided a drawer for such offerings, happy apparently for the shop to be used as a 'safe house' in return for the many services Rick continued to render. I hoped she knew what she was doing, and turned a blind eye.

Our most exotic visitor was Dante Horowitz, an unlikely name for any man, least of all for a dress designer, though his name was nowhere near as unlikely as his creations. Half Italian and half Russian-Jewish, with a face like Ivan the Terrible, Dante was a 'celeb' in the modern design world, Gail assured me in a voice as near to awe as I'd ever heard from her. The majority of his clients were pop singers and rock stars, with a sprinkling of Hollywood glitterati thrown in. What all of them had in common, Gail said, was a total dedication to catching the camera's eye, and certainly none of Dante's designs could ever have failed to do that.

Yet from time to time Dante went too far: from

the Valhalla of his imagination appeared creations which even his boldest clients declined to wear. And this was where we came in: Gail had a few clients who would wear anything. Dante's first appearance at The Outfit was after we'd been open about a month. He swept in, awarded Gail a regal nod, gazed about him, and swept out again. He always did this, Gail explained: it was his way of announcing he intended to return – 'a sort of curtain-raiser. Hold your breath!'

The next day he did return. He left his chauffeur in the Lamborghini outside, and strode in bearing a large package wrapped as if it was a royal wedding-dress.

Gail was out to lunch. I was in charge, and the shop was empty for once. Dante gave me an eagle-like glare and with an extravagant gesture of his hands commanded me to open the package. I did so. It contained three dresses. I removed them from their tissue-paper with obsequious care while he continued to glare at me, making subterranean noises in his throat. Then I laid them out one by one. They were lighter than cobwebs, and not very dissimilar from cobwebs: all of them were silk, and all of them very obviously transparent.

'You like them?' he said challengingly. 'Then put one of them on. This one.'

And he lifted up the most cobweb-like of the three – a sort of grey mist that hung in the air over his arm. I gave a gulp, and muttered something about going down to the changing-room. Dante clicked his fingers dismissively.

'Just do it. Nobody is here.'

(Except, *he* was.)

'Quick! I need to see.'

(See what? Mostly *me*.)

So I did. I turned my back and unzipped my dress as coolly as I could manage, and lifted a thousand pounds' worth of grey mist over my head and shoulders. But it didn't stay there. The dress wasn't simply transparent: it was topless. I thanked God I was wearing a bra.

Dante didn't share my thought.

'Ridiculous. Take it off!'

I gave another gulp. All right, I thought; I am not a vicar's daughter; at least I shall be able to dine out on this; I bet Caroline's never been asked by a world-famous dress designer to strip, least of all in a shop. So I unhooked my bra and let it drop to the floor.

And at that moment Josh walked in.

There have been moments when I'd have given anything to spin time backwards and take another road. And this was one of them. A numbness overtook my brain. I closed my eyes – perhaps for only a few seconds, but when I opened them again Josh had gone.

'Yes!' Dante was saying, running talon-like fingers through his hair. 'I was right. Madonna was wrong.' Then for a moment the ice-cap melted. 'It suits you: you have the right skin,' he added. 'You should keep it.'

Oh absolutely, I thought. A topless cobweb was just what I'd always wanted: it would be ideal for those informal evenings when a few neighbours called in for a drink; or when Ralph's mother came to dinner; or if I wanted a quiet stroll on the common; or a parents' meeting at Rachel's school; perhaps even a christening. Perfect! Oh, Mr Horowitz, how have I managed to live so long without you?

'Then I shall give it to you,' he said sternly.

I tried to cover my breasts with my hands and my confusion with a smile, and thanked him. Then I thanked him a second time, not knowing quite what else to say; whereupon he gave another subterranean grunt, looked dramatically at his watch, and walked away leaving me partly clothed in a grey mist, and with a high-pitched humming sound persisting in my head.

The Lamborghini roared away. I grabbed my clothes and made a dash for the changing-room. A moment later one thousand pounds' worth of cobweb floated to the floor.

Gail was still out at lunch when I returned, and the shop was empty. I'd half hoped it wouldn't be, then I couldn't even have contemplated doing what I was burning to do – phone Josh. I looked up the number and put one hand on the receiver. Did I dare? I hadn't set eyes on the man since our 'shop-warming' more than a month ago. And what on earth could I say? I rehearsed a few possibilities.

(Breezy) 'Sorry you couldn't stay: I was just seeing if a dress might be suitable for us.'

(Pathetic) 'Josh, how awful; I feel so embarrassed; I don't know what to do. I hope you didn't think . . .'

(Cool) 'Well, you saw my bra last time: now you've seen me without it.'

(Honest) 'So, what the hell am I supposed to say to you after that? For God's sake invite me to lunch, or something – anything!'

Then my rather shattered dignity began to reassemble itself, and I knew I wanted to do nothing. And at that point Gail returned, followed a moment later by a customer. I didn't feel like any lunch, and stayed behind to help Gail bring out a number of suits – a Joseph, a Caroline Charles and a Jean Muir. The woman was going to look dreadful in all of them, but she carried them grimly downstairs to the changing-room, and I slumped wearily into a chair.

'What's the matter, darlin'?' Gail asked. 'Any disasters?'

'No!' I said. 'Just a few embarrassments.'

And I showed her the three dresses Dante Horowitz had left. Gail held them up one by one, and guffawed.

'Well, I can think of one or two of our customers who won't be rushing in to buy these,' she said. 'The question is – who might? Princess Michael? Oh, I don't think so, do you? Janet Street-Porter? Possible, I suppose.' Gail gave another hefty laugh and swept her hair back from her eyes. 'You'd look pretty good in them, mind you, Angela. You should try one on.'

I gazed at her.

'I already did,' I said.

Gail wasn't often upstaged.

'You what?'

I told her about my intimate little scene with Dante Horowitz, and Gail's eyes widened.

'What's more, he gave it to me.'

And I held up the grey cobweb.

Gail peered at the cobweb, then at me.

'Mary, mother of Jaysus,' she exclaimed. 'He *gave* it to you. That old queen?'

It was my turn to be upstaged.

'Queen?' I said. 'You mean . . . ?'

Gail burst out laughing.

'Dante Horowitz! Didn't you know?' She looked at me with a wry smile. 'Darlin', Dante would be about as interested in your boobs as he would in a couple of turnips on a barrow. No offence meant, you understand, but that's how it is. So you've nothin' to worry about. Nothin' at all!'

I kept silent about Josh, whose eyes hadn't exactly suggested he was gazing at two turnips on a barrow.

I was writing out some receipts when he came in. Gail was downstairs in the changing-room with a customer.

'I've managed to catch you alone this time,' he said. '*And* dressed.'

His mouth gave that humorous twitch at the corners which I remembered. He looked weather-worn and deeply sunburnt – dressed in jeans and an open shirt which looked as though they'd travelled the globe with him and become a part of what he was.

'You've been away,' I said, hoping it didn't sound too much like Thank God you're back. 'Where?'

'Angola,' he answered. From the tone of his voice he might as well have said Margate. He grimaced. 'Not recommended. Marginally better than Somalia. And you?'

Well, I thought, I can play this game too.

'Pimlico Square,' I said.

The mouth twitched again, and he laughed.

'Exotic place. You see all sorts of unexpected things.'

I wondered if he was deliberately trying to embarrass me, or just sending little messages in case I imagined he'd just called in for a chat.

He accepted some coffee, and while I prepared it began to pace casually round the room, gazing at the clothes on the racks and every so often at me. Again I noticed the long scar at the base of his neck; it stood out palely against the suntanned skin, and I was aware of how taut and muscular his body was – as I was sure I was meant to. I cursed him for having the self-confidence to gaze at me like this, totally at ease, choosing what little to say, allowing his face to say so much. It was like being stalked by a panther.

I cursed him because I liked it.

He took the cup of coffee and perched himself on the edge of the table. His eyes were taking in the receipts I'd been writing out, the contents of my shoulder-bag, the jacket over the back of my chair, the note I'd scrawled reminding me what to buy from the supermarket on my way home. I was being anatomised.

He drank the coffee and handed me the empty cup.

'About photographing you,' he said suddenly. He must have seen my look of surprise because he added with a smile – 'I asked you the last time we met. Remember?'

My surprise was that *he'd* remembered. I said something indeterminate like, 'Oh yes!' and set about the earnest business of washing the coffee-cup.

'I've had an idea,' he went on. 'I'd like a chance to talk to you about it.'

I suppose if I'd been honest I'd have said – 'For Christ's sake, Josh Kelvin, I've been having all sorts of ideas for the past month or so, and if they're anywhere near the same as yours then I'm in deep trouble.'

Instead I said, 'Oh, really!'

Perhaps that put him off because he stood up and began to move towards the door with that same lazy ease with which he appeared to do everything. Then he paused.

'Perhaps you feel like dropping in for a drink before you go home?'

The speed of the mind never ceases to amaze me. In the split second that followed I'd already decided Rachel would certainly much prefer a take-away this evening, and probably Ralph would too. And I was on the point of saying, 'Yes, I'd like that very much,' when Gail's voice sounded breezily from behind me.

'Someone suggesting a drink? Jaysus, I could do with that.'

I hope my look throttled her; but it was too late.

'Join us, of course,' Josh was saying politely. 'Just press the bell.'

Maybe my face that afternoon offered a few hints of my irritation to Gail's shrewd Irish eyes. Had she done it deliberately, I wondered. The older woman determined not to be left out? I couldn't decide. Fortunately we were too busy to talk. At five-thirty there were still three customers in the shop. At ten to six the last one departed with some firm encouragement from Gail.

'You know, me darlin',' she announced wearily. 'We're going to have to get an assistant. We can afford it. Come on, let's lock up and hit Mr Kelvin's booze.'

I would have preferred to hit her.

As Gail climbed the stairs ahead of me I noticed with satisfaction that she had blotchy legs. I convinced myself that there was no way Josh Kelvin would be keen to explore more of them. Good! Even so, it would help if she could trip and sprain an ankle or two. I remembered a trick from school: you gave someone's foot an imperceptible tap as they lifted it, so that it hooked itself round the other one and sent them sprawling. Then I felt bad. 'Angela Merton,' I said, 'you're *not* a schoolgirl any more.'

The door of Josh's flat was ajar.

'Be with you in a minute,' came a voice from what I assumed was the kitchen, followed by the popping of a cork.

We stepped into a warm and exotic place. All around was the ethnic paradise of a world traveller: kelim rugs around the walls, African masks, Australian bark-paintings, gourds, Navajo pottery, and in the window a busty Indian carving which reminded me rather too closely of myself in my grey cobweb earlier in the day. Here and there little trinkets were arranged on low tables where lamps cast a reddish glow on to Arab bolsters and an enormous Persian carpet. It all reminded me of a Victorian painting I'd seen in Caroline's house, called *The Harem*.

And no doubt, I thought, that is precisely what this place is. At any moment I expected a turbaned slave to bring in sweetmeats and beguiling perfumes, and cursed Gail for being here.

Josh appeared with a bottle and three glasses which he placed on one of the low tables. He caught my eye as he did so, with the faintest shadow of a smile. I cursed Gail again.

'Cheers!' she said, raising her glass.

I did the same without saying anything. The last thing in the world I wanted was good cheer.

Then Gail began to chat – telling stories, laughing, impersonating people, dishing out scandal, finding one subject after another to spin her charms around, and to charm Josh. I didn't feel so much jealous as simply absent. I might have been drifting out to sea on a raft.

I let my eyes wander. There was a pile of black-and-white photographs on a nearby table, and I reached over for them.

'May I?' I asked, making my one contribution to the evening so far.

'Of course,' Josh said, turning to me.

Then Gail was at it again, chattering away centre-stage. Josh left me to his photographs. Or, a part of him did, because now and again he would steal a glance in my direction, and his eyes flick from the photographs up to my face and back again as if trying to fathom what I was thinking. And our eyes would meet in mid-journey. It was electric – Josh trying to read my mind as I tried to read his through his pictures, all in the silence imposed by Gail's chatter. It was like a secret liaison, and I loved it.

The photographs were of Africa – shot very close, and intense, so intense I found myself holding them further away from me. I drew in my breath sometimes. There was an old woman dying, insects feeding off her skin. Then a young woman, hardly more than a child, breast-feeding her child; but the woman had only one arm. There was a young man in a US flak-jacket brandishing a Kalashnikov and grinning; behind him, just visible, a heap of the dead. Another was of a fat general, sweating, a baton in his hand and a sneer on his face.

Josh was glancing at me again. Without a word he reached over and slid another pile of photographs in front of me. Gail went on talking: the Irish stories were in full flood.

The second pile were all photographs of women. It seemed to be London. A girl was flying a kite. A woman was scrubbing a step. A prostitute was half shadowed in a doorway. A barmaid was laughing through cigarette smoke. A mourner was weeping by a grave. A model was teetering along the cat-walk.

They all possessed the same extraordinary intensity, as though he knew each of these women intimately. More than that, it was as though he'd somehow photographed their thoughts, their secrets, at the same time as he was showing me his own. I'd never imagined photographs could do that. And for a moment I found myself thinking about Ralph, who was an actor in order to become other people; whereas Josh, when he took photographs, became himself. I wasn't sure where this thought led me, but I was intrigued and puzzled.

The last picture made me shiver. I had a feeling it had got slipped into the pile by mistake. A young woman was lying naked on a bed. She was lovely, and she was gazing at the photographer with the faintest of smiles. Looking at her I knew instantly what had been said a moment before, and what would happen a moment later. I wanted to see the photographer's face.

I looked up and saw Josh's face – and knew.

Instinctively I closed my eyes.

Then I realised the room was silent. Gail had stopped talking, and was gazing at the two of us. Josh was refilling our glasses. I placed a hand over mine and shook my head.

'I must go,' I said hurriedly, and got up. Gail did the same.

Josh let her go first.

'We'll talk about the idea another time,' he said quietly, holding the door for me. 'It's for a book. Those were some of the pictures you were looking at.'

He pressed my hand lightly as I left.

Angela, I said to myself as the door closed; what kind of fire are you playing with?

But I knew the answer perfectly well.

'Be careful!' Gail said as we stepped outside. And she gave me one of her sideways glances. 'Just be careful!'

The trees in the square looked rich and burgeoning. Renato was waving at me from the window of the Trevi. On the way to the Underground I changed my mind and hailed a taxi. Now I could *afford* a taxi. Then I settled back and watched London pass me by. Crossing the river the water seemed so serene – and so was I, conscious of having just shifted my moral barriers a significant distance back from the safe and narrow path I'd been treading for so many years.

As I opened the front door Ralph looked up and smiled.

'Working late?'

I couldn't answer for a moment. 'Working late?' I realised, was precisely what a wife is supposed to ask when her husband has been dallying with the secretary. It came as quite a shock. Then, smiling back, I gave him precisely the answer a husband is supposed to give.

'Yes, darling,' I said.

I took two days off for Rachel's half-term. Gail dismissed my protestations and assured me that Rick would be perfectly happy to stand in for me, and in any case she'd certainly be doing the same herself before very long. The Derby wasn't too far away, and she hadn't missed that for fifteen years. She always won, she claimed, and needed a second day off to recover from the hangover.

'But we definitely need a full-time assistant, darlin',' she added. 'Perhaps I'll persuade Timothy to leave The Emporium. He's wonderful with the ladies; a man of his persuasion is no threat, you see. They all strip off in front of him without a qualm. I bet he knows as much about female anatomy as Bill Wyman. Or your photographer friend upstairs. How is he, by the way?'

She was hanging up some new suits which had just come in, and gave me another of her sideways looks.

'He wants to photograph me,' I said.

'Yes, I bet he does. I could see it in his eyes.'

She gave a chuckle.

'For a book,' I added.

'Yes, of course, darlin'.'

She was laughing to herself. And that was the

end of the conversation. I couldn't help feeling fool-ish.

So I took my two days off, and Rachel didn't seem to notice. This left me wondering what to do. What exactly *did* housewives do day in, day out? What did I used to do? More to the point, what did the unemployed husbands of housewives do?

That was when I learnt that time was elastic.

'Do you need anything from the shops?' Ralph asked.

'We could do with some lamb chops,' I said. 'But I can easily pop out when I've finished the ironing.'

'Don't worry: I'll do it,' he insisted.

He took two hours over it.

'You never realise how prices differ from shop to shop, do you?' he announced when he got back.

I did know, only too well, but it never took me two hours to find out.

'I think I'll go and get an evening paper,' he said a little later. 'Shall I collect the dry-cleaning at the same time?'

I looked up from the ironing.

'If you like. But it can wait.'

He did it all the same. And by six o'clock there wasn't the minutest item in the *Evening Standard* unab-sorbed: Ralph could have told me which two-year-old was tipped to win the Apprentices' Cup at Pontefract, and what the weather was like in Albania.

And after six it was time for a drink. Ralph used

to have a wonderful cellar. Now he hunted for the 'bin ends' at Wine Rack, and spun the bottle out.

'We can afford to buy a case now, you know,' I said, glancing at the almost empty bottle of Vin de Pays des Côtes de Gascogne.

Ralph felt proud, and didn't answer. I resolved to visit Oddbins tomorrow, and to hell with Ralph's pride.

Or he would read sometimes, more to fill the hours, I realised, than to fill his mind. Occasionally the phone went – and it was never his agent. Afterwards there'd be a long silence. I wished he'd go and see someone: get him out of the place, get him out of himself. The trouble was, Ralph never used to have time for friends; now he had only time, and it hung about the house like a life-sentence.

It saddened me – and shocked me – to see a man searching for so many ways of shrinking the long hours. It was such a waste. I understood the problem perfectly well – Ralph was an actor, and wasn't allowed to be one. And he was gentle and uncomplaining. He often said he loved me. And we made love – a bit. We also went to bed early, Ralph in order to shorten the day, me not to be alone. Then I wouldn't be able to sleep. I'd lie there listening to the night sounds – the drunks coming back from the pub, the distant sound of a party, the sudden shriek of one of Fatwa's victims.

And I wished I was going back to work tomorrow.

On the second day Rachel was again whisked off in a Volvo by some beaming mother of many, and I decided I needed to call on Caroline. She was pleased to see me, and we sat in the garden. It was like old times, except that now I couldn't imagine how I used to do this day after day.

She was in her usual state of animated resentment, and looked tired, as people who do nothing often do. She complained about Patrick, about the children's boarding school, about the neighbours' dogs, about anything she could put her mind to.

'How do you manage to look so dreadfully happy?' she said in an aggrieved voice. 'Is it that lover of yours? Why won't you tell me who it is, and what he's like? It's the only thing I don't like about you – you're so bloody secretive.'

I'd grown used to ignoring Caroline's little fantasies. It made no difference contradicting them: Caroline believed whatever she chose to believe, and nothing would ever shift that.

'I'm bored with men,' she went on. 'I'm going to become a lesbian. Will you let me practise on you?'

'I don't think you're bored with men, Caroline,' I said. 'I think you're just bored.'

She looked at me sharply, and I thought she was going to be angry. Instead she put her chin in her hands, and made a face. Then she looked at me again.

'Of course I am. Bored to tears.' She sighed, and got up. 'Bored. Bored. Bored. I'm a rich bitch with nothing to do. D'you realise, Angela, I'm not even qualified to get a job in Woolworth's? I've never been educated except at a finishing school. I've got one more O Level than Princess Di. I've never been taught anything useful except how to smile and what to wear at Henley; and all it's landed me with is the heir to the smallest county in England, with a prick to match.'

Now she was laughing.

'God, I miss you! I haven't talked to anyone like this for months.'

Suddenly her face brightened, and she shot to her feet.

'I know,' she exclaimed. 'I've got it. Why don't I come and work for you?'

5

Partners

———————— o ————————

For the best part of a week I racked my brains for a way of telling Caroline 'No!' without inviting her eternal wrath. I paced the common in the early mornings seeking inspiration from nature and rehearsing what I might conceivably say. Several approaches came to mind.

(1) 'Caroline, it's terribly sweet of you, but don't you think Samantha needs you more?' (That wouldn't work because Samantha would be only too delighted to be left with the au pair girl, and enjoy some peace in the house for once.)

(2) 'Caroline, we simply couldn't afford to pay you what you're worth.' (This seemed a promising line until Caroline volunteered that she had no intention of being paid for her services anyway.)

(3) 'Caroline, most of our clients are truly ghastly.' (They weren't, of course: the only truly ghastly ones were friends of Caroline.)

(4) 'Caroline, [this one said with a teasing smile] do

you think that the heiress to half of Rutland would really wish to be seen working in a cramped little second-hand shop?' (But when I tried this one on, she flung it back at me: 'Don't be ridiculous, Angela; what better practice for the smallest county in England than the smallest shop in London?')

Finally I came at it straight.

'Look, Caroline, you'd have to work with Gail too, and you know you can't stand her.'

Caroline looked at me in astonishment.

'What *are* you talking about, Angela? I love the Irish. I was brought up with Irish servants, and they were wonderful.'

I gave up.

The next task was putting it to Gail.

'Would you mind just giving her a chance?' I pleaded. 'She almost certainly won't stick it out for more than half a day; but it would let me off the hook.'

We'd closed the shop for an hour and were sitting in Renato's.

'Jaysus!' Gail said, shaking her head and stabbing mournfully at her lasagne. 'The things I do for you.' She took a long gulp of chianti. 'But I'm telling you, darlin',' she added, waving her fork menacingly in front of her, 'one ugly word from that bitch and I'm off: you can run your own fockin' shop.'

'You wanted an assistant,' I reminded Gail hopefully, 'and I've got you one for nothing. That can't be all bad.'

She gave me a withering look.

'Oh yes it fockin' well can.'

I dreaded the day of Caroline's promised arrival; and it was preceded by several days of high-voltage silence from Gail as we waited for the hurricane to strike.

It arrived on a Monday morning in a not-unfamiliar way. At about ten o'clock in the morning I caught the sound of a furious row in the street outside the shop. I recognised the male voice; it was the antique dealer on the other side of us from the wine merchant, and from what I could hear the gist of his complaint was that some unspeakable person had nicked his parking space. Didn't the bloody woman know about residential parking permits? Damned shoppers from the suburbs; why didn't they get a bus? He would see what the police had to say about it.

Then a second male voice chipped in. This time it was the wine merchant himself, who'd given me huge discounts on the champagne for our shop-warming. He wasn't sounding particularly friendly right now. What did the woman think this was? A camping site? Occupying not just one parking space, but *two*. How was he supposed to get his deliveries with that ruddy great trailer occupying half the road?

There was a general chorus of agreement from other male voices which seemed to have gathered for the occasion. Then all of a sudden there came another sound, higher-pitched and considerably louder than the others, and which cut through their protestations like a knife.

'Fuck off! Can't you see I work here?'

That was all. Seconds later the shop door was flung open and Caroline swept in.

'Bloody peasants. Who are they?'

Gail had already disappeared urgently downstairs, and I feared she might already be leaving by the back entrance. I sought refuge by the espresso coffee machine.

'Welcome Caroline!' I said. 'Everything all right?'

She ignored me, and turned back towards the door.

'You'd better come and give me a hand. Are you alone? Where's What's-her-name?'

I followed her outside, averting my gaze from the explosive faces of the antique dealer and the wine merchant. The dark-blue Mercedes was parked at a diagonal, half of it straddling two parking spaces, the other half occupying the pavement. Protruding into the centre of the road was a trailer attached to the rear bumper of the car by a length of rope, much of which dangled beneath it and some distance out the other side.

'Here!' Caroline announced, folding back the roof of the trailer. 'I've brought you some presents.'

And she had. By the time Gail could bring herself to emerge from the basement Caroline and I had laid out a black velvet suit with a Bruce Oldfield label, a

Versace midnight-blue chiffon dress slashed from the hip, an Esteba tweed jacket, cream-coloured Joseph leggings and jumper with a cashmere throw, a navy-blue Jean Muir suit and a Hartnell ball-gown decorated like the night sky with pearls.

'Mary, mother of Jaysus,' Gail managed to exclaim. 'And whose might these be?'

Caroline, who invariably preferred a frown to a smile, awarded a special one to Gail.

'Yours,' she said.

And that was how it began.

Up to that moment Gail's face had been a thunder-cloud. I knew the moment she surfaced from the basement that her mind was set on an immediate and decisive showdown with Caroline: Gail would make it quite clear who ran this place, and the 'spoilt bitch' would be out within the hour. Her face said it. Her hands said it. Even her walk said it as she came up the stairs.

But she underestimated Caroline, just as I did. That languid condescension – 'Why don't I come and work for you?' – wasn't at all what it had seemed. Caroline wasn't coming here because she was bored. She was coming here to make her mark. That was what she always did in life: that was what life was for – having Caroline's mark left on it. Right now Gail was the one she had to master, and she'd thought carefully about how best to do it. She was like a boxer who'd been squatting on a ringside stool for quite long enough, and was now burning to get in there and slug it out; which meant getting in the first punch when the opponent wasn't expecting it. And what more disarming a blow to a born street-fighter like Gail than a gift – of a kind that only Caroline could make? And here it was, laid out for Gail to admire.

End of contest. The look on Gail's face said it all.

This, after all, was Caroline's world, I realised: it had probably been so ever since the very first time 'Mummy' summoned whoever the top designer was to make her daughter look the most stunning young thing of the year. How could a former shop girl from Wicklow, or an ex-bank clerk from Ipswich, possibly understand anything about clothes that really mattered? It simply wasn't in their bones.

I could see from her expression that Gail knew this, while hating to admit it. Making a huge and begrudging effort she decided to tolerate Caroline, at least until the chance came to trip her up.

It never did.

Caroline's talents weren't of an obvious kind – except for her *chutzpah* which was frighteningly obvious to all. After the police towed her car away on that first morning she managed, after a number of well-placed phone calls, to have it towed back again by the late afternoon, by now immaculately clean and wax-polished, and well in time for her to drive us both home.

'It's fun working there,' was her only comment on the day.

She was actually smiling.

To my surprise she turned up again the next day, and the next, and the next.

This wasn't the only surprise. In the mornings Gail and I were normally at the shop a good deal earlier than Caroline. But on about the fourth or fifth day I arrived to find her already in occupation, rearranging some of the clothes on the racks, and humming to herself. The coffee machine was hissing and belching steam, and next to it rested a wad of fifty-pound notes.

'Oh, I told Amanda she had to have the Hartnell ball-gown,' she announced without turning her head or saying good morning. 'She needed it before driving to the country for the weekend, so she had to pick it up early. And she only had cash on her.' Caroline walked over to the coffee machine, turned it off, then picked up the wad of notes. 'It must have been about five thousand new, I imagine, and I've only worn it once, so I asked her for fifteen hundred. Here you are.'

Feeling shell-shocked, I thanked her, entered it quickly in our sales book and went straight to the bank via the back entrance, which was quicker, praying this wasn't the morning for being mugged. A large car was parked on the edge of the communal lawn close to where Rick had roasted chestnuts at our shop-warming. I recognised it immediately as Caroline's. It bore a large red sticker on the windscreen which read '*Fortescue Estate Maintenance Department*'.

'Excuse me, Caroline,' I said on my return. 'What's that on your car?'

She only half bothered to look at me.

'Oh, just something Rick printed up for me till I get my resident's parking permit.'

'And who's Fortescue?'

She gave a shrug.

'I dunno. I thought it sounded right.'

So Caroline was already twisting Rick round her little finger. I began to think she was possibly going to prove an asset after all.

Gail was taking longer to arrive at the same view. The two of them had hardly spoken since the first morning. I doubted whether Caroline's blissful childhood experiences of Irish servants were exactly being reawakened, but at least she didn't treat Gail as though she was one. Gail for her part seemed happy to keep a suspicious distance, occasionally bridged by a nod of respect when Caroline dealt with a particularly awkward customer as if to the manner born.

What finally won Gail over was an afternoon during Caroline's second week at the shop. She still hadn't missed a working day, and her only complaints had been about the car she'd needed to buy for the new au pair girl to do the school run, before she'd discovered the au pair couldn't drive. Much of that morning had been taken up with Caroline interviewing terrified girls to replace her, making each candidate drive the Mercedes round and round Pimlico Square to prove they were up to it. Most of them left sobbing, but by the evening Caroline had grabbed one and insisted on taking her straight home. Protestations in broken English were grandly ignored: the girl could give in her notice to her present employer in the morning when she went to fetch her belongings, Caroline insisted. After all, what on earth did the girl need a nightdress for anyway? She made it sound like a nappy.

But on this particular afternoon there were no such dramas. Domestic life on the common was settled, and so was Caroline. She even smiled at Gail, who didn't know what to make of it.

Suddenly a meek woman of around forty came into the shop, doing her best not to be noticed, which couldn't have been difficult. I could see Caroline eyeing her. Gail knew the woman well enough to leave her alone.

'Husband's a junior minister – trade and industry,' she whispered to me. 'Awful prick. She'll choose something black: the dullest thing we've got. You wait.'

Gail was right. The woman reappeared from the changing-room dressed for a funeral – possibly her own.

Caroline took one look at her and decided to step in.

'Whoever told you to wear black?' she said loudly. 'I bet it was your husband: the man must be a complete ass. Get it off.'

Somehow Caroline managed to make it sound as if she was doing the woman a personal favour. I could hear Gail beginning to grind her teeth. But the junior minister's wife was evidently accustomed to being spoken to in this way, and looked grateful.

'What you need is this,' Caroline went on, reaching for a grey Lanvin suit with a Prince of Wales check. I knew the garment: a startlingly beautiful French woman had brought it in only a week before. I thought Caroline must be out of her mind; the skirt was at least six inches shorter than anything the junior minister's wife can ever have worn in her life. As for the jacket, it needed someone with a minute waist and high breasts, and from what I could judge this dowdy creature possessed neither waist nor breasts.

'Put it on!' Caroline insisted.

The woman took the suit without a word and turned towards the staircase. But Caroline had hardly begun.

'Wait a minute!' And she rummaged in one of the baskets of accessories and pulled out a navy-blue blouse. 'You'll need this as well.'

A look of wonder was beginning to appear on the woman's face. Then Caroline started to rummage in the other basket which contained scarves, belts, gloves and various other accessories. She held up a navy leather belt with a silver clasp, and looked at it critically for a moment.

'Yes! This too! Now go and try them on.'

I could see Gail was preparing to commit murder, but Caroline didn't seem to notice. Her eyes were fixed on the empty staircase as if she'd already re-created this woman in her mind and was waiting to admire her handiwork. Minutes of high-voltage silence passed. And then the woman re-emerged. At first I wasn't certain it *was* the same woman: she looked ten years younger, and quite stunning. How on earth had Caroline detected under the widow's weeds that the woman had incredible legs and a wondrous figure? I glanced at Gail: her expression reminded me of my maths teacher's face at school when the class rebel quite unexpectedly came up with the right answer.

Caroline had won again.

I knew then – and I could see that Gail reluctantly did too – that Caroline understood something which neither of us did: it wasn't just knowing about clothes, but how you put an entire outfit together so that it worked, so that a customer left with a feeling of having been transformed, almost reborn. From the look of gratitude on the woman's face you might have thought she'd thrown away her crutches at Lourdes.

Encouraged by her first miracle, there was no stopping Caroline.

'Good!' she said, rubbing her hands together. 'Very good! Now we can really start. It's Ascot soon, of course.'

The junior minister's wife looked a little confused.

But Caroline was already striding over towards a row of pegs along one wall. After a moment's contemplation she whisked down a huge hat.

'Yes, that's the one.'

Having placed it on the lady's head and adjusted the angle to her satisfaction, she stepped back and nodded approvingly. The woman's eyes were widening like Cinderella's.

By now Gail and I were immobile spectators.

Caroline gave a grunt of satisfaction, and a little nod.

'Well now! Let's see,' she said. 'You'll be going to Ladies' Day at Wimbledon, won't you?'

The woman seemed to be trying to say something, but Caroline was already among the racks. She yanked out a yellow-and-white linen suit.

'This is the one. Caroline Charles as you can see . . . And this hat. I assume you'll be in the Royal Box, so nothing with a brim: you don't want to poke the Duke of Kent's eye out, and you'll want the television cameras to see you're there.'

I glanced at Gail and gave her a wink. But Gail's eyes were too wide to wink back.

'Now, what about Glyndebourne?' Caroline was saying. 'You're going to need an evening dress. I'll find you one. Not long dresses this year: just above the knee.'

Before long an overladen figure in a pill-box hat made a bewildered descent to the changing-room.

Caroline walked nonchalantly to the window and gazed out into the street, humming contentedly to herself.

Then, as the woman returned magnificently attired for Ladies' Day at Wimbledon, Caroline's face lit up.

'Oh, one other thing – I nearly forgot. Cheltenham; the Gold Cup. Now, what have we got for you? Scarves – let's see!' And she bent down over the accessories basket and started pulling them out one after another as if it was a magician's hat; and from the look of wonder on the woman's face you might have thought it was. Caroline chanted out the designers' names like a roll-call. 'Gucci. Dior. Hermes. Saint-Laurent . . . This one, I think, don't you?' And she handed it over. 'Now the hat. Take a look . . . God, no! Certainly not that one! Everyone was wearing wide-brimmed hats last year . . . No, there simply isn't the right one for you here, I'm afraid. You'll have to come back next week. Afternoons are always the best for me. Shall we say Tuesday?'

And there the performance finally ended. Caroline looked thoroughly pleased with herself. She wandered meditatively about the shop while Gail totted up the bill and the woman fumbled eagerly for her credit cards.

'What a nice woman, whoever she was,' she announced, having bundled the junior minister's wife into a taxi laden with her unintended purchases. 'Her husband may get a surprise, I suppose,' she added. 'But I'm sure that's what he deserves.' And she laughed. 'How much did we make? It must have been quite a lot.'

Then, turning to Gail with the most delightful

of smiles, she said, 'Oh, I do enjoy working here. Thank you!'

So now we were three.

I hadn't seen or heard anything from Josh for several weeks. Various theories were put through the bath test.

(1) He'd decided he didn't fancy me after all.

(2) He respected my marriage.

(3) He expected me to pursue him.

(4) He was too busy.

(5) His wife had returned from wherever.

(6) His current mistress had threatened to cut it off.

That was six baths, and none of my theories managed to survive the test.

(1) He obviously *did* fancy me. A lecherous eye is a lecherous eye.

(2) Men like Josh never respect anyone's marriage, including their own.

(3) They also find it much more exciting to pursue than to be pursued.

(4) Who had ever met a rampant male too busy for sex?

(5) The wife, if indeed he had one, was certain to be of the disenchanted or meek variety, and in either case unlikely to be a deterrent to a prowling libido.

(6) A man who had survived being shot at in Beirut was most unlikely to be intimidated by a kitchen knife.

No, there had to be another reason. Meanwhile I found it hard to decide whether I was hurt or relieved.

I came to the conclusion I was both. In the seventh bath I tried to make them cancel one another out; but this also failed. Nor was the hurt merely to my pride: it was a hurt to that area of the imagination which builds glittering castles in the air and leaves one with a sensation of delicious and imminent danger. The sense of relief, on the other hand, was in realising that I was now released from having to face that delicious and imminent danger.

As a result, after I'd dried myself and dressed, I hugged Rachel and put my arms round Ralph in a surge of warm and tearful gratitude.

Rachel reacted with, 'What's the matter, Mum; are you all right?'

I wasn't. But then on the next day all was revealed. Rachel came in to breakfast bearing the morning paper.

'What are Nazis?' she asked, placing the *Independent* magazine on the table in front of me.

Ralph gave her a carefully considered answer while I peered at the magazine. On the front cover was a photograph of a torchlight march through the Brandenburg Gate in Berlin: the marchers were protesting against racist violence in what used to be East Germany. There was something disturbing about the photograph – the stark faces, the dazzle of the torches, the gesture of the man closest to the camera: I knew immediately that Josh must have taken it.

I turned to the feature inside – and I was right. There were six pages of black-and-white photographs. A tattooed skinhead was beating up a Turkish immigrant, who was screaming. A number of paramilitaries in a beer cellar were leering and making fascist salutes. Figures in pyjamas were fleeing a burning hostel. Then there was another photo of the Berlin peace march. This time the camera had caught a woman who looked like the young Marlene Dietrich: she was grasping a banner in a phallic pose and at the same time awarding the photographer a mischievous smile. Ah yes, Josh, I thought: that was you all right. I bet you laughed and called out 'Ich bin ein Berliner' in order to catch her eye.

I was going to be late this morning: it was that sort of day. Ralph was auditioning. He was nervous and wanted to talk. Not that auditioning was a rare event: Ralph was always doing it – he was becoming the world expert in being turned down for lousy parts. But this time there seemed a glimmer of hope, and it certainly wasn't a lousy part. There was to be a revival of *Uncle Vanya* – a shoestring revival, his agent had added, which I imagined (rather uncharitably) might explain why Ralph was being suggested for one of the leading roles – the doctor, Astrov.

'Olivier played the part,' Ralph said proudly.

I didn't say, 'Certainly not for the money they've got to offer.'

But – Jesus, I hope he gets it, I thought. The money didn't matter so much any more. Ralph's sanity did.

As soon as I'd helped calm Ralph's nerves Rachel marched in to announce that she'd lost her recorder. I felt like saying, 'Thank God!' Instead I spent a quarter of an hour searching for it. Then the doorbell rang, and I found myself confronted on the doorstep by our least favourite neighbour in tears.

'Your cat!' she sobbed. 'Your horrible cat! She scratched my lovely Marmaduke so badly he's had to have ten stitches. You ought to have her put down.'

I was late. I was on edge. I wasn't in a sympathetic mood.

'If you stopped treating your dog as a child substitute it might learn to fend for itself,' I snapped.

I wasn't proud of myself. Fatwa, curled up blissfully on the sofa, clearly was.

By the time I eventually reached Pimlico Square all fantasies about Josh were at a great distance from my mind.

'I'm sorry, Gail,' I said as I burst in.

A rich smell of coffee filled the shop, and already I felt better. Gail was chuckling.

'That makes two of you, darlin'. Caroline's in bed with flu – or with somebody. One sugar?'

'Bless you,' I said.

The shop was empty. I perched gratefully on the edge of the table with my cappuccino, stirring spirals of brown sugar into the froth.

'Nobody been in?' I asked.

'Nobody who matters. Just a friend of yours.' There was an impish look on Gail's face. 'What's his name now? He did say, but I've quite forgotten.'

I was used to Gail in her bog-Irish mood. The performance often lasted quite a while.

'Anyway, never mind the name. Not at all a bad-looking feller. A bit rough for my taste, but there's ladies who like that sort of thing, I suppose – quite a few of them, I'd say, judging by the look in his eye and that way he has of walking: you know, sort of pivoting from the crutch like Yul Brynner used to? Now, what was it he said to tell you? Something or other. Oh, my memory's terrible these days: it's what comes of having to look after this place all by meself because the fockin' staff can't get here on time.'

Gail's monologue was mercifully cut short by the arrival of a customer.

'Here, darlin'!' she said to me quietly as she rose to greet the woman. 'The gentleman – whoever he was – left you this.'

And she slipped a note into my hand. I felt like a schoolgirl being secretly dated by the boy at the desk in front. It was just a folded sheet of paper with '*Angela*' scrawled vigorously on the front, and I wondered if Gail had read it. Yes, of course she had!

I opened it. There were just a couple of lines hastily written.

'Do you like German sausage? If so, please come

and share it with me at lunchtime. I want to see you.'

That was all. Nothing about being away for weeks without a word. No apologies. But then, why should there be? I tried to tell myself none of it mattered anyway; it was just a game, and what was all this nonsense about German sausage? I don't much care for the stuff, as it happens; and if I did I could perfectly well go and buy it from Marks & Spencer's.

But my words faded away. Another voice a great deal louder was saying – 'Forget the bloody German sausage, Angela; for heaven's sake, girl, he's probably just bought it from Marks & Spencer's himself. He *wants to see you*: that's the point. So what do *you* want?'

This was disgracefully easy to answer. I wanted to see him. I wanted to see him very much. And in my stomach I felt frightened.

I phoned and said, 'Yes!'

There was a brief silence at the other end; then – 'Good!' And I was left marvelling at how a man could convey quite so much in a single word.

Gail and I were too busy to talk for the remainder of the morning; and I was relieved. In a brief pause between customers she said only one thing.

'I have to tell you, darlin', I'm not a discreet person, but I'll be making an exception in your case. Just be careful!'

She'd have made a wonderful Mother Superior, I decided.

She was also right. Absolutely right. When I pressed Josh's doorbell it was as though my shoulder-bag held a large stick of dynamite. Yes, I needed to be very, very careful.

The buzzer went. The door clicked. I had two flights of stairs in which to decide precisely how I was to behave. After the first flight I'd entirely convinced myself: this was to be a perfectly civilised lunch with a friend who was keen to photograph me for a book. What could be wrong with that? All right, I was attracted to him: so what? If all of us were to spend our lives avoiding people we were attracted to we might as well go and live in convents or on a desert island.

That seemed to settle the matter.

Then, at the beginning of the second flight I had an inconvenient thought. What did Gail mean by, 'Be careful'? Did she mean – 'Be careful because your marriage, family and future happiness could be put at risk'? Or did she mean – 'Make sure you're not found out'? Or even – 'Make sure he's wearing a condom'?

This disturbed and confused me. I was tempted to hurry downstairs and phone Josh from the shop to say I was too busy after all. But since I'd already pressed the buzzer I could hardly do that. I had to go through with this. Be calm and resolute, I told myself. Dignified. Cool. Above all, do *not* be inveigled.

None the less I ran a quick comb through my hair, then tousled it with a quick shake of the head. My mouth was dry, and my heart sounded as though it was fitted with an amplifier. Why did the mind not have greater control over these things?

The door to the flat was open as before. Inside, the room was littered with cameras, lenses and tripods, and Josh was standing there in shirtsleeves. He was tanned and smiling.

Sometimes mere seconds can fill an ocean in the mind, and one swims about desperately in search of a life-raft. This was one of those moments. What on earth was I doing? I was a married woman and a mother; I'd never been unfaithful; and yet stepping into this room it was exactly as though I was stepping into another man's life. I felt weak; I felt naked; I felt frightened. And out of all this mess in which I wallowed emerged just one little word.

'Hello!'

It came out as a squeak.

'I'm glad you came,' Josh said, laughing. 'Sorry about the chaos. I only got back last night.'

And he handed me a glass of wine with that disarming ease with which he appeared to do everything. Taking it, I spilt some. He calmly gave me the second glass, which I carefully took in both hands in case I spilt it too. This was absurd, and I glanced about me for something to concentrate on. I noticed that the table was laid for two, with a loaf of French bread and a long triangle of Brie; and on two plates were spread thin slices of smoked salmon, with half a lemon by each.

'I decided against the German sausage,' Josh was

saying. 'I didn't think you'd want to spend the whole afternoon digging it out of your teeth.'

He cleared the cameras away, and we sat and drank wine. I was beginning to feel something approaching normal. Perhaps I could cope with this after all. He was courteous and attentive, leaning back against the sofa with his legs stretched out, gazing at me. He talked: I didn't much. There *was* a book, he explained, in case I'd thought he might have invented it. It was one of those books which photographers occasionally get invited to put together by some whimsical publisher for no obvious reason, and which get remaindered in six weeks. Did I mind being remaindered in six weeks? And he laughed. *Women of London* was the idea, he said, if you could call it an idea. But it was fun to do – people who caught his eye, people of all kinds. He didn't say what had caught his eye about me; I couldn't help thinking of the nude which had got slipped into the pile of photographs by mistake the last time I was here. I wondered what I'd say if he asked me, and what it might be like reclining naked before his camera in the half-shadows here in this room.

But he didn't ask, and I was relieved at not having to answer. Instead he talked about travelling, about being a photographer – running away into a worse world, as he put it. How it ruined your private life: he'd been married once, he said almost with a shrug, then let the subject drop. I realised he was a lonely man; his cameras saw more of him than his friends did, if he had any. Yet he dealt with people so easily. I liked him, and I wasn't frightened of him any more. I *could* cope. Nothing was in danger. And gradually I felt free to talk. He coaxed it out of me. I was married, wasn't I, he asked; and it was easy to say yes. I told him about Ralph – he knew of him of course, he said, from a good many years ago. I even told him about the boutique, and how I'd sneezed my way into his bed. He laughed again. His face was warm, and I began to like him even more. Perhaps I'd even be able to tell Ralph about him: I might even invite him over to dinner. Rachel would enjoy him too: he might take her photograph, and she could be proud of it at school.

Sitting there, talking and drinking wine, I couldn't understand why I'd been in such a state of confusion. This was so natural. It was easy. How delightful to be able to have male friends. Why on earth not? I'd entirely misjudged this man, and misjudged myself. Angela Merton, I told myself, you've been an ass.

Josh was glancing at his watch.

'You know, we should eat. I invite you to lunch, and all I do is tell you my life story.'

'I like it,' I said, smiling.

The smoked salmon looked wonderful, and I was ravenous. Yes, this was a delightful and civilised occasion. I was enjoying myself, and there was nothing whatever to worry about. He pulled back a chair for me – and then . . . as I sat down he ran his fingers very slowly down my spine.

That was all. No words: just a touch of the hand. At

the fourth vertebra my vision blurred. By the tenth I was shaking. By the eighteenth I was making pleading sounds. If God had given us more than twenty-six I'd have been in heaven, although He might not have seen it that way. As it was, in the space of a few seconds that invisible hand had brushed away my sweetest self-deceptions, along with my appetite, my powers of speech, and all my worthiest resolutions. And having known nothing of what I wanted only a moment ago, suddenly I knew everything. No, I would *not* be telling Ralph about Josh, or inviting him to dinner. I would keep this deliciously and dangerously private.

I put out my hand and touched his face. We kissed. He held my breasts. My fingers were in his hair. Then I drew back at arm's length, and gazed at him. It was so simple that I almost laughed. I wanted him. We would have an affair – of course. Not this minute, there wasn't enough time, and I wanted time. I wanted the evening and the night and the morning. I had no idea how I'd arrange it, or what might happen after that, and I had no wish to think about it. I felt joyful – joyfully wicked and joyfully free. I wanted Josh, and that was enough.

And it was enough to answer yes to dinner one evening very soon, and yes to the question, 'Could I stay?'

Then I left, running my hand down his arm until I let it fall, and on the staircase turning my head with the promise of a kiss. I felt light as air.

'Well, Angela,' I told myself as I stepped into the street; 'you're about to lead a double life.'

I'd always imagined that the chief hazard in planning adultery would be the enormous sense of guilt. But it wasn't so at all: I was quite shocked by how unguilty I felt, and by how easily I radiated serenity and goodwill. I took Rachel to the zoo, to the puppet theatre, to violin lessons, on river trips, attended countless school functions, read favourite stories to her interminably, and arranged elaborate summer picnics in the country. Perhaps all this *was* guilt in disguise; none the less it certainly didn't feel like it. I was propelled through each weekend and each evening by a fresh and wonderful energy which I was well aware seemed to originate in the region of my crutch.

As for Ralph, life with him could hardly have been more harmonious. Now that I had serious reason to doubt whether I really loved him, I found it rewardingly easy to be loving. On the day he heard he'd got the part in *Uncle Vanya* I quickly found a baby-sitter and whisked him off to a lavish dinner in Chelsea. I wore a shamelessly low-cut dress which Gail insisted I have – a Sonia Reykel, black, with a tiny skirt printed with gold butterflies: no outfit could possibly have been more flighty. Ralph's eyes became almost as predatory as in the days when I'd felt the need to 'outplunge' the bimbos who used to drape themselves round him. I didn't even feel guilty that I kept imagining them not

142

to be Ralph's eyes feasting on me, but Josh's; or that I knew I'd be wearing this very same dress on my first evening with him – in his flat, while he cooked, and I'd lean towards him and dare him to concentrate on the *crêpes Suzettes*.

Ralph swore he'd never seen me look so beautiful. And I swore to him that I'd seldom been so happy – which was entirely true. I was alive. I don't believe I'd ever felt so alive.

I was also perhaps being an out-and-out bitch – not because I intended to be, but because there were voices in my head saying, 'You shouldn't,' and which I was wilfully refusing to listen to, preferring instead to heed more urgent and seductive voices which were saying, 'Go for it, Angela! Go for it!'

Altogether it was a strange time of transition, and of release. I found it hard to sleep, and equally hard not to smile.

No, the hazards were never those of guilt. They were external hazards. Josh was away for three weeks – would he always be away? And I had no choice but to wait for him to return and phone me. Before he left he'd given me a necklace with an aquamarine pendant, and his fingers had laid the pale stone carefully between my breasts. Now, whenever I put it on secretly, I could feel his hands. And when I removed it I felt frightened that those hands might never come back, that *he* might never come back – because there were always gunmen where he went, and I found myself wishing he was something safe like a garden photographer. But then would he have been so sexy?

Another hazard, not surprisingly, was Caroline. I carefully told her nothing about Josh, but since Caroline always assumed that if anyone was happy it was because they had a lover, she didn't really need to be told anything – except the identity of the man in question. In fact if I *had* told her about Josh I might never have aroused her God-given instinct for tactlessness. One particular morning took the prize.

'That photographer friend of yours, I haven't seen him for a while. Harriet says he's got an incredibly pretty assistant he takes away with him, though how she knows I've no idea since he dumped her after about five minutes; according to Amanda he's only into one-night stands anyway. I am too, rather: I wonder if he'd be interested. I might invite myself one evening and find out. I know a bit about photography, and he might like to show me where he works. After all, if you've got a darkroom you might as well make good use of it, don't you agree, Angela? Then I can tell you what he's like in case you might decide to try him out yourself.'

Thank you, Caroline!

It was a great way to begin a Monday.

Gail, who knew everything without needing to be told, saw the colour of my face and squeezed my arm.

'It's a load of rubbish, darlin',' she whispered. 'He's not like that, I promise you.'

I was comforted for about five seconds; then I wondered how the hell Gail knew.

This was bad. And I hadn't even gone to bed with the man. It seemed to me I was in danger of enjoying the longest unconsummated affair in London.

Caroline's own interests were becoming focused rather surprisingly on Renato. She adored handsome Italians, she announced: they always made you feel uniquely wonderful. I felt like saying that it mightn't take Renato long to discover that Caroline was uniquely awful most of the time, and that in any case he was entirely dedicated to widowerhood and to the eternal virginity of his daughter. Caroline's attraction was greatly stimulated by being addressed always as 'my lady', Renato not being slow to reward a customer wealthy enough to order white truffles every lunchtime. She was also enraptured to hear that he owned a farmhouse with a vineyard near Siena where he went each August; and since August wasn't far away she'd taken to dangling every possible hint of the joys she could bestow on him if only he were to invite her out there. Renato never seemed quite to get the point.

'My lady would find it so very primitive,' he volunteered after a particularly broad hint one lunchtime.

'*Primitive*,' Caroline screamed as we made our way across Pimlico Square towards the shop. '*That's exactly what I need*. Sex among the vines. Grapes squashed all over me. Sweat. Wine from leather flasks.' (I didn't point out that leather wine-flasks were Spanish.) 'Cicadas.

Nightingales in the dawn.' (Not in August, Caroline.) 'Oh God, naked lust in the Tuscan night!' (Nor did I point out that in a Tuscan August most of the naked lust would be among holidaymakers from Surbiton between drunken renderings of 'O sole mio'.)

'And what would you do about Patrick?' I enquired unkindly.

Caroline shot me a look of amazement.

'Patrick?' It was as though she'd never heard of him. 'I wouldn't *do* anything about Patrick. I never *do* anything about Patrick. Now I'm tired of fellatio there's nothing left to do.'

'And the children?' I persisted.

Another look of amazement.

'That's what nannies are for, Angela. They can all go off to the Club Med: they'll have a much better time, and the nanny can get herself pregnant. Isn't that what's supposed to happen at a Club Med?'

She paused reflectively with one hand on the door of the shop, and her face became suddenly gentle.

'You know, what I'd really like is to go away just with you some time. I like you so much, and we never have a chance to talk any more.' I was touched, and squeezed her hand. Then she laughed. 'We could gossip and tear our friends to pieces for a week, by which time we'd be thoroughly randy and could send for our lovers to join us. Isn't that a great idea? Let's do it. Oh, why not?'

The daydream was broken by the arrival of a

customer who said, *'Danke schön'* rather nervously as we stepped back to let her enter the shop. She was dressed in February grey.

Caroline surprised me by addressing her in fluent German. The woman began to explain something rather falteringly, lowering her eyes from Caroline's critical gaze and fidgeting nervously with her fingers. Everything about her was downturned; her air of self-abnegation was so painful that I longed to wave a magic wand and release her from the misery of being visible. But then Caroline led her over to the back of the shop and began to make her a cup of coffee. They stood talking and drinking there for five or ten minutes, and the woman began to relax. Then she smiled. And suddenly she looked beautiful.

Eventually Caroline began to pace the shop, eyeing the clothes on the racks while the woman stood nervously beside the coffee machine, watching her. Then after a few moments Caroline gave a contented nod of the head, and plucked a garment off one of the racks. I glanced at Gail, who had closed her eyes. It was the most flamboyant outfit we had in the entire shop: a Bruce Oldfield design in flame-coloured chiffon and silk which had been brought in by a Mexican dancer who'd found the skirt too short even for her. Gail had expressed grave doubts that we'd ever sell it.

But there were no such doubts in Caroline's voice.

'Das ist es!' she said.

The German lady hunched in her February grey obeyed orders and disappeared towards the changing-room. Caroline turned to Gail.

'Well, that should liven up the royals. She's the German ambassador's wife, and there's a formal reception at Windsor Castle tomorrow.'

By now the shop was filling up with customers, and Gail and I attended to them while Caroline waited impatiently at the head of the stairs. Five minutes passed. Ten minutes. Twenty. Finally Caroline called out something loudly in German and marched down towards the changing-room. A moment later I heard sounds which reminded me strongly of Caroline whipping Samantha into her school uniform. The customers in the shop began to look alarmed while Gail and I tried to pretend that nothing was happening.

Something *was* happening. A few moments later more urgent sounds of coercion drifted from below. Then up the stairs, her face still flushed with tears, emerged a figure dressed apparently all in flames. They licked around her body as she moved, caressing her shoulders, her breasts, her hips, and swooping just low enough to brush the fringe of one of the briefest skirts I'd ever seen, below which were a pair of astonishing legs. I wondered if the violent sounds might have been Caroline stretching them on a rack. Caroline herself followed behind, smiling contentedly; she was carrying over one arm the suit of February grey, and over the other a brassière, a cotton slip, a woollen pullover, a pair of heavy stockings, a suspender-belt and several other items of formidable underwear.

'Well!' Caroline announced. 'What d'you think?'

It was the only time I'd ever heard applause in the shop. The German ambassador's wife was blushing with unaccustomed pleasure. Caroline gave me a broad wink.

'Jaysus!' said Gail, gazing at the apparition. 'If that doesn't bring down German interest rates, nothing will.'

'Or put the interest up, if I were the ambassador,' I suggested. Gail chuckled.

'Yes, if there's another fire at Windsor Castle, we'll know why, darlin'.'

The German lady changed back into February grey, and departed with her parcel. The downcast expression had returned, but as she left she awarded Caroline a knowing and grateful smile.

'She hates her husband,' said Caroline once the woman had gone.

'You mean, she told you?' I asked.

Caroline gave me one of her patronising looks.

'Angela, you can always tell. She's frightened of him because she's frightened of what she'd like to do.'

Caroline's shafts of insight always surprised and intrigued me. And once again she was perfectly right. Three days later the German lady returned to buy some accessories. She was wearing a light summer suit which showed up her figure, and her dark hair fell attractively over her shoulders. Her eyes were bright, and when she caught sight of Caroline she hurried over and embraced her. They chatted away in German by the coffee machine, and from time to time Caroline went over and rummaged in one of the accessories baskets and made an addition to the small pile of purchases on the table. But most of the time they just talked animatedly, and drank coffee, until it was almost time to close the shop. Finally the woman looked sharply at her watch and hurried over to the window. A large official-looking Mercedes had drawn up outside. After a final kiss on both cheeks she waved goodbye to Caroline, then to Gail and me, and almost ran out of the shop clasping her purchases. Caroline called out something in German which made the woman turn and give a girlish laugh. I watched as a chauffeur in immaculate silver-grey opened the rear door. For a moment I caught sight of a dark-suited figure take her packages and then lean forward to embrace her, before the darkened window closed on them both.

'Well, Caroline,' I said. 'You seem to have done the trick all right, if Herr Excellency comes to fetch her in the ambassadorial car.'

Caroline gave a rather private smile.

'Yes, I did, didn't I. You're right, it *was* the ambassadorial car. But not the same ambassador. She switched embassies on the night of the royal reception. He happens to be the Italian ambassador.'

Gail gave a toss of her red hair, and a raucous laugh.

'That's OK. It *is* the Common Market, after all, darlin'.'

I was still stunned.

'Caroline, how on earth do you do it?' I asked.

She put on an expression of puzzled innocence.

'Me! It's nothing to do with me!' she exclaimed. 'I just listen, and they tell me the truth.' Then she turned to Gail. 'You're a good Catholic girl, you'd understand,' she went on. 'It's called the confessional.'

I said I thought you had to have one of those whispering boxes you sat in while the priest wanked and pretended to give you good advice. Caroline just laughed.

'But we've got one.' And she pointed to the espresso coffee machine. 'There! That's where they confess. Nobody needs a priest.'

Gail clapped her hands delightedly.

'How right you are, darlin'. Nobody needs a fockin' priest. But wouldn't you say we needed a name? Our personal confession box has to be called something. You can't expect me to say to a customer – "Have you confessed to espresso, dear lady?"'

'All right, Gail,' I said. 'As a good Catholic girl, give it a name.'

She looked thoughtful for a moment. Then her eyes lit up.

'Well now,' she said, looking important. 'I learnt

a bit of history from the nuns at school. And I seem to remember the most famous and ruthless confessor of all time was a Spanish gentleman by the name of Torquemada. And after all, the machine must be almost that old. So, how about it? Torquemada? And now for Jaysus Christ's sake,' she added, opening the small cupboard next to the espresso machine, 'let's have a fockin' drink.'

And so Torquemada it became. We had a good many drinks to celebrate, after which Caroline and I wisely took a taxi home. And on the way amid much laughter we raised an imaginary toast to the Grand Inquisitor of the Spanish Inquisition whose fiery spirit now inhabited a coffee machine which I'd rescued one fine spring morning from a dump in Pimlico Square.

The taxi dropped Caroline at her mansion and I walked a little unsteadily back across the common to our own house. Life seemed wonderful and absurd at the same time, and I had a powerful feeling that both the wonder and the absurdity of it had only just begun. The absurdity was related to Torquemada who'd been dead five hundred years, and the wonder to Josh Kelvin who was five hundred miles distant and, as I sincerely trusted, very much alive.

And somewhere, holding a precarious balance between the absurdity and the wonder, lay my real and ordinary life – my husband, my daughter, my home, my shop.

Ralph was reading *Uncle Vanya*. Rachel was watching television with Fatwa on her lap.

'Hello, Mum, are you all right?' she said.

I wasn't entirely sure.

6

Torquemada

───────── o ─────────

To have an espresso coffee machine that was equipped with confessional powers wasn't something we could reasonably expect anyone to believe. Indeed, once the joke had worn off we tried not to believe it ourselves. And yet, however much we tried to rationalise its effect on people, it was undeniable that the smell and promise of coffee lured customers to the back of the shop, and once there they proceeded to talk in the most personal and uninhibited way as though they'd never had the chance to do so before. In a remarkably short space of time Torquemada had extracted almost as many guilty secrets through the administration of caffeine as his namesake in the Spanish Inquisition had managed through medieval instruments of torture. And to acknowledge this unexpected spiritual role I'd taken to giving its brass and chromium face a respectful polish from time to time, until Torquemada now grinned out across the shop inviting customers to approach and unburden their tormented souls. And this they did almost as if they had no choice – as if they were bewitched.

I also noticed that nearly all the women who came to confession only did so after they'd tried on some new suit or dress which they'd chosen from the rack. When they first came into the shop they'd appear self-conscious and hardly utter a word; but once they emerged from the changing-room in a fresh guise they'd make a bee-line for the coffee machine and immediately volunteer the most startling facts about their lives – their marriages, their affairs, their miseries, longings, dreams, fantasies, fears and disappointments. It was as though the clothes they selected – or we selected for them – freed them from the prison of their daily lives, and drove them to seek the comfort of the confession box. Shedding their clothes was like shedding their skin.

Torquemada came spectacularly into his own one sleepy August afternoon. A woman Gail knew slightly arrived at the shop in a tense and agitated state. She was about Caroline's age – in her mid- or late thirties – with dark hair sternly swept back to reveal features that must have been gently beautiful not long ago, but were now hardened and a trifle grim. It was more a mask than a face, but a mask that revealed what lay behind it, which was certainly not happiness. She was a woman who seemed to lower the temperature of the room as she entered.

Gail walked over to her. They talked quietly for

a few moments, then together they looked carefully through several of the racks before Gail pulled out a Jean Muir dress in navy-blue silk and handed it to her. The woman gazed at it uncertainly before making her way downstairs to the changing-room, holding the dress gingerly before her as though it might explode.

There were no other customers in the shop, and Caroline was on holiday. So Gail and I were alone. She came over to me, glancing at the staircase as she did so.

'Darlin', I have a feeling this is going to be one for the confession box,' she said. 'D'you want to bet what it is?' Gail raised her eyes to heaven. 'How about . . . Husband's having an affair? Wouldn't you say that's obvious? You can always tell. Certainly not the first time, judging by her face. Serial infidelity! Ah well, that means next week we'll probably have the girlfriend in, sobbing that the bastard's gone back to his wife. Then – you wait! – it'll be the turn of the girlfriend's husband, and he'll be escorting some bimbo he refers to as his niece. I tell you, it's a fockin' merry-go-round. They're all so predictable.' Gail gave another glance towards the staircase. 'And it's always the women who manage to feel guilty, as if it's their fault their husbands like to wave it about. So what d'you reckon for penance, then?' She laughed. 'Two Jean Muirs and a Paul Costello? Better than a hair-shirt anyway.'

At that moment a customer came into the shop. I went over to serve her, and as I did so the sad-looking woman re-emerged from the changing-room. The new customer was one of those who take ages wanting nothing, and out of the corner of my eye I could see Gail administering coffee, admiring the woman's dress, and all the time listening with grave concern.

It was a good half-hour before she finally ushered the woman out, and the shop was empty again.

Gail slumped into a chair.

'Jaysus!' she moaned. 'If they ever allow women priests in the Catholic Church, promise you'll never let me say yes! Besides, I could never keep the fockin' silence: it'd be all over town in twenty-four hours . . . So, d'you want to hear it, then?'

Of course I did.

'Well!' she said, settling back comfortably. 'I wasn't far wrong. There's this woman – Rebecca, her name is. She's married. OK! Three kids. Husband's some kind of legal hotshot – a QC, or something like that. Rich anyway, and money's gone to his prick. Marriage has been on the rocks for quite a few years, perhaps always. He has affairs; she doesn't, or so she says. She never used to mind that: she doesn't fancy him much any longer. All she cares about are the kids. Lives for them. All right, no problems – until hubby meets this Cruella de Vile creature. Scheming bitch. Unmarried. No money. String of lovers. Pussy power galore. Gets QC firmly by the balls. Demands he get a divorce. Fancies herself the future Lady Something-or-other with a house in Hampstead, country cottage, and a little place in the Dordogne. Screw the kids: he can pack them off to boarding school. Open up the caviar and say "Thank God!".'

Gail paused to attend to another customer, then left the woman to pick through the accessories baskets before settling back into her chair next to Torquemada.

'Right! So what's to be done? Rebecca doesn't mind losing her husband particularly, but not to some bitch who'll grab all his money and bar the door to his kids: Rebecca'd be left coping with the little buggers full-time. And as he's a smart lawyer he's likely to squeeze her dry in the courts while Cruella squeezes his balls to make quite sure he does; and she'll end up living on a shoestring in Acton. God save us! Where have you heard that story before, Angela darlin'?'

She laughed, and got up to smile at the customer and wrap up a couple of scarves.

'Thank you, madam. Please call again,' I heard her say sweetly.

As she returned to the back of the shop Gail ran a tired-looking comb through her resistant hair, making it look even wilder, and sat down again heavily.

'"What can I do?" she kept asking me, as if I should know. Jaysus, Angela, I wish that fockin' machine of yours could spew out answers as well as coffee. Anyway, the point is she's got this ghastly weekend she's going to – *with* legal-prat husband, would you believe it? Some smart affair in the country. Good for his career, he says. Holy Moses, I'd shove his fockin' career up his arse, I told her. And what's more,' Gail went on, 'she wants me to look out a whole load of other stuff – a suit for country walks, a day dress, God knows what else. And she's coming back on Monday to pick them up. I ask you! And d'you know why she's happy to do all this?' Gail's eyes were round with disbelief. 'Because she fancies that Cruella will see the pics in Jennifer's Diary and be so pissed off she'll give hubby QC the old heave-ho. The stupid fockin' cow; doesn't she know that the Cruellas of this world are like Exocets – once they're locked on to a target you can't shake them off?'

Gail simmered down; other customers came into the shop. And that, for the time being, was that. I didn't think any more about it.

And very soon I had other things on my mind. *One* other thing, to be exact. Josh phoned. It was a rainy morning, the shop was crowded, and the call was from Milan. Now, there are moments for pillow-talk on the telephone – 'British Tele-Come', Caroline calls them. But this wasn't one of them: there didn't seem much point in having my breasts admired from half-way across Europe, and since Josh had yet to explore the rest of my body I wasn't turned on by having it described to me in rich detail. Who was he using as a role model, I wondered.

'I know my plans at last,' he explained when the anatomy lesson had ended. 'I'll be back after the weekend . . . And I miss you.'

'You're the one who went missing,' I answered somewhat frostily.

The truth was that my stomach had done its familiar acrobatics the moment I heard Josh's voice, and if he could have seen a print-out of my thoughts the message would have read: 'Oh God, hurry back! I want you!'

But I was wet from the rain, I was busy, and ruffled. How was it possible to lead a double life if one half of it consisted of sitting in a bloody shop and receiving early-morning phone calls from Milan — most probably from a man who'd just spent the night humping some accommodating signorina. Maybe she'd only left the room a moment ago because he insisted he needed to smooth-talk his wife.

I decided it was far worse being jealous of women in general than it was of just one. If Josh really did have an 'incredibly pretty assistant' he took around with him, as Caroline claimed, at least I could scratch her eyes out, whereas I'd have some trouble blinding the entire female sex.

'Could I see you Tuesday lunchtime?' Josh was saying.

I would like to have kept up my frosty voice and answered, 'Perhaps — if I'm still here.' But of course I didn't.

'I'd love that,' I said. 'And I've missed you too.'

Gail was eyeing me as I put the phone down. She showed a customer to the door, then wandered back towards the coffee machine, glancing at me as she passed.

'Believe me, darlin',' she said, running her fingers through her cloud of red hair. 'The first infidelity's always the worst.'

That made me smile. It also seemed to put the whole matter into perspective. It really wasn't obligatory, I told myself, to fall in love with a man simply because I fancied him rotten. Nor was it obligatory to cause pain and suffering to my husband by telling him all about it. A double life didn't mean that one of those lives needed to be at war with the other: there was such a thing as peaceful co-existence, and that was what I must achieve. It was no more than men had been getting away with for centuries, after all.

Something else too was occupying my mind. We were doing extraordinarily well in the shop. We were making money – rather a lot of it. There was suddenly the prospect of all sorts of things I could now afford. My bank manager even invited me to lunch, flavouring the *steak tartare* with offers of business loans, investment advice, pension schemes and high-interest accounts 'designed specially for the young executive' – which I assumed to be me. I liked the 'young' better than the 'executive'. By the end of a bottle of Nuits St-Georges I felt able to tell him I'd only had lunch with an *assistant* manager before, and that was many years ago in Ipswich. It was probably a good thing I refused the cognac or I might have regaled him with the assistant manager's views on the size and significance of men's noses. I might even have congratulated him on being the first bank employee I'd met socially who hadn't played footsie-footsie under the table or attempted to explore my cleavage while talking meaningfully of 'hidden assets'. But I decided this would be behaviour unbecoming to a 'young executive', and smiled agreeably instead.

I also came to realise that much of the success of The Outfit was due to the recession. The prosperous 1980s had been tough, Gail explained. There was so much money pouring into the pockets of the upwardly mobile that wives and mistresses could afford designer clothes by the dozen – always new of course. But now that the south-east of England had been well and truly clobbered the outlook was dramatically changed. Men whose businesses were going under, and who were struggling to save their homes from being repossessed by mortgage companies, were keeping their women on a tight rein while still expecting them to look as chic or stunning as wives and mistresses should. And this was where Gail's message fell on grateful ears: namely that you could acquire five or six designer outfits second-hand for the price of one new.

'There's something very satisfying, darlin', about making money out of people who've lost theirs,' Gail announced one lunchtime.

We were sitting at the back of the shop munching smoked salmon sandwiches. Rick had breezed in with the salmon earlier in the morning with an ''ow abart this!' Then he'd departed with a cheery, 'Caviar next week wiv any luck.' Gail as usual had said nothing, and

I'd asked nothing. Rick's little miracles were better left unquestioned, and we ate the salmon quickly in case the police arrived.

There were just the two of us in the place. Caroline was still away. Having failed to achieve her bacchanal with Renato in Tuscany, she'd settled for a gruesome holiday with Patrick and the children in Sardinia, and was due back the following week, God help us! Caroline's purgatorial holidays were always endured twice – once by herself at the time, and once by those around her when she returned in fury. Rachel's Brownies Camp was also next week, and but for Josh's return I'd have been tempted to volunteer to help out. Anything! Cook. Wash up. Deal with head-lice. Clean out the latrines. Anything to be absent from Pimlico Square during the week of Caroline's return.

'You know, darlin', I can't help liking the miserable old cow,' Gail was saying. 'There's something about the English upper classes you hate to admire, but you do because you envy it, don't you? It's the generosity of the totally selfish. How the hell do they manage it? I certainly can't. I'm no more selfish than the next person, but I've no generosity in me at all. Not an ounce of it.'

Gail looked around her with an air of surprise.

'Jaysus,' she exclaimed, 'I'm becoming a fockin' intellectual.' Then she laughed. 'And if business goes on like this I'm going to be fockin' rich, too.'

Was it really possible that we were going to be rich? I found it hard to believe; none the less I cultivated delicious fantasies of what I might do if it were true.

One of the things I could now afford without the aid of fantasy was an au pair girl. I'd never imagined matching Caroline in such a ladylike self-indulgence. Nor could I possibly give the poor creature a choice of palatial suites in which to relax and entertain her friends: not that relaxation was ever much on offer in Caroline's household. All we had was a tiny extra room which I always suspected was only there because the dimwit of an architect found he had a space he couldn't account for, and decided he'd better punch out a window.

The girl I engaged through an agency was Portuguese. I showed her the room with some trepidation: she was a large girl, and I wasn't sure she'd fit into it. However, she smiled and said 'very nice', which surprised me until it transpired these were the only words of English she knew. Her name was Magdalena, and she was pretty in a hairy way: I wondered if Ralph would fancy her, since he likes hair, and was a little shaken to realise I didn't greatly mind if he did. Rachel took to her immediately, and decided to teach her to say more than 'very nice', which wasn't a huge success. She also decided the girl needed to love Fatwa, which wasn't a success either. Fatwa seemed to think Anglo-Portuguese relations would be improved by the offering of a half-eaten rat presumably ambushed on the compost-heap. If only Magdalena had abandoned her hysterics for a moment while I carted the corpse away she might have added a useful four-letter word to her English vocabulary. Alas, she became just as frightened of Fatwa as the local dogs were, and for a while I feared she might suffer a similar fate.

But at least Magdalena could drive. She could do the school run now that Ralph was rehearsing, and get Rachel tea or supper if either of us was late home. She could also – and I cringed at the thought that this was what clinched my decision to employ her – hold the fort when Ralph was touring with *Uncle Vanya* and I chose to be unavoidably detained overnight.

In short, I had high hopes that Magdalena would prove an essential key to my double life, and made a point of being 'very nice' to her to make sure she didn't leave. As a result, the first words she learnt after 'very nice' were 'I love you', which was gratifying for me though I feared it might land her in a heap of trouble once she discovered the local disco.

I was seeing less and less of Ralph. I'd usually be asleep when he returned from rehearsals late in the evening, and he'd be asleep when I left for the shop in the morning. This reduced marital rites to a spartan minimum, which made me lust after Josh even more. Then at weekends I was occupied with Rachel, and if Ralph and I did find time for a drink together, or an evening walk along the towpath, he invariably wanted to talk about *Uncle Vanya*, or more specifically about himself in *Uncle Vanya*.

'Such a marvellous character, Astrov,' he announced as I thought we were enjoying the sunset over the river.

'You know, I've never played a part I could identify with so entirely.'

It was as though, having lost his identity for so many years, Ralph had finally rediscovered himself as somebody else.

For a while it worried me having a husband I felt I didn't know any longer. Then I came to realise there was poetic justice in this. If, when we made love, Ralph imagined he was somebody else, well – so did I!

Caroline's interpretation of 'Residential Parking Permit' was that it permitted her car to take up residence wherever she chose. On the Monday morning she announced her return from holiday by parking the Mercedes in the forecourt of the police station across the square, there being no other available space, she said. The police constable who followed Caroline into the shop had the wit to point out that at least they wouldn't have to tow it very far, but perhaps Mrs Uppingham might care to move it before *they* did. But 'obstructing the law in the pursuit of its duty' was never a concept that meant much to Caroline, especially after a holiday where the law had done nothing but obstruct her by insisting that even in Sardinia she needed a passport, driving licence, credit cards and a return air ticket. Visiting a local church topless hadn't gone down well either, in spite of Caroline's protest that it had been a hot day and the church was almost on the beach. Besides, if God had made everything then He'd presumably made her breasts too, she claimed, in which case He wasn't likely to be offended by the sight of them.

The *carabiniere* had made a careful inspection of God's work before agreeing that the Almighty had done his job well. Sadly the priest took a different view, and so did the local magistrate. But at least the prison cell hadn't been hot, a good deal less so than the temper of the British consul. Mrs Uppingham had been strongly advised not to return to Sardinia.

The car was towed away.

Caroline's sun-tan suggested that neither church nor prison cell had occupied too much of her time on holiday. Neither, she made it clear, had Patrick or her children. The former had discovered the local golf-course, the latter an amusement arcade. Here the Swedish au pair had been serenaded by every rutting male on the Costa Smeralda, collecting numerous proposals and even more numerous propositions, several of which she'd accepted once the children were in bed. Caroline herself was comforted in her loneliness by a Formula One racing driver from Rome who she claimed had three balls, though she admitted that his ardour may have caused her to miscount. 'He certainly burnt up the track,' she said laughing: 'none of your twenty-second pit-stops.' All the same, he was a gallant Roman gentleman, she insisted: it had been he who had driven all the way to Cagliari to fetch the British consul.

'Not bad for a week's holiday,' I suggested.

Caroline was one person who had no need of

Torquemada to draw out the dark secrets of her life. They were laid open before us like a market stall, enriching an uneventful Monday morning and surprising several customers unaware that Caroline lowered her voice for no one.

Hers wasn't the only return to occupy my mind that morning. Every half-hour or so I wondered what area of the huge sky held a little plane containing Josh, thankful all the same that August wasn't the season for electric storms, iced-up wingflaps or flocks of giant birds, and that Arab terrorists had been quiet since Lockerbie. My double life none the less rested precariously in the hands of Alitalia.

Earlier, over one of our rare breakfasts together, Ralph had emerged from his cocoon of *Uncle Vanya* just sufficiently to quote me a line from it. 'A woman can only become a man's friend in three stages,' he pronounced: 'first, she's an agreeable acquaintance, then a mistress, and only after that a friend.'

I puzzled over why this particular line had grabbed him so forcefully. Of all Chekhov's words of sad wisdom in *Uncle Vanya*, these struck me as among the least wise. Maybe Ralph decided they were blindingly true – true of him, true of us. Well! Yes, I thought, I had indeed been his mistress, and looking back on those years they seemed now to have been the best – the years when I was sweet and young, and we revelled. But when had I ever been 'an agreeable acquaintance'? That didn't sound like me at all. And now 'a friend'? Was that what I'd become? An image formed in my mind of two people growing old in silence by the fire.

I had my own fire, and it frightened me sometimes how fiercely I wanted it to burn.

Another plane went over. I glanced up from the window to see if it had Alitalia markings; but it had gone.

By midday Caroline's holiday confessions had run out and she was turning her attention to her missing car. I overheard snatches of conversation as she made various insistent phone calls – phrases like 'vandals', 'police corruption' and 'stolen from under my nose' occurred rather often, none of which seemed to pay much attention to the truth.

As she put the phone down, it rang again immediately. Caroline answered it and without a word passed it to Gail. I heard her say, 'I'm sorry, Rebecca,' and then, 'I'll see if there's anything we can do, darlin': I'll ring you back.'

I remembered that Rebecca was the woman who was supposed to be going off to the smart country-house weekend with the husband who was screwing Cruella de Vile.

Gail's voice changed alarmingly once she'd replaced the receiver.

'Stupid fockin' cow! She can't come and collect all those clothes after all because poor little daughter's got a sniffle. And there they are, all wrapped up and waiting.'

'What about a taxi?' I suggested.

Gail glared at me.

'Eight hundred pounds' worth of designer clothes! Not fockin' likely.'

'Then I'll go with them,' I said. 'Where is it?'

'Hampstead. Leinster Parade.'

Gail was looking grudgingly grateful. And then Caroline chipped in.

'Leinster Parade! But Amanda lives there, and I'm meeting her for lunch. I'll tell her to drop them in.'

And so a very small problem seemed to be solved.

But the name Amanda went on ringing in my ears. Wasn't she the one who was supposed to have had a one-night stand with Josh? How many Amandas did Caroline know? I was damned if I was going to ask; none the less I was determined to have an extremely good look at the bitch.

I very much wished I hadn't. I very much wished I hadn't even been there. Amanda came into the shop with Caroline early that afternoon. She was about six foot, most of it leg, with a cascade of blonde hair and a sun-tan which largely took the place of her blouse. Caroline didn't improve matters by insisting on introducing me as a friend of Josh Kelvin – 'you remember, darling, that sexy photographer who ... all right, I won't embarrass you! Angela rather fancies him: you'd better tell her what you told me, Amanda.'

I swallowed hard. There must, I thought, be

a weapon to use against Caroline; but where did one find it?

At least Amanda had the decency not to say anything. But with an all-over sun-tan like ·that I decided she probably didn't need to. She wasn't even wearing a wedding-ring. I loathed her.

I wasn't happy that evening. Ralph was rehearsing; Rachel away at Brownies Camp; Magdalena was out, no doubt telling people, 'I love you.' It was a warm late-summer evening, and I was alone. I poured myself a glass of wine and sat in the garden. A bat was stitching to and fro in the dusk between the plane trees, and a blackbird was scolding at Fatwa somewhere in the bushes of the neighbouring gardens. I wanted Josh to phone and say he hadn't forgotten me. But if he had been able to phone, what could I have said? That I wanted him and I was frightened. That I was free and not free. That my marriage was stale but I could never imagine bringing myself to end it. That I wanted him to have half of me, and only half.

But which half couldn't he have? That made me laugh, and I poured myself another glass of wine. Well, the half that was restless, that was on fire, that was still young, that longed perhaps too much for what I'd never really had in my life and didn't even know how to describe, except that it was to do with being with someone very hungrily and very close. It was the half that was going to have a wild and wonderful affair with Josh.

And what if Josh could give me only half of himself too, and I had to share him with some other woman – a woman like Amanda, all legs and self-confidence and sun-tan? It hurt me to think of that, and yet it was all I could offer him myself, so what else could I expect? Oh, sod it! There had to be an answer to this. I poured myself yet another glass of wine and sat gazing at the darkening sky. Yes, of course there was an answer: there was all the difference in the world between taking a lover when you've grown tired of your husband, and sharing that lover with another mistress. That seemed perfectly clear to me.

It was about the only thing that was clear to me, because at that point the wine began to hit me like chloroform. The trees around me became a blur in the night. Overhead the bat kept dividing into two, and joining up again – just like my double life, I thought.

In the morning Caroline's dark-blue Mercedes was outside the shop as usual, astride two parking spaces and a portion of the pavement. How she'd retrieved it from the police I decided not to enquire, but I noticed that it now gleamed, the dent in the front wing had been removed and the bumper straightened. It also displayed a House of Lords sticker on the windscreen, and one saying 'Charity Commissioners' on the rear window. Then the truth struck me. Of course! Caroline deliberately got the car towed away whenever it badly needed to be repaired and polished. The people she knew in high places were obviously very high indeed.

She never mentioned the episode again. Instead she eyed me fiercely up and down.

'Christ, Angela, who are you about to seduce?'

I probably changed colour. I wished I could have brought myself to say – 'Look, Caroline, I'm about to have an affair with Josh. I've never had one before and I'm bloody terrified, but I want it very much. I'm bored with my marriage and I need something to put some zip into my life. So, will you please try to be understanding and not embarrass me every time you open your mouth. It so happens I'm having lunch with him today; I'm as nervous as a kitten, and it took me over an hour this morning to decide what I should wear.'

Instead I said – 'Oh, I'm just having lunch with a friend.'

Of course she didn't believe me.

'Huh!' she said.

At about the sixth attempt I'd settled for a cream-coloured Armani linen suit, with a short skirt to prove it wasn't only Amanda who had good legs, and a white cotton T-shirt – extremely tight with no bra: tastefully shameless, I decided, especially as my nipples are very dark and the floppy jacket was one of those that look as though they're about to slide off any minute; all of which I hoped would concentrate Josh's mind quite wonderfully, and cut the small-talk to a minimum.

Caroline watched me suspiciously all morning. Gail was alternately amused and protective.

'Darlin',' she said quietly while Caroline was occupied with a customer, 'if it helps your nerves, you look terrific. If I had your figure Rick wouldn't see me for dust. So, what's the perfume to be?'

'Diorissimo.'

She laughed.

'Lily-of-the-valley, eh! To put him in mind of country matters ... Jaysus, I'm vulgar. And there's you thinking sweet thoughts.'

I wasn't.

Suddenly the door opened and the lofty Amanda walked in. For a moment my heart sank. Then I noticed she looked a wreck. Her eyes were hollow and her skin blotchy. She blinked, and gazed about her as if she'd forgotten why she was here. Gail didn't seem to notice anything was wrong, and breezed up to her.

'You managed to deliver the clothes to Rebecca all right, then.'

Amanda just nodded.

'Well, actually,' she said in a stumbling voice, 'I'm not sure Rebecca's going to need them after all.'

Caroline was saying goodbye to her customer, and glanced at Amanda sharply as she did so. Then she hurried over.

'So, what the hell's happened to you?'

The three of us were now standing round Amanda.

Suddenly the woman's face broke into a bewildered smile.

'Maybe I should feel terribly guilty,' she said with an uneasy laugh. 'But I don't! . . . I don't at all! I feel wonderful!'

Then the story came out. She had indeed delivered the clothes. Rebecca lived just a few doors down the street, but Amanda had never actually met her before. They got on immediately, and together proceeded to go through the various outfits Gail had selected. Between trying on one garment after another Rebecca raided the drinks cupboard, and the two of them sipped Bloody Marys as the room became strewn with evening dresses, blouses, skirts, jackets, belts, scarves and God knows what else. By the second Bloody Mary Rebecca was protesting what a ridiculous weekend this was going to be, and why on earth had she agreed to go on it just because Angus, her pig of a husband, had decided it was better for his career to be accompanied by his wife rather than by his mistress? Why the hell couldn't Angus fall for some civilised bitch rather than Cruella de Vile? There'd be no problems, and she and the new lady of his life could get together and agree on such things as money, sharing the children, who got the house, pictures, furniture, and so on. Then whoever-it-was could have Angus with her full blessing and good riddance, Rebecca said. They might even become friends so long as she promised never to talk about Angus.

As for this wretched weekend, she wished she'd

never agreed to it. As far as she was concerned he could take any woman he liked so long as it wasn't Cruella de Vile. She didn't even like the clothes much. They'd suit Amanda much better, with her sun-tan and long legs: why didn't she try them on while she was here? And while she was here, why not have another Bloody Mary? They had the house to themselves. The kids were away. And Angus was always back late from chambers, or else he'd be enjoying a delicious *cinq à sept* with the shapely Cruella.

'So I did!' Amanda said. 'After two-and-a-half Bloody Marys I was ready for anything.'

She tried on one outfit after another. Between sips of Bloody Mary and much improvised dialogue Amanda acted her way through Rebecca's ghastly weekend. She dressed for breakfast. She changed for the country walk. She changed for tea. She made charming conversation. Then with a final sip of Bloody Mary she set about changing for dinner. The evening-dress was pink satin, tightly clinging, and bare to the waist at the back. So Amanda peeled off everything except her pants and hoisted the dress over her head, thrusting one arm through the sleeve, and then the other – which stuck.

Cursing the Bloody Marys and the designer of the dress, she struggled. The dress totally shrouded her face and hair: she could see nothing. Rebecca, trying to assist, began to laugh. The laughter was infectious: it took over. The two of them just stood there helpless. There was nothing either of them could bring herself to do.

Rebecca was doubled up; Amanda made feeble semaphore gestures above her head, and hoped no one in the houses opposite could see her. Suddenly Amanda could feel a gentle summer breeze blowing across her bare torso, and imagined Rebecca must have opened a window. She was about to mumble, 'For God's sake shut it,' when she heard Rebecca give out a gasp; then, 'Quick! It's Angus.'

Amanda gave a last frantic tug at the evening dress. There was a slight ripping sound and with an effort she managed to ease it away from her face and down almost as far as her waist, just in time, though her arms were still firmly stuck. With relief she opened her eyes to find an astonishingly handsome man standing in the doorway. He had a delighted smile on his face – as well he might: Amanda realised at that moment that she'd put the dress on the wrong way round. Her elegantly bare back had become her elegantly bare front – and she couldn't move.

'Oh, I love it! I love it!' Caroline exclaimed. 'And what happened? Go on!'

Amanda gave an embarrassed laugh.

'Well, *I* couldn't move,' she said. 'But *he* could. And he did. I realised he wasn't only rather beautiful, he was a man of experience, because with a devastating smile he reached over and calmly found a zip at the side of the dress which I'd never realised was there. "That should make it easier," he said, "though I must say I prefer it as it is."'

And that, Amanda explained, was just the beginning. She looked round to say something to Rebecca, and found that she'd gone – heaven knows where. This might be an eccentric moment to feel the hand of destiny, she thought, but destiny it was. It was laser beams. Pure laser beams.

Suddenly all the things Rebecca had said only an hour before about wishing Angus would fall for some civilised bitch floated back into her mind.

'"Well, I *am* a civilised bitch," I decided. "So here goes. Rebecca's left me the field of play. Let's play." And we did. We spent the night together – in my house – and he was wonderful.' She laughed again. 'I always did want a man who understood about zips.'

'And what about Cruella de Vile?' I asked.

Amanda looked coy all of a sudden.

'Oh, that's all right,' she said. 'Angus phoned her this morning and told her to piss off. Then, after he'd gone I phoned Rebecca. I was terrified she might have changed her mind. But she hadn't. She was delighted – had even slipped quietly out of the room hoping for the best. She's calling in this afternoon, by the way, to bring back the clothes. She's sorry she won't be wearing them, but she hopes you'll appreciate that they've served so much more valuable a purpose.'

Caroline said nothing, but her face wore an expression of the purest pleasure. I made Amanda a cup of coffee, giving the machine an appreciative pat by way of saying 'You did a good job there, Torquemada.'

Amanda sipped her coffee, and glanced at her sun-tan in the mirror.

'And I'm about to enjoy an old-fashioned weekend in the country,' she said with a laugh. 'This time maybe I should wear my evening dress the right way round. What do you think?'

Josh was waiting at the head of the stairs. For a moment I felt I hardly knew him: then I felt I'd known him all my life. The 'lived-in' shirt and jeans. The careless shock of dark hair. The long scar above the collar-bone. The weathered face. The slightly taunting smile. I gave a start as I caught sight of him, and his eyes made me naked as I stood there. Oh my God, I thought, here we go.

The language of silence was powerful: words would have seemed blundering and foreign. As I stepped towards him he extended his arms, and my jacket seemed to find its way effortlessly to the floor while his eyes and hands explored me. I closed my own eyes, and my fingers were in his hair, and down his back. Our clothes tormented us, and we clung together, saying nothing. I wanted this. How I wanted this!

'When can you stay?' he murmured after a while.

'Tomorrow!' I said.

'And then?'

'Another tomorrow!'

I didn't much care if the empty corridor witnessed where Josh's hands and lips were; and even after I opened my eyes it was a second or two before I realised that the corridor wasn't actually empty. There was a woman standing there.

I gave a jolt. She was cool, beautiful and dressed to kill. I was hot, dishevelled, and half-undressed to kill. Worse than that, she was awarding me a self-assured smile as though she knew perfectly well how to cope with this, and had probably done so a great many times before.

I did the best that two hands can do to restore my clothing, and made a grab for my jacket which was lying at the woman's feet. But she calmly picked it up first and handed it to me with that same crushing smile.

This was not a moment to be defeated. I gave what I hoped was a dismissive laugh, and turned away.

'Well!' Josh said, and his mouth puckered with irritation as he gazed at the woman. 'Stella, you could have chosen a better moment.'

'If you will leave the door open!' she answered, walking into the room. 'I just forgot something.'

It was the confident smile that got to me.

'What was it? Your Dutch cap?' I said, and stalked towards the open door. Josh grabbed my arm.

'Angela – wait! This is my agent, Stella Neale,' he said. 'She's a very old friend. I'm sorry. She wasn't supposed to be here.'

'I'm sure she wasn't,' I said. 'But in a busy life scheduling must be a real problem, Josh – fitting everyone in. Even very *old* friends.'

Stella ignored the remark and impassively took a

file from the table. Then she hesitated as she passed me on the way to the door, and held up the file.

'It's all right, I promise you.' She sounded kind suddenly, and put her hand on my arm. 'I only *manage* Josh's affairs: I'm not *having* one.'

She gave a soft laugh, and left.

Still grasping my jacket, I sank into a chair. Josh took it from me, then knelt down and held my hands.

'You certainly know how to deliver a punch,' he said.

I just looked at him. I was still feeling angry. Jesus, I'd behaved like Fatwa. I didn't know I could do that. Of course, it was all a cover. A heap of doubts and guilts had surged up in me in those few moments. Here I was, a married woman, a mother, playing with fire like a teenager and already getting burnt. This was absurd: this was what it would always be like. Suddenly I wanted my safe and ordinary life. I didn't want a life of cat fights. I wanted to be away from here. I even wanted to be at Brownies Camp with Rachel.

That made me laugh. Josh was still looking at me, holding my hands. I needed him to say something. Instead he raised my hands to his lips and kissed them.

'What are you thinking?' Josh asked.

'That I'd rather be at Brownies Camp in Frinton with my daughter than have to go through that again.'

This time he laughed.

'So, what are *you* thinking?' I said.

Josh got up and began to pour out two glasses of wine.

'You really want to know?'

'Yes!'

He passed me one of the glasses.

'I'd rather tell you tomorrow,' he said, perching himself on the arm of the chair, his fingers combing my hair.

'Bastard!' I said, and pulled his hand down on to my breast. 'What a total bastard you are.'

He chuckled.

'I know.'

I laid my hand over his.

'And you only want to see me tomorrow so I can cook dinner for you,' I said.

'That's right!'

'And when you wake up in the morning you won't even remember my name.'

'Of course not!'

'And after that you'll have to catch a plane to Rome because you promised Gina or Marcella or Sophia you'd be there a week ago.'

'All three!'

'And on the way back you might just have to stop over in Milan because Paola misses you so much.'

'Absolutely!'

'And then of course there's the sweet little wife and kids tucked away in the country.'

'Yup!'

'Not to mention your pretty little assistant who thinks you're simply wonderful.'

'Afraid so.'

'And we mustn't forget your beautiful agent who's such a very *old* friend, must we?'

'Certainly not!'

Josh got up to fetch the bottle of wine.

'As a matter of fact Stella and I did have an affair,' he said, without even turning to look at me.

I gave another jolt.

'What?'

'Two affairs, to be precise.'

I swallowed my wine rather quickly.

'At the same time?'

Josh gave a laugh, and refilled my glass.

'It was a while ago,' he went on.

'And what happened between the two affairs?' I asked, wondering what was going to come up next.

'She got married.'

I just looked at him, putting my head on one side.

'Of course!' I said. 'People do. And then?'

'She became unmarried, and we became friends. Very good friends. It goes to show, doesn't it, that friendships can be more durable than marriage.'

'And what about affairs? Are they more durable than marriage?'

He laughed.

'Oh, definitely!'

'Josh,' I said, trying to pull my thoughts into some sort of order. 'What am I doing here? You're dreadful.'

He looked at me quizzically.

'And what about you? You're married. So, what are *you* doing here if I'm so dreadful?'

This time I was cornered.

'I know,' I said. 'I think I'm probably being very silly. Don't you think we ought to stop this?'

For an awful moment I thought he might say yes, and wondered what I would do. To my relief he came over and placed his hands on either side of my face.

'No!'

I kissed him. Then I smiled.

'Well, you can't have two affairs with me, can you, because I'm married already, as you know.'

He laughed again.

'Then we'll have both affairs together.'

'And how long will they last?'

Josh got up again and put down his empty glass.

'Oh, a week or two, I should think. Until I have to go back to Gina in Rome and Paola in Milan. And of course there's the little wife.'

I aimed a kick at his shins. He sidestepped neatly; then he took a couple of steps forward, hoisted me into his arms, and carried me to the door, somehow managing to close it after him with his foot.

'I know it's supposed to be the other way round,' he said, 'carrying the lady into the house, not out. But

I'm hungry, and so are you, and there's nothing to eat in the flat until my delicious little assistant comes back with the shopping.'

With that he carried me down the stairs and out into the street, jacket dangling, from time to time pausing to plant a kiss on my breasts. I decided a struggle might attract even more attention, and merely prayed that Caroline wouldn't see me – or the wine merchant, or the antique dealer, or Renato, or the bank manager who'd referred to me as a 'young executive'. Only Gail would have understood, and loved it.

He put me down on the far side of the zebra crossing, and with his arm somewhere under my T-shirt we walked to a wine-bar where Josh assured me they served wonderful tortillas.

We sat at the bar and Josh ordered two glasses of white Rioja. The barmaid glanced at us both, and smiled knowingly. I suppose what we were, or were going to be, was written across our faces. I gazed at Josh over the rim of my glass, and felt euphorically happy. It was the kind of happiness you pretend is for now only, knowing all the time that if it was for now only you wouldn't be happy at all. The hours between now and tomorrow night seemed like a warm sea to float on, and the current would carry me there.

The tortillas arrived – and so, apparently from nowhere, did a girl. She was maybe sixteen, hair tossing about her shoulders, radiant, and with a pert body that seemed almost accidentally to be covered by a few clothes, as if this were a desert island and she'd had to make do with seaweed. Josh looked surprised and delighted. She threw her arms round his neck, and he hugged her.

'Josh, Josh, Josh,' she was saying. 'What a surprise! I didn't know you were back. How was it? It looked lovely from your card. Am I still going to come and stay with you at the weekend?'

I might have thrown my glass of Rioja in his face. But I didn't, and I was glad.

'Angela,' Josh said, disentangling himself from the girl's arms. 'Meet my daughter Jessica.'

Laughing, I put my arms around him too. For once Josh seemed almost bashful. I noticed Jessica give me an approving glance, and an even more approving glance at my wedding-ring.

'I must go,' she said, looking amused and very pretty. And she gave Josh a peck on the cheek. 'I really look forward to it. I'll ring you, shall I?'

With that she danced off across the bar to join a Neanderthal youth whose jeans had suffered the death of a thousand cuts.

'Any more like that?' I asked.

Josh shook his head.

'No! Jessica's my only one. Still at school – when she can be bothered.'

'She doesn't live with you?'

'No!'

So, here was the big question.

'With your wife?'

There was a pause.

'My wife's dead.' Josh looked down at his hands as if to avoid my face. 'Cancer. Jessica was two. She lives with my sister.'

Saying nothing can be worse than saying the wrong thing; and I couldn't even say the wrong thing. I put my hand in his. He gently squeezed it.

'It's all right,' he said quietly. 'It's thirteen years now.' Then he smiled, and that taunting look returned. 'Besides, life isn't all that bad, considering. My work's fun apart from the odd bullet. And of course there's always Gina in Rome and Paola in Milan, and quite a few more you don't know about – you'll meet them all one day: I'll throw a party. Kelvin's harem party. Would you like that? My pretty little assistant can arrange it while I'm in LA with one of the girls you don't know about.'

'Please!' I said.

He squeezed my hand again, and his eyes wandered over my T-shirt.

'You do have an incredible body,' he said. 'As if I needed to tell you. Does it require special treatment?'

'I hope so,' I said.

He laughed.

I glanced at the clock. It was half past two.

'Josh, I have to go.'

'Well! So long as you don't sell anyone that T-shirt. Promise me? And if you decide to wear it tomorrow you probably won't get any dinner; and I was going to cook you something very special.'

'I promise,' I said.

I didn't tell him I intended to wear something a great deal more revealing than that. We could always, after all, have dinner in the interval.

By the door I hesitated. I wanted to say one more thing. I wanted to say hundreds more things, but one thing specially urgently.

'Josh, will you be going away again soon?'

He just looked at me for a moment, then slipped an arm softly round my waist.

'How could I?' he said.

Those three little words felt like a gift from heaven.

The afternoon would have wafted by somewhere wonderfully far from my mind if it hadn't been for a bizarre chain of events. There were few people in the shop: a late-summer weariness seemed to hang over the place. Rick had called by, affronted by having received a tax claim. Gail was complaining about needing a holiday; Caroline was complaining about the holiday she'd already had. All three of them looked at me sharply from time to time. I'm afraid I had Josh in my eyes, and it showed.

Suddenly the door burst open, and Rebecca rushed in. She'd brought back the clothes, she explained breathlessly, and please could she borrow some money for the taxi? I hardly recognised her for the downcast lady who'd bleated on about the weekend she didn't want to go on with her pig of a husband. It was as though her spirit had been given a face-lift. The sun-tanned Amanda had clearly worked wonders on the pig, and Cruella de Vile was now only a memory.

'I'm free! I'm free!' she exclaimed, having disposed of the taxi and placed the unwanted clothes on a chair. She clapped her hands and performed a little dance across the shop.

Then she stopped, looked at me, at Rick, then at Gail, and finally at Caroline.

'Well! Any ideas?' she said, and did a flirtatious twirl in front of the mirror. She seemed about ten years younger.

Caroline was still looking grumpy, and her mouth was turned down at the corners

'What sort of ideas?' she grumbled.

'Oh, I don't know. Somebody rich. Somebody free. Somebody attractive,' Rebecca went on. 'Somebody I can have fun with.'

I wasn't sure how serious she was – maybe it was just the joy of being rid of both husband and Cruella at the same time. But Caroline was never one to refuse a challenge, even a challenge offered in jest. She gazed at Rebecca. Then the clouds lifted from her face, and her eyes sparkled.

'Well! Let's see!' she said.

She continued to look hard at Rebecca. Finally she walked calmly over to the counter and picked up the telephone. Without saying anything she tapped out a number, glancing at her watch.

'He should be there now, I think,' she said, apparently to herself.

There was a pause, then Caroline turned her back to us. I heard her say, 'Hurlingham Club! Could you page Lionel . . . ?' and I couldn't catch the rest of the name. 'Tell him it's Caroline Uppingham, and it's urgent.' There was a long wait. Rebecca was beginning to look uncomfortable. Then – 'Lionel! . . . I don't care if you *are* in the middle of a match. Listen!' Again Caroline turned her back and I couldn't hear the rest of the conversation, until after a few moments she swung round to replace the receiver and said in a loud voice – 'Right, Lionel! Be at the Connaught at seven. You keep a table there anyway, don't you! . . . Yes, of course I'll tell her: don't be such an idiot.'

I never did find out who Lionel was, how he came to spend his afternoons at the Hurlingham Club, what the match was, or why he should keep a table at the Connaught, though I assumed he was an ex-lover of Caroline's, and if so he was certainly rich and idle and entirely under Caroline's thumb. One of the many things I'd learnt about her was that the payment she extracted for her favours was to keep her men forever in thrall. They all apparently adored her, and they all of them obeyed her. If Caroline Uppingham determined that Rebecca was the right woman for Lionel, then Rebecca *was* the right woman for Lionel, and that was that.

It was Rick who broke the bemused silence after Rebecca had departed.

'Bloody 'ell!' he exclaimed. 'Women pay a dating agency an 'undred quid a session plus twenty-five for every old fart with bad breath who takes 'em out, and you just done the lot over the blower for free. You got a fuckin' goldmine 'ere, you three.' He pointed to Torquemada. 'What with Talking Mother – or whatever yer calls 'er – to get them blabbing, and Caroline who knows everybody and a few more, yer can't lose. Marriage brokers. Marriage breakers. Make a fortune, and 'ave an 'ell of a lot o' fun.'

I'd never heard Rick string more than six words together before.

'Don't be ridiculous, Rick,' muttered Gail, still looking sour. 'Stick to shoplifting.'

But Caroline was looking anything but sour. There was an expression on her face I'd seen many times before. It was exactly the expression she must have had when Nanny told her spinach was good for her; or when Mummy produced some chinless scion of an ancient family for her to spit out in pieces; or when the headmaster at Eton informed her that she'd omitted to put her son down for the school early enough.

It meant trouble.

'Rubbish! It's a *brilliant* idea,' she announced. She spread out her hands to create an imaginary banner. 'I've got it! The Outfit. Designer clothes. Designer partners. We fit you out for both.' Then she laughed. 'Second-hand, of course.'

As she watched Caroline, Gail's face took on a look of astonishment, and she gave a quick toss of her forest of red hair.

'Jaysus, you're right!' she said. 'You're fockin' right! I've always fancied myself as a procuress.' Gail sat heavily on the edge of the table and gazed at Caroline very seriously. 'It's only common sense, darlin', isn't it?' she went on. 'After all, if you want a new house you need a buyer for your present one first, don't you? It stands to reason. Why has no one thought of it before?'

She turned to me with a smile.

'Angela, me darlin', if you could manage to get your mind out of bed for just a moment, how about coming up with a suitable title?'

I didn't even have to think. It came straight off my tongue.

'Outfit Enterprises,' I said.

After all, wasn't I about to embark on my own enterprise?

7

Enterprises

———————— o ————————

I slept badly. I kept thinking that the night before one's first infidelity was very like the night before one's wedding. Not my own wedding, it was true, but the proper old-fashioned kind, with the bride-to-be lying there in the darkness all gift-wrapped in anticipation of the next night – half dreading it, half wondering how she could possibly get out of it, and what on earth would happen if she didn't enjoy it?

Then I told myself not to be such an idiot, and of course I'd enjoy it. I wasn't like my parents, who'd moved gratefully into separate bedrooms as soon as I was conceived. I'd always enjoyed making love with Ralph – at least until recently when it had become a rather infrequent mechanical exercise while Ralph thought about *Uncle Vanya* and I thought about Josh.

There were lots of other differences too. For a start I was breaking a vow, not making one. Then, if it wasn't a success I could always come back and stitch the vow together again like invisible mending, pretend it was a mere aberration, an unfortunate mistake, just one of those things that happen when you're not paying proper attention. It wasn't as though I needed to live with my mistake. I didn't even have to see him again if I chose not to. Josh was supposed to be heavily into one-night stands, according to Caroline, so maybe this would simply be another one. Thank you, and good morning!

All this was rubbish too, of course. I knew that. If it was so unimportant, then why couldn't I sleep? And why was I indulging in this absurd dialogue with myself? It was like being interrogated by some earnest sex counsellor who had absolutely no idea who I was, or what my situation was.

I heard the clock strike two.

So, what *was* my situation? Oh no! Not again! I needed to switch off. I needed to sleep. But I couldn't sleep. I wanted Josh, and I felt sick thinking how much I wanted him. But – Christ! – if I didn't get some sleep now I might just pass out tomorrow night after the first glass of wine.

Sleep! For God's sake, Angela, sleep!

I grew more and more angry trying to will myself to sleep until I heard the clock strike three.

To my bewilderment, it seemed to strike again almost immediately. This time I counted eight. I opened an eye. It was daylight. I didn't know where I was, or whether tomorrow night had already been and gone. My dreams of Josh still raced between myself and the day.

I blinked. Ralph was gazing down at me. I felt myself give a start. Did my dreams show on my face? Had I talked in my sleep? Instant panic!

'You were very restless,' he was saying, still gazing at me. 'Are you all right?'

My mouth felt dry.

'Just hot, I think,' I mumbled.

Well, that was true at least.

Then Ralph started talking about *Uncle Vanya*. He was excited. He was nervous. It was barely two weeks before the play opened. A theatre had been booked in the West End for November; meanwhile there was a brief tour beginning in Brighton. He paced up and down the room, still talking. By now I was wide awake, trying to listen, trying to care. He felt sure his career was about to begin again. Everything was going to be wonderful from now on. People were already saying they'd never seen anyone play Astrov so intelligently since Olivier. I made appreciative noises. Yes, of course I'd be at the opening night, I said. We could have a late dinner afterwards, couldn't we? And I'd stay the night at his hotel. Then breakfast in our room overlooking the sea. Would he like that?

Ralph laughed.

'You make it sound like an affair. A night in a hotel in Brighton.'

I winced, and said nothing.

It was late. I dressed quickly. Magdalena was preparing breakfast. I wished she wouldn't: I needed the day to begin myopically and with delicate whispers. Magdalena was singing something frightful in Portuguese. How could I make her less happy? What's more, she'd discovered porridge, which was a terrible mistake. I don't know what she did to it but it always arrived looking like a dead jellyfish. It shivered as she placed the bowls in front of us. Usually it was just Rachel who had to deal with the mess; but now that Rachel was away at Brownies Camp Magdalena had decided we needed to suffer instead. Ralph was too polite to say anything, and I was too feeble. Besides, I dreaded offending the girl in case she departed in a huff, taking with her the key to my double life.

I made an effort to pull my thoughts together. My alibi for tonight was only a half-lie – well, three-quarters! The truthful bit was that a famous designer was holding a private show of his new creations in Canterbury where he lived – by invitation only. I was one of the privileged. The invitation had arrived at the shop by special messenger, and I'd immediately recognised the name of the man who'd once marched into The Outfit looking like Ivan the Terrible and proceeded to make me put on a topless cobweb, which for some inexplicable reason he'd then presented to me. And Josh had chosen that precise moment to put his head round the door. My embarrassment had remained indelible in my memory, and so had the man's name – Dante Horowitz.

The untruthful bit was that I'd told Ralph the occasion was late in the evening, so I'd need to spend the night in Canterbury. In fact it was mid-morning, which was why I was now flustered and late, contemplating Magdalena's dead jellyfish and racking my brains how I could possibly make it palatable to Fatwa.

'I don't know where I'm staying yet, darling,' I said coolly. 'But you'll be back from dress rehearsals late, so there's not much point my trying to ring you. I'll see you tomorrow evening.'

I was quite shocked by how easily I lied.

Ralph just nodded. His thoughts were already deeply buried in *Uncle Vanya*.

Then I went upstairs to pack. I took out my Number One seduction number which I'd tried out on Ralph a few weeks ago – with such success it had almost rekindled our marriage. It was the Sonia Reykel dress Gail had insisted I have, just about modest enough to hide my navel, and with the minuscule black skirt printed with gold butterflies. Gail knew perfectly well why she'd given it to me, of course, just as she knew perfectly well I'd be wearing it tonight, even if not for very long. She'd announced only yesterday that she'd always wanted to be a procuress, and evidently she was starting with me. All this seemed to contradict her repeated warnings of 'Be careful!'

I had no intention of being careful, and Gail knew it.

Perhaps she really meant, 'Don't get hurt. But how

could one be careful about having an affair, except by not giving anything worth while? Wanting someone wasn't like having an investment portfolio: paying out dividends while making sure you kept the capital intact. In any case, I wasn't a teenager. I wasn't a novice. I wasn't going to throw myself at Josh and say, 'Take me; walk all over me; love me or I'll kill myself.' I was nearly twenty-nine. I had a husband. I had a daughter. I had a life – a life that was going to be miraculously more complete once I had a lover who could cherish me, desire me, fuck me, laugh with me. A double life, with no guilts, no recriminations, no divided loyalties. Render unto Josh . . . Why not?

'But Angela? I asked myself, 'how the hell are you going to manage it?'

I didn't know, and I didn't care to know. Today I was on air.

And with that thought I reached into the wardrobe and pulled out the grey cobweb Dante Horowitz had given me. I'd never had the nerve to wear it. But perhaps . . . perhaps . . . once the Sonia Reykel with the gold butterflies had done the preliminary work, then over the coffee and brandy I might just retire to the bathroom for a moment and float the cobweb over me and nothing else. And I'd feel his hands very gently smoothing the cobweb away, and letting it fall. Then letting his own clothes fall. And then . . . well!

I laid the gossamer dress on top of the other and closed the suitcase. I was smiling. I couldn't help thinking that, apart from Ralph's, and long ago the assistant bank manager's peeping through his flies, I'd never seen another man's cock. I'd been swept off the market at eighteen, and that was that. Now, at the age of almost twenty-nine, didn't this make me a deprived woman? It was extraordinarily unfair when I came to think of it. After all, men see women's breasts all the time, on every topless beach, on page three, in every stationer's window, in fashion ads. But never a cock in sight, let alone an erection. Was it that men were just prudish? Or merely anxious to hide reality under a priapic myth, in the hope that once they'd got you in the dark you wouldn't notice the discrepancy?

My own speculations about Josh's anatomy continued to occupy my thoughts all the way along the M25 – so lustily that I failed to spot the Canterbury turning and plunged straight into the Blackwall Tunnel. This, I decided, was taking Freudian symbolism altogether too far; so I firmly set matters of the night to one side, and bent my mind to the more immediate matters of the day. To Canterbury!

I had no idea what I was supposed to be doing there. I never went to fashion shows, and I would never have come to this one but for the demands of my alibi. There was a little map on the back of the invitation, so there was no problem about finding the place. The Horowitz house was set in a village a short distance outside the city, and was called The Old Rectory. From the outside it looked suitably gabled and grim, and as I drove in I found myself imagining I was the 'old rector' making a sentimental return to see how the new occupants were faring.

I soon realised that the rector would have learnt a surprising thing or two about his new flock. I was greeted formally at the door by a man who was entirely naked except for a mask over his face and a blue bow round his prick. Well, I thought, I hadn't expected to see one of those quite so early in the day: no wonder it was 'by invitation only'. But invitation to what? Curiosity overcame my inclination to turn tail and run.

'Angela,' I told myself firmly, 'this is all part of life's rich tapestry: do not be daunted.'

So I wasn't. Having plucked up courage to greet the man with the bow round his cock I found myself in the main 'salon'. By now I was ready to expect anything, and was quite disappointed to find that no Roman orgy was actually in progress, and that everyone in the room wore at least some semblance of clothing, though the rector might not have defined it as such. Not that it was exactly a formal fashion show, with models mincing along the cat-walk and sturdy ladies perched on fragile golden chairs. The windows and walls were draped from ceiling to floor in black, and from somewhere behind the blackness hidden speakers emitted a cacophony of jungle shrieks alternating with sounds of desperate panting which could have been a missionary fleeing a tribe of cannibals or a couple enjoying the ultimate orgasm: it was hard to be certain which. The lighting, set high around the blackened walls, was programmed to fade almost to darkness every now and again, then suddenly to strobe brightly – green, red, ice-blue, indigo, ghostly white – before settling down to normal for a while. Everywhere lingered the pervading smell of musk.

In the midst of these theatrical displays the room was crowded with people of several sexes who were drifting about holding glasses of champagne in long fingers and saying nothing while they gazed at themselves and each other in tall mirrors – which were positioned everywhere. No matter where I looked I could see myself ten times – and in different colours according to the whim of the lighting. The men, heavily in the majority, all wore make-up and perfume. Several of them were well-known designers I vaguely recognised. The women who drifted aimlessly about the room resembled stick-insects with nipples. These, I realised, must be the models. They flitted and fluttered among the perfumed crowd like anorexic ghosts, gazing about them with huge and unseeing eyes while the young men gazed at one another and held hands. The models all shared a certain family likeness. The famous Horowitz cobwebs floated on them as if the strobe-lights had caught the spiders unawares.

I hid behind my champagne feeling like an earth-mother from an alien planet, and occasionally smiled.

No one returned my smile. No one seemed even to notice I was there, which was something of a relief: conversation might not have been easy.

It was a curious sensation, being invisible, and after five or ten minutes I was beginning to enjoy myself in an odd kind of way when I noticed a pair of eyes fixed on me at the far end of the room. There was no mistaking the messianic ferocity of that face. It was Dante Horowitz, the maestro himself. I was still trying to decide whether I should go up to him and say 'Hello!' when I saw him begin to thrust his way through the crowd towards me, sweeping the stick-insects and the perfumed boys aside. He was exactly as I'd seen him when he entered the shop that day, and instinctively I knew what was in his mind. There could be no doubt about it: he intended a repeat of my disrobing act. I was to be his performing bear – or performing bare, more likely! He was even grasping the dress intended for me, holding it delicately aloft so that it wafted under the strobe-lights with the transparency of summer mist.

The other hand was beckoning me.

There was only one thing to do. I ducked. And I fled. The stick-insects followed my departure with their large and unseeing eyes. The man at the door was carefully retying his bow, his masked face bent low over his naked belly.

Suddenly the whole affair seemed so outrageously ludicrous that I burst out laughing. I tapped the man on his bare shoulder.

'Good thing it's not a clip-on, isn't it?' I said, giving the bow a little tug.

The man raised his mask and looked aggrieved.

Somehow I thought I recognised the face, and smiled to be on the safe side. Then I hurried away before Mr Horowitz could pursue me with his summer mist. I didn't dare look back.

It was midday. I drove into the city and sought normality in the cathedral shop. I bought a T-shirt for Rachel and a tea-towel which featured Chaucer's Canterbury pilgrims. Dante Horowitz would have fitted that company well, I thought. Then I sat in the cathedral listening to the organ fill the nave with Bach. A few more years in the rag trade, I decided, and I might even turn to God.

The afternoon passed slowly. I window-shopped. I bought a couple of paperbacks. I found a local museum. I had tea with home-made scones and raspberry jam. Then around four-thirty I headed back towards London. It was vital that I miss Caroline. Gail had said she'd wait for me – I'd certainly need a stiff drink, she said. Before one's first infidelity a drink was essential, she assured me. It calmed the nerves, stifled the guilt and stoked the libido: 'God knows how teetotallers manage? Perhaps that's why they're always so fockin' self-righteous,' she added.

All the way back I wondered what Josh was thinking. I hoped he was thinking of me.

'Well!' said Gail as I entered the shop. 'How was it?'

'Weird!' was all I could find to say.

She gave her storm of red hair a violent shake, and laughed.

'I know. The men all looked like girls, and the girls like boys. Cadogan was there, I assume?'

'Who?' I asked.

'On the door. He usually is. Dante's boyfriend – "Dante's Inferno" he's usually called. An MP. That's why he wears a mask. Member for somewhere feudal: takes his membership rather literally, I seem to remember. True-blue Tory, of course: Bow Group, as you may have noticed. I take it he *was* wearing his bow? Right colour and all? A grateful constituent gave it to him apparently, though I'm not sure what he was grateful for.'

She could keep a straight face no longer, and gave a huge guffaw. I stared at her in astonishment.

'Gail, I think I need that drink,' I said.

It was seven o'clock – a warm September evening. It felt strange to be going downstairs to the changing-room where every day our customers would disappear to transform their appearance and sometimes – as it increasingly seemed – their lives. I looked at my own transformation in the mirror and wondered how much my life too was about to change. From now on I was going to have to live with a secret. I pondered over why it was that I didn't mind. Then I realised that I'd been living with a secret for many years – that my life with Ralph was incomplete, and becoming increasingly so. Perhaps it always had been incomplete: I'd married the glamour of him, not the man; he'd married a pliant mistress, not me. It wasn't that I was anxious to leave him: we were friends, we had Rachel, we knew each other, we'd been through a lot together. Habits are binding. But I needed more than this – I wanted the electric charge without which life is grey. Oh Josh, lighten my darkness!

How strange that crucial moments in one's life can pass by almost unnoticed. I suppose this was the day when, had I been brave enough to acknowledge it, I knew that my marriage was over; that whatever might remain of it from now on could only be a hollow echo, which I might still listen to out of fear of the silence beyond. But I wasn't ready to be that brave.

A warm breeze touched my bare shoulders: I wondered if we'd have the windows open tonight. A warm breeze and moonlight. His body and mine, exploring one another. I shivered.

I looked at myself again in the black Sonia Reykel dress. If I was about to live with secrets, I decided, then I'd better not wear this outfit too often. The only secret was how it managed not to fall off. But at least no one was likely to take me for a stick-insect.

It was nearly half-past seven. My witching hour. I tossed my hair loose over my shoulders – my witchy look. That would do. I felt nervous: the butterflies on my skirt must have escaped from my stomach. That made me smile. A few dabs of Jean Patou 'Joy', a last glance at the mirror in case I'd broken out in spots during the last two minutes, and I was ready.

'Bijaysus!' Gail exclaimed. She stared at me and made a face. 'I don't know. When your mother offered up a prayer for you, she must have asked for a double helping.'

She jangled the keys and followed me towards the door, setting the burglar alarm and turning the lock behind us. Then she looked at me for a moment.

'Well, all I can say, me darlin', is that you're the best advertisement for adultery I've ever seen.'

I waited a moment or two until she'd turned the corner. Then I pressed the doorbell. With my suitcase in one hand I felt sure I was advertising my intentions to the whole of Pimlico Square. I glanced towards the Trevi restaurant and was relieved to see that Renato wasn't standing at the window.

The door clicked open unannounced. Well, this was it! I stepped inside, and looked up. Josh was standing at the head of the stairs, gazing down at me. He was wearing black jeans and a white open-necked shirt. The long scar on his neck disappeared into the forest of dark chest hair. Christ, that was sexy! He was leaning on the banister rail with a casual smile: how was he managing to look quite so bloody relaxed? Practice, I imagined. How many dozens of women had he let in with that buzzer, saying nothing, then gazing down on them as if they were room-service he'd ordered up? 'It was *Tarte aux pommes* you requested this evening, wasn't it, Mr Kelvin?'

The stairs seemed endless. I felt as though all my gold butterflies had returned to my stomach and were doing a barn-dance in there. I knew Josh was watching me: with a dress like this, how could he not?

Finally I reached the upper landing. I stopped. The butterflies didn't. I managed to raise my eyes towards him, and as I did so the small smile on his face faded. Without saying anything he reached down, took the suitcase and guided me politely into the flat. Then he closed the door and took both my hands in his. His eyes widened, and he gazed at me for a moment; then he let go of my hands and began to run his fingers as soft as feathers across my throat and shoulders and down into my cleavage. By now my butterflies were going berserk, and my mouth was dry.

He just went on looking at me, his hands clasping my hips.

'So!' was all he said, quietly, as though nothing else needed to be said. 'So!' I wondered how one little word could manage to convey so much, and be quite so reassuring. It meant, 'So here we are . . . at last . . . alone . . . You are beautiful . . . and desirable . . . and I want to make love to you before another word is spoken . . . So!'

I smiled.

'So!' I echoed.

I closed my eyes. He drew me towards him and kissed me.

Then he lifted me in his arms and carried me into the bedroom. It was dusk. I could feel a light breeze from the open window. My dress slipped away, and the breeze was on my naked body. So were his hands and lips; and mine on his. I had never known hunger like this: it astonished me, bewildered me. It was as though I'd never been awake until now. I kissed every part of him, wanted every part of him. And I sank with him on to the bed and we made love as the warm night stroked our bodies. We feasted in the darkness and in the moonlight, and it was like the first night of my real life. Then we slept in each other's breath, woke again, and again the night was all touch and hunger. He was my lover, and everything felt new.

Somewhere a clock struck midnight. Josh's head was between my breasts. His body stirred, and I heard him give a little groan.

'I was supposed to feed you, wasn't I,' he murmured.

I ran my fingers down his back.

'You did,' I whispered.

There was silence, followed by a chuckle.

'That's all right then.'

He raised his head and took my breasts in his hands, curling his tongue round one nipple, and the other.

'We could even have a midnight banquet,' he said quietly. 'It's waiting for you.' I could just make out the outline of his head silhouetted against the window as he looked down at me. 'Would you like that?'

I stroked his face.

'Surprise me, then.'

He eased himself off the bed.

'Wait here a second.'

He moved silently out into the sitting room. I could hear a door being opened, and the muffled sound of feet moving to and fro in a room beyond.

After a while I heard him call out very softly – 'OK!'

I got up. A blade of light shone from an open door at the far end of the sitting room. I picked my way carefully among the furniture towards it. I'd never realised there was another room.

I stood at the door silently for a moment, taking in what was before me. There in the soft light was our midnight banquet. The flicker of dark-green candles lit up a mahogany table set with silver cutlery and slender glasses. In the centre a salmon was laid on a porcelain dish, with thin wafers of cucumber arranged along the length of it, and rings of yellow pimento carefully placed around the edges. On one side was an olive-wood bowl filled with green and red salad; on the other a tureen of mayonnaise was decorated with tufts of dill. A glass bowl piled with peaches rested beside a glass wine-cooler.

From the darkness on the far side of the room came the sound of a champagne cork. Josh came over to the table and placed the bottle in the cooler.

Then he turned and his eyes roved over me.

'I love your body in the candlelight.'

'And yours,' I said. Beads of sweat still glistened

round his neck and shoulders. His body looked powerful and muscular. I'd never seen him naked in the light before. 'And I'm happy,' I added.

He smiled, and reached for two glasses.

'Thirsty too?'

He poured out the champagne, and handed me a glass. I gazed at him over the rim, and he raised his glass.

'You look wickedly sexy.'

'Good!' I said, and raised my own glass. 'And now you must tell me, Mr Kelvin, when did you last dine naked with a woman?'

He put on a look of surprise.

'Oh, I do it all the time, Mrs Merton – of course. Particularly at midnight.'

'Beast!'

And he laughed.

Then he motioned me to a chair, and we ate. Suddenly it seemed absurdly formal to be using knives and forks, and we resorted to fingers. I licked his, and he mine. Then we kissed, tasting each other's champagne. Eating ripe peaches without a stitch of clothing on felt gorgeously voluptuous. The juice dribbled down my body, and Josh leaned over and licked it off my breasts. I shuddered.

'You planned every bit of this, didn't you?' I said a little breathlessly.

'Of course!'

Josh sat back in his chair with that mischievous

look in his eyes which I'd noticed the very first moment we'd met.

'Well, I planned something for you too,' I said.

He leaned over, resting his chin on his hands.

'I can't wait.'

'Oh, but you must.'

I ran my fingers down the dark scar on his neck, and kissed him. Then I got up and went back into the bedroom. I lifted Dante Horowitz's grey cobweb from my suitcase, and floated it over my body. If I'd had a mole or two on my skin I suppose it might just have covered them, I decided.

I went back into the candlelight.

'Remember this?' I said, watching the expression on Josh's face. 'Only this time it's for you. I shall be your lady of the cobweb. I hope you aren't frightened of spiders.'

For a second he looked surprised. Then it was as though I'd pressed an electric switch in his body. He rose, and so – with the precision of a guardsman – did his prick.

'Josh,' I said laughing as he stepped towards me, 'the last time I saw one of those before tonight it had a blue bow round it. But I promise you it wasn't saluting me like that!'

Josh merely seized me. The cobweb sank to the floor, and so did I. Scented with champagne and peaches, we made love in the candlelight.

*   *   *

Outfit Enterprises felt like one of those ideas which seem brilliant when you're pissed, and embarrassing the next morning. What was more, my own enterprise had quite swept it from my mind.

But it certainly hadn't been swept from Caroline's mind: if anything it had expanded. Having lost the taste for doing absolutely nothing with her life, Caroline was now bursting to organise the world — or at least that part of the world which found its way regularly into our shop.

So concentrated was her mind that she didn't appear to register the bleary and dishevelled condition in which I confronted the morning, having descended the stairs a little shakily from Josh's flat and discreetly hidden my suitcase behind Torquemada. I was feeling deeply grateful for Caroline's distracted state, since for the past year the minutest switch of mood on my part she'd instantly attributed to my having acquired a new lover. It tickled me that, now I really did have a lover, she didn't even notice. She was inflamed by a spirit of creative mischief.

'Come on, Angela,' she said briskly, 'what the hell's the matter with you this morning? Come up with some of your famous ideas.'

I couldn't. Far from plotting to rearrange other women's marriages, I was much more preoccupied with my own, and what might possibly be left of it after my night of gorgeous infidelity. What would it feel like to be going home this evening? What would I find to say to Ralph? Would he take one look at me and know immediately that I'd been fucked stupid all night by another man? And if this was the beginning of my double life, how was I going to keep the two safely in separate compartments?

Quite apart from my own preoccupations, the whole idea of Outfit Enterprises struck me as trivial and thoroughly foolish – precisely the sort of manipulative game that was bound to appeal to someone like Caroline who always imagined she could run other women's lives far better than they could. Because she was a genius at picking the right clothes for people, she assumed the same genius applied to picking their lovers and mistresses.

'Think of it,' she announced loudly during a pause between serving customers. 'The scores of miserable women we've had in this shop who'd give anything to palm their husbands off on the right woman if only someone would show them how. All they want is an excuse. So, let's give them the best excuse of all – fix their husbands up with someone else. What have we got to lose?'

The wife of a prominent Methodist minister who'd been quietly searching for a middle-aged suit among the racks looked round with a surprised expression. Caroline evidently hadn't noticed her.

'Jesus!' she went on. The minister's wife caught a familiar name and began to listen in earnest. Caroline was getting into her stride. 'You get married in your twenties. That means you could be waking up to the same face on the pillow for sixty years! God, what a prospect! You're not going to tell me any man's got enough juice in him to go that distance; so it makes perfect sense to hand him on before his sell-by date, doesn't it? Then you can start again. Oh, wow!' And she began to smile dreamily. 'Just imagine! Away-break weekends trying out replacements. Life begins at Trust House Forte.'

This made her laugh. It didn't make the minister's wife laugh. Then suddenly Caroline looked at us both sharply.

'But the snag is – who does the husband go off with? There's never enough money to support two families – everyone knows that; and it's always the first wife who comes off worst. The last thing you want is for some conniving bitch to take him for every penny he's got. So ...' and Caroline stabbed a finger on the counter like a government spokesman at the despatch-box, 'you have to find him Mrs Right. That's the answer, isn't it? The perfect divorce!'

She waved her hand in a triumphant flourish, and swung round to receive the imaginary applause from what she took to be an empty shop. Facing her was the Methodist minister's wife, her eyes round as marbles, her jaw hanging open like a torn garment. For a moment, words seemed to form on the woman's pale lips as Caroline gazed at her. Then the jaw snapped shut.

She shook herself slightly, blinked, and strode out of the shop.

There was silence for a few seconds. Gail and I just stared at one another.

'Ah well, me darlin',' said Gail eventually. 'There goes one wife who won't be on our lists.'

Caroline just shrugged.

Then, late in the afternoon, something occurred which made me wonder if Caroline had set it up quite deliberately in order to prove her point. A nervous-looking woman in her forties came into the shop and began to peer among the racks as though she hoped nobody would notice her – which wouldn't have been particularly difficult. She was dressed in autumnal tweeds and wore an autumnal air. Her hair had been abandoned to pepper and salt, and make-up had long since abandoned *her*. I had a suspicion that her husband might have done so too.

Caroline and I were busy with other customers, and Gail took charge. A garment less reminiscent of the Scottish Highlands was eventually found for her, and Gail coaxed her downstairs to try it on. When she emerged, looking distinctly less downcast, she accepted a cup of coffee and sat with Gail at the back of the shop, close to Torquemada.

It wasn't until it was almost time to lock up and she was still sitting there that I began to take any notice.

Gail's red hair was looking more than usually wild – always a sign that Torquemada had extracted a particularly gruelling confession. The woman, her face by now radiant with spent tears, finally departed downstairs to change back into her autumnal tweeds, and shortly afterwards left the shop grasping the suit Gail had found for her.

Gail gave a sigh.

'Another one; only a bit worse than usual!'

Caroline caught the scent of gossip, locked the shop from the inside and perched herself on the counter, a glass of wine in one hand and her legs dangling.

'Well?'

'Poor fockin' bitch!' said Gail, shaking her head.

She was right: it was a familiar story, only worse. The woman was married to a university physics professor who was being tipped for a Nobel prize, Gail explained. It seemed that he'd clawed his way to the top after being supported for years by his wife, who'd given up her own research job to take in typing at home and cope with four kids, one of whom was mentally handicapped. Hubby had screwed round a bit, as ambitious men do. That had hurt, but she'd managed to accept it because at least he was considerate to her: except that now he'd fallen crazily in love with a twenty-year-old student who, he said, made him feel like Robert Redford. He felt young again. This was to be his new life. The world was at his feet.

'And so, when she wasn't in his bed, was the student,' added Gail with a laugh.

'He felt desperately guilty, of course,' she went on, 'but a man's gotta do what a man's gotta do, and all that shit. Lots of, "You've been a good wife to me, darling, but some things are bigger than us both."' Gail mimicked what she imagined a physics professor's voice might be like, with her left hand on her heart. '"Yes, you've been an absolutely wonderful wife, and – believe me – I hate to see you unhappy. I really do. And I want you to know we'll always be friends. But I simply cannot give up this chance. She gives my life and my work new dimensions."' Gail gave a loud sniff. 'Where have you heard that fockin' nonsense before, I ask you? Makes you want to throw up.'

Anyway, she went on, the fates had dictated that the professor should live with his gorgeous crumpet, marry her, start another family perhaps. And all his horizons were golden.

'Great, isn't it! Jaysus, the wife's horizons are as black as fockin' night. Poor bitch! Mind you, she'd be happy to see the bastard disappear up his own quantum theory – he's a boring old fart, apparently. But there's no way a university professor's salary – even with a bleedin' Nobel prize – is going to stretch to two families and God knows how many children. And what's more, would you believe it?' Gail gave her hair a particularly violent shake. 'D'you know what the wife found out? That the bimbo's been getting into practice for the past year with half the male staff of the physics department.'

'Research on their part, I suppose,' I said. 'Isn't that what physicists do – search for black holes?'

Caroline looked quite shocked.

'Angela, you're disgusting.'

Then she laughed.

'Not very black, I wouldn't think. "Entry" signs everywhere – floodlit!'

Gail gave us both a severe look.

'A couple of filthy-minded schoolgirls, you are,' she said, half concealing a smile.

Then she helped herself to a glass of wine.

'So, what do the tea-leaves say?' Gail continued. 'That the bitch'll marry the Nobel prize, strut her stuff as Lady Someone-or-other till the novelty wears off, then in five years' time she'll have exhausted the professor's funds along with his potency, and trade him in for a younger model. And that'll be easy enough: uncle's a fockin' divorce lawyer. Which means that Prof will be shown to have a drink problem, probably violent with it, grope the au pair girl, kick the dog, Christ knows what else: then she'll get the house, custody of the kids, plus maintenance which will wipe out his entire pension. And meanwhile there's sweet little Wifey Number One stuck in a two-up two-down in fockin' Balham with a mentally handicapped teenager, a pile of typing, a chronic depression and a mortgage. So there you go, me darlin's! How's that for paradise on earth?'

There was a silence. Gail started tidying up the invoices. Finally Caroline swung herself to her feet.

'It's obvious, isn't it? She should have found the stupid old fart a better bet. Someone who'd be good to him *and* her.'

'When you think about it,' I said, 'it's just like the rag trade. You buy a dress you love; then when you've worn it enough you don't just throw it out for anyone to pick up, do you? You bring it along here, and we find just the right person for it. Right fit. Right style. So why not the same with husbands? Right fit. Right style.'

I laughed. Caroline looked at me with a half-smile.

'Jesus, you're crude, Angela!'

Then a mischievous look began to spread over her face.

'But that's it!' she exclaimed. 'Outfit Enterprises! Our first client! How about that?'

Gail swigged the last of her wine, glanced suspiciously at Caroline, then at her watch, and reached for her coat.

'You're fockin' mad, you two. I'm off.'

Perhaps we were mad. And yet suddenly the idea didn't seem trivial any more. It seemed extraordinarily clear.

'Sisterhood! That's all it is,' I said. 'Having a say in a man's sex life, just as men have always had a say in ours.'

Gail was lingering by the door. Then she turned, and gave a grin.

'Oh, is that what it is? Sisterhood! Jaysus Christ! Then we'd better call ourselves Sisters of Mercy. I'm a fockin' Catholic – remember?'

We locked up and left. I prayed Caroline wouldn't

comment on my suitcase. But she was far too pre-occupied.

'God, we'll have fun, Angela. Mayhem! That's what it'll be. Bloody mayhem!'

As she drove off she leant out of the car window.

'We must get together and plan it,' she shouted. 'Come round one evening and we'll get smashed.'

The word 'smashed' was all but lost in the sound of tearing metal from the car in front. Caroline didn't appear to notice, and accelerated away through the red lights, the front wing of the other car dragging behind her.

I drove home feeling unbelievably weary. It had been a long night and a long day. I was also not a little apprehensive. Would 'home' feel quite the same?

On that late-summer evening the common already wore the dank air of autumn. The house martins were darting low among the chestnut trees – a promise of rain. My neighbour the ad-man was striding up to his front door bearing a large bunch of flowers for his sad wife – a promise of guilt. Across the cricket-pitch hobbled a three-legged dog – a promise of Fatwa. I half expected to be greeted with a present of the missing leg on the doormat. Instead, there was a card from Rachel bubbling with the joys of Brownies Camp, signed with a smiling face and a rash of kisses.

Christ! Next week it was back to the school run. I realised that a whole year had passed since Caroline had first butted into my life. And in that time I'd taken on a thriving business and a thriving lover. Caroline was responsible for neither really; and yet I would have done neither without her. It was Caroline who gave me the courage to step outside the safe stockade of my life, to risk things, to go for bust as she once put it, laughing: 'since you've got one, honey, use it!'

I had a bath, changed into T-shirt and jeans, and urged Magdalena to go out for the evening before she had a chance to prepare me something ethnic for supper. Then I made myself a cheese omelette, opened a bottle of wine and set myself to work out the official version of yesterday evening, in case Ralph enquired. I ran it carefully through my head several times, smiling at the thought that while Ralph was rehearsing, so was I.

I was still trying to decide whether to tell him about the MP with the blue bow round his cock when Ralph walked in. He hardly glanced at me. He looked drawn and anxious: I doubt if he even remembered I'd been away.

'Hello, darling!' I said, as one does.

There was a sort of grunt that had pain in it. Then – 'Hello!' No 'darling'. No, 'Lovely to see you'. No, 'Let me put my arms round you.' No, 'How I've missed you.' He clearly hadn't, and wouldn't miss me if I weren't there at this moment. Nor perhaps tomorrow and tomorrow and tomorrow – and Lord, I thought, if it was *Macbeth* he was playing he'd be quoting that at me any minute now.

Instead of which it was – 'There's one bit of this bloody part I simply can't get hold of, and it really bugs me.'

He looked overcast with middle-age suddenly, the eyes weary-looking, all wickedness drained from them, the face set in lines that weren't laughter-lines.

'Tell me!' I said.

It was right at the beginning of the play, Ralph explained. Astrov is talking to the old children's nurse. She's telling him he used to be young and handsome, and he's not any more. And he drinks too much.

'Then I have to say – "Yes, in ten years I've become a different man." And I can't seem to get the tone right.'

I mumbled something about how the line sounded straightforward enough to me, but then not being an actress maybe I couldn't grasp the complexity of the problem. But Ralph wasn't listening. He was pacing the room and shaking his head, tuned in to his own gloom. He took the glass of wine I poured him like a robot. I made a face to myself and thought – 'This is extremely boring.' I wanted to say – 'For Christ's sake, however you say the fucking line the audience are going to understand what you mean. All you're trying to explain is that in ten years you've become a different man, and that's hardly a thought that would have taxed Aristotle.'

Then I realised. Of course. Ralph wasn't playing Astrov, he was playing himself. It was true: the two of

222

us had been together ten years, more or less to the day, and in ten years Ralph had indeed become a different man. A much more boring man. No wonder the line stuck in his throat.

I was beginning to wonder if Ralph had ever really cared for me at all, and whether his only real love was what he projected of himself on to the parts he played. Ralph in love with himself making faces in the mirror: and if I happened to be standing between himself and that mirror, then some of that love fell on me. Until I moved – and suddenly I wasn't there any more.

Or was I being horribly unfair? As I gazed at Ralph I tried to see the man I'd loved – had wanted to live with, grow old with. Was he still there, and was it really me who had changed? For the first time I felt a twinge of guilt. My head was still swimming through my night with Josh. My body still lay with him: I could feel myself giving off an anti-magnetic force, pushing Ralph away.

'Would you like me to get you some supper?' I said warily.

He looked at me as if he hadn't heard.

'"In ten years I've become a different man!"' he exclaimed, wringing his hands, and with a hunted look on his face. 'Does that sound better?'

No, it wasn't just me who had changed.

'It sounds absolutely fine, darling. Now, would you like some supper?'

'"In ten years I've become a different man,"' he said again, more sadly this time.

This, I thought, could go on for ever. I poured myself another glass of wine and sought refuge in the evening paper. And between the lines of the latest evasions on Bosnia by the Foreign Secretary I heard Josh's voice – 'I love your body in the candlelight.'

So I became a lunchtime lover.

I did wonder what Josh got up to in the evenings, though I hoped that if I was demanding enough in the middle of the day he wouldn't be able to do much harm at night. I wasn't entirely confident of this, Josh's appetite being what it was – he seemed to be permanently erect while I was more or less permanently horizontal: and in the afternoons I kept a weather-eye from the shop window to check what edible blondes were mincing up to his front door and pressing the bell. Unfortunately, now he was working from home doing a lot of fashion work, there were rather a lot of these and I took to dousing my jealousy by phoning up on his work line to make sure. I shouldn't have done, and Josh sounded irritated.

'I'm working, sweetheart. No, I'm *working*!'

So I stopped phoning and tried to trust him.

All this brought out the Irish in Gail, who alternated between being a secret accomplice and Mother Superior. Even her speech became a caricature of her Wicklow origins.

'Bijaysus, darlin', how the fock can I be sellin' dresses to some old tart wid you humpin' away up

224

dere like the thunder o' God and me pretendin' it's the fockin' plumber?'

Caroline, her mind focused ever more sharply on Outfit Enterprises, continued not to notice. Her only complaint was that I was no longer free to join her for a lunchtime pasta at the Trevi.

'Are you slimming or something, Angela? Ridiculous, with a figure like yours!'

I suggested she ought to be happy, she could now have Renato all to herself; but that only produced a grimace. Since the failure of her bid to get invited to Renato's Tuscan farmhouse for a summer romp among the vines, she'd given Renato up as a potential lover. Or so she claimed.

'What happened to the Formula One racing driver from Rome, Caroline?' I asked. 'The one with three balls?'

She gave me a fierce look. Presumably he'd gone on round the circuit, or found another pit-stop.

'Angela, you're free this evening, aren't you!' she ordered, ignoring my enquiries about the racing driver with three balls. 'We need to talk about Enterprises. What we're going to do, and how we're going to do it. Make it about seven.'

It was a while since I'd been to Caroline's house. Patrick, she explained, would be out at some City booze-up. Ralph, I knew, was at a full dress rehearsal and would be back late. Magdalena promised to provide Rachel with some Portuguese national dish she'd been threatening us with for weeks – something she called '*teckvai*'.

'I make *teckvai*,' she announced, glowing.

For Rachel's sake I enquired what exactly it was, but Magdalena merely spread her arms wide and smiled like the sun, which I understood to mean that it contained just about everything you might care to mention – some sort of Portuguese equivalent of *paella*, I imagined, probably flavoured with Portuguese man-o'-war, which I remembered was a kind of poisonous jellyfish. I mentally prepared a note for Rachel to take to school once she'd fully recovered, and left Magdalena money to do some late shopping. Rachel would help carry it all back, she assured me. God knows in what state I'd find the kitchen when I got back.

Caroline opened the door without interrupting the call she was making on her hand-phone. I stood gazing out at the garden while she continued to issue a string of commands. I remembered it was a 'late shopping' evening, and pictured some cringing assistant at John Lewis on the receiving end.

Finally there were indications that Caroline had given the poor girl enough punishment for one day.

'I've got to go, Mummy!' she said loudly. 'I'm in the middle of a board meeting.'

As she said this I caught sight of a note-pad on the drawing-room table. Caroline had scrawled in bold red letters across the top of it – Bawd Meeting.

'Right! So what's the first step, d'you think?'

she asked, marching into the room and handing me a vodka-and-tonic that almost took my eyebrows off.

'The first step, Caroline,' I said, 'is not to drink more than one of these till we've got something down on paper.'

'Huh! Are you as bossy as that with your lovers?' she retorted sulkily. 'I bet they don't get you in the submissionary position.'

I laughed. Caroline slumped into a chair and swigged half her vodka-and-tonic.

'So, go on. Let me have it,' she said.

I attempted a résumé of where we'd got so far. That there were all these wives who were longing to pass their straying husbands on to Mrs Right, I reminded her. That they needed to be sure the new wife was sympathetic to their needs, would be good to the children and not bar the door to them or deprive them of access to their dad. That preferably she should be the sort of nice, kind creature who would take them for a week or so when the ex-wife found herself invited to join Richard Gere on his yacht. In other words, there had to be complicity between the two women.

'That's the ideal scenario,' I said. 'How's it sound so far?'

Caroline knocked back the rest of her vodka-and-tonic, and got up to pour herself another.

'Fabulous!' she exclaimed, waving the bottle high above her head before swooping it down towards her glass. 'And who do I get?'

I could see this was going to be a difficult meeting.

'Caroline, you're a director of the company, not a client. And directors don't nick the goods from the shop window.'

She looked at me fiercely.

'Shit! Then I resign.'

'No you bloody well don't,' I said. 'We need you.'

Even as I said it I was beginning to wonder about that. None the less I pressed on.

'Well, first of all we have to draw up a list. Thanks to Torquemada we've got plenty of candidates already. Then we need to approach them individually — very very discreetly. OK?'

(I already had visions of Caroline's special brand of discretion — 'Right! When did you last have a fuck with your husband? On election night! Jesus Christ! So you'd like him to bugger off. Right? What's his taste? Blondes? Brunettes? Bimbos? Fat? Skinny? You don't know. God Almighty! Well, is he any good at it? You don't remember. Can you believe it? Never mind; forget it. Just leave it to us. That'll be fifty quid. And another five hundred when we succeed. Next client!')

But Caroline was too busy with her vodka-and-tonic to do more than nod. She was into the third by now.

'Then we put the word about,' I said, carrying on bravely. 'Among friends. Friends of friends. So it

228

snowballs. Just like The Outfit. Perhaps a tactful little card placed here and there. We need a selling tag to put on it. What d'you think? Something innocent-sounding, like "Pastures New". How would that do?'

Caroline took a huge glug at her drink, and spluttered.

"*Postures* New"! I love that. "Postures *Nude*"! Even better.' She gave a hiccup of pleasure and began to wave her glass about like a child's kite in the wind. 'Christ, I'm getting pissed, Angela. It must be your fault.'

I began to think I'd be better off at home sharing Magdalena's '*teckvai*' with Rachel. I decided to have one more go, hoping some of it might survive Caroline's hangover. By now she was into her fourth mega-vodka, and the note-pad still had nothing on it below the lonely heading – Bawd Meeting.

'So, we've done all the interviewing and we now have our clientele. Right!' I said. 'The next step is to find out as much as possible about the husbands, so we can match them to the right replacement. And that means another, careful interview with each wife to elicit exactly what their men like best – their habits, their foibles, their fantasies, and so on.'

Caroline began to shake her head violently. The vodka caught the momentum and spurted on to her sleeve.

'No! No! No! No! No!' Caroline's forefinger made a determined effort to point in my direction. 'Only one way to find out about husbands.' (She made the word 'husbands' sound like a swarm of bees.) 'Try them out!' The forefinger did a descending spiral before plunging into her groin. 'So ... that'll be my job, Angelela.' My name was proving difficult. 'Consumer research. Chief test-pilot, that's me, Angelela. Fly them all! In the cockpit!' She hiccuped resoundingly, then washed it down. 'Fuck it, Angelela, why can't I articu-thing? Whoops!' She rose unsteadily towards the drinks tray and collided with the sofa. 'Ooooh dear! You got me drunk, Angelela. Whydidyoudothat?' Then a mystified look smeared across her face, and the forefinger took off again in my general direction. 'You know, Angelela, I'm the heiress to the smallest county in England. So maybe ... maybe ... I'll findabiggerone.'

She gave another tremendous hiccup, and laughed.

'Isabrilliantidea! Abslutelybrilliant! We gonnastartomorrow.'

At that moment Caroline's daughter Samantha put her head round the door.

'Could you help me with my maths homework, Mum?'

Then she took one look at her mother and gave me the knowing glance of a girl very much older than nine.

'Perhaps not,' she said, and retreated. I took her cue, and got up. Caroline followed me, aided by the walls on either side. Her empty glass flagged me towards the door.

'So we gonnastartomorrow, Angelela! Orright?'

From the far side of the road I glanced back and waved towards the figure wedged diagonally in the doorway. It was almost dark, and the bats were weaving and stooping between the trees on the common. There was the distant screech of an owl. Ralph's car wasn't back yet.

'So, how was the "*teckvai*"?' I enquired, closing the front door quietly behind me.

Rachel raised her head from the same maths homework.

'Scrummy!' she said, grinning.

8

Cupid

———————— o ————————

Caroline stalked into the shop late even for a Monday morning. She threw an imperious glance at two customers who were nosing among the racks, then advanced towards Gail and me brandishing a sheet of paper.

'Is this a joke?' she exclaimed in a penetrating voice. 'Which of you did it?' She glared at me. 'I bet it was you, Angela. Just your kind of humour. Well, fuck you!'

With a snort, Caroline slammed the sheet of paper on the table in front of me. The two customers froze among the racks.

'I don't know what you're talking about,' I said, feeling ruffled. 'What is this anyway?'

And I picked up the offending document. Gail leant over to peer at it, holding back a cascade of red hair with one hand as she did so. Then she gave a laugh.

'Caroline darlin',' she said, straightening up and placing both hands on her hips like a washerwoman. 'I ask you, would anyone who knew you waste a postage stamp sending you bumf about an "introduction agency" called Soulmates? We all know you've got no fockin' soul.' With that she picked up the sheet of paper and her eyes began to flick down the page. 'And what's more, darlin',' she went on, 'look what it says here – "Soulmates will not allow anybody of doubtful character or motive to join". Well, that rules you out, doesn't it?' She continued to read, then looked up again at Caroline and shook her head. 'It's obvious, if you took the trouble to read it. Listen to this. "We mail our survey questionnaire throughout an entire postal code at random, in the hope of reaching people who will be glad to receive it." Small fockin' hope in your case.'

By now Caroline was looking sulky. Her tantrums were supposed to induce subservience, not a reprimand, least of all mockery. It still rankled with her that Gail, so obviously of the servant class in her eyes, refused to behave like one. Caroline decided to divert her irritation back to me.

'So tell me, clever one, what are we doing trying to set up a dating agency when people like this are doing it already?' She made a grab at the sheet of paper and slapped it back on to the table. '"Soulmates,"' she growled. 'What a lot of cock!' She looked up and saw me laughing, thought about another tantrum, then settled for a chilly smile. 'A lot of cock! That's exactly it, isn't it! Perhaps that's what *I* need. And who wouldn't, living with Patrick!'

Gail had moved away from the battle zone to assist

the two customers who were still truffling warily among the racks, keeping their heads down and pretending not to listen. Caroline gave a sigh, poured herself a cup of coffee and seated herself heavily on the edge of the table.

'Jesus! Monday morning!' she sighed. 'And some bastard's pinched my parking space.' Caroline regarded the whole of Pimlico Square as her parking space, zebra crossings included. Her eyes began to wander disapprovingly over the customers, then returned to the offending sheet of paper. 'So, what *are* we doing, Angela? You're in one of your silent moods. How is Outfit Enterprises going to be so different from this? Just tell me!'

I glanced through the Soulmates leaflet while Caroline sat there impatiently swinging her legs and drumming her fingers, waiting for a chance to pounce.

Within thirty seconds it was so blatantly obvious what was different about Outfit Enterprises that I hardly knew what to say. It was only a matter of days since Caroline had delivered a peroration on the need for unhappy women to achieve the perfect divorce. Now it seemed that the winds had blown the idea clean out of her head. But then Caroline, I remembered, was often like this. Suddenly it would enter her head that she had only one more O Level than Princess Di. This would give her the excuse to miss the point of something entirely: vast opportunities were then opened up for her to rage about some injustice wrought upon her by an evil world until it was finally brought to her notice, usually with an exasperated shout, that it wasn't like that at all. By this time everyone's nerves were thoroughly jangled, except of course Caroline's: her face would take on the softest of smiles, and with the most ingenuous voice she'd say, 'Oh really! Now I understand. But you've no need to shout.' And she would have had a lovely time.

That was exactly the scenario on this Monday morning.

'Caroline,' I said. 'Look!' I held up the Soulmates leaflet in front of her and pointed to the section headed '*Personal Profile*'. Her eyes picked out the question – 'What is your occupation?' She laughed.

'Shop assistant. Unpaid.'

'No, not that,' I said.

'What is my weight? I'm not answering that.'

'No, Caroline – here!'

'You mean the bit that says am I male or female?'

'Go on!'

She read out the next line.

'"Are you Single/Divorced/Legally Separated/Widowed?"'

'Exactly!' We were getting there at last. 'The one thing it doesn't say is – "Are you married?" Get your mind round that. There are dozens and dozens of agencies who find partners for people who *aren't* married and would love to be. The people we want to help are the opposite – they're women who are already married and would love not to be – who are longing to find just the right substitute to lift their dreadful husbands off their hands.'

Caroline looked wide-eyed.

'I get it!' she said. 'Of course! Forgive me, I've got a mind like a sieve.' Which was putting it generously.

My chief concern now was that Caroline might spend the rest of the day asking every female customer who came into the shop if they'd like help getting rid of their ghastly husbands. I could see her sharply assessing them as they came in; but for once tact imposed a restraining hand.

I left the shop before her that evening. As I did so something caught my eye on the central island in Pimlico Square. Caroline's dark-blue Mercedes was parked neatly between the Gents' and Ladies' lavatories, blocking the entrance to both. A number of policemen were taking some interest in this phenomenon, from time to time peering more closely at the car and making notes. I wandered over as unobtrusively as I could. Sellotaped to the outside of the windscreen was a well-worn notice printed in bold letters – *'Police Already Informed'*. But the constables seemed more intrigued by the interior of the car, so as I sauntered past I glanced inside. The glove pocket was wide open, and on the passenger seat lay a spillage of other printed notices which likewise bore the signs of much use. I only had time to spot a few of them. On top of the pile was *'Doctor on Call'*; next to this – *'Disabled Driver'* and *'Fortescue Estate Maintenance Department'*. Only partly obscured was *'Bomb Disposal*

Unit'. On the floor lay *'Westminster City Council, Pest Control'*, and propped against the gear-stick *'International Council of Churches — Latvian Delegate'*.

They were all of them well familiar to me. And so was the sight of the tow-away truck easing its way towards us through the rush-hour traffic.

Outfit Enterprises began to take off with bewildering speed, so much so that I found little time to consider my own life, let alone my double life. Sometimes, driving home in the evening dusk, I'd recall with amazement that less than a year ago I'd been a loyal and impoverished housewife and mother whose mental horizons stretched about as far as the school run and the 'Special Offers' counter at Waitrose. It was true that I was still a housewife and mother; loyalty, however, had managed to slip from me as smoothly as Mr Horowitz's cobwebs, while impoverishment seemed to be going the same way just as effortlessly as more and more victims of Mr Major's recession trooped into the shop to trade in their finery for more affordable rags.

As for mental horizons, sometimes I could sense the hand of my Rotarian father reach out from the grave to shield my eyes from the temptations they saw shining around me. That he should have a daughter who had taken a lover would have been hard enough to bear in Vine Cottage. I tried to picture my father's face. Yet it tickled me to reflect that, in his lifelong bid for middle-class status, my adultery would have been less painful to him than having a daughter who'd stooped to flogging second-hand clothes in a shop. At least, I told myself, I wasn't shaming him publicly by doing either of these unmentionable things in Ipswich.

All the same, I wished he wasn't dead. He died too soon: there had never been time to discover a real father behind the proprieties which encased him. Whenever I'd questioned them, he'd turn away. Then a drunken truck-driver on the A12 turned him away for ever.

I preferred not to think what he would have made of Outfit Enterprises. At least I would never have to explain that.

It was Rick who got us moving, rather abruptly. I'd expected at least a week would pass before a suitable printing machine fell off the back of a lorry so that he could make us our new advertisement cards. Yet there he was, back in the shop sharp at nine the next morning carrying a GPO mail-bag.

"Ere you are, sweetheart,' he announced, dumping the bag on the table. 'Five hundred of 'em. Deckle-edged. Decided against "By Royal Appointment" but thought you'd like the gold lettering. All right, chick?'

And there the cards were. '*Pastures New*' – the gold standing out against a pastoral green background. The wording that followed had given us the worst headache. We'd spent hours pondering over it in Renato's restaurant over lunch, day after day. How in a single brief sentence could one possibly reach out to women who had adulterous or unsatisfactory husbands without sounding like marriage guidance counsellors (if the wording was too soft) or a bunch of old slags (if it was too blunt)?

Caroline hadn't helped.

'I've got it,' she announced one lunchtime, stabbing at her prosciutto. 'Listen. It came to me playing tennis at the Hurlington Club yesterday. Just seven words – "Isn't it time you changed your balls?"'

Gail and I looked at one another.

'No, Caroline!' we said in unison.

'You mean it's too subtle?'

'Not exactly, Caroline.'

She looked aggrieved for a moment, then with a mouthful of prosciutto began to laugh.

'Then what about "Exchange and Part"?' she spluttered.

'Getting closer,' I said. 'A bit short.'

'Just like Patrick,' Caroline mumbled.

Once again our bawd meeting seemed to be getting out of hand.

'The thing about advertising,' Gail chipped in, looking serious, 'is to target only the people you want, and no one else.'

'Go on, then,' I said wearily. 'Your turn.'

Gail drained her wine-glass and gazed about her.

'What about "Cleave him unto others,"' she suggested.

Caroline made a face.

'Oh, not the bloody marriage vows, please. Who wants to be reminded of those?'

But they did remind me of something. I suddenly had the germ of an idea.

'Maybe Gail's right,' I said. 'The marriage vows. Now wait a moment, how do they go? ... That bit about till death do us part. I know! Simple! We just turn it round – "Why wait till death? Part now!" How's that?'

There was silence for a few seconds. Then a smile began to spread across Caroline's and Gail's faces.

'She's done it again,' said Gail, refilling her glass.

So that was what our cards read. In large letters *'Pastures New'* – in an inviting summery script blossoming with wild roses. A bit over the top, I thought, but it certainly made you feel happy to look at it. Then underneath – *'Why wait till death? Part now!'* – rather grandiose in gold considering the bluntness of the message; none the less, the effect was undeniably striking. And *'Outfit Enterprises'*, with our address and phone number along the bottom of each card; nothing could have been more discreet and businesslike. We gathered round to admire them as Gail opened the package. Rick had made an excellent job of it.

'Marry a thief and you marry an artist – I've discovered,' said Gail whimsically.

There was no question of payment, Rick insisted. He had his professional honour, and by now we'd learnt to respect it.

For the first day or so I was shy about disposing of our little green cards. I did leave one on Josh's scattered clothing after we'd made love during a long autumn lunchtime – scrawling, after '*Pastures New*', 'and long may you graze, my darling', which was a bit forward of me, I realised, but I adored our midday lust after wine and smoked salmon, and no longer felt like being reticent about it. I loved Josh's body and what it did to mine; and afterwards I'd float dreamily through the afternoon, watched by Gail with a knowing smile, and by Caroline with a frown. How she never suspected, I never knew.

And how it would all end, I never knew either. I was living in the present, and each tomorrow was merely an extension of it. Two lives seemed altogether better than one.

Gail shared none of my scruples about the cards. She just slipped them like little time-bombs into the pockets of any garment we sold. For customers she knew particularly well – or customers who'd already made tearful confessions to Torquemada – she'd press a card into their hands with a cheerful, 'Just a new line of ours you may find interesting, darlin'.'

As for Caroline, she didn't bother with either words or scruples. She simply placed a pile of cards near the door by the coat-rack, others in the changing-room and the loo, and spread a fan of them in front of Torquemada. Each morning she checked on how many had gone the day before.

'We'll be reprinting soon at this rate,' she announced.

The response caught us unprepared. Even Caroline,

who liked to think every woman's marriage was a bondage she longed to shed, was surprised.

'I knew I was right,' she said. 'But I didn't know I was *that* right.'

At first only a few customers took the bait, slipping unobtrusively towards the back of the shop on the pretence of acquiring a cheap scarf or belt, then taking one of us nervously aside with a, 'Do you really think you can help me?' But then, as the days passed, there were more and more of them. They began to arrive in flocks – it was like an autumn migration. We could tell by their faces what was on their minds. Never in his long and distinguished service had Torquemada gushed and hissed out so much coffee. Our resources of manpower and caffeine were stretched to the limit.

We listened.

We interviewed.

We took notes.

We opened files.

We kept a register.

And after the shop was closed we held hasty bawd meetings debating how we could possibly manage to hold things together. Important decisions had to be made, and made quickly.

The most pressing issue was – space! It became rapidly obvious that we couldn't possibly operate two businesses in our existing premises, particularly since it was hard to tell which customers required which service. Inevitably we made a few mistakes. The wife of a prominent Tory peer, who came into the shop to dispose of her Joseph suit, was dumbfounded to be asked by Caroline who her husband had been screwing at the recent party conference in Brighton. Even after the lady stalked out of the door Caroline remained unabashed, insisting that since she herself knew perfectly well who the husband had been screwing in Brighton, she'd assumed quite reasonably that this was why the stupid woman was here.

To avoid further misunderstandings we agreed that we urgently needed new premises. And this urgency increased daily as the message of Pastures New spread. In no time, for every woman who entered the shop keen to part with her Lanvin dress, there were now three who were even keener to part with their husbands.

Here I managed to pull off a coup. The antique dealer next-door had always taken a shine to me: the way he'd caress the cabriole legs of a Queen Anne card table left me in no doubt what he hoped he might be stroking next. None the less I liked him and would call in for the occasional cup of coffee, keeping my own legs safely crossed.

One day, leaving the shop late, I ran into him as he was locking up. As I greeted him I noticed he looked ashen. I asked him if he was unwell. He hesitated for a moment; suddenly I noticed there were tears in his eyes. I became ridiculously protective and put my arm round him, whereupon he half collapsed. Then his story gushed out. He was on the verge of bankruptcy, he explained.

The antiques trade had plummeted – no Americans were buying, the continentals found London too expensive, and the Japanese had never understood about furniture because they always sat on the floor. What was more, the buyer of his lease had that very morning withdrawn from the deal. The poor man was in despair.

'How long is the lease?' I asked.

'That's just the trouble,' he said. 'Only three years. Too short to be worth anyone's while.'

Except maybe ours, I thought.

'Well, perhaps we could buy it,' I said tentatively. An office for Outfit Enterprises right next-door – it was exactly what we wanted.

He seemed incredulous for a moment. Then his face brightened and he looked perplexed and eager. I asked the price and he stuttered as he named it, then immediately reduced it as his face began to register panic that I might say no.

I didn't. I thought we could probably afford it, so I said yes, provided of course – I added calmly – that my partners were of the same mind. I could scarcely recognise myself talking like this: I felt a tycoon. So, there on the pavement a gentlemen's deal was immediately struck, and assuming all was well we agreed to hurry it through. Then I left him striding down the street, still a little bewildered, but occasionally giving his rolled umbrella a jaunty flourish.

Not for the first time I found myself reflecting how, like undertakers at a time of plague, we were being handsomely served by Mr Major's recession; though at that moment I felt less like an undertaker than a pirate on the high seas.

The news of my coup met with a mixed reception the following morning. Caroline, never one to concern herself with legal niceties, was keen to move in right away.

'Why don't we ask Rick if he'd knock a hole in the wall for us? Then we wouldn't need to wait for a key.'

Gail, who had a hangover, wanted time to reflect.

'You're roshin' things. Fockin' amateurs, the pair of you. For a start, how are we going to get our money back? Tell me that. Jaysus Christ, this is supposed to be a business, and we haven't even decided what we're going to charge!'

Even Caroline saw the point of that, and we agreed to turn lunch into a special bawd meeting. So at one o'clock we locked up the shop for an hour and made our way over to the Trevi. Renato caught the conspiratorial look on our faces as we came in and gave us a quiet table in the corner. Gail's hangover had by now turned into an urgent thirst, which Renato anticipated by setting a carafe of chianti in front of her. Caroline was in unusually high spirits: she'd received an invitation that morning for a weekend in Monte Carlo from her Italian racing driver – who would no doubt be suitably well fuelled after the Monaco Grand Prix, she trusted, pouring herself a generous glass of Gail's chianti. As for me, I was due to spend a candlelit evening with

Josh, having arranged for Magdalena to cook Rachel one of her famous Portuguese 'teckvais' which always went down far better with my hungry daughter than anything I ever undertook to prepare for her.

None of us had the slightest idea what scale of fees we should charge, and it seemed unwise to ring up Soulmates for advice. Obviously we must insist on a registration fee, modest enough not to put anyone off, but sufficient to cover basic costs should our endeavours fail. We already had more than eighty potential clients on our files, and we agreed that two hundred pounds sounded about right. Towards the end of Gail's bottle of chianti we'd raised it to two hundred and fifty. This first payment was to be for the preliminary interview with the wife, plus the more searching one to follow which was designed to ascertain the husband's specific likes, foibles, weaknesses, fantasies, recreations, sexual predilections, religious and political leanings, and so on right down to his taste in socks and underwear. It would also cover the next stage of Enterprises, which was the drawing up of a short-list of potential female candidates, and the delicate enquiries we'd need to make in order to find out if they were willing to embark on such an adventure. Most important of all, the fee would cover arrangements for the present wife to meet the chosen few and select from them her preferred successor. Finally we would undertake to arrange an appropriate clandestine meeting between husband and woman in question.

Altogether, two hundred and fifty pounds seemed a give-away price for such a service.

Then came the crunch – what should be our fee for a successful ... we weren't at all sure how we should refer to it?

"'Wife swap'" I suggested.

But that was thought to sound corny and sordid – the sort of thing you read about in the Sunday tabloids, taking place between consenting vicars in Sidcup.

Caroline thought 'cock swap' would be better, then she refined it to 'male organ transplant'. I was looking blank, and Gail was shaking her head.

'No, no, darlin', you've got to think decent, for fock's sake.'

'All right,' I said. 'How about "organ relocation"?'

Gail looked thoughtful for a moment.

'A bit better. You're beginning to get the right tone.' Then she clasped her hands together piously and gazed at us with a mischievous smile. 'I have it. "Marital realignment" – that's how we should be thinking of it. "Marital realignment." There's a ring of respect about it for the holy state of matrimony, you see, and that's very important.' Gail swept a froth of hair from her face and looked wise. 'I tell you, it's a simple lesson I've learnt in life: when people plan to do something wicked, they need to feel God's on their side.'

So, what were we to charge for a successful 'marital realignment', as we now agreed to call it?

Caroline immediately named a sum which would

have made a sizeable dent in the national debt – which Gail and I swiftly vetoed. I suggested it ought to be linked to the husband's income, but short of a means test this was thought to be impractical; besides, no man could be relied on to make an honest declaration of his earnings, and we'd have no access to Income Tax returns – which everyone knew were dishonest anyway.

There was a pause until once again Gail came up with the answer.

'Look! There's only one way to do this. We simply take a percentage of the divorce settlement.'

Eureka! It seemed a beautifully democratic solution. Wives awarded very little by the courts would pay us very little, while those given golden handshakes would fill our coffers.

There remained only the question of what percentage we should ask. I plucked a figure out of the air and suggested 2 per cent. Caroline gave a snort, said we weren't a bloody charity, and raised the stakes to 50 per cent. Gail thought it should be 10. Finally we settled on 5.

And that was our lunchtime business done.

It was two o'clock – time to reopen the shop. We got up from the table and paid a smiling Renato the bill. Clusters of men around the restaurant eyed us with some interest as we made our way to the door. I found myself wondering what they imagined three women had been discussing so earnestly over lunch and a bottle of chianti – one wild-looking redhead, one impeccably turned-out blonde, and me the dark raven with the smile on her face. If only they'd known that the smile, which of course they took to be for them, was simply at the thought that maybe one or two of their wives might very soon be our clients.

'D'you think everyone will assume we hate men?', I asked nervously as we crossed the square on our way back to the shop.

Gail was still in her wise mood. She glanced at me with a quizzical smile.

'Darlin', if you're a feminist there are always people who think you hate men.'

She was right. I wondered why I'd asked that question, and what kind of reassurance I'd wanted. In my entire life it had never occurred to me to hate men, even assistant bank managers who showed me their willies, or lager louts with BO who squeezed my bum in the Underground. All the same, I was conscious of an area of fog in my brain, and somewhere hiding in that fog lay a certain unease. It was to do with Ralph, and with Josh: it was to do with what I felt about the man I lived with but no longer desired, and what I felt about the man I didn't live with but desired with every muscle in my body. And perhaps it was also to do with all kinds of emotions I wasn't prepared to deal with: that one half of my double life was full of safety and emptiness, while the other half was full of risk and joy. How much easier it would be if I could love the one and hate the other. But neither 'hate' nor 'love' really fitted: there was only 'indifference' and 'need'. You couldn't hate a man you were merely indifferent to. On the other hand, did you necessarily love the man you needed? I didn't know. Perhaps I didn't want to know. I only knew about a kind of hunger. Oh God, I did! My body quivered – even in the middle of Pimlico Square! – at the thought of my evening with Josh. It made me feel weak. It made me feel joyful. It made me smile.

'What are you grinning about?' said Caroline crossly. She was always cross when I was happy. Then she rounded on me. 'What d'you mean – "Do I think people will assume we hate men?" Of course they will, and why not? I love hating men – it's terribly sexy. A blazing row and a good fuck: there's nothing like it. That's what's so dreadful about Patrick. He refuses to have a row, and he's a lousy fuck.' There was a pause; then she looked wistful. 'Christ, I can't wait for the weekend.'

It was Caroline's turn to smile, and Gail gave us both an old and wily look. We crossed the road and Caroline turned the key of the shop with the vigour of one whose thoughts were already feasting on her racing driver with three balls.

Maybe it was the prospect of her Formula One weekend in Monte Carlo which spurred her to further action. Gail and I were already resigned to muddling along with Outfit Enterprises at the back of the shop until the premises next door were finally ours. It would be a month at the very least, the solicitors informed us.

We would manage somehow. But Caroline, perhaps still thinking of her racing driver, said, 'Balls!' and promptly swept out of the shop.

She was gone less than half an hour. About five o'clock she returned with a serene expression on her face. Ignoring three customers who were waiting to be attended to, she went straight to the telephone, flicked through Yellow Pages and tapped out a number.

'Is that Pickfords?' I heard her say after a moment or two. 'Right! I need a large van at nine o'clock tomorrow morning. Pimlico Square.' She gave the number of the shop next door. 'The name's Uppingham ... Nonsense! I'll pay by American Express Gold Card. And don't be late.'

She put down the phone.

'Well, that's settled,' she said. 'We can move in.'

I left a customer searching for a scarf in one of the bins.

'What do you mean?' I asked, mystified.

'That we can move in,' she repeated. 'Tomorrow!'

Then she told me. Nothing could have been simpler. Caroline had been to see the antique dealer, cast an eye over the contents of his gallery, and bought the lot.

'I need some good furniture,' she said.

The key Josh gave me to his flat had seemed such a precious thing – a secret door into his life. He had slipped it down the front of my blouse as I left early one afternoon, saying with a smile – 'Keep it safe'; and

I'd kept it there between my breasts until the evening, imagining it to be his hands.

But a secret door into Josh's life was proving a mixed blessing. Until now I'd visited him only by arrangement. I'd never needed to think, Is this a good moment? Will he be busy? Will someone else be there? Will he be there at all? Now all these questions confronted me whenever I decided to call on him. I realised that my key didn't only open a secret door into his life, it also opened a door into his secret life.

Suddenly I was made to feel an intruder. On the very first occasion I used the key – having plucked up courage all afternoon – I found the flat littered with a woman's clothing. A T-shirt dangled from a standard lamp, a mini-skirt lay on the coffee-table and a pair of wispy lace panties by a half-open door. It was a trail of hasty undressing. I froze. Then I caught sounds of cheerful humming, and realised they came from the bathroom. To hell with that, I thought; I needed to know, and know quickly.

I put my head round the door. For a second all I could see through the steam was an extremely pretty, dark-haired girl stretched out in the bath, her feet playing with the taps and her fingers drumming the side. She stopped humming as she saw me, but made no effort to cover herself.

'Hello!' she said, squeezing bath-water out of her hair. 'You're Angela, aren't you? Dad's just popped out to the off-licence.' She gave a giggle. 'He's furious 'cos I should be at school.'

I mumbled a 'Hello Jessica' and backed away into the sitting room. The humming resumed. And shortly afterwards Josh duly returned.

A couple of days later I tried again. This time I found the door of the flat already open and a fiercely lacquered woman in tweeds standing by the window grasping a large clipboard. Sounds from next door told me Josh was still at work in his studio. I gave a weak smile and was preparing to seat myself quietly on the sofa with a magazine when the lacquered woman barked at me – 'Get undressed, then. You're late!' With that she opened a large suitcase, drew out a pink nightgown and tossed it to me. 'Put it on!' she ordered. Then she looked at me sharply. 'You're a bit old, aren't you? And far too much bust. I shouldn't bother.'

I bridled. Then, remembering Marilyn Monroe, I threw the pink nightgown back to her.

'Keep it,' I said sweetly. 'I only wear Chanel Number Five in bed.'

Josh was effusively apologetic: the photographic audition for a nightwear advertisement had gone on rather long. And he introduced me to the lacquered lady while an anorexic model wandered in wearing an identical pink nightgown.

I almost returned the key after that.

The next time was only a little less uncomfortable. At least I found the door of the flat closed, and there was no lacquered lady inside. Instead I found myself face to face with Josh's agent, Stella Neale; she was standing by the coffee-table with a sheaf of photographs under one arm and a possessive smile on her face. This was the woman, I remembered, who'd had not just one affair with Josh, but two. I also remembered I'd been exceedingly rude to her the only other time we'd met.

Again Josh was at work in the studio next door: I could hear his voice giving instructions to yet another model – 'Head back a little. That's it! Close your eyes . . . and open them quickly – now! Great!'

I wanted to know if she was pretty. I wanted to know what she was wearing. I wanted to know if she was wearing anything at all. But I couldn't see. Stella was smiling. I wanted to like her: it would have made the two affairs seem smaller.

'Contact lenses,' she said in a loud whisper. This puzzled me for a moment until I realised Josh must be doing an advertisement for them. Well, at least the girl was unlikely to be naked if she was advertising contact lenses.

I smiled back at Stella. She was extremely elegant, in her late thirties I imagined. My newly professional eye began to assess the designer clothes, wondering if they would look as good on me.

She was looking at her watch.

'He won't be long,' she added. 'Then you'll have him to yourself.'

There was a note of such complicity in the way

she said it that I felt myself blushing. Did she and Josh talk about me? And what did he say? What did she say? I was longing to take her aside and ask her what it had been like having Josh as a lover; and why had it ended? – why had it ended *twice*? But I couldn't; instead we just stood there next to one another, both of us gazing at that half-open door and listening to Josh apply his talents to the dreary business of contact lenses.

'You know why he takes these jobs?' Stella said quietly, without turning her head.

'Money?' I suggested.

She smiled, and this time she looked at me. She had beautiful eyes, and I thought of how often Josh must have gazed into them, damn her!

She shook her head.

'Because of you,' she said.

Again I felt myself blushing. I tried to grasp what she meant: then I realised it could only be so he wouldn't have to travel – so he could be here for me. I gazed at Stella gratefully: I don't know why I felt grateful to her, except that it was as though she were my guardian angel – as though she were making me a gift of Josh, with her blessing. Passing him on to me. And at that moment he appeared. I wanted to throw my arms round him, but with Stella there, and the model next door, I could only stand there wishing they'd both go away. I looked at the scar on his neck, and wanted to kiss it. I wanted to touch him.

Josh was helping the model into her coat and seeing her to the top of the stairs.

'Hasn't he photographed you yet?' Stella asked.

I shook my head.

'He did say he wanted to include me in some book,' I said.

Stella gave me an amused smile.

'And you believed that?' She glanced towards the door: Josh was still talking by the staircase. 'My darling, I think if there were a book I'd know about it.'

Now I was even more confused.

'I suppose so,' I said feebly. 'After all, you are his agent.'

Stella just looked at me.

'I also know Josh very, very well,' she added.

I wanted her to tell me everything he'd said to her about me. I wanted to know everything she'd said. I even wanted to ask her what I should do. But there was no chance to say anything more. Josh came back into the room; and a few minutes later Stella left. Josh kissed me. I longed to ask him so many things, and couldn't.

Why was I so confused? The thought that I might actually love Josh terrified me. I hadn't reckoned on that sort of vulnerability. I'd embarked on my double life thinking I could share myself out – render unto Josh . . . render unto Ralph . . . Suddenly it was all getting dangerously unbalanced. It shook me to think that Josh was turning down work abroad in order to be close to me: this was a gift I could never repay. I was married.

I had a daughter. And how long would it last like this? He would tire of it – surely he would. Soon he would find someone else to fill his hours without me, someone to fill his nights. How long would it be?

I went home disturbed and unhappy. On the common the autumn leaves were damp and golden under the street-lamps. Caroline's lights were burning: she must be back from her long weekend with the racing driver. How easily she managed this sort of thing, for all her tantrums and her rage. There was a security about her which I didn't possess. Perhaps there was an honesty about her I didn't possess. I was playing a game that I could only lose. I began to wish it was only a game; then I could give it up. Close the board. Put the pieces away in a box. Goodbye Josh!

But it wasn't like that. I opened the front door. Rachel looked up, smiling.

'Daddy rang. He says he's booked a room in Brighton.' She tossed her dark hair back from her face and gazed at me. 'Why d'you have to go to Brighton, Mum?'

'For his play,' I said, hearing the lack of enthusiasm in my voice. In a few days there'd be Ralph's first night, and I'd have to be with him – a late-night dinner and a Brighton hotel. It disturbed me to realise how little I was looking forward to it.

'Will Daddy be famous?' Rachel asked.

'Maybe, darling.'

'Oooh!' she said.

* * *

257

By eleven o'clock all Caroline's antique furniture had been loaded into the removals van. For the past two hours Gail and I had been casting a fascinated eye on the proceedings next door. Neither of us was bold enough to ask what she'd actually paid for the stuff. We both assumed that, being Caroline, she'd struck a cruel bargain with the near-bankrupt dealer; at the same time, seeing the ornate and unlikely objects being shifted into the van, we agreed that she must still have parted with a sizeable fortune.

'A fockin' museum she's got there,' commented Gail as a fantastically carved Venetian throne was being edged slowly up the ramp. 'Maybe Patrick fancies himself as the Doge.'

I thought of our own farmhouse kitchen chairs which I'd picked up for a fiver in Clapham during our darker days, and wondered if I'd ever dare ask Caroline to our house again.

I was also intrigued to know what the hell she intended to do with it all. The Venetian throne was followed by what appeared to be a medieval instrument of torture, but was apparently a Victorian trouser-press. After this came a set of what Caroline informed me were eighteenth-century chairs in the Chinese style: they looked so fragile I imagined that one of her more vigorous dinner parties would reduce them to chopsticks in no time. Then came a satinwood sewing-table. I smiled at the sight of it: what tickled me was the thought of a sewing-table belonging to Caroline, who had never sewn on a button in her life.

Finally the van moved off – and we moved in. Suddenly we had space. Oceans of it. Our original plan had been to knock a hole in the wall between the two premises. But we decided to scrap this in the interests of cost and privacy: after all, it was perfectly easy to walk next door, or if discretion were needed one could simply nip in the back way via the rear entrance. We arranged for a direct telephone link, and that seemed enough. We also agreed that we could live with the antique dealer's red flock wallpaper. Gail thought it looked aristocratic. She also persuaded Rick to paint Outfit Enterprises over the antique dealer's name, though not before I'd squashed his preference for a pictorial sign to match the one hanging outside our shop. It was bad enough, I explained, having to live day after day with a portrait of myself unzipping my dress; I was not going to tolerate a second portrait depicting me as a naked siren beckoning from the waves, which was Rick's bright idea of how we should advertise our Enterprises.

'I'd do a good job. Honest!' he explained.

Gail looked quite shocked, and rounded on her husband severely.

'Jaysus, Rick, we're not a fockin' call-girl agency. We're perfectly respectable marriage breakers.'

Rick seemed peeved, and began to mutter. We were making a big mistake, he said. We weren't fulfilling our potential. There were pots of money to be made, and we were trying to be all respectable. That was no way to do business. He had another brilliant idea too: would we care to hear it? I thought, 'No!' and said, 'Yes!' I didn't want to disappoint Rick a second time. He glanced down at us from the top of his ladder, and cleared his throat.

'Well, you got all these classy customers – see! Dozens of 'em. Ain't yer?'

Yes, Rick.

'Important geezers. Not just tarts and bimbos. Film stars. Rock stars. Bishops. Big names. Personalities. OK?'

Yes, Rick.

'And they're famous fuckers, ain't they?'

Some of them, Rick, yes! Not so sure about the bishops.

'Well, they're not a bunch of wankers, anyway. They like to wave it abart a bit, don't they? Superstuds. Right?'

Sort of, perhaps, yes, Rick.

'They want everybody to know what a lot they got? True, in'it?'

Maybe, Rick.

'Right! 'Ere's the idea, then. We 'elp 'em spread the word.'

Oh really! How?

At this point Rick put down his paint-brush and looked serious.

'Simple. Listen now. These geezers – vain as hell!

OK? But they can't 'ave every bit o' crumpet, can they? No time. So what do we do? We persuade 'em to 'ave a cast made of their erections. Then we sell 'em as dildoes. Limited edition. Signed of course. Go like a bomb, I tell yer. Call it "Infit Enterprises". All right?'

There was a stupefied silence. Gail finally broke it.

'Jaysus, Rick! How often have I told you to stick to shoplifting?'

From time to time that afternoon I glanced nervously out of the window, just in case the sign Rick was painting looked like turning into a graphic illustration of his brilliant idea. But, glum and dour though he remained, he never deviated from the script.

Mercifully, once steered away from his fantasies, Rick proved himself to be invaluable as well as remarkably canny. We already possessed umpteen files on the women who'd responded favourably to Pastures New: now the next stage was to arrange 'in-depth' interviews with the same women about the husbands they wished to dispose of. This was likely to prove far more demanding, and would certainly require a filing system a great deal more sophisticated than scrawled notes hastily shoved into folders.

We gazed at each other blankly. But Rick, who by now had appointed himself the provider of all sorts of office equipment we might possibly need, had no doubt about the answer.

'Yer goin' to 'ave t'get a computer, sweetheart, ain't yer?'

And of course he was perfectly right. A computer! That was clearly what we needed. My heart sank. Who on earth was going to operate the thing? All I knew about computers was that they identified the generation gap more vividly than anything I could think of. For instance, why was it that Rachel, rising nine, could use them at school and find them 'easy-peasy', while for me, rising twenty-nine, it was like being seated at the controls of Concorde? I shuddered at the thought of people's marriages and divorces being at the mercy of my computer illiteracy.

Caroline didn't share my horror, but this was more out of ignorance than experience. All she knew about them, she explained languidly, was that they had something to do with 'software' — and, frankly, she already had quite enough of that living with Patrick.

So we could probably rule her out.

Gail was altogether more tricky on the subject. She did sort of understand about computers, she claimed; none the less she was, she reminded us, Irish, and that wasn't always a very reliable qualification when it came to working with high technology. We might regret it, she warned us. After all, it would be most unfortunate, wouldn't it, if some high Tory lady from the shires paid the registration fee in order to be rid of her husband, only to find that the computer paired him off with a lesbian wrestler?

Before we had a chance to question her excuses, Gail then came up with the answer. There was a young nephew of hers, she said, who was a computer whizz-kid. Only twenty. Not trained, but he certainly knew more than most people who were. What's more, at present he was unemployed. We should take him on, she suggested. It wouldn't cost us very much: he'd welcome the experience. Besides, it was clearly going to be impossible for just the three of us to run a shop, *and* an agency, *and* do all the computer filing as well. We'd blow up, and so would the business.

Of course, she was right. I felt a strong sense of relief. And Gail went off to phone the unemployed nephew.

The next few days were like a countdown. Business in the shop continued as usual, as if nothing new were about to happen, but next-door there was an air of animated suspense. Rick produced a brand-new Mackintosh computer, apologising for the fact that we'd have to pay half-price for it. He realised he'd let us down, he said, but sometimes his own sources let *him* down, which was what had happened on this occasion. If only we'd been able to give him more time. It would never occur again, he promised.

And the following morning Gail produced the nephew. He was tall. He was twice as Irish as Gail. And he had her red hair — only somewhat longer: it swept round his shoulders like a wild and golden mane.

And – Jesus! – he was handsome. Gail introduced him with an air of cool pride.

'This is Eamonn. He's a good lad, even if he does look like a tramp.'

He didn't. He looked gorgeous.

Eamonn shook hands with the shy arrogance of a young man who knows that the hand he shakes is trembling. Mine was. I felt old. His eyes took in my age, my figure and my thoughts.

Caroline became entirely silly in his presence, and afterwards petulant.

'Well, Angela, you're far too young to have a toy-boy. I'm certainly not. Gail, is he a virgin?'

Gail smiled.

'There are no virgins in my family, Caroline.'

At that moment customers began to trickle into the shop, and Caroline's plans for seduction became diverted. But I noticed how throughout the day any lull in trade would find her taking a surprising interest in the new computer, and a regular supply of coffee made its way next-door.

'Where does Eamonn live?' she enquired casually as we were about to lock up. Gail said he had a bedsit somewhere in Balham. Caroline looked disdainful. 'Can't be very comfortable,' she said. 'Tell him we've got plenty of spare rooms at home if he feels like it.'

'Feels like what?' I asked with a smile.

Caroline pretended she hadn't heard.

Gail was perfectly right about Eamonn: his mastery

of the computer turned out to be as impressive as the sight of him operating it. For the first few days we worked a shift system – two of us minding the shop while the third sat with Eamonn going through all the notes we'd kept on our clients. After that we left him to it, apart from Caroline's frequent visitations bearing coffee.

'I've invited him for the weekend,' she announced after one such visit. 'It must be awfully lonely in Balham on one's own.'

Gail looked at me knowingly.

'I don't imagine Eamonn's lonely too often,' she said.

And as if to prove the point, he wandered into the shop a short while later as Gail was dealing with a Lanvin model who'd brought in a dress. The girl had been sullen until that moment. Suddenly the eyes widened, the lips moistened, and a pretty hand gave a provocative flick to her dark hair. She wriggled like an insect caught on a strip of fly-paper. Caroline glowered. And to make it worse, Eamonn awarded the girl a careless glance as if to say, 'OK, but you'll have to take your place in the queue, doll.'

Then he turned to us. He had finished, he said, scarcely noticing the girl depart. All the notes were now on the computer. So what did we intend to do next?

The four of us stayed behind late that evening. We'd reached the point when we now had to move in earnest. We'd also reached the point when I seriously felt like backing out. It all seemed to be getting too much. I had my own life – my own double life. How could I possibly become involved in so many other people's lives? Buying and selling designer clothes was one thing; it was fun, it was rewarding, and the people whose troubles and heartaches I encountered were little more than birds of passage. But to engage in the business of marriage partners, marriage break-ups, conspiring with unhappy wives to free them of their husbands; this was something else altogether, and I began to wish we'd never thought of it.

I plucked up courage to say as much quietly to Gail. She looked at me; then she squeezed my hand and gave me one of her wise smiles.

'You don't have to think of yourself as a suffragette, you know, darlin',' she said. 'We're not fightin' a fockin' cause. It's a service – that's all. If it works, it works. If it doesn't, no one's the worse off. Let's just give it a whirl.'

That evening we decided to lay our plans for Stage Two. From Monday we'd start making appointments for our clients to come and be interviewed in depth about their husbands. They'd need to bring a photograph, plus anything else that might help us build up a picture of the men concerned. Most of all, they'd need to bring with them a great deal of honesty. Torquemada would help at the beginning, as he invariably did. A liberal supply of alcohol was to be kept in readiness for the more painful stages. Rick had already thought of this and installed an immense drinks cupboard, which I noticed had *'Royal Garden Hotel'* engraved above one of the glass doors. The contents, I had my suspicions, may well have come from the same source.

Eamonn was to take over in the shop whenever one of us was engaged next door. Afterwards he would be entrusted with the task of feeding the information into his beloved computer. He seemed quite happy about this, as well as being surprisingly clued up on the subject.

'Data profiling – that's what we need,' he assured us. 'That's the "in" thing. They use it at Scotland Yard.'

It sounded wonderfully professional. I was already shedding many of my doubts. Our computer was clearly going to perform miracles of psychological analysis. I couldn't wait to see it in action.

'What are we going to call it?' I asked. 'We can't go on referring to the thing as "our computer", and "Mackintosh" sounds like a raincoat.'

Caroline thought it should have a name that suited its role as a sort of agony aunt.

'We should call it "Proops",' she suggested.

'Almost certainly libellous,' I said.

Gail was making tut-tutting noises.

'No! No! Where's the romance in you, for fock's sake?' And she gave the computer a gentle tap. 'Don't you see, this little creature could make a thousand people fall in love.'

Caroline and I looked at her with surprise.

'So what *do* you want to call it, then?' I asked.

Gail made a balletic gesture to suggest a bow and arrow.

'It's obvious, darlin', isn't it? We have to call it "Cupid".'

9

Birthdays

───────────── o ─────────────

How the hell was one supposed to dress for a first night in Brighton? Was it vanity or enslavement, I wondered, that caused women to agonise about such things, while men just dragged the same old suit out of the cupboard?

What was more, I had fifty-odd miles to drive, and I was already late.

'It's an old-fashioned production,' Ralph had said on the phone. 'None of your Chekhov in jeans. This is *Uncle Vanya* as it should be,' he added portentously.

But what kind of audience would it be? As old-fashioned as the production, or quite the opposite? Youthful glamour or hearing aids? Ralph hadn't been much use: all he could volunteer was that Laurence Olivier had lived in Hove nearby. For weeks Ralph's thoughts had been entirely focused on the challenge of following in the great man's footsteps. I didn't say so, but I couldn't help feeling this was a somewhat foolhardy comparison for an actor whose achievements consisted of a romantic TV series ten years ago, and since then half a dozen bit parts and a play at the Royal Court which had closed after four nights. I crossed my fingers for Ralph, but feared the disappointment might be terminal.

None of this helped me decide what to wear. In the end I made a few hasty decisions. Definitely *not* one of Mr Dante Horowitz's grey cobwebs, I thought: I wouldn't want Vanya to forget his lines. But also *not* the navy-blue shift from British Home Stores which I used to wear to parents' evenings at Rachel's school because it hid the size of my tits and so gave me a chance of being taken seriously by her teachers. I chose something that I hoped was half-way between the two – a Bruce Oldfield suit in deep-pink silk, with a short skirt and a fitted jacket worn open to reveal what Gail liked to describe as a '*bustière*'. After all, a star's wife should be entitled to one mildly *risqué* concession, and this was it: the '*bustière*' was in multi-coloured pinks rather like a stained-glass window, with a golden bee embroidered on one of the panels just above the left nipple. I'd only worn the garment once before, for Josh, who'd promptly removed it with a 'Where the bee sucks, there suck I.' Oh, what it was to have a literary lover!

Well, Brighton, I thought as I left the hotel room – let's see what you make of this.

It was a blustery October evening. In the theatre foyer the furs were out. My ticket was waiting for me in an envelope in Ralph's handwriting. I'd half expected a note inside, but there wasn't one. Then I thought how nervous he'd be, and felt selfish. I wasn't quite sure what else I felt. I knew I wanted him to do well! Ralph had staked everything on this performance: too much perhaps, after all those years of waiting. God, how I would have loathed an actor's life. To be such a slave to whim and fashion. To be able to initiate nothing at all – just wait, wait, wait for the nod of chance which might never come.

The one-minute bell rang as I made my way along the row to my seat. Several wide eyes settled on the golden bee.

Then the lights dimmed.

The curtain rose on my husband in a park. He was pacing up and down, spruce in his Victorian-looking outfit and wielding an elegant stick. The silver and black of his clothes matched the avenue of birches on the painted screen behind him. He looked good.

'Beautiful set!' the lady next to me whispered to her companion. 'And that's Ralph Merton. Remember him? Hasn't he changed!'

Yes, he had; though I noticed that the photograph in the programme still showed him as he was when I first knew him. The glamorous stud Ralph Merton. It came as quite a shock to see him gazing at me again with that knowing half-smile, just as he had on that day in the boutique when I'd trembled as he came in and promptly sneezed all over him. It was a long time since I'd seen that smile, and it reminded me how much I'd changed too.

He not only looked good: he was good. Stylish. The way he moved. And the voice, deep and resonant, with a touch of mournful irony to suggest he wasn't quite telling the truth. The way, right at the beginning, when he waved away the old nurse with, 'No, I don't drink vodka every day'; and you knew he almost certainly did. It was so cleverly done. Yes, Ralph, you've got it, I thought. You really have. And I relaxed.

In the silence around me I could sense the attention sharpen on to him whenever he entered. I felt a surge of pride. Then gradually I began to let the play enfold me; it was as if I was in a room with people talking, and sometimes I'd hear what was being said, and sometimes I wouldn't because my own thoughts muffled their voices. I'd have made a lousy critic, I realised. My mind follows its own paths and only sometimes returns to the main track.

For a long time I didn't understand what it was that my thoughts were following. Even in the interval I was puzzled. In the bar people were saying how good the production was; wasn't that man who played Astrov excellent; no wonder it was going to the West End. And again I felt proud.

Then it all began to come together. All those weeks when I'd listened to Ralph talking about the part of Astrov, how attuned he felt to it, how he felt it was him. And now I was watching him, it was as though he really *was* Astrov.

I kept hearing the same thing over and over again, in slightly different words.

'How could I help ageing? . . . My brains are still functioning all right, but my feelings are somewhat duller. I don't wish for anything, I don't feel I need anything, I don't love anybody.'

'I have my own special system of philosophy, according to which all of you, my good friends, appear as insignificant as insects . . . or microbes.'

'I don't love human beings . . . I haven't cared for anyone for years.'

'As I said, my time's over, it's too late for me now . . . I've aged too much . . . I believe I could never really become fond of another human being. I don't love anybody, and never shall now. What still does affect me is beauty. I can't remain indifferent to that.'

The words kept playing and replaying in my head like a loop-tape. I was watching my own husband telling me who he was – what he had become: it was as though Ralph were a ventriloquist, and Astrov his doll. I half expected to see a pole sticking out from below Astrov's jacket, with Ralph's hand holding it and making the head and mouth move. It was extraordinary, and it was a revelation. Could this really be the man I'd once fallen for, who'd swept me out of a Chelsea boutique, who'd shared his golden days with me, and then the long grey days? Now I began to understood what those years of failure had done; how beneath the ease and the charm they'd robbed him of all ability to think of anybody else. That was when self-obsession had set in. 'I don't love anybody, and never shall now.' Actors are only the

273

parts they play, and if there aren't any parts, what are they? A silent shell listening in vain for its own echo.

Oh Ralph, how you've always needed a place in the sun. And now maybe you've found it again. But if you have, dear husband, will it be me you care about? And will I ever be able to care about you? Because I've changed too; I'm no longer the blushing teenager who sneezed all over you. Our constellations have moved apart.

I could hear myself clapping as the curtain fell. The applause went on and on. Ralph was standing there smiling, bowing, linking hands with the cast, stepping forward as the curtain rose for the third, fourth, fifth time. Now people were on their feet. They were cheering. They were cheering Ralph. And I remembered him saying that if you could get a Brighton audience to stay awake, let alone clap, you were on to a winner.

Ralph was going to be all right. I knew that. He'd found his place in the sun again.

I went round to the stage door. There was an excited mob, many of them young. I thought of going to his dressing room, but I decided not to. Instead I stood at the back of the crowd, and after fifteen minutes or so there he was. He was smiling, being gracious. People were pushing forward with programmes for him to sign. He went on smiling. Two girls were almost hanging on to him: he had his arm round one of them while he jotted something on her programme. I remembered that line of Astrov's – 'What still does affect me is beauty. I can't remain indifferent to that.' Yes, he was proving the truth of that all right. It was exactly as it was in the old days, with bimbos like limpets on his sleeve.

Except that it wasn't like the old days. Then I would pluck the limpets off. Now I was just standing back: I don't believe Ralph had even seen me. I watched him. I watched him smiling, being adored, handing out his favours – and for all I knew his telephone number at the hotel. After all, I'd be gone tomorrow, and he could enjoy whoever he liked. Little rays of sunlight sharing his bed.

The same lines kept going through my head – 'I haven't cared for anyone for years . . . it's too late for me now . . . I could never really become fond of another human being.' But then, you didn't need to be fond of anyone to enjoy a little adoration and the occasional favour, did you. Little rays of sunlight come and go. I smiled at the unintentional pun.

He saw me, pushed his way through the crowd and gave me a kiss that was rather less intense than the one he'd just awarded to a succulent little blonde. But he was so happy. I told him how wonderful he was, how proud I was of him, how brave he'd been all those years, and now everything was going to be all right for him.

Ralph didn't reply. He just beamed. He was lost in it all, dazzled by the sunlight.

Then we joined the cast, and the rest of the evening swam with wine and adulation. Triumphs were relived, old jokes retold. Finally, a little after midnight we left the restaurant and staggered through cool empty streets back to the hotel. He collapsed into bed and passed out. I drifted into sleep with uneasy thoughts.

In the morning I ordered breakfast in our room overlooking the sea while Ralph pulled on his clothes and hurried out to gather the morning papers. When he returned he tossed them down on the bed and gazed at them fearfully for a moment: his face had the look of a criminal in the dock waiting for the verdict of the jury.

'All right, let's know the worst,' he said.

He opened the *Guardian*. There was nothing. Ralph groaned.

'Bastards!'

I tried to tell him the *Guardian* always preferred news a day late, when it had matured a bit. But Ralph wasn't comforted, and looked despondently down at the other papers lying on the bed. I reached for the *Independent* and turned to the reviews page. And there it was. A rave.

Then the *Daily Mail*. A rave.

The Times. A rave.

The *Telegraph*. A super-rave.

Several papers carried photographs of Ralph. His performance was said to shine out above the rest. There were even comparisons with Olivier.

I handed him the reviews one after the other.

'I'm so happy for you,' I said. 'That's the best birthday present you could ever have given me.'

Ralph looked up.

'Your birthday!' He looked startled. 'Oh yes, your birthday! When is it? I forget.'

'Tomorrow,' I said.

He nodded.

'Of course!'

Ralph's eyes dipped back to the reviews. And in that brief silence I remembered another of Astrov's lines yesterday evening – 'Our situation is hopeless – yours and mine!'

Back home, Magdalena greeted me with two messages. Fatwa had wandered in this morning covered in blood, followed shortly afterwards by a hysterical lady dog-walker carrying a mauled bundle of fur. Magdalena had done a great deal of 'Afraid Meesees Merton is not eere', whereupon Rachel had the good sense to ring the vet, who was well accustomed to these lucrative emergencies and arrived offering reassurances to the lady that spaniels often looked much better without their tails – so Rachel told me later with a grin.

The second message was to ring Gail at 'the chop'. So I phoned 'the chop' and got Caroline. She expressed indignation that I'd taken the day off, and then reluctantly passed me on to Gail, who spoke so softly I could barely hear her.

'Darlin', a certain gentleman is anxious to give you a birthday breakfast tomorrow. I can't imagine who, but you're to be there at eight. He's sorry he didn't give you more notice.' Then she added in a more decisive whisper – 'For fock's sake, I wish you'd tell Caroline about your lover: this secrecy stuff's killing me.' She cleared her throat and raised her voice to its normal pitch. 'And by the way,' she said, '"marital realignment" is going beautifully. Half-a-dozen interviews already. Cupid's doing his stuff like a dream.'

I put the phone down wondering about my own 'marital realignment'. What did it mean when your lover remembered your birthday and your husband didn't?

Rachel had made me a wonderful card which she'd painted at school, she told me. It had gold stars all over it, and quantities of what looked like vampires but which Rachel assured me were angels.

I gave her an enormous hug, and promised her a special supper this evening – which I'd already prepared, having won a fierce battle with Magdalena, who'd been keen to offer me a very special '*teckvai*' for the occasion. 'In Portugal always "*teckvai*" for birthdays,' she insisted. As well as every other day apparently, I thought: don't the Portuguese ever tire of their national dish? Then, with my eye on the gathering rush-hour, I hurried out to the car and drove off for Pimlico Square. Christ, I told myself, I'm entering my thirtieth year and I feel like a teenager playing truant: soon I shall be starting a working day pissed on birthday champagne.

I let myself into Josh's flat wondering what surprise he'd prepared for me. But the room was empty: there was no sign of him, or of any kind of surprise. I hesitated.

'Josh!' I called out nervously.

There were sounds from the bedroom. Then the door opened, and he came out carrying a large briefcase. I blinked. He was wearing an elegant dark suit with a purple tie and a neatly folded handkerchief protruding from the breast pocket.

'Happy birthday!' he said, rather formally.

I gazed at him. I gazed at the briefcase. I gazed back at him. Was this some kind of joke?

'Going somewhere, are you, Josh?' I asked.

He nodded.

'Yup! With you! Just a last-minute thought.' A smile began to spread over his face. 'Are you ready?'

I nodded, feeling puzzled. Why on earth did he need to dress up for breakfast? He followed me down the stairs and into the street. Then he steered me across the empty square.

I never knew Josh had a sports Jaguar. I realised I'd never thought about him away from his London flat; yet here was a man who travelled the world. In fact, there were an awful lot of things I didn't know about Josh, and that felt rather exciting. Without saying anything he pointed in the direction of the car, and I got in. He still didn't say anything, merely tossed the briefcase in the back and started up the engine, giving me a sideways glance and brushing my leg with his hand. We headed westwards towards Chiswick against the block of morning traffic, then over the river and on to the M3. It was a soft autumn day, and Josh slid the roof back so the wind caught my hair. The trees were turning bronze and gold, and a few thin clouds were combed across the sky. I laid my head back and watched them pass, enjoying the sexy feeling of having been kidnapped. Josh looked composed and extremely dashing in his dark suit, and he wore the taunting smile of a man guarding a secret.

After a while I broke the silence.

'You did say "breakfast", Josh, didn't you?'

He gave me another sideways glance, and nodded.

'Just a continental breakfast, I thought.'

I decided to ask no more questions and we continued in silence. Eventually we turned off the motorway somewhere near Basingstoke, and I began to keep my eyes skinned for country hotels. It did seem an awfully long way to drive just for breakfast, even if it was my birthday. Then I began to worry about the shop: I was going to be terribly late by the time I got back. It was already nearly nine o'clock. Should I ring Gail? I noticed that Josh had a car-phone.

He must have seen me looking at it because he gave a chuckle.

'Don't worry,' he said. 'It's all fixed.'

'You mean you've already told Gail?'

'Of course!'

He still had that shadow of a smile on his face. We passed several likely-looking hotels: two or three times Josh slowed down before shaking his head and murmuring, 'No, I don't think so, do you?' And he'd drive on.

When he did finally turn off the road there was no hotel in sight at all, only what looked like a tin barn at the end of the lane through the trees.

'Ah yes, this is better,' Josh said brightly. 'This will do. The roof leaks a bit, but I don't imagine it'll rain today.'

The teasing smile had grown broader.

The track ran round the side of the barn, and I could see there was a large open space beyond. The Jaguar slowed almost to a halt as we bumped on to the grass. I looked at Josh. Then, as we edged round to the front of the barn I looked ahead of me – and gulped. It was an airfield.

For the next half-hour I felt too shell-shocked to be clear what was happening. Men in overalls appeared, whom Josh seemed to know; and he went off with them, taking his briefcase with him. As he did so he turned and pointed casually towards a little yellow machine parked on the grass with its nose in the air and thin struts under each wing. I stood gazing at it, horrified. No one, but no one, I thought, is going to get me into that bloody thing: this is supposed to be the day of my birth, not the day of my death.

Josh reappeared. He must have seen the blanched look on my face, because he took my hands.

'You're frightened,' he said. 'Don't be. You'll love it. I promise.'

Promise! How could any man promise something like that?

'Frightened? Oh no, Josh, not really!' I said. 'It looks lovely.'

I gave another glance at the flimsy yellow butterfly. Clearly the merest gust of wind would rip the thing to pieces. Its wheels looked about as solid as the contraption Rachel and I had cobbled together last year to push Guy Fawkes in.

'You'd be surprised how comfortable it is,' he added.

I certainly would. The cockpit was the size of a hamster's cage. A piece of string seemed to be hanging from one wing. Something on the tail flapped.

'And the view's sensational.'

I'm sure. A sensation I'd do anything in the world to do without right now. Oh God, I wished we could go home.

'And you mustn't worry about feeling airsick: it's a beautifully calm day.'

Jesus, I was feeling sick already, and my feet hadn't even left the ground.

'You don't seem all that convinced.'

I forced a smile. I was *not* going to spoil Josh's present to me, even if it killed me – which I feared it might.

'Oh, I am, Josh!' I said. 'Entirely convinced. After all, I've flown dozens and dozens of times.'

But never in something made of paper and string. Then I looked back. The little yellow butterfly had its nose in the sun. It seemed to be waiting. I swallowed.

'Josh! It's absolutely wonderful. Really!' And I threw my arms round him. I hoped he didn't feel me quaking, or if he did that he thought it was lust. 'And now, are you going to tell me where we're going?'

Josh opened the cockpit and began to help me clamber in.

'Certainly not!' he said. 'Except one thing – it's in France.' And he laughed. 'Didn't I tell you it was going to be a continental breakfast?'

Once inside the cockpit I was aware of the same phenomenon which always puzzles me when I'm in a Mini – that it was twice as big inside as out. I strapped myself in next to Josh, who now had all kinds of gadgets round his head, and something that resembled a toothbrush suspended in front of his mouth. The two empty seats behind were strewn with maps and flight papers. I looked nervously around for a parachute, inflatable raft, life-jacket, fire extinguishers, oxygen mask, tranquillisers, gin bottle and anything else that might conceivably help save my life. I could see none of them. Then the engine started up and the propeller flicked hesitantly into life before accelerating so fast that suddenly I could no longer see it – had it fallen off already? We began to move, and I closed my eyes. My life felt such a little and fragile thing. I wondered if I could very quickly discover God, and if he would register my conversion in time to come to my aid.

I kept my eyes closed until I began to feel surprised I wasn't dead. To make sure, I plucked up courage to open just one of them for a split second. This achieved, I started to feel curious: if I wasn't dead, then perhaps I should try to enjoy it. So I opened both eyes and gazed about me.

It was as though someone had waved a magic wand, and I'd woken to a dream in the sky.

Josh turned his head.

'Are you all right?'

I nodded. I was much more than all right. After the terror and the relief I'd begun to feel exhilarated. This was wonderland: just the two of us surfing on the clouds, weightless. I wanted to laugh. I wanted to sing. I wanted to park the plane in the sky and make love. I thought of this time yesterday – an unwanted breakfast in a Brighton hotel with a husband who'd forgotten my birthday. I looked down in case we might be passing over Brighton now; but all I could see was the frayed thread of the coastline, and the sea flecked with tiny spots of white. I laid my hand timidly on Josh's knee – I wasn't sure if one should do such things to a pilot. But he smiled and put his arm round me. Then he leaned over and unbuttoned my blouse.

'It's all right; no one can see,' he said.

I was much more worried about the plane. Could it fly itself? Otherwise I could imagine the tabloid headlines tomorrow – 'Topless mother ditched in Channel'. I longed to put my hand on his prick: after all, if there *was* an automatic pilot may be it could take care of the joystick, in which case I could enjoy the real one.

Meanwhile Josh's fingers were continuing to explore me like Braille; my breasts, my stomach, between my legs. Oh my God! I gave a deep shudder and came; and in the rush of an orgasm I gazed up and saw the sky tilt over my head until the clouds lay below me and the sea was upside-down.

'Did I do that?' I said breathlessly once the sky had returned to its proper place, and the plane appeared to be the right way up again.

Josh was laughing.

'Of course! The power of sex. Simple aerodynamics.' He leaned over and kissed me. 'Happy birthday, darling!'

I hugged him. My heartbeat sounded louder than the engine.

'Is this why you learnt to fly?' I asked. 'So you could make your ladies loop the loop?'

He smiled.

'The best cure I know for fear of flying.'

I ran my hand under his shirt and dug my nails into his back.

'Beast! I want you,' I said.

I wanted to say, 'I want you always.'

He glanced at me.

'I always want you,' he answered like an echo of my thoughts. 'You know that.' Then, as if he'd said a little too much – 'Look down there!' he added, pointing. 'Perhaps you should make yourself a tiny bit decent: we're nearly there.'

His hands were making adjustments to the controls, and the sound of the engine changed. I could feel the plane descending. Then Josh was saying something in French on the radio and I could hear the crackle of another voice on the other end. And out of the window there were the cliffs of France, almost as high as we were. I could see the sun shining on gabled roofs. Dinky Toy cars were passing beneath us along the coast road.

'Where are we, Josh?' I asked, fixing the last buttons of my blouse and smoothing down my skirt.

'Le Touquet,' he said.

Now we were at the height of the trees and houses on either side. We dipped. We glided. We dipped again. My stomach felt taut. There was a slight bump, and then another. Well, at least this time it was a proper runway; there was even a man with two ping-pong bats waving us in. My stomach relaxed. I looked at my watch. It said eleven o'clock: that must be midday by French time.

I felt as excited as a child. I couldn't believe it. We were in France!

'Christ, Josh!' I said. 'My passport! I'm an illegal immigrant – on my birthday!'

Josh didn't react. He was busy flicking at various switches on the control panel. The propeller slowed and the engine cut. He reached up and slid back the roof. The sun poured in. Then he looked at me, fished in his pocket and produced a small wallet, which he opened. A printed card said '*Press*' in important letters. He returned it to his pocket with a smile.

'Besides,' he said, 'the airport manager's a mate. I'll just tell him you're my mistress. He'll understand.'

I laughed.

'It's a strange thought, isn't it? I suppose I am your mistress.'

'In that case,' he said, 'perhaps I'd better start treating you like one.'

And with a surprising show of strength, Josh grasped me by the waist and lifted me out of the plane. Christ, that was well-practised, I thought: he must have lifted an awful lot of women out of planes.

We were both of us standing on the tarmac. Josh was retrieving his briefcase and flight papers.

'Much more than a mistress,' he said quietly. 'You're my love!'

I felt a sudden shock: it was the first time either of us had ever used that word. Standing there in the middle of an airfield being told 'you're my love' – it was as though we'd travelled somewhere and could never return. I wanted to say something back – some awkward bumbling words from the heart; but I didn't know what words. Instead I squeezed Josh's hand. He put his arm round me.

'Now let's see,' he said calmly as we made our way towards the airport terminal. How did he manage to be so composed?

A sign read 'Douane'. Josh led me in the direction of a smaller sign that read 'Passage Interdit'. He flashed his press card at the gendarme and mentioned someone's name. The expression on the gendarme's face immediately changed from surly to respectful, and he began to tap out a number on his mobile phone. He spoke a few words, then handed the phone to Josh who began to rattle away cheerfully in French. I couldn't catch what he was saying. Then he returned the mobile phone to the gendarme, who hooked it back on to his lapel and gazed at us quizzically.

I heard a door open somewhere above us, and the sound of hurried footsteps. A portly little man of about fifty appeared at the top of the stairs, blinking, and smiling hugely. Josh embraced him, then introduced me as '*mon collègue*'. Well, at least it wasn't '*ma maîtresse*'. Josh explained that the gentleman was the airport manager, a long-standing friend. 'Excuse us one minute,' he added gravely, whereupon the two of them moved away towards the door. I assumed they were discussing the small matter of my passport, and began to gaze about me with what I hoped was insouciance.

The conversation didn't last long, and I heard little of it. But a few words caught my ear – one word in particular, used rather frequently by the airport manager. '*Milord!*' Several times it was '*Bien sûr, milord!*' and as they turned back towards me – '*A votre service, milord!*'

Josh beckoned me to accompany the two of them, and we walked round the side of the terminal to where a pair of iron gates opened on to a private car park. An important-looking black Citroën glistened in the sunlight, and I caught sight of the word '*Officiel*' affixed high up on the windscreen. The airport manager led us towards the car and took a set of keys from his pocket.

'*Bon voyage!*' he said, handing them to Josh with a salute, at the same time awarding me an appreciative smile and an even more appreciative glance at my legs. I stepped into the Citroën, sank back into the upholstery, and we drove off.

'Josh,' I said as we left the airport, 'are you going to tell me what that was all about?'

He looked at me out of the corner of his eye.

'Later, perhaps,' he said. 'Meanwhile it *is* your birthday, and aren't birthdays supposed to be full of surprises?'

I didn't argue. After all, my birthday surprises had already included a flight to France and an orgasm in the sky. What, I wondered, was likely to happen next?

Half an hour later I knew. Josh turned on to a by-road which hugged a long wall of the kind built to keep the peasantry out. After a while the wall was broken by a lordly entrance flanked by twin reclining goddesses in stone. With a crunch of gravel we turned into a spacious park whose drive was lined with immemorial trees which guided us in a noble meander towards a *château*. Around the entrance numerous seals of gastronomic approval hung like heraldic crests. Two uniformed lackeys opened the car doors simultaneously, whereupon we were steered through a gilded hall by a man so effortlessly dignified that I couldn't help glancing to see if perhaps he was wearing the ribbon of the *Légion d'honneur* on his lapel.

At the entrance to the dining room the man turned and addressed us. '*Un grand plaisir, Monsieur Kelvin . . . et madame.*' I noticed the slight pause before he added '*et madame*', just enough to suggest that I might be someone more important to *Monsieur Kelvin* than merely *madame*. Oh God, I thought, how I love the sophisticated innuendoes of the French. I felt less like a mistress than a queen.

We were ushered to a table by the window. Curtains swooped up on either side of us like a throne. Beyond the window fallow deer were grazing on boundless acres. A peacock dragged its tail along a manicured and English-looking lawn. A shell of a fountain spilt a curtain of water into a stone basin. In the distance rose a stone column surmounted by a figure in heroic pose.

I tried to take it all in. Then I looked back at Josh, and reached out to take his hand.

'What can I say?'

He laughed. 'That you like this – I hope.' The *maître d'* was setting two glasses of champagne in front of us. 'Have you ever had vintage Krug?'

Of course I'd never had vintage Krug. I'd never even heard of it. I tried to look ladylike and composed, and the *maître d'* gave another bow.

'*Bonne anniversaire, madame.*'

So Josh had told them that too. Or maybe Josh always brought his mistresses here on their birthdays, and the management discreetly understood the system.

I wondered if they all had orgasms in the sky first, but decided I preferred not to know the answer – at least not now.

Gradually the lunch unfolded. It was a slow and majestic ceremonial. We had *foie gras* with truffles. We had turbot. We had venison. We had wild mushrooms. Between courses we had morsels of God-knows-what which tasted like heaven and somehow made me hungrier for the next course. We had a soufflé made of fresh pineapples. And as an accompaniment to it all we had a bottle of something that was brought to us with the solemnity of the Holy Grail, and which Josh informed me was a *premier cru* from a famous *château* I'd never heard of.

It was half-past three when we rose from the table. My head was full of wine, and full of questions I was burning to ask.

'Thank you for a wonderful, wonderful birthday,' was all I could say.

And I floated in a dream all the way back.

The tiny airstrip near Basingstoke seemed such an unlikely point of return. But there was the tin shed. There were the men in overalls. And there was the Jaguar, exactly where we'd left it.

'Now Josh, please, a few explanations,' I finally managed to utter as we drove off. 'The plane. The *château*. The car. All that *milord* stuff ... I mean ... just tell me, will you?'

He chuckled.

'All very simple,' he said. 'You may be disappointed. I borrowed the plane from a friend. I use it for work sometimes: not very often. The *château* — I just picked it out of the *Guide Michelin*: I'd never been there before. And the car — well! It so happens the airport manager thinks I'm Lord Snowdon, and that tends to help. I don't like to disillusion him, and as you can see it can be rather useful. No, the whole idea came to me yesterday morning, and I just sat down and made a few phone calls.'

'Oh Josh!' I said, laughing. 'I do love you!'

I love you! It just came out. Until I heard myself say it I hadn't been certain if it was true.

Back home, Rachel said the same thing.

'Mummy, I do love you.'

I never knew words like that could hurt. Suddenly my double life felt like a rack. I unwrapped Rachel's present with unsteady hands, doing battle with the Sellotape. It was a coloured plastic till with a tiny key and a bell. For the shop, she explained: now I'd have somewhere to put the money, wouldn't I.

I hugged her; then I turned away.

'Mummy, why are you crying?' she asked.

Eamonn, with his miraculous instinct for computers, was proving more and more invaluable, and was now proudly registered as an associate director of Outfit Enterprises. Only Caroline wasn't wholly enthusiastic, her view of him temporarily soured by his behaviour as a weekend guest. She was now treating him rather haughtily, while Eamonn himself appeared a little sullen.

Gail waited until Caroline was ensconced next-door before regaling me with the account Eamonn had given her of what had actually taken place over that weekend.

'You have to believe this, darlin',' she said. 'God strike me dead if we aren't truthful in my family.'

I bore in mind that no Irishman ever saw a small rat, and hoped God's attention was elsewhere.

Eamonn, she explained, had arrived at the great house early on the Saturday evening, more than a little overawed by the guest suite to which he was ushered, the size of the double bed, and especially by the whiskered ancestral portraits which glared down on him wherever he looked. However, Eamonn was an accommodating lad, Gail assured me, and had brought along his only suit and his very best manners. If he had any suspicion of how he was expected to sing for his supper, he kept it well to himself. He had no objections to this being the age of the older woman, and in any case Eamonn was never one to say no to a good offer.

There were only the three of them at dinner – Caroline and Eamonn, plus Patrick who was already a little drunk. A sullen maid was in attendance. Eamonn found himself confronted by a battery of different glasses spread in front of him, and hadn't the faintest idea which to use for what. He'd already made a mistake with the champagne, and to save any further embarrassment

Caroline chose to lean over and pour the claret for him – which was sweet and charming of her except that she was wearing a blouse so loose it almost poured itself with the wine, along with most of Caroline that was underneath it.

'Well, that was fine, darlin',' said Gail. 'Eamonn knows a good pair of breasts when he sees them. But the young lad's not a fockin' monk, and nature has a way of responding to beautiful things, doesn't it just? So there was my nephew suddenly with this fockin' great erection right in the middle of dinner, and nowhere he could decently put it.' Gail paused to wipe away a tear. 'The trouble was – poor lad – you see, he'd had a small disaster with his zip while he was changing; and what's more his pants were those little skimpy objects that aren't meant for emergencies of this kind. They were under stress, shall we say?' Gail was now doubled up with laughter. 'Oh Mary, mother of Jaysus, can you imagine the scene, darlin'? There's Eamonn trying to cover himself with his napkin, and Caroline trying not to notice and spilling the wine all over the table. And Patrick nodding off half asleep and noticing nothing.'

There was a pause while Gail recovered, holding her stomach with both hands.

'But that was only the beginning, darlin',' she went on, glancing towards the door in case Caroline had decided to return at this moment. 'Poor fockin' Eamonn was praying for the meal to end, with his prick now flat as a little worm and not too much conversation flowing across the table. And then suddenly after the cheese and the sorbet Patrick shook himself awake and announced he was going to drag Eamonn off to the pub. So off they went, leaving Caroline bootfaced and the maid clearing up the dishes, with Eamonn nipping upstairs to change his trousers and thinking that a good pint of beer might drown his miseries.'

Well, the pub proved to be exactly the right tonic, Gail explained. It wasn't the sort of pub that welcomed beautiful young men like Eamonn every night of the week, and the warmest welcome of all came from one particularly buxom barmaid who kept stroking his hair and showing him Caroline wasn't the only woman around who could put a healthy body on display for his benefit.

'So up he rose a second time. At least this time his zip held, me darlin'; though not for very long.' Gail gave another glance at the door. 'Around closing time Patrick wandered off, leaving Eamonn with the barmaid and saying knowingly that he'd leave the front door on the latch. Now, Eamonn's no fool, and to be aroused twice in one evening was already provocation enough for a young fella. So, what did he do? What would any young man do? He took the girl back with him, didn't he? There was this double bed, and the door on the latch. And the rest you can imagine, darlin' . . . except that you can't, because around midnight Caroline came tiptoeing up to his room, pleased to see the light still on, but not quite so pleased to get a glimpse of a female rump bouncing up and down, and young Eamonn in much the same condition that had so excited her at dinner – except that this time there was no napkin to cover him, only a fairly large barmaid from the Rose and Crown.'

At this dramatic moment in Gail's story two customers wandered into the shop, leaving me with a mental picture of Caroline's face as she contemplated a scene straight out of the pages of the *Kama Sutra*.

'Poor young fella,' Gail went on in low tones, having left her customers peering through the racks. 'Between the undulations of the barmaid he caught a glimpse of this woman by the door with her eyes popping and her mouth hanging open. It was a terrible situation, he realised; but with satisfaction so nearly upon him this wasn't exactly a moment for sorrow, and at the third time of asking, so to speak, he got his rewards as nature intended. And so did she, he said, except that her little crics were so shrill they caused Caroline to slam the door behind her. Darlin', 'twas a miracle it didn't set the burglar alarm a-ringing.'

The two customers were by now looking around seeking assistance, so there was a further break in Gail's story. When they'd finally departed she calmly poured herself a cup of coffee and perched herself on the edge of the table.

'Poor Eamonn!' she said again. 'You have to imagine him, all mortified and shrivelled away. What was he supposed to do? He decided to wait till all was quiet, then he quickly ushered the girl out of the house – not very gallant of him, I'm afraid – and went miserably back to bed, planning to sneak away at the crack of dawn and maybe off to Ireland by the first plane.

'But he hadn't reckoned on Caroline,' Gail went on. 'As he crept down the stairs she called out to him from the kitchen – "Breakfast, Eamonn?" Well, what the fock could he do? He sat down at the table, feeling tired and a bit hungover, and trying not to look her in the eye. She had her apron on, and this frying-pan, and there was bacon and eggs, sausages, tomatoes, all the fockin' lot. Enough to make him feel ill at the mere sight of it. And she was smilin' sweetly. "Mushrooms? Fried bread, Eamonn?" she was asking. He could only nod. "And was the bed comfortable? Did you sleep soundly?" she kept enquiring. Meanwhile there was all this sizzling and spitting going on, until finally she brought over this steaming mountain of a plate. "Good to see you've got such a healthy appetite, a vigorous lad like you; need to keep your strength up," she went on, still with this lovely smile . . . and tipped the whole lot down his crutch. "I know you like it hot," she added, without dropping the smile for a second.'

Gail was shaking her head, with a look of wonder on her face.

'Darlin',' she said, 'she's a grand girl to be sure, is Caroline.' Then she gave another laugh. 'And d'you know,' she went, 'it was Eamonn's birthday – his twenty-first! The day he became a man.'

Caroline made only a brief reference to the event a

couple of days later, commenting in a bemused way that, strange as it might seem, she'd never watched another couple making love before. It wasn't a particularly elegant spectacle, she added: more striving than pleasure, she thought; they hadn't seemed to know quite what to do with the rest of their bodies, which was a shame, but then skills were things you acquired with practice, weren't they? She would have made a much better job of it herself, she made quite clear. What a pity Eamonn had felt the need to go off to a public house when a far superior service was available at home. And she shrugged her shoulders.

'He's only a young lad, darlin',' explained Gail a little indignantly, aware that family honour was at stake.

'I know he is,' replied Caroline wistfully. 'And that's exactly why I wanted him.'

Eamonn, for his part, had become rather subdued, focusing his attention studiously on the computer, and filing away the reams of notes we'd been taking on our women interviewees. Caroline worked with him quite unconcerned, though I noticed that she now left him to fetch his own coffee.

Then, one afternoon the atmosphere changed.

'Well, that's the last interview done,' Caroline announced, striding into the shop when mercifully there were no customers to overhear what she was undoubtedly about to tell us. 'Here's the breakdown!' And she brandished a folder of papers which Eamonn had just printed out. 'Really, you wouldn't believe what some of these women like to get up to,' she said. 'And as for their husbands! I never knew I'd lived such a conventional life.'

Jesus! I thought. If Caroline is conventional, what am I?

She laughed. I'd rarely seen Caroline so happy. For the past few weeks she'd taken on the role of chief interviewer. Gail on the whole preferred to remain in the shop, and with my own marriage on a slippery slope I tended to duck out of asking other women about theirs. Not so Caroline. She loved it. And to my amazement she appeared to be doing the job brilliantly, her natural incisiveness dragging out answers to questions no one else would have dared ask. There had been a constant flow of shattered women emerging for restorative cups of coffee after a session with Caroline, gasping out their praises for this woman who, they said, had probed deeper into their lives than all the analysts and psychotherapists they'd been expensively weeping over for years.

'Well, here's the roll-call of permanently unfaithful husbands,' she went on, pulling out several sheets of paper from the folder. 'Want to hear it?'

Of course we wanted to hear it.

Caroline adopted the stance of a town crier in the middle of the empty shop, the sheaf of papers held out in front of her.

'Right! In no particular order, here we go! Members of Her Majesty's government – three! And that includes a minister of state with special responsibility for home affairs: well, at least there's a man happy to mix business with pleasure.' Caroline gave a raunchy laugh. Then she went on reading. 'Other Members of Parliament – twelve! That's eight Tories, three Labour, and one very Liberal Democrat: I don't need to tell you who that is. Next, peers of the realm – three! Rather a low count, I'd have thought, but then I suppose most of them are rather old. Judges – eight! I'd have thought they were even older, wouldn't you? But perhaps they're circuit judges rutting away in Macclesfield. Now how about this: senior BBC management – four! I assume that's all in the cause of keeping standards up. And you'll never guess who the prime culprit is. If we sold that to the tabloids we'd be quids in.'

Caroline's eyes began to skim down the list.

'Then lots of boring ones. Assorted businessmen – twelve! Merchant bankers, stockbrokers, etc. – sixteen! Property developers – six! Permanent under-secretaries – three! Permanently on top of secretaries, more like it. Doctors – five! Funeral directors – one! Christ, who'd want to have an affair with an undertaker? Perhaps he's a necrophiliac – how are we going to dig up the right partner for him, I wonder?' Caroline gave a giggle, then cleared her throat. 'University lecturers – four! Directors of charitable trusts – two! Frightfully middle-class, all this, isn't it! No, here we go: scrap-merchants – two! Boxing managers – one! Swimming instructors – six! Why are swimming instructors such a randy lot, d'you suppose? It must be all that flesh: teaching nubile girls the breast-stroke. Well, that's the end of Samantha's swimming lessons.'

Caroline turned over another page.

'Then there's Odds and Sods — ten!' She giggled. 'And there's a few of them too.' There was a pause while she continued to scan the sheet of paper. Her eyes lit up.

'Now, here's the prize. Bishops — two! And you remember that one who's been frothing against women being ordained? Well, here he is! Has two mistresses — one on the Isle of Wight, the other on the Isle of Man. I suppose at least it keeps them apart. And now ... wait for it. Archbishops — one!'

She looked up triumphantly. Gail let out a groan.

'Jaysus, I hope he's Church of England. If it's the Archbishop of Dublin you can forget it.'

'It isn't,' said Caroline coyly, enjoying keeping us guessing. 'Well, we've got eighty-four husbands who are screwing around and making their wives miserable,' she concluded, replacing the sheaf of papers in the folder. 'Not bad for a beginning.'

Gail was making whistling noises between her teeth.

'What a fockin' classy clientele we have, to be sure. And what a filthy lot of bastards they are running this country.' I thought she was about to say that this sort of thing couldn't possibly happen in Ireland. But then her face brightened. 'And if we find the right women for just half of them,' she went on, 'we'll be fockin' millionaires.'

That was the first list, and it felt as though we were in possession of dynamite. I was terrified by the thought of leaving it in the shop overnight: a burglary, and Watergate wouldn't be in it. We'd never got round to acquiring a safe because Gail had always gone round to the bank safe deposit the moment we'd locked up in the evening. But this was different.

'How quickly can we get hold of a safe, Gail?' I asked.

Gail didn't even answer. She just picked up the phone.

'Rick, darlin',' I heard her say. 'We need a safe . . . No, just a small one, large enough for a few sheets of paper and a computer disk.' There was pause, and then she nodded. 'OK. An hour!' And she turned to me. 'Rick knows about safes. After all, he's opened enough of them.'

And she laughed. I often wondered what we'd do it he was ever nicked, and whether we'd be sent down with him. I decided to place my faith in Caroline being related to someone who'd rescue us.

The safe duly arrived, hauled in by Rick and some tattooed ruffian who no doubt had helped him find it. The shop was full of customers at the time, and several of them glanced at the two men suspiciously. For petty cash, I assured them. We installed it at the back of the Enterprises office, and arranged with Rick to have it cemented into the wall the following morning.

Eamonn looked up from the computer as we were

about to return to the shop, and handed us another sheaf of papers.

'There are your two lists of women,' he said. 'I've just printed them out.'

So this was the second part of the operation. We already had the list of happy philanderers; now here were the unhappy wives, and a second list of women who were prepared to take the philanderers on. A number of the wives had volunteered to appear on both lists, no doubt hoping for better luck next time. They had one thing in common only: their lives were made a misery by their husbands' affairs, and by the thought that one day they would be ditched in favour of some bitch who'd take everything. And they had all of them jumped at the idea that they could conspire – with us – to find just the right woman to succeed them. They were all of them paid-up members of what Gail insisted on calling our Sisterhood of Mercy. Our message had got through – 'Pastures New. Why wait till death? Part now!' I was proud of that.

So now we were approaching the real business. This was the nitty-gritty. We had to match them up.

'This has to be where Cupid comes into his own,' I said.

Caroline was looking puzzled.

'Well, it's no good a computer just spewing out information about people,' I went on. 'We've got to program Cupid properly.'

'And what the hell does that mean?' asked Caroline.

'You ask it questions,' I explained.

A contemptuous expression came over Caroline's face.

'Don't be ridiculous! How can you ask a computer what it had for lunch?'

I could see this was going to be difficult, and tried not to look exasperated. Gail came to my rescue.

'You don't ask it about lunch, you fockin' *ee*jit. You ask it to search.'

But Caroline refused to be put off her train of thought.

'You mean, you send it out for a walk?'

I looked away. Gail was beating her head with the palm of her hand.

'Listen, Caroline darlin'.' I could hear her trying to remain calm. 'The whole point of a computer is that it sorts out information. You tell it what to look for. If we're going to match some poor woman to some fockin' bastard, we've got to know if he's the sort of arsehole who likes blondes, or big tits, or the missionary position, swinging from the chandelier, Swedish massage, or whatever else he likes. You've got to have a *criterion* – and that's a fockin' big word for me.'

Caroline seemed to get the point at last.

'OK,' she said. 'So, how do we do it?'

Between us we explained that data profiling meant picking out the key characteristics of the person in question. The wives had already told us the main causes of their marriages having gone wrong – what it was the husbands wanted that they simply couldn't share, or couldn't provide. Incompatibility often came down to quite a simple thing, we said; it could be rooted in just one or two differences in personality which were irreconcilable. Something, for example, that the husband particularly liked but the wife didn't. Something he longed for and she couldn't give him. It could be as straightforward as a passion for golf, or Indian curries.

We thought we'd done rather well. Caroline said nothing for a long while, riffling through the copious notes we had on the eighty-four husbands we were targeting. Finally she looked up and gave a nod to indicate that all was now totally clear.

'Oral sex!' she announced. I was about to gulp, then realised this would be quite the wrong thing to do at that particular moment, and hid a smile. 'Yes!' Caroline went on. 'Oral sex! Forty-eight of these husbands want it.' She gazed at Gail and me, looking extremely pleased with herself. 'That's simple then, isn't it? All we have to do is to find forty-eight women who like it too.'

Gail had closed her eyes. I suggested that perhaps this wasn't quite enough, and that other male predilections should be taken into account too. This sent Caroline into another lengthy research among her papers. From time to time she made jottings on a note-pad.

'All right!' she said eventually. 'How about this? Sixteen husbands insist on the missionary position. Five like it in the bath. Seven won't do it on the Lord's Day. Six can only do it when drunk. Four can't ever do it

305

because they're always drunk. Three like to dress up as vicars. Two make their wives urinate . . .'

At this point Gail gave a little scream.

'For fock's sake, Caroline, can you try and be serious!'

I found myself wanting to ask if doing a 'loop the loop' at five thousand feet might be on Caroline's list somewhere. Instead I suggested calmly that sexual tastes might not be quite everything that mattered when it came to data profiling, and that perhaps *coq au vin* might sometimes be as important as cock.

Gail laughed. Caroline frowned. Mercifully, two customers entered the shop, which brought our meeting abruptly to a close.

As we locked up that evening Gail waited until Caroline was distracted by the collection of parking tickets on the windscreen of her Mercedes. Then she turned to me with a tired smile.

'We'll just go through the notes quietly tomorrow, shall we, darlin'? Caroline's got a lunch at the House of Commons – no doubt with one of the MPs on our list. We can decide what really matters, just the two of us; then we can let Eamonn get on with it. The quicker we get this done, the better.'

It meant not seeing Josh, but for once I decided my double life should take second place. And God knows, maybe sorting out the mess of other women's marriages would help me sort out the mess of my own.

'Then we can get down to the "mix 'n match",'

Gail was saying. She gave a laugh. 'After all, darlin', that's what we do in the shop every day, isn't it – mixing and matching people's clothes. The only difference is, now we're doing it with people's lives. Bijaysus! Where's this all going to lead?'

10

Mix 'n' Match

——————o——————

When the day came, Gail hung a notice on the door –
'*Closed for Stocktaking*'. The three of us then made our
way via the back entrance into the small office we'd
partitioned off from the main area of Outfit Enterprises.
This was Cupid's domain, and where Eamonn had spent
weeks poring over his beloved computer while it worked
its magic on the mass of data we'd been feeding it. We
trusted that by keeping Caroline well out of the way we'd
managed to program Cupid correctly, but in any case we'd
very soon know. Eamonn had carefully arranged his list of
suitable pairings in a mountain of folders, each one bearing
the name of a husband we were targeting.

I was surprised by how much I was getting into
the spirit of this enterprise. My early reticence had quite
evaporated; the prospect of sorting out other people's lives
sounded so much more rewarding than trying to sort out
my own. Maybe it was a displacement activity; none the
less I felt cheerful and rather wicked.

Eamonn's folders lay on the table in front of us. Out of curiosity I began to flick through the first dozen or so, noticing the names of quite a few public figures.

'It's a sort of Dishonours List,' I suggested.

Caroline liked that, and impatiently seized another pile of folders.

Eamonn felt the need to point out, before we actually looked inside the folders, that there had been problems. Cupid had not proved infallible. There was no way, for example, that a high court judge who needed to recite the whole of 'Horatius guards the bridge' before he was able to ejaculate could be found an ideal partner from among our existing clientele. One would need to advertise in some suitable literary journal, which might provoke scholarly misunderstandings as well as being a gross breach of confidentiality. On the other hand, Cupid's profile of a millionaire rock star with a *palazzo* in Tuscany, debenture seats on the Centre Court and a taste for fine wines could be easily matched by at least half the women on our books.

'OK,' I said. 'So we toss a coin for the rock star, and leave His Honour standing erect on his bridge. What about the rest of them?'

Caroline was now looking excited.

'Screw the rest of them,' she exclaimed. 'How old's the rock star? Where's the file on him?' Having failed with Renato's Tuscan farmhouse, she was clearly hoping to score with the *palazzo*. 'You know, I haven't slept with a rock star for nearly twenty years,' she added wistfully. Her face fell. 'Christ, I feel old!'

Before Caroline had a chance to sink into being maudlin Gail produced coffee and suggested we share out the folders between us, discarding any pairings that were obviously a dead loss and earmarking those that invited immediate attention.

She then handed them out. There weren't quite as many as there might have been, she explained. More than a quarter of the husbands had proved totally unmarketable, including the judge who liked to recite 'Horatius' while on the job; so their profiles had been set aside at least until we could recruit a fresh intake of women, or we felt compelled to return our registration fee to the disappointed wives. This meant that there were about twenty folders for each of the three of us, Eamonn being excluded on the grounds of inexperience in spite of his recent athletic performance with the barmaid at Caroline's house.

It was an extraordinary morning. As I worked my way through the folders, the most improbable joys and absurdities of people's lives began to be spun out in front of me: reading their files was like reading their souls. I was transfixed. Of course, no one knew these men better than their wives – this was self-evident; probably the men themselves would be appalled to discover just how much they did know, and how much *we* now knew. Touchingly, what came through to me was how deeply their wives had once loved them. If they had never done so they would never have known them so well; and had they still loved them today *we* wouldn't have known them so well. There was a certain tragic irony in this. Only the ruthless detachment of dead love had given us their portraits.

The best part of an hour passed before any of us said anything. It was like taking part in a game of patience. Gail, red hair cascading around her as she bent over the folders, mouthed the odd word of surprise. The occasional laugh burst out of Caroline. We all of us set certain folders aside from time to time: I chose three pairings which seemed to me to have been made in heaven. Gail appeared to do the same. Caroline, I noticed, had picked out just one.

Finally she turned to us with the single folder in her hand.

'Well!' she announced. 'You programmed the computer, you two. Want to listen to this?'

Caroline proceeded to open the folder. Eamonn took no notice, but went on thumbing through his girlie magazine.

'Here we have the assistant head of religious broadcasting,' she announced. 'He's forty-two. Enjoys cricket, fell-walking and reading Trollope. Author of a number of biblical studies, in particular a volume on the theological significance of the serpent in the Book of Genesis. Doesn't smoke or drink. Patron of a youth club in Ealing. Regular lay preacher. Strongly opposed to the wearing of church vestments. Hasn't slept with his wife for five years. Believed occasional infidelities at ecumenical

311

conferences. Present lady-friend a maths teacher at a local comprehensive.'

Caroline paused, and looked up at us with a thin smile.

'Now here's the woman Cupid imagines would be ideal for this godly gentleman – a striptease artist whose act is accompanied by a seventeen-foot boa constrictor!'

Caroline's eyes were boring into first me, and then Gail.

'Marvellous, isn't it! What a triumph of computer programming! Congratulations to you both. That'll teach you to do things behind my back.'

She gave a snort, then turned for support to Eamonn who was still quietly poring over his girlie magazine.

'Well, Eamonn!'

Eamonn raised his eyes from the centrefold and lazily tossed his hair back from his eyes.

'So what's wrong?' he said.

Caroline looked at him fiercely.

'What d'you mean – "What's wrong?" You were listening, weren't you? Or were you too busy drooling over those tits?'

Eamonn nodded wearily.

'Yeah! I was listening.'

His eyes returned to the tits. Caroline gave an exasperated flutter of the hand and thrust the folder under Eamonn's nose.

'Explain! That's all. Explain how these two dimwits

here have managed to program our computer to produce a result like this.'

Eamonn reluctantly put down the girlie magazine.

'Yeah! No problem.'

He took the folder from Caroline and began to skim through it, pulling out an apple from his pocket as he did so, and biting into it. Caroline was looking increasingly irritated. If she'd had another pan of bacon and eggs in her hand I felt sure she'd have tipped it down his crutch. Gail caught my eye, and winked. Eamonn was getting his own back.

'Makes sense all right,' he said eventually without looking up. 'The boa constrictor – well! The guy's written a book about serpents, hasn't he? Forget the Book of Genesis – that's what the computer's picked up.' A look of bewilderment appeared on Caroline's face. Eamonn went on reading. 'He's also strongly against wearing vestments: OK, so is she – she's a stripper. Right?' Another pause. Caroline's fingers began to twitch powerlessly. 'And he likes Trollope. Well, if you look here, the girl describes herself as "a bit of a trollop at heart", doesn't she?' Eamonn gave Caroline a patronising look. 'Computers can't make mistakes, you see, Mrs Uppingham. They make connections. You can't expect a computer to understand the difference between one kind of trollop and another, can you now?'

Then Caroline surprised me. She placed her hands on her temples, gazed at first one of us, then another – and laughed.

'The truth is,' she said after a moment, 'a striptease artist with a boa constrictor is probably exactly what our lay preacher could do with. You don't write books about the serpent in the Garden of Eden without having temptation fantasies, do you?' Caroline rose to her feet and thrust her hands into the pockets of her jeans. 'Well! Let's bring them together then. Religious broadcasting will never be the same again.'

Gail looked at Caroline indignantly.

'You Protestants, you're all the same,' she said. 'Fockin' hypocrites!'

It was my turn next. I had nothing so colourful to offer. My chosen three were plain and obvious by comparison. A feminist publisher, a games mistress at a London girls' school, and a stunningly attractive ex-model – these seemed perfectly matched to a junior minister for the environment, a boxing promoter and a successful divorce lawyer.

Gail's selection sounded a good deal less convincing. Neither Caroline nor I were at all sure about Cupid's pairing of a leading plastic surgeon with a pockmarked Indian waitress, or an Arctic explorer with a lady sales rep for Häagen Dasz ice-cream. As for the high-powered lady marine biologist, was her ideal partner for life really likely to be the under-chef of a Battersea fish-and-chip shop?

Clearly we had some fine-tuning to do on Cupid, even though Gail insisted we were just bigoted and class-ridden Anglo-Saxons who didn't understand the beauty of God's ways.

'What the fuck has God got to do with it?' Caroline retorted.

'You're just heathens, the two of you,' retorted Gail, looking ruffled.

I wondered what being heathens had to do with it too. Gail, I noticed, invariably brought her Roman Catholicism out of mothballs whenever she was stuck for an answer.

Finally at midday we declared 'stocktaking' to be concluded, and reopened the shop. By this time we'd managed somehow to agree on what action was to be taken next. For each of the husbands who were promising targets Cupid had provided us with a short-list of suitable women, all of whom of course we'd already interviewed. Now we would need to show this list to the present wife, who would express her preference and then agree to meet the woman who might possibly replace her in the marital bed – or more to the point, as Caroline suggested, would replace the mistress in the extra-marital bed. Then, if the two women got on well, the next move was up to us: we needed to devise a scheme for the husband to meet his wife's chosen successor, crossing our fingers that Cupid had got it right.

I suggested that this was going to be our biggest headache: how the hell would we do it without the husband suspecting? Gail agreed. Caroline on the other hand didn't think it mattered a damn whether the husband suspected or not.

'Look!' she said fiercely. 'They're all of them wom-anisers, aren't they? If their roving eye catches sight of someone they fancy they're not going to ask what the hell she's doing there, for Christ's sake. If Robert Redford turned up in my house, d'you imagine I'd stop and ask myself if Patrick had decided to give me a birthday present?'

'No, darlin',' said Gail. 'Of course not! You'd ask him to sign your autograph book, wouldn't you?'

It was at this point that we broke up the meeting. What we now needed was to decide on perhaps three test cases. The only remaining question was – which three?

We were occupied with customers for the entire afternoon. There was no chance to exchange further thoughts, but every so often one or other of us would give a knowing look and slip next-door to consult the files. For several hours there was this animated conspiracy of silence. In the shop we busied ourselves matching women's outfits, while in our heads we were busy matching men with other women. It wasn't until we finally locked up at nearly six o'clock that we could get together again and pool our thoughts.

Gail suggested diplomatically that we each choose one test case.

Caroline opted for an MP – perhaps the one she'd had lunch with, I wondered, which made me suspect her motives. None the less she produced an excellent idea for how to bring about the meeting with the chosen lady, whoever she might turn out to be. This was to be a constituency lunch: it would be easy enough to arrange this through the man's wife. Thank God he wasn't MP for the Western Isles, Caroline added.

I chose an actor with the National Theatre. On his files I'd spotted that he suffered from chronic back trouble as a result of overdoing it as Coriolanus. The lady who was first on our short-list happened to be a successful physiotherapist. Great! I thought. There was nothing like a 'hands-on' approach in these matters: it would cut out a lot of awkward preliminaries.

Gail picked a television news presenter. His face told us what his file corroborated – that he loved good food. Cupid had earmarked for him a lady whose business was to supply lunches for City boardrooms. We also knew that the man's birthday was next month. Gail was sure that his wife would be only too happy to lay on a lavish party for the occasion, without of course disclosing that his real birthday present was to be the chef.

So there was our plan of action. For a bunch of amateurs we felt we were doing exceptionally well.

'It's becoming like a military campaign,' said Caroline cheerfully.

'Then perhaps we should think of it as D-Day,' I suggested. 'Divorce Day!'

Before long Torquemada was enjoying a new role. In addition to employing his confessional powers, he was now helping to bond three wives to the women chosen to replace them. I'd feared that these meetings between pairs of women might prove an utter disaster, and when it actually came to it they'd loathe one another instantly. Far from it: in all three cases the rapport was instant. Between buying and selling outfits I managed discreetly to overhear enough to be reassured that Cupid had done a quite wonderful job, and that all three of our first choices appeared to be precisely right.

After initial introductory chatter over coffee the resident wife would take her successor for more intimate discussions in the Enterprises office next door, which we'd now equipped as a sitting room where we could offer drinks. I was strongly reminded of the rigmarole of selling a house, with the present owner proudly showing off the best features of something she was actually dead keen to get rid of – the lovely bedroom, the elegant staircase, the custom-built kitchen, the immaculate services, the garden which was so lovely in spring. And of course, like selling a house, all the real rubbish was carefully concealed – no one would want to put off a prospective buyer at this early stage.

Then, as the three vital meetings drew closer, Caroline came into her own.

'We've got to dress these women exactly the way we know the men like them to be,' she insisted. 'It's no use them being the perfect match if they don't *look* the perfect match. Otherwise the husbands may not even notice them.'

With the resources of the shop at our disposal, we

agreed that this should present no problems: we had outfits on our racks to suit all possible tastes.

However, it turned out to be much less easy than we expected. Consulting our files to discover how these husbands' ideal women were supposed to dress, it became clear that male fantasies had played a powerful role. For instance, how on earth could the elegant and sophisticated lady we'd chosen for the Member of Parliament possibly attend a constituency luncheon wearing a see-through nightdress? No more appropriate was the idea of the TV presenter enjoying a birthday dinner prepared by a chef in a Balenciaga ball-gown with diamonds in her hair. The actor was easier – at least he was only going to have his back wrenched and massaged: even so, the prospect of our physiotherapist plying her trade in a topless swimsuit was beyond even Caroline's exotic imagination.

'I'll do my best,' she said, laughing. 'Let's deal with them one at a time.'

The first call on Caroline's skills was to sort out the Member of Parliament, who was forty-ish, rather dashing, tipped for a cabinet post in the next reshuffle, and at present enjoying a hot-and-heavy with his ambitious private secretary. She was the one who had to be removed at all costs.

The MP's wife had arranged plenty of constituency lunches before; so this was no problem. It was a south London constituency. A local hall was booked; the party faithful were marshalled; a junior minister agreed to give the welcoming address, touching only lightly on unemployment, Maastricht, the NHS, compulsory tests for schoolchildren and VAT on domestic fuel, and coming down heavily on popular issues such as drug abuse and law and order. The wife's potential successor was a young woman by the name of Rowena, whom she swiftly co-opted on to the organising committee, so entitling her to a place on the platform and – more important – to the informal 'get to know your Member' gathering for drinks after the meeting. The wife assured us that no woman had ever found it difficult to get know her husband's member if she'd really tried; so, provided Caroline did her job, all should go smoothly. She herself would keep a tactful distance, having already made quite sure that her husband's current mistress would not be present. She didn't disclose how.

Caroline's big test came two days before the crucial event. We'd arranged for the wife's successor to come in at one o'clock, when we could conveniently close the shop for an hour. Gail and I were in attendance in case we were needed. The present wife was there to give advice. Caroline had already done her homework on the husband's data profile, and decided that the closest we could get to the man's fantasies of a see-through nightdress was a Versace outfit which an Italian model had brought in the previous week on the grounds that her boyfriend was embarrassed to be seen with her in public. Caroline proudly held up the dress to show us, and as I gazed at it Dante Horowitz's grey cobwebs seemed positively nunlike by comparison. If it had been a fishing-net, all the fish would have escaped. The ratio of bare spaces to actual material was roughly three to one.

'For fock's sake, Caroline,' said Gail, looking horrified. 'The woman can't wear this to a Tory party meeting!'

Caroline clicked her tongue, and scowled.

'And why on earth not?' she retorted. And she reached over and picked up the MP's file. 'His wife here says her husband's dream is an intelligent and successful woman with long dark hair, high breasts, good legs, and who moves like a snake. Isn't that right?' The wife gave a nod. 'Well then! Rowena's got a degree in chemistry. She's a highly paid researcher for a top pharmaceutical company. She's beautiful. She's exotic-looking. She's got fabulous legs. And if she's worried about the breasts, well, her hair's quite long enough to cover them – at least for the meeting. So, what's wrong?'

I closed my eyes. I had visions of Rowena being hurried off the platform wrapped in a policeman's overcoat, and Outfit Enterprises hastily closed down under a hail of public indecency charges.

At that moment Rowena walked in. Gail and I retreated into the background and began to eat the sandwiches which Renato had kindly prepared for us.

'She's certainly beautiful,' I said in a low voice. 'Why is she so keen to marry this bloody MP?'

Gail gave a shrug.

'You know what Cupid came up with, darlin'. They share all the same interests. She looks like his dream. Maybe he's her dream. After all – British establishment, security, social position. Remember, she may have the brains and the looks, but her father's a Cypriot waiter. So, she's an outsider who longs to be an insider. Common enough situation, don't you think?'

Caroline and the wife were now leading Rowena down to the changing-room. Gail and I finished our sandwiches and waited expectantly. If Caroline can persuade the woman to wear that outfit, I thought, she's more of a genius than I ever knew.

The silence downstairs seemed interminable. We glanced at our watches. On the pavement outside customers were pressing their noses to the door and glancing at their watches. We pretended not to see them, and busied ourselves making coffee. Suddenly a throttled cry could be heard from the changing-room below, followed by another, rather more shrill. I made a face at Gail, who ran her hands through her hair and looked down at the floor. Now we could hear Caroline's voice – insistent, cajoling, unyielding: it was the voice of imperturbable authority, precisely the tone I'd heard so often when Caroline was persuading Samantha to get off to bed even if she did have a favourite TV programme to watch. I'd never known Caroline lose one of these battles. But Gail was looking at me balefully.

'Jaysus, we're in trouble now, darlin'!'

I shook my head.

'You wait!' I said.

And I was right. Ten minutes later we heard the door of the changing-room open, and Caroline and the wife made their way up the staircase into the shop, followed at a short distance by Rowena. The woman's hands were gripping the stair-rail as if she might fall, and she had exactly the wild and thankful expression I'd seen so often at funfares on the faces of women who'd just stepped off the Big Dipper for the first and certainly the last time.

'She looks absolutely stunning,' announced Caroline. 'Doesn't she?' she said emphatically, turning to the wife who gave a perplexed nod. 'And her hair's exactly the right length. You just have to remember never to shake your head,' she added, giving Rowena an encouraging smile.

She's done it again, I thought.

Caroline carefully wrapped the Versace dress in tissue-paper and slid it into a carrier-bag. Then she gathered the various accessories she'd selected to be worn with it, placed these in a second carrier-bag, and handed both to Rowena.

'Wonderful! I'll see you the day after tomorrow,' she said reassuringly. 'Now I'll get both of you a cab.'

Rowena murmured some sort of thanks, gave Gail and me a bewildered smile, and followed Caroline and the wife to the door. We heard Caroline's voice shrieking across Pimlico Square.

'Taxi!'

A short while later she returned. She was shaking her head.

'Christ! I need a drink,' she said, collapsing heavily on to a chair. 'That was a close-run thing.' She closed her eyes for a moment or two. 'You may think Rowena is a modern woman of the world,' she went on. 'But can you imagine what she'd never thought to tell me before?' Caroline was now gazing at us enquiringly. 'Well, for a start that her family are Turkish-Cypriot, not Greek. That she was brought up a Muslim. A strict Muslim!' Caroline let out a little giggle and reached for the drinks cupboard. 'Well!' she continued. 'All I can say is that I've learnt something today.' She gave us an impish smile. 'I now know what a fundamentalist bra looks like!'

Gail was wide-eyed.

'You mean she actually took the fockin' thing off?' she said.

Caroline laughed.

'No! *I* did! With a hacksaw!'

I was shaking my head.

'And this is our first test case,' I said incredulously. 'You're not seriously telling me it's going to work, Caroline?'

She looked at me, surprised.

'Work? Of course it'll work,' she said crossly. 'They're perfectly suited, those two. The bra was the only thing left of Rowena's fundamentalism, and she'd probably be burning it right now if it weren't incombustible. As for the MP, his secretary-mistress will be out of the door in two minutes flat: you wait.' Then a coy expression came over Caroline's face. 'You don't think I have lunch at the House of Commons for nothing, do you?'

When Caroline got it right, she got it spectacularly right. A week after her rough handling of Rowena, Gail pushed a copy of one of the tabloids in front of me as I came into the shop.

'Well! What d'you think of that, darlin'?' she said.

There in the gossip column was a photograph of the Tory MP with his arm round the beautiful Rowena, and above it the headline 'MP's wife seeks divorce.'

'Didn't take long, did it?' Gail added with a chuckle.

I read the piece the gossip columnist had written; and there it all was. Rowena had graced the platform with her dark hair cascading almost to her waist. The MP's speech about open government had been punctuated by meaningful glances at the open dress the young lady close to him was wearing. At the informal gathering afterwards he made a point of complimenting her on her hair, her lovely dress, and much else. Shortly afterwards they were seen to leave together in order – as the columnist delicately put it – to become 'better acquainted'. It was understood, he added, that the MP's wife was fully aware of the situation, and was taking appropriate legal action.

There seemed no choice but to believe it, though for a while I assumed it was just a fluke; or that Caroline had exercised some kind of black magic during her lunches at the House of Commons. But then a week later another newspaper carried the story of how a certain actor with the National Theatre had fallen helplessly in love with his physiotherapist. The lady was said to have done a miraculous job: she'd repaired his back and wrecked his marriage simultaneously.

Caroline, who had said almost nothing all week, was beginning to look inordinately pleased with herself. Then the following Monday a phone call was put through to her by Eamonn from the Enterprises office. The shop was crowded at the time, though naturally this in no way deterred Caroline.

'You mean, they went off together for the weekend?' she said loudly. 'Where? . . . To Paris! . . . The Meurice. Good! Yes, I told her to insist on that. The beds are huge, and the staff are very discreet. I've often used the place myself.' By now most of the customers had forsaken the racks and were goggle-eyed. Caroline, phone in hand, preferred to talk straight through them. 'So you think there'll be no problem about the divorce, then . . . You mean the press have got hold of it already? Oh well, I suppose he *is* rather well-known! Congratulations anyway. Call in and have a drink . . . Yes, today will be fine. Any time after six, when the bloody customers have gone.'

From the look on their faces I didn't think the bloody customers had any intention of going. Caroline put the phone down.

'Well! It must have been a good birthday party,' she said, beaming. 'That makes it three out of three. Not bad for a start, is it?'

And Caroline began to serve customers as if nothing had happened at all. She was suddenly all grace and charm.

We'd by now reached an agreement as to how duties could best be divided between us. With all three test cases I'd done the organising, which had been a series of delicate operations. Caroline had undertaken the social side, making sure people were where they should be, when they should be, and looking exactly as they should. Gail preferred to remain in the background, running the shop with Eamonn and dealing with the stream of telephone calls to the Enterprises office next door.

'Angela,' she said to me one afternoon. 'Things are hotting up. I really don't understand it.' She looked exhausted. 'Twenty-eight phone calls in one day. Fockin' madness, darlin'. We're going to need more staff.'

With a percentage of three divorce settlements already coming our way, we decided we could well afford a receptionist. A local employment agency supplied one straight away, and two days later she arrived. Her name was Karen, she came from Orpington, and her mini-skirt had the effect of distracting Eamonn from his girlie magazines. He also started wearing a particularly disgusting aftershave until Gail objected.

'Jaysus, Eamonn!' she said quietly, so that Karen shouldn't hear. 'How d'you expect people to come in here and talk decently about divorce when the place stinks like a fockin' brothel?'

Eamonn awarded Gail the sort of look young men give their stuffy aunts. But at least it put an end to the aftershave.

Even with a receptionist our resources were still

being stretched to the limit. I had less and less time to see Josh, which distressed me. The days when I'd been a lunchtime lover whenever I wished seemed like a lost paradise. My birthday flight to France was a beautiful memory. I was teetering on the edge of being in love with Josh, but on recognising this I had backed away in panic. I'd begun to use work as a shield. Excuses for not seeing him were also excuses for not acknowledging my feelings for him. When I'd first gone to bed with Josh I'd reckoned on a lover, not a man to love. This confused and frightened me. I was scared of losing him, but just as scared of breaking up my life in order to be with him. Rachel, more than anything, was the tie. How could I possibly cause her that pain? And I threw myself into work in order not to have to think about it. I hid behind other women's broken marriages to avoid facing the breakdown of my own.

At the same time I loved it here. I loved the turmoil of what I had to recognise was success. After the first three test cases Enterprises didn't just subside, as I'd imagined might happen. It boomed. It blossomed. Clients poured in. The divorces poured out. 'Why wait till death? Part now!' – the message had caught on.

It also caught on with the press. Gail's friend Conor, who'd written a glowing piece about us when we first opened the shop, rang up one morning to say he wanted to come and see us.

'You'd better take him out to lunch, darlin',' Gail suggested.

I protested that I had no idea how to talk to the press: why shouldn't she do it? After all, she knew the man: I didn't.

'Nonsense!' Gail answered firmly. 'I'm Irish. Conor never believes a word I say. And he ought to know: he's Irish too. Besides,' she added with a laugh, 'I'd probably get drunk and be horribly indiscreet; as for Caroline, she'd be indiscreet drunk or not. No, you've got to do it, darlin'. Anyway, you've got the face and figure. He'll love it.'

She was right. He did love it. And so did I. Half-way through lunch I realised that talking to a gossip columnist somehow turned you into a gossip. Far from being ultra-careful about what I told him, I kept blurting out all sorts of things I should never have said. I even told him extremely indiscreet things about myself – how I'd once worked in a bank where the assistant manager had flashed me his willy – how I'd met my husband in a Chelsea boutique and sneezed all over him – how I'd got the idea for The Outfit from Caroline's garage sale. Only a supreme effort stopped me telling him about Josh, and how he'd given me an orgasm doing a loop the loop over the Channel.

'Christ, Angela!' I said to myself near the end of a bottle of Chablis. 'Keep your big mouth shut!'

Then I realised that, unlike nearly all the men I'd ever had lunch with, Conor wasn't just putting on a show of chat while wondering how he could possibly get my knickers off. He actually wanted me to tell him things. That was his business. And of course, with a fatal sense of relief that he wasn't trying to seduce me, I gratefully obliged. This, I thought, must be the power of the good journalist.

Finally, over coffee he made me a business proposition, though it was so carefully couched that it hardly sounded like one. Perhaps, he said, one of us might care to tip him the wink from time to time about some prestigious divorce, or – to use my own phrase – an interesting 'marital realignment'. He laughed as he said it. There would be no question of payment, of course, he explained; that would be sordid, wouldn't it. But it would be easy enough to run a piece about The Outfit 'in parallel', as he put it. No apparent connection between the two stories, he explained; but everyone who read gossip columns understood the code, and how to fit the two together. That was the sub-text – much more powerful than the actual story, and of course it drastically reduced the number of libel actions. It was known as 'imaginative editing'. Would this seem a reasonable arrangement, just between ourselves, Conor asked with a confident smile? Then he thanked me for lunch, switched off his professional eye, and said he wished every woman he interviewed was as desirable as I was.

When I told Gail about the offer she gave a whoop of pleasure. Then she looked very serious.

'Darlin', we have to handle this very, very carefully. And that means not breathing a word to Caroline.'

I never realised at the time just how invaluable it could be to have a gossip columnist on one's side. But then, as winter drew in and our enterprises continued to expand, I kept noticing little references to us in Conor's column. There'd be a photograph of one of our budding divorcees with his radiant new lady; then, next to the tittle-tattle about the two of them would be a shorter piece – in italics – about the tearful ex-wife-to-be, and how she was consoling herself by purchasing clothes at that wonderful shop in Pimlico Square called The Outfit, where everyone was to be seen these days.

There was never any mention of Enterprises as such. We were, as Conor had put it, the 'sub-text': we were ghosts at the divorce banquet, and everyone who read his column seemed to know we were there. I became conscious – just through the things people kept saying to us – that our modest agency was acquiring a certain *cachet*, an aura even. The word was being put about. As proof of this, all sorts of new clients kept arriving. They'd pretend to be searching for clothes among the racks for a while until gratefully accepting the offer of a cup of coffee; then their eyes would immediately alight on our *'Pastures New'* card discreetly propped up against Torquemada. They'd pick it up with a look of faked surprise, and say, 'How very interesting!' and within minutes they'd be seated next-door with Caroline having their marriages shredded. Eamonn would promptly get to work, and in no time at all there they'd be, looking agonised in Conor's gossip column, but comforting themselves for the loss of their husband of twenty years with the purchase of a fetching Lanvin dress from that wonderful little shop in Pimlico

Square. It was no longer necessary even to mention its name. People knew.

We began to feel like alchemists; as though we possessed some kind of magic formula for sorting out people's personal lives. It was even suggested – Caroline brought back this tit-bit from a dinner party – that we were secretly advised by several leading London psychiatrists. How else, the woman had suggested, could our phenomenal successes be accounted for?

How indeed? *We* didn't know. But we never denied anything. Our silence was golden. We just smiled – and the world took our smiles to be a yes.

And of course it was extremely easy to smile. How otherwise could we express our amazement that such fame should have come our way through the combined efforts of a coffee machine, a computer, and the guesswork of three women who knew a lot about designer clothes and a little about human nature?

I began to feel we were living in the middle of a human kaleidoscope. Everyone's life around us seemed to be forever changing; and so, less dramatically, was my own. Ralph's tour with *Uncle Vanya* was finally over, and the play was about to open in the West End. It was strange having him at home. For the past months I'd grown accustomed to 'home' being just Rachel, Magdalena and me, with Fatwa strolling in and out – sometimes bloodstained, sometimes not. And always the pungent smell of '*teckvai*' about the kitchen when I was back late. But now there was Ralph too; and suddenly he didn't seem to belong. He was like a stranger to me – a stranger who was perfectly easy to talk to, easy to be with. We never argued. We made no demands on one another of any kind. It was as if being parted had freed us of something, freed us of personal tensions, freed us of the habits and obligations of love. Now we just *were*. We existed under the same roof like two pieces of furniture.

'Do you feel like making love tonight?' Ralph would ask. He might have been offering me a biscuit.

'No thank you, darling. Not tonight,' I'd hear myself say. And we'd roll away from one another. It was cold, and he wore pyjamas. I stared at the ceiling.

Sometimes in the night I'd lie awake thinking of Josh inside me. My body was his. Yet I wasn't with him. These were the long hours when I tried to understand what I should do. But I always seemed to fall asleep before I could find the answer.

And in the morning there was breakfast.

Josh had begun travelling again. He said it was nothing to do with me – these were jobs he simply couldn't afford to refuse – there were Jessica's school fees to pay, new cameras to buy, and God knows what else.

But it was to do with me – I was certain of that. He'd made a bid for me, and I'd backed away. Josh wasn't one to come straight out with what he wanted: he demonstrated it by the things he did – my birthday flight to France, giving me a key to his flat, taking on commercial work so as not to be away from me. He knew perfectly well that I understood: it was another kind of sub-text. And by ignoring it I'd rejected him. So he'd taken a step back. I could feel him making space for himself – getting back into his old life. I wasn't free: he was. It was as simple as that. I tried not to feel jealous. In any case, what right did I have to his loyalty? He'd leave me a note in his flat telling me when he'd be back. Often I never even knew where he'd gone, though one day I saw photos of Sarajevo in the paper. Ravaged faces stared out at me. The photos were Josh's, and I was terrified. He was living in danger, and I was living with Ralph. I tried to see the absurdity of it – they were like two figures in a weather-house, Josh and Ralph: when one was out, the other was in.

'I'm used to being on my own,' he said one lunchtime after he'd returned. We'd been making love. His hand was on my breast, and he was smiling, his body propped on one elbow as he gazed at me.

What did 'alone' mean in Sarajevo, I wondered. Could you ever be alone when at every street corner some sniper had you in his sights?

Then one morning he wasn't there when I let myself into his flat. He wasn't expecting me, and there was no note. I went into the bedroom, and the bed was unmade. There were two dents in the pillows, and on the floor beside the bed lay a bra. I felt sick.

And I didn't even know where he was.

If this was what Josh meant by 'being alone', I didn't think I could bear to go on seeing him. At the same time I could hear his voice, not so much accusing as horribly truthful – 'But you're with your husband, Angela.'

That was the worst day. That was when I knew what I was losing – what I might already have lost.

I'd have preferred any evening other than this one to be attending Ralph's opening in the West End. What took me was a kind of hollow loyalty. Ralph had got me one of the best seats. The theatre was packed: clearly a buzz had got about – this was a production not to be missed. Men I scarcely knew came up to me before the curtain rose, and said nice things about Ralph; then, eyeing me up and down, said nice things about me. They were all people I recognised as being 'in the know' – theatrical agents, critics, producers – people who'd carefully avoided us for years. But now they were smiling, and dropping hints, making it clear they had Ralph's future in their sweaty hands. I wanted to put my hands round their necks, and squeeze.

'Yes, he *has* had wonderful notices, hasn't he!' I agreed three or four times.

I made my way to my seat. The programme was an altogether glossier document than the one for Brighton, but beyond noticing that Ralph's photograph was of the same youthful charmer as before, I looked no further. Instead, my eye was drawn to a woman seated a row in front and a little to the left of me. She was about my age, perhaps a bit older; incredibly slim, with no apparent bust, and a halo of blonde curls crowning a doll-like face in which were set such enormous blue eyes that I found myself wondering if they closed automatically whenever she lay down. She appeared to be on her own.

It wasn't until after the curtain rose that a little bell

began to ring in my head. Hadn't I seen this woman somewhere before? I tried to think where. Was it in the shop? She looked as though she might well be a model. No. I didn't believe it was the shop. I went through the possible alternatives in my head. Could it have been the hairdresser's? Renato's restaurant? Rachel's school? Still the answer seemed to be no.

I turned my attention back to the play. Ralph was wonderful – there was no doubt about it. He was far more polished than at Brighton. He was passionate. He was sad. He was moving. The audience was growing excited by his performance: I could feel a tension in the darkness. I watched him deliver his lines with such skill, modulating his voice until it became almost mesmeric. They were lines so familiar by now I found myself reciting them with him. 'I believe I could never really become fond of another human being. I don't love anyone, and never shall now. What still does affect me is beauty. I can't remain indifferent to that.'

It was then that something snapped into place in my head. Of course! Brighton! That was where I'd seen the woman before. She'd been sitting in the row in front of me – just like tonight. And she'd been alone. *And* she'd been outside the stage door, I remembered that too. She hadn't been one of the women who'd crowded round Ralph as he came out, touching him and jostling for his autograph. She'd been standing back – alone, watching. Well, I thought, maybe she was just some lonely theatrical groupie with a crush on Ralph. There were always women like that: they loved to adore from afar. But to adore from the best seats in the house? The row of seats almost certainly allocated to the cast? No!

Other memories floated into my mind – little things I'd paid no attention to at the time. Now they were like pieces of a jigsaw, and they began to fit. Silent phone calls on days when I should have been at the shop, but had stayed at home because Rachel was unwell. The smell of perfume on Ralph's clothes, which I'd assumed to be his leading lady kissing him goodnight after rehearsals. Even the hours he'd take over buying a couple of pork chops. Now here was the piece of the jigsaw that seemed to pull all the others together.

I didn't know what to think. I didn't know what I felt. I gazed at the woman in the half-darkness. All I could make out was that halo of blonde hair. Could it really be true? Could it really be that she was having an affair with Ralph?

Well, supposing he was, what *did* I think? At that moment my mind was like one of those fruit machines, with pictures whirling round before my eyes, and me anxious to see what combination would come up when they finally stopped.

It took a few moments before they did stop. And suddenly I knew. Yes, I felt jealous – but only a very little. Rather shamefully little. More than that, I felt fascinated – the thought that Ralph might not be at all the man I'd always believed him to be – that he too might be leading a double life. But most of all – and this came as a revelation and a shock — I felt an enormous sense of relief. It was as though chains were falling from my body.

But hang on, I told myself: I musn't overreach myself. The important thing first of all was to find out.

I thought of going up to the woman after the performance and introducing myself as someone else. 'Excuse me, but I'm sure we've met before.' But where the hell would that get me? I could hardly say — 'Do you know Ralph Merton, and would you mind telling me whether you're having an affair with him?' I'd do much better to go straight up to her in the foyer and confront her with — 'Hi! I'm Angela Merton. Are you fucking my husband?' But then supposing I was wrong, and she turned out to be some junior employee of the theatre company happily married to an insurance salesman in Epsom?

No! I'd have to do better than that.

I waited for Ralph after the show, and he was elated. The applause had been thunderous. He'd stood there bowing and bowing. People had cheered. Outside the stage door I'd again spotted the woman with the blonde halo, but she waited only until Ralph appeared, then walked away. Maybe she knew her lover's wife would be here, and merely wanted to size up the competition. She was older than I'd thought, it pleased me to notice. And she had bad legs. *And* no tits. My little scrap of jealousy was soothed.

It was late. We drove home. Ralph's euphoria filled the journey. I made him an omelette, and he fell into bed with a 'Goodnight darling.' I stayed up for a while. The house was dark and silent. I gazed about me at so many familiar things. Christ, I thought, my husband's having an affair, and I'm happy! What am I going to do about it?

I woke in the morning with a plan. Ralph was still half asleep when I left for the shop. The common was crisp with frost, and ice-patterns had formed on the car windscreen. I turned on the heater, tuned in to Paul Gambaccini on Classic FM, and joined the rush-hour traffic.

It was such a simple plan. There was only one small problem – I needed the privacy of a telephone. And I needed to wait at least until midday because the theatre office wouldn't be open.

At half past twelve I suggested to Karen that she might like to take an early lunch; then I whispered to Eamonn that he might care to join her. He'd been infatuated with her mini-skirt for so many weeks that he needed no persuading. This left me the Enterprises office free. I checked that both Gail and Caroline were busy in the shop; then I phoned the theatre and asked for the manager. There was a long pause before a rather disgruntled voice the other end said simply 'Yes!'

This was my moment. The star's wife was about to pull rank.

'I'm sorry to trouble you,' I said. 'I'm Ralph Merton's wife. I'm afraid there was a slight mix-up over tickets last night. I wonder if you'd mind telling me how many tickets my husband reserved for yesterday evening's performance.'

The man muttered a kind of apology, and asked if I'd mind waiting just a moment. It seemed like an awful lot of moments, and I glanced about anxiously in case Caroline chose to appear, or perhaps Karen, indignant at being touched up in the pub by Eamonn. Eventually there was the sound of breathing on the phone, and the voice said, 'Are you still there, Mrs Merton?' I said yes, I was. There was more breathing.

'Last night! Um . . . Here we are. Yes . . . Tickets for Mr Merton,' the voice continued. 'Um . . . Just two, madam.'

Two! Ah-ha!

'Would you mind telling me who they were for?' I asked.

More breathing.

'Um! Yours, madam. And one other – for Mr Merton's cousin, I believe he said it was.'

Ralph doesn't have any cousins; at least none that he'd ever owned up about.

'Do you by any chance have the lady's name?' I said lightly.

I prayed he wasn't going to say it was a man.

'Um! Yes. I think it's written here. Yes – a Mrs Heather Claridge. And may I ask, madam, what the confusion was? Perhaps you'd care to leave a message for Mr Merton. I'll give it to him when he comes in.'

Oh God, no, I thought. Suddenly I could hear Caroline stomping up the stairs from the rear entrance.

'Oh no! No! I wouldn't want to trouble him,' I

answered hastily. 'It's nothing really. I can sort it out perfectly well. Don't worry. A great many thanks.'

And I quickly put the phone down as Caroline appeared.

'Sneaking off to phone your lover, I see,' she announced accusingly. 'When are you going to tell me who he is?'

I smiled at her.

'Well,' I said sweetly. 'He's not a racing driver, and he's only got two balls. Will that do for now?'

She frowned. And then she laughed.

'You know what I'm going to do this afternoon, Angela?'

'Tell me,' I said tamely, my mind rather more on what the doll-like Mrs Claridge chose to do with her afternoons.

'Well! I'm going to program in Patrick. I've decided I want to know what his ideal woman is. And I need Cupid to tell me.'

I was tempted to ask why she suddenly needed this information after fifteen years of marriage, but I didn't particularly want to prolong the conversation. I had more urgent matters of my own I was anxious to pursue.

'But there's just one problem,' she went on, settling herself comfortably in a chair. 'I need your advice.'

'What is it, Caroline?' I asked, surprised. It was the first time I'd ever heard her ask advice from anyone. She leant forward and gazed at me very intently.

'Well, it's his prick!' she said. 'I know one's supposed

to be truthful, but do I have to tell the computer he's only got four inches? Because if I do, his ideal would have to be a dwarf or a pygmy, wouldn't it?'

I could only laugh. Her look suggested that I shouldn't have.

'Caroline,' I said, trying to keep a straight face. 'Perhaps you just shouldn't mention it at all. Simply avoid it.'

That made her smile.

'I usually do,' she said.

I left her, and returned to the shop. On my mind was a certain fluffy-haired blonde with big blue eyes and no tits. How on earth was I going to find out who this Mrs Heather Claridge was?

11

Adultery Tours

———————o———————

The obvious person to talk to was Gail. She was a natural accomplice for whom all manoeuvres of the human heart were what gave life its zest. She was also the only friend who knew about Josh: and if there was sometimes a note of envy in her voice that I should have a resident lover upstairs, this was never tinged with malice. Being a fair amount older than me, she was good at withdrawing behind the wisdom of the much-married, and at enjoying my adventures vicariously. The idea of tracking down Ralph's little admirer would, I felt sure, appeal to her sense of mischief. She might even be able to help.

I waited until a day when Caroline decided to take time off for Christmas shopping, and invited Gail to lunch. Enterprises was slackening off: purely temporary, Gail assured me – people tended not to push for divorce during the season of goodwill, but just you wait till the New Year, she added with a chuckle, as if she had long experience of such matters. So we left Eamonn in charge of the shop, trusting that he wouldn't seize the opportunity to close it for an hour while he swept the mini-skirted Karen off to the changing-room for a quick 'mix 'n' match'.

Renato greeted us with delight and showed us to a table by the window; and from here we could enjoy a good view of Caroline's Mercedes glistening in the rain on a double yellow line opposite. Since the day when her collection of printed notices had been confiscated by order of a local magistrate she'd opted for a more resourceful device, Rick having run up a set of false wheel-clamps for her. These were only made of cardboard, but they fitted nicely over the tyres and the wheel hubs, and in their bright-yellow livery they looked punitive enough to meet the approving gaze of police officers as they strolled by.

'Where is she today, our lady?' enquired Renato, handing us the menu and awarding me an appreciative glance.

'Shopping,' Gail answered without raising her eyes from the wine list. 'So if you hear an explosion in Harrods it won't be the IRA.'

'Terrible people!' said Renato, missing the point.

Gail looked up from the wine list to give him a reproving glare. Renato dropped his smile, and turned to me.

'Very special today, An-gel — a Greco,' he said, pointing to the wine closest to my cleavage. 'From near Rome. My uncle.'

I tried to remember how many uncles Renato had claimed during the time we'd been coming here.

I ordered the Greco, and thought of the very first time I'd invited Gail to an Italian restaurant, when The Outfit was merely the germ of an idea in my head. And she'd told me about her life, and I'd plucked up courage to invite her to become my partner. It was bewildering to think how much had happened since that previous winter day. Could one become a different person in a single year, I wondered. Then I had a husband and the school run; now I had a business, a lover and a crumbling marriage. Sometimes I felt I'd gone astray; more often I felt I'd been released.

The risotto arrived, and out of habit we talked about how the shop was going, and whether Enterprises was really going to expand as it had shown every sign of doing. Gail knocked back her first glass of wine appreciatively, then gazed knowingly at me across the table.

'Well, me darlin', you didn't invite me here to discuss second-hand clothes, did you? What is it?'

I shook my head.

'So, what is it? Trouble with Ralph, or trouble with Josh?'

I gave her a wan smile.

'Both,' I said. 'But mainly trouble *about* Ralph. I think he's having an affair.'

Gail looked at me wide-eyed.

'Mary, mother of Jaysus!' she said, pouring herself another glass of wine. 'That makes the two of you, doesn't it! You're a lucky girl to be sure.'

For a moment I felt rather put out.

'What d'you mean – "lucky"?'

Gail laughed.

'No! Truly I didn't mean it. I'm sure you're wounded and all that. Jealousy's a terrible thing to be sure.' Still laughing, she reached out and patted my arm. 'But seriously, darlin', you can't be entirely surprised now, can you? There are you havin' it off upstairs until the lights are quiverin' on the walls and the customers thinkin' it's a fockin' earthquake. And your poor dear husband sittin' there at home learnin' his lines. Honest to goodness, hardly what you'd call "democratic"?'

Gail's Irishness always took on a note of caricature whenever the subject was either sex or Roman Catholicism.

'But you only *think* he's havin' an affair, you said,' she went on, dropping back into her normal speech.

I explained about the woman in the theatre. How I'd seen her once before at the first night in Brighton. How she'd been at the stage door – both times. How I'd phoned the theatre and found out that Ralph had reserved two tickets – one for me and one for another woman.

'A married woman!' I added, not quite sure if that made it better or worse. 'Heather Claridge, she's called.' I gazed across the table at Gail. 'What I need to know,' I said, 'is how the hell I can find out about her.'

Gail looked amused for a moment, fingering her empty glass.

346

'Claridge! Well, maybe she's married to the hotel. That would make it easy now, wouldn't it?'

'Thank you, Gail,' I said. 'Have some more wine.'

She looked gratefully at her glass as I refilled it.

'You know,' she said suddenly, her face brightening. 'I think me darlin' boy'll do it for you.'

I was too astonished to say anything, and Gail turned her attention back to her wine-glass. I knew better than to enquire what particular kind of shoplifting might possibly give him the low-down on Mrs Heather Claridge. I would trust Rick, and wait patiently.

We finished our lunch, and I called Renato for the bill. Outside the rain had turned into a downpour. We only had one small umbrella between the two of us, and made a dash for it. Then half-way across the square a curious sight caught my eye, and to Gail's annoyance I insisted on stopping in the pouring rain to work out what it could possibly be. Almost immediately I realised.

'Look, Gail! You have to look.'

Reluctantly she turned her head, rain streaming from her cloud of red hair.

'Jaysus!' was all she said.

And both of us burst out laughing. Gathered round Caroline's car were several gentlemen of the law. They were peering with some puzzlement at the wheels of the Mercedes, from which drooped several soggy and yellowish objects that had once resembled wheel-clamps.

*   *   *

I'd grown accustomed to keeping a secret from Ralph; but now I was having to keep two secrets from him, which was an uncomfortable burden. Part of me longed to confront him with, 'Are you having an affair?' But supposing he looked me straight in the eye and admitted, 'Yes, as a matter of fact I am,' I'd then feel obliged to say, 'Well, as a matter of fact so am I!' and where would that leave me? There was a time for honesty, but not yet.

On the other hand, supposing he were genuinely startled and said, 'Certainly not!' and it turned out he really did have a fond cousin I'd never heard of, that would be infinitely worse. I'd have cast myself as a jealous and prying wife, and given him an entirely false impression of what was on my mind.

I could no longer deny to myself that my marriage was at an end; yet for a long time I'd been ruled by an instinct not to rock the boat, trusting to the belief that indecision would somehow be my saviour, whatever the outcome might be. But suddenly, with the appearance of Heather Claridge, matters seemed altogether more urgent. What was the point of trying not to rock the boat when it was clearly sinking anyway? Wouldn't it be better to reach for a lifebelt and jump quickly? In any case, how long could I reasonably expect Josh to wait? I knew that he loved me, but the sands of love might very soon run out. There was nothing tragically romantic about Josh: when he finally tired of living alone, spicing his solitude with the occasional one-night stand, he might easily settle for some woman who didn't persist in clinging to the wreckage of her present marriage. And I would slide into a long middle-age, saying to myself, 'If only . . .' like so many other dreary women I was forever meeting in the shop.

I didn't want to be like that. *I wasn't bloody well going to be like that.*

Yet whenever I keyed myself to this brave resolve, I kept imagining a little face peering up at me, and I'd hear Rachel's quavering voice – 'Aren't I going to have a mummy and daddy any more?'

That tore me apart.

Josh was infuriatingly understanding. I wished he could have been angry, or selfish, or pleading. Then at least my two choices would have been clear: was I prepared to run the risk of breaking up Rachel's life, or not? Instead he insisted on agreeing with me.

'You're right! Of course Rachel's happiness is important.'

And he'd say it in such a matter-of-fact way, as though it didn't really affect anything – as though I'd somehow missed the point, and there was a perfectly straightforward solution which I hadn't thought of. Then he'd make it worse by undoing my blouse and caressing my breasts. And I'd want him desperately, and instead of crying all over him I'd make a groaning noise and pull him down on to the floor.

'I love you, Josh,' I'd blurt out, a little breathlessly. 'I love you and I want you.'

Then he'd be huge inside me, and I'd forget everything else.

'It'll work out,' he'd say afterwards as we lay gazing up at the ceiling.

He wouldn't say how it would work out. Sometimes I wondered if it actually suited him to have our lives like this: he had a pliant mistress who made no demands beyond seeking his body. Wasn't this what men were always supposed to want? Sex and freedom. A life of appetites and escape. The word 'love' could always be whispered every now and then to brighten the little lady's dreams and keep the affair on the boil. 'Women like sex as a means, men like it as an end,' Gail assured me once, though admittedly this was before she got to know Caroline.

'Do you really believe it'll work out?' I'd say hesitantly.

And Josh would laugh.

'I know so.'

But how could he know? I was in love with a man of secrets. And then, as if to prove it, he'd change the subject – lying back on the bed while he watched me dress.

'I bought a cottage last week,' he announced one lunchtime.

I blinked.

'You what?'

'In Cornwall. Overlooking the sea. You'll like it.'

'Josh! . . .' What on earth could I say? I made a banal remark. 'Did it cost you an awful lot?'

He laughed, got up and began to pull on the loose black sweater I remembered him wearing the very first

350

time I talked to him, at the Outfit opening party; and I'd wanted to know what his body was like underneath it.

'Not specially,' he said. 'After all that bloody commercial work I thought I deserved some reward.'

I felt hurt. I'd hoped the reward was me. What made it worse was that I knew it could have been me. And I found myself wondering who he'd take down there, make love to overlooking the sea as the sun went down? Josh must have seen the look on my face because he put his arms round me. I snuggled into the black sweater.

'It won't run away,' he said quietly.' And he stroked my hair.

But would he run away? I wanted him so much. I wanted a life with him. Something about his gentleness reassured me it *would* all work out – and that behind those eyes laughing at me, he knew how.

Then he changed the subject again.

'I hear Ralph's landed a big television part,' he said.

Josh so rarely mentioned Ralph that I gave a start.

'How did you know?' I asked.

He smiled.

'Stella Neale told me. She's an agent: she tends to know everything.'

I nodded. It was true. Ralph had been rung up only yesterday. It wasn't just a big part; it was a big, big part. The serial could run for years if they got it right. It could be just like the old days – only this time there'd be no 'Ralph Merton's Ipswich eyeful' to hang on his arm.

Suddenly it was as though I'd left Ralph already.

'We'll sort it out with Rachel, won't we?' I said. 'She'll be all right, won't she?'

Josh kissed me. Then he smiled.

'I don't see why not.'

In the run-up to Christmas the total resources of Outfit Enterprises were apparently being requisitioned by Caroline. I hadn't taken her particularly seriously when she announced that she intended to program in Patrick in order to discover his ideal woman. But I was quite mistaken. She'd never worked so hard on any of our clients, she said; but then she knew so much about Patrick that it was a formidable task feeding Cupid all the essential information. Eamonn was proving invaluable, she was happy to acknowledge, selecting from a mass of data the habits and personality traits that would help pinpoint the woman of Patrick's dreams.

'It's a dangerous game she's playing, to be sure,' was Gail's verdict. She and I were alone in the shop, and we could make out Caroline's strident voice next door, insisting on something that Eamonn presumably deemed irrelevant. 'Whoever Patrick's dream-girl turns out to be, she'll murder the poor bitch.'

I was shaking my head.

'She claims she's going to give him the girl for Christmas.'

Gail gave a surprised smile.

'At the top of the Christmas tree, d'you suppose, darlin'? Or maybe in his stocking.'

'Well!' I said. 'Then at least he'd be able to unwrap her in bed, wouldn't he?'

Gail's laughter was cut short by the arrival of a customer.

It was never easy to assess the seriousness of Caroline's *idées fixes*. She was convinced, she kept telling me, that her marriage to Patrick was an utter disaster – perhaps it always had been, but just recently this had become glaringly obvious to her. It was this business of dealing with so many other women's marital disasters that had opened her eyes to her own. Perhaps her fling with the Roman racing driver with three balls had something to do with it too, she added. In any case, it wasn't really Patrick's fault, she admitted generously: no doubt there were lots of women around who'd be only too delighted to marry the heir to the smallest county in England, even if he did have a cock to match. She was just totally the wrong sort of woman for him. She felt thoroughly bad about having been so foul to him all these years when he honestly couldn't help it, and now she was keen to make up for past sins by presenting him with a woman who'd truly love and cherish him.

All this was while strolling with me on the frosty common one Sunday afternoon.

'What about the children?' I asked, thinking about Rachel and my own collapsing marriage.

Caroline looked astonished, and snapped off a stem of frozen bracken as if such foolish questions should be treated likewise.

'Children?' she said. 'What on earth have they got to do with it? They're away at school most of the time anyway, thank God! And after that they'll go away for good.'

I didn't believe a word of this. Caroline's devotion to her children was unswerving. It was just that to be forced to consider their needs right now would muddy the pure waters of her argument.

'Sex!' she said loudly. Several lady dog-walkers some distance away stumbled over their extension-leads. 'It's just like food really, isn't it! You wouldn't want the same dish every day, would you – specially when it's such a meagre helping?' She laughed, then stopped and looked at me. 'But maybe you would, Angela. You're the faithful sort. I bet you've never had more than one lover at a time.'

Caroline's assertions about me to my face never required an answer. They merely added to her store of 'truths' which she carried around with her. And if at a later date I should protest that she was entirely wrong, Caroline would glare at me and announce indignantly – 'But Angela, you told me so yourself only last week!' It all made me wonder what her view of my life really was. One day I would have to sit her down with a large vodka-and-tonic and ask.

Caroline was now swishing the stem of dead bracken about like a golf-club.

'You know, the best lover I ever had was MP for Maidenhead,' she went on whimsically. I noticed two of the dog-walkers abruptly change direction. 'As a married woman I couldn't help finding it rather embarrassing that it had to be *Maidenhead*. I used to say to him – "Howard, can't you find a constituency that's more appropriate, for Christ's sake? Laycock, or Nether Wallop, or something?" Then they went and made him Chief Whip. People thought I was being punished for adultery, so I was faithful to Patrick for a while after that. He was terribly sweet about it.'

Caroline's reminiscences always somehow ended up with Patrick, just as I felt sure she always would.

It was growing cold, and dusk was drawing in with long skeins of mist. I turned up my coat collar and together we walked back across the open common.

'Well, Angela! Tomorrow I should know,' she announced as she reached the gate of her house. 'Eamonn's promised that the data on Patrick is all safely stored; so we'll see what Cupid comes up with, won't we?' And she gave a little laugh. 'Jesus, I do hope the woman's not married to a friend of mine. That would be awkward, wouldn't it, having the husband come round threatening him with a poker on Christmas Day. Poor Patrick!'

I didn't see much of Caroline the following morning. The pre-Christmas rush was on, and our stock was becoming seriously depleted.

'Don't worry!' Gail assured me. 'It'll all come back in the New Year. That's when people have a good clear-out. Start afresh. New outfits. The same with marriages. You'll see.'

It was midday when Caroline appeared from the office next-door, looking shaken and holding two sheets of paper. The shop was crowded, and she could only thrust the papers into my hand as I was busy making out invoices.

When the customer had gone I glanced at them. The first sheet appeared to be a data profile; it was headed simply 'Patrick Uppingham – the Hon'. There followed what I took to be the personality breakdown of her husband which Caroline had so carefully prepared with the help of Eamonn. I didn't bother to read it, but turned quickly to the second sheet of paper. This began with the words 'Identity of partner', followed by a sequence of question-marks. Below the question-marks was a brief and somewhat garbled account of a woman who seemed to possess a number of rather unusual characteristics: these were listed separately as though it had been beyond Cupid's powers to gather them into a single recognisable human being. The woman was described variously as 'under 5 ft tall', 'club-footed', 'alcoholic' and 'possessing pointed breasts'.

During pauses between serving more customers, I pondered on this strange animal who didn't seem to match any of the women on our books; so at least there was no danger of Patrick being presented with her for Christmas. Her unusual characteristics began to make some sense once I recalled the few things I knew about Patrick – the size of his prick, his drinking habits and his passion for golf (though 'club-footed' seemed rather a crude misunderstanding). As for 'pointed breasts', I could only assume this to be some sort of amalgam of his sexual predilections and his love of race meetings of all kinds – Cupid must have picked out the phrase 'point to point'.

I shook my head. Thank God, I thought, we never let Caroline loose on the computer when it came to a serious piece of data profiling.

But it was the final two entries which really baffled me, because Patrick's ideal partner was described on the print-out as needing to be a 'Jehovah's Witness' and a 'female astronaut'.

Now, nothing I knew about Patrick had ever suggested a craving to be God's witness on earth, or to leave this earth in the company of an alcoholic midget with pointed breasts. This was a complete mystery to me, and it remained unsolved until after we'd locked up the shop that evening. Caroline was by now thoroughly miserable: she couldn't understand what had gone wrong, and was pleading with us to help her. So Gail and I duly sat down and examined Patrick's profile very carefully, searching for clues which might explain this apparent yearning for a partner who soared high towards the stars as well as towards God.

Being a good Catholic, it was Gail who spotted God.

'Caroline darlin',' she said. 'It says here that Patrick is active in Neighbourhood Watch. Right? In fact, he's what's described as the "local co-ordinator".' She paused, and a flicker of a smile appeared on her face. 'But I don't think you'll find that the bumf the police send him is actually called "The Watchtower", as you've claimed.'

Caroline looked indignant, and said nothing. Then it was my turn to comment. One particular entry had mystified me.

'What is this organisation Patrick belongs to called the "International Ballistics Society"?' I asked.

'Oh, that's easy!' she said, regaining confidence.

And she explained that Patrick had always been fascinated by rockets, missiles and so on. She assumed it was penis envy, Patrick being so small, she said with a laugh; anyway, these booklets kept coming through the post – they were all headed 'IBS' in large letters. She never bothered to look at them: it seemed such a childish hobby, and she hated everything to do with warfare.

I thought for a moment. Then I remembered Ralph coming home once with a booklet exactly like that. He'd been unwell with chronic stomach pains, and had gone to see his doctor.

'Caroline,' I said tentatively, 'I think you'll find that "IBS" stands for "Irritable Bowel Syndrome".'

It was exactly as Gail predicted: during January and February our racks became loaded with designer outfits that lady customers had purchased before Christmas, while next-door our files were even more loaded with profiles of the husbands they were anxious to shed.

We'd lost count of the precise number of successful pairings Cupid had already arranged, though we were proud of the fact that they included two bishops, one Greek patriarch, one cabinet minister, two other MPs, four members of the House of Lords, two judges, three privy counsellors, not to mention several actors, barristers, civil servants, captains of industry, as well as a professor of moral philosophy at one of the ancient universities and – a rather special prize – the chairman of the London Marriage Guidance Council. There was also a Chief Superintendent of Police: this was a major coup for Caroline since it meant she'd have no further trouble parking her Mercedes wherever she chose. Caroline herself was more proud to have paired off the Controller of BBC 1, having at first refused the brief from his wife on the grounds that no other woman in her right mind would have him.

'Not a Roman Catholic among them,' Gail pointed out smugly. Her faith she may have lost long ago, but never her loyalties.

Caroline replied archly that Catholics just preferred to live in sin, that being what they understood best after all, which ruffled Gail's feathers. And anyway, Caroline persisted, how was it that Gail herself had managed to be married three times? This forced Gail to confess that she'd never actually married the first two, whereupon Caroline laughed and suggested this proved her point.

I parted the two combatants with a drink, and Anglo-Irish relations were restored.

'Fockin' Protestant!' Gail muttered as a parting shot.

In the midst of all these New Year celebrations Rick

appeared late one afternoon and beckoned me with a flick of the head. There were customers in the shop, so I followed him outside. I always knew when Rick had serious information to offer because he invariably chose the street as the only place to impart it, as though he were in Brezhnev's Russia and every building was bugged.

It was snowing. But Rick was undeterred, merely pulling down the peak of his cap and peering at me from under it.

'Well, sweetheart!' he announced. 'This Claridge lady – you got trouble there!'

I asked what kind of trouble, and began to feel uneasy.

'She's a star-fucker for a start,' he said. 'Bit of a ball-breaker, I'd say. Pushy. Some sort of PR business – films, telly mainly. Twice married. Thirty-six. Likes to look twenty-six. Cleaned both 'er 'usbands out apparently. Just wound up an affair with that geezer – what's 'is name? – you know, the one who plays the young detective in that series, what's it called? – you know the one, all about Oxford and stuff. Taken 'im for a real ride. Looks like a doll, and be'aves like a shark – a bleedin' great white shark.'

Rick gave a nod as if to say, 'That's more or less it.'

'And Ralph?' I said nervously. 'What's he got to do with her?'

I sounded so coy asking that. Why couldn't I say, 'Is my husband screwing the bitch?'

Rick didn't answer. He flicked the snow off his sleeve

360

and reached into his breast pocket. He handed me a scrap of paper.

'Recognise the writing?'

Of course I did. I just stared at it, my hand shaking. Snow kept falling on the paper, blurring the ink. There were only three words scrawled on it, but they said everything. *'Darling, sleep well!'*

I folded the damp scrap of paper, mumbled a 'Thanks!' to Rick and went inside. I realised I hadn't even asked him how he got the note. Had he burgled the place?

So Ralph was screwing her. I felt bewildered, and lots of things I didn't understand. Thank heavens it was almost time to close the shop. I excused myself early and, without even thinking why, went into a pub round the corner from the square. I ordered a large gin-and-tonic – which I never drink – and sat up at the bar with my chin in my hands. After a few moments a young man seated himself next to me and started to chat, eyeing me carefully while he rambled on about the weather. Without looking up I quietly told him to fuck off. 'Be like that, then, sweetheart,' he said huffily, and rejoined his mates.

The gin-and-tonic didn't do a lot for my brain: my thoughts chased each other round in circles like the blind leading the blind – perhaps I should learn Braille to read my own mind, I wondered. The idea made me smile. The barman thought I was smiling at him and imagined I wanted a refill, and I had to place my hand over the glass: this was not the moment to get smashed. Or perhaps it was exactly the moment, but not here. I gazed out at the snow silently falling.

There was something hypnotic about the snow. I realised I must have been gazing at it for at least five minutes; and when I looked back at my empty glass everything seemed clearer. No, I didn't even feel particularly unhappy. In a way I was relieved. That Ralph should be having an affair somehow felt right: it underlined the obvious, that we had drifted far apart and that both of us needed to move on. So long as it had only been me who was leading a double life there had been an air of agreeable pretence about our existence – a sort of painless charade. But now both of us had a double life, that pretence had suddenly collapsed. The barriers were down. At last we'd be able to confront one another on equal terms. We no longer needed to behave as though nothing had changed. We could agree to tear our marriage up – 'Ralph, you start from that end, I'll start from this, and we'll meet in the middle and say "Goodbye".' It didn't even feel particularly frightening to contemplate: not so much a matter of biting the bullet as agreeing to a truce. Yes, it would be civilised; there'd be no recriminations. We'd just 'sign off'. We'd even meet for lunch sometimes – as friends: talk of the good times, what we owed to one another, what we'd achieved together, all the things we'd fought for. We really hadn't done badly, had we? Better than most.

Yes, that all sounded good.

But would it really be like that? I wanted that second

gin-and-tonic, and the barman was beginning to eye me suspiciously as if I were a hooker.

I paid him and walked out into the snow.

So, would it really be like that? Some of the things Rick had said about Heather Claridge kept floating back into my mind. 'She's a star-fucker. Bit of a ball-breaker. Twice married. Cleaned both 'er 'usbands out.'

What if she cleaned Ralph out too? What would that do for me? And for Rachel? Suddenly I felt just like those dozens of married women who'd been coming to us for help. Mine was exactly their situation: however many times had I heard it? My marriage is dead; my husband is entangled with another woman. She wants him all to herself. She wants nothing to do with his wife, children, mortgage to be paid ('let her move to a smaller house'), school fees ('there are good comprehensives, aren't there?'), house repairs ('she works, doesn't she?'), car repairs ('what's the bus service for?'), visits from the kids during school holidays ('aren't there supposed to be summer camps, for Christ's sake?'), phone calls at drinks time saying one of the children has been taken ill ('Jesus, can't we ever have a moment of peace?').

Oh God! And now me!

Suddenly an amicable truce seemed a fragile and unlikely thing.

The car tyres made a soft, muffled sound on the snow. Ahead of me the flakes spiralled in the headlamps, and hung like a curtain over the dark river, blurring the lights on the bridges. London was being buried in white.

And how the hell could I bury Mrs Heather Claridge? All of a sudden it occurred to me. Outfit Enterprises! Why shouldn't I do for myself what I'd done for so many other women?

This brilliant thought occupied me all the way home. The common was ghostly pale, and the trees silent with snow. Neighbours' cars were ungainly white bumps ranged along the kerb. A few commuters were picking their way cautiously along the pavement. This place no longer felt like home.

'Mummy! Where's Daddy?' Rachel asked as I came through the door.

I shook the snow off me, and smiled at her.

'At the theatre I expect, darling,' I said, lying. I couldn't exactly say, 'With his mistress.'

I gave her a hug.

'I'm going to make a snowman tomorrow,' she said excitedly.

I wondered where she'd put the carrot this time. Oh, how I loved this little creature. Right now I was glad she didn't look at all like Ralph.

'Now, darling,' I said enthusiastically, 'would you like me to cook you something a bit special for supper tonight?'

Rachel's pretty face took on a slight frown, and she looked away.

'Magdalena's promised me a "*teckvai*",' she said awkwardly. Then she glanced back at me, and smiled. 'But you could have one with us, Mum. Would you?'

Suddenly it sounded a good idea.

'All right!' I said.

I might as well try this famous Portuguese dish at last, I thought. After all, Magdalena might not be here all that much longer. Then I looked at Rachel. 'But do tell me, darling; what exactly is "*teckvai*"? I've never known.'

Rachel looked puzzled.

'What d'you mean, Mum?' she said. And she gazed at me as though she realised senility had set in. 'You just ring up the Chinese restaurant and ask for it.'

It was my turn to look puzzled.

'*Chinese?*' I said.

'Or it can be Indian,' Rachel explained, her voice sounding patronising. I was beginning to feel irritated.

'Or Russian, I suppose,' I snapped. 'Why don't you stop playing silly games with me, Rachel? Just tell me. What is "*teckvai*"?'

Rachel broke into a giggle.

'Oh Mum,' she laughed. 'You say it just like Magdalena. "*Teckvai*."' And she imitated my accent, fluttering her hands above her head and giving another giggle. 'Why don't you say "take-away" like everybody else?'

I marked the computer disk 'RM', which preserved at least a semblance of secrecy, and kept it carefully in the safe. There wasn't much on it as yet, but then I could only make use of Cupid when his services weren't being required 'professionally' – as Gail liked to put it.

'All I can say, darlin', is I hope you make a better

365

job of it with Ralph than Caroline did with Patrick.' Her red hair was looking more than usually storm-tossed as she strode in out of the February gales, shaking the rain off her voluminous overcoat. 'We can't have you pairing Ralph off with some alcoholic female astronaut. I know he's a star now,' she went on, enjoying her own exuberance, 'but he mightn't wish to be launched up there quite so soon.'

It was true that Ralph was a star. Rehearsals had already begun for the big TV serial, and the publicist had seen to it that glamorous photographs of Ralph Merton – looking as though all life's mysteries could be solved behind those searching eyes – were appearing in all the right publications in the company of all the right people. Even the Controller of BBC 1, now happily paired off with one of our unfortunate clients, was to be seen smirking up at him from somewhere below Ralph's elbow, which amounted to a papal blessing. I was happy for Ralph; happy that his years in the wilderness were finally over; happy that fame and flashbulbs now distanced him from anything we could possibly call 'our life together'. I hadn't said a word to him about Heather Claridge. We moved in separate orbits, and for the time being at least I was happy about this too. It gave me time to think, and time – when there *was* any – to address myself to the question of what Cupid might consider vital to know about the character and needs of my husband.

This was already proving to be far harder than I'd imagined, and I began to have some sympathy with Caroline. I knew by heart all the kinds of questions we normally put to our female clients about their husbands: these had always seemed perfectly straightforward, to be answered with scarcely a moment's hesitation. Or so I thought. But now I had to do the answering myself it wasn't quite like that. I could manage the shirts, ties and socks he preferred, his taste in music (bad), books (highbrow), art (non-existent), food (indiscriminate), wine (plentiful), entertainment (solemn), as well as a list of harmless aversions – dinner parties, church services, gardening, dogs, physical exercise, Cilla Black, the Pope.

None of this seemed to get me very far. Cupid kept gazing at me as though the computer screen was a big yawn. So I tried to think about Ralph's sexual habits: maybe then Cupid wouldn't look quite so bored. In any case, if I was to identify the perfect woman for him these were obviously things I needed to address myself to very precisely.

So I sat staring at Cupid for a long time thinking about Ralph and sex, and wondering what might interest the machine most. Damned computer, I said to myself; I wish it could speak to me, give me some help. What *was* special to Ralph about sex? Well, he preferred the missionary position, preferably late at night, and he always snored afterwards, though not before asking me if it had been 'all right' – which irritated me. He didn't like oral sex – or maybe he did: I'd never tried (why hadn't I?). Did he fantasise? I didn't know, I'd never asked him. Did he masturbate? Presumably. Everyone did, according to

Caroline, though I didn't much myself (was I missing out on one of life's golden pleasures?). What parts of the female anatomy turned him on most? Well, he liked breasts, though perhaps I was making a false assumption here – after all, Heather Claridge hadn't got any. And he liked hair – spread over a pillow. But what kind? Mine was dark and straight, Mrs Claridge's was blonde and bubbly; so where did that get me? And what about eyes, teeth, hands, legs, voice, perfume, make-up, clothes? What about the things he liked women to talk about? Did he like them to be bold or shy? Powerful or submissive? Did he like them to flirt with other men at parties? Did he . . . ? I heard myself give a long sigh. I hadn't the faintest bloody idea.

In fact I decided that even after more than ten years I didn't know a great deal more about Ralph than Caroline knew about Patrick. By now I was thoroughly depressed. And Cupid still looked bored.

At this moment Caroline marched in. She had an interview in five minutes, she said fiercely, and what the hell was I doing? I quickly whipped the disk out of the computer and slid it into my bag, not wanting her to see me lock it in the safe.

Over the next few days I tried and tried again. I racked my brains. I made a lot of guesses. I remembered things about Ralph I thought I'd forgotten, little things that suddenly felt deeply significant and would surely supply the key. And at last I imagined I was getting somewhere. Finally I took my courage in both hands, and instructed Cupid to print me a profile of Ralph's perfect woman.

Cupid buzzed and murmured. I dreaded Caroline walking in again, but thank heaven she didn't. I watched the computer at work. I imagined it to be some sort of divine creator, moulding Ralph's ideal companion out of clay, and that the woman would step out before me, radiant and grateful, a creature perfectly in tune with all my own needs and wishes as the ex-wife-to-be, who would never cause problems over the mortgage, or school fees, or summer holidays, or Christmas. She would be a friend whose gratitude for my gift of Ralph would shine upon me like eternal sunshine. Cupid had already helped dozens of discontented wives: now he was going to help me.

The computer stopped. I waited. Nothing happened. I envisaged Cupid making a meticulous arrangement of all my data, honing his skills, taking his time to get the answer absolutely right. I was tense with anticipation. This was to be the moment of truth.

Finally a single line appeared on the screen. It said '*Information not accepted*'.

I stared at it. I couldn't understand. I wanted to shake the smug little bastard. I wanted to order it to try again. Perhaps it had nodded off, so in frustration I pressed various buttons to try and wake it up. As a result the screen went blank. Now what was I to do? I swallowed my irritation and decided to coax it, pressing the buttons more gently, caressing them: computers after all must be delicate creatures – all that refined and incomprehensible 'high tech' they were full of. There was another pause. I waited. Then the words reappeared: '*Information not accepted*'.

In exasperation I reached for the instruction booklet. I discovered you could ask a computer to tell you why things had gone wrong. The trouble was, it didn't explain how you actually did this. I wished I'd had the courage to ask Eamonn to help me. Instead I turned to the section of the booklet called 'Troubleshooting', and pressed the appropriate buttons. There was another lengthy pause while it made important-sounding noises. I began muttering to myself – 'Come on. What is it I've failed to do? Tell me! Tell me! Tell me!' Eventually I detected a hopeful murmur and a decisive click from within Cupid's brain; and then a quite different message flashed up on the screen. This time it was just a single word.

'*Error*'.

'Oh fuck!' I shouted. Jesus Christ, as if I didn't know that already! If my marriage hadn't been an 'error' I wouldn't be consulting this bloody computer, would I.

I stared at the machine for a minute or two, helpless with frustration. I wanted to smash the thing. Then, angrily, I switched it off, and took a deep breath. 'Angela,' I said to myself, 'why don't you just stick to selling second-hand clothes?'

I sat there for a while feeling wretched and humiliated. How did it come about that we could wave a magic wand over other women's failed marriages, and I could get absolutely nowhere with my own? It seemed grossly unfair. I wished I'd never embarked on this absurd exercise.

Then from somewhere within me a voice said – 'Why on earth *did* you?' And I couldn't answer. So why had I done this? I got up and walked round the empty room bombarding myself with the same question – why had I done this? And still I couldn't answer. This confused me: perhaps I'd forgotten why. No, I told myself, I hadn't forgotten. There was nothing to forget. Everything suddenly seemed clear. I'd done all this nonsense with Cupid on the blind assumption that I was exactly like all the other women who came here with their desperate problems. But I wasn't like them – my situation was nothing like theirs at all. The women who came here were trapped: they had no independence, no life of their own, and any future life they might have was threatened by the new woman in their husband's bed. None of this was true of me in the least. I wasn't trapped; I already had my independence; I had a life of my own; I even had money of my own. Besides which, there was a man in my life whom I loved. So, whatever Ralph chose to do was entirely his affair, not mine. If there was another woman in his bed, I really didn't much care. And if Heather Claridge was a dangerous bitch, well – let him find out. She couldn't touch me. Rachel would be living with me. Ralph was a good father: he'd never allow himself to be cut off from her. And if the next Mrs Merton produced more children – fine! Rachel would have brothers and sisters, which she'd always wanted anyway. And I wouldn't have the stress and the sleepless nights raising them. Good luck!

It was as if the winter had rolled away. I walked over to the window: the sun was glistening on the bare

371

branches, and across the square the first buds on an almond tree were bursting.

I glanced back at the computer. The perverse little bugger, I thought; why did it have to say '*Information not accepted*'? Why couldn't Cupid have said what he really meant – 'Angela, you don't need me'?

Well, at least I'd got the point in the end. And I began to feel grateful. I decided to tell Cupid so. This was ridiculous, but never mind. I switched the machine on again and tapped in – '*Thank you!*'

The screen lit up. Then two words appeared.

'*You're welcome!*' it said.

And I burst out laughing.

It felt as though I'd climbed a mountain and could at last gaze down on what lay before me. It was clear and bright. There were no dark clouds. Well, there was one: Josh was away for nearly two months in the Far East. He'd be all over the place, he said, but if I needed him I should leave a message at the Mandarin Hotel, Hong Kong. I did need him. God, I needed him! Josh had given me a fire-opal ring before he left. A wave of longing came over me as I looked at it, and I transferred it to my wedding finger – just for now, I decided, when I was alone. Then I sat down and wrote him a letter: 'Darling Josh, I love you. Please come back safe,' I began. Christ, how banal our truest sentiments can sound, I thought. Is there no originality about loving? What else could I say? I added another banality, sketching one of those little smiling faces on the notepaper; and after that I added – 'I can't remember if you asked me to come and live with you, or not, but please may I? Very soon?' There was nothing more I could say after that. Then I signed it – 'Angela (the one with long dark hair who did the loop the loop, in case you've forgotten)'. And I added a rash of kisses.

Now it was just a question of when I'd confront Ralph. I hardly ever saw him these days; but then, I'd hardly seen him for months – probably a lot less than Mrs Claridge had. So, what would I say to him? Much more difficult – what would I say to Rachel? I still dreaded that. Maybe it was cowardly of me, but I decided to get used to the idea of leaving Ralph first; the moment to break it to Rachel would choose itself, I felt sure.

It was exciting and frightening to be living in limbo.

'What's the matter with you, Angela?' said Caroline fiercely one lunchtime. 'You're buzzing like a top.' Inevitably she assumed I had a new lover. 'It's disgusting,' she snorted. 'Can't you keep it to yourself? Christ, I'm envious!' she added with a reluctant smile.

I'd scarcely exchanged a word with Caroline for weeks: we'd been busier than ever, both in the shop and in the office. But today we'd managed to sneak out for a quick lunch at Renato's, just the two of us, with Gail grumbling that she'd never again go into partnership with a couple of middle-class layabouts who left her doing all the work while they went and pissed it up. Caroline had rounded on her as we left the shop – 'Gail, I'm *not* middle-class.'

And she proceeded to order champagne as if to prove it.

'Angela,' she said, gazing thoughtfully at the risotto with white truffles which Renato had specially cooked for her. 'Has it occurred to you that we palm all these husbands off on other women, and then we just abandon them?'

I looked up from my seafood salad, wondering what on earth she was getting at.

'What else are we supposed to do?' I asked.

Caroline began to play with her risotto as if searching for something to complain about.

'Well, some sort of follow-up service. You know, like you get when you buy a new car.'

I laughed.

'Ours are second-hand cars,' I said flippantly.

Caroline frowned.

'Angela, I'm serious. If they don't have a good time then they won't get their divorce and we shan't get our percentage.'

Sometimes, I thought, the rich can be amazingly mercenary.

'So what d'you expect us to do?' I said. 'Ring them up and say, "This is your friendly divorce agency anxious to make sure you're having a nice time"?'

Caroline clicked her tongue in irritation and gave the risotto another suspicious rake.

'Just something we could offer them,' she said. 'Something romantic. A place to go. I don't know – for God's sake, you're the ideas person, Angela.'

Not having any ideas, I found myself looking round

the walls of the restaurant. Renato had hung them with aerial views of Rome and Venice, interspersed with arty photographs of Tuscan vineyards no doubt owned by yet another of his uncles.

'I suppose we could always set up a travel agency,' I said without thinking.

Caroline's eyes widened.

'Brilliant!' she exclaimed. 'Jesus, what a brilliant idea! A travel agency. Angela, have a glass of champagne.'

Was it really such a brilliant idea? After all, there wasn't exactly a shortage of travel agencies. Why one more? But Caroline was already off and running. Her eyes had that intense look that had penetrated police cordons, customs barriers and the doors of exclusive men's clubs. She never even finished her risotto.

'She not well, Signora Caroline?' Renato enquired in a sad voice as we left.

That afternoon we hardly saw her. She monopolised the phone in the offices of Outfit Enterprises, leaving us to make emergency rearrangements for several lady clients. After an hour of being displaced, Karen enquired whether she might take the rest of the day off since there was nothing she could usefully do while Mrs Uppingham was there, and every so often Eamonn appeared in the shop looking weary and disgruntled.

'She's still at it,' he'd say with a sigh. 'Tell me, is there anyone Caroline isn't related to?'

Then, just before five-thirty, she emerged with a complacent look of triumph on her face.

'Right! Outfit Phase Three!' she announced in a loud voice. 'Want to hear it?'

And she slumped into a chair, ignoring two customers who were still lingering in the shop.

We listened, and went on listening long after the last customer had departed and the shop was closed. She'd been convinced, Caroline explained, that our successful clients deserved a golden start to their new lives, and that we ought to be in a position to offer such a service. So she'd made a number of phone calls – Eamonn had already informed us that she'd made at least twenty, including several to countries he'd never heard of. And the result, she assured us, was rather promising, if we'd care to consider it.

An uncle of hers – 'some sort of duke', she said vaguely – owned a controlling interest in a modest-sized airline registered in Guernsey. Due to the recession the foreign travel business had hardly been lively of late, and one or two of his smaller aircraft were about to be mothballed at considerable cost to the company. The uncle was even considering having to sell a grouse moor or two. So the idea of expanding into what Caroline had assured him was an exceptionally classy package trade appealed to him strongly: what was more, he was quite likely to be personally acquainted with a number of his potential clients already, either in the House or possibly at Balmoral, Caroline had informed him. Caroline laughed as she told us this, admitting that she may have exaggerated a little.

That wasn't all. For clients who might prefer a

more relaxed consummation of their new relationship, she went on, she had a first cousin who was managing director of a passenger shipping line. His company was suffering a similar loss of custom due to the economic climate, particularly in the luxury cruise market. His ships had been sailing for the West Indies half empty, and cruises among the Greek islands were faring little better.

'Alistair's terribly keen,' Caroline assured us. 'He thinks it's a splendid idea, though he's a stuffy old fart. I gave him the perfect title – "Divorce through Joy Cruises". And do you know – he was stupid enough to find that vulgar.'

Gail and I exchanged looks, and I pretended to examine my nails.

'However,' Caroline continued, 'Alistair's got a brother who's much more broad-minded. He owns a small chain of hotels – the Canaries, Morocco, Crete, St Lucia, Hawaii, places like that. They're all secluded – cater very much for honeymooners; and they're custom-built with exceptionally thick walls so you can't hear other couples hurling abuse at one another next door.'

Caroline looked pleased with herself as she said this. I felt sure that her own honeymoon must have required extremely thick walls.

She still hadn't finished. Here was the crucial link, she explained, opening the drinks cupboard and pondering on what to select. A brother of hers happened to own a small travel agency, and he'd agreed to organise and co-ordinate absolutely everything we wanted – cruises, flights, hotels, whatever was needed. What was more, she went on, Outfit Enterprises would get a 20 per cent cut on every single piece of business we offered him.

'And that has to be real money for doing virtually nothing,' she added, pouring herself an enormous vodka-on-the-rocks. 'And now wait for it! He's also been thinking of moving to larger premises. I told him the newsagents next to our office was closing, so why didn't he move down here to Pimlico Square?' Caroline looked at Gail and me triumphantly. 'Then he'd be slap on our doorstep, you see. And what's more, d'you know what his agency's called? I promise you – it's "Adult Tours"! In other words, they don't do family beach holidays for the kids.' She took a contented gulp at her vodka. 'So I told him that was simply wonderful: all he'd have to do was to add three more letters when he came to paint the sign on the window, and he'd got it. "Adultery Tours!" How d'you like that?'

There was silence. Then Gail said, 'Oh, Jaysus!' I poured myself a vodka almost as large as Caroline's and said nothing. I wasn't certain how much of all this I could actually believe. But then, I hadn't been any more certain about Outfit Enterprises either, yet within a few months we'd become a success story. So maybe Caroline was right.

'Well, here's to Adultery Tours!' she said, raising her glass. 'And to you, Angela. It was your idea after all. You're a bloody genius!'

I raised my own glass, wondering what on earth I was raising it to.

It didn't take long to discover. If I'd imagined Caroline's 'follow-up service' to be a mere whim which would vanish into thin air, I was quite mistaken. The next morning – and indeed for much of the week that followed – Caroline worked like a navvy setting up her new empire. She was down at the newsagents enquiring about the lease on behalf of her brother. She was on the phone to one successful client after another, offering them cruises to the West Indies, 'honeymoon' flights to the Mediterranean and the Canaries, luxury hotels on secluded islands, all at rates which couldn't possibly be matched by any other travel agency, she assured them. I even overheard her throw in a 'lovers' safari' to Kenya, which she'd never mentioned before, but apparently yet another relation owned a game park equipped with a Treetops-style hotel where visitors could sip their sundowners while gazing at pachyderms wallowing in mud.

'Makes you feel incredibly randy watching rhinos, I assure you,' she explained. 'I suppose it's those horns. No wonder the natives sell them as aphrodisiacs.'

'I wouldn't know,' I said. 'I've only ever seen rhinos at the zoo, and I can't say they turned me on particularly.'

Caroline decided I obviously had no imagination, and went back to the telephone and the cause of Adultery Tours.

Perhaps Caroline was right that I had no imagination. Or maybe it was just busy elsewhere. I'd still heard nothing from Josh. Several weeks had gone by since my letter, and

I felt adrift. It was easy to go on telling myself that he was probably thousands of miles away in the Burmese jungle or on the Great Wall of China; none the less, the great snare of the world seemed so vast and dangerous. It wasn't only Beirut and Sarajevo that had snipers, and weren't photographers always regarded as spies by totalitarian regimes – and weren't all regimes in the Far East totalitarian? I longed for him to come back and tell me that in future he was only going to do commercials for contact lenses and ladies' nightdresses; I'd rather be jealous of anorexic models pouting at his camera than live in dread of the midnight ring on the doorbell from some stuttering police constable – 'I'm sorry to have to tell you . . .

It was nearly spring. I'd known Josh a full year. We'd been lovers almost as long. I wondered how long Ralph had known Heather Claridge. It was of purely academic interest, but I longed to know who had betrayed the other first. I felt quite competitive about it. If Ralph had done the deed before me, then it rather devalued my own infidelity. I liked to think that the cooling off of my desire for Ralph was entirely due to me, and that my passion for Josh had been a pure and unprovoked expression of lust with no moral justification whatsoever: that it was just naked and selfish need. I wasn't sure I was proud of this thought, yet I knew it to be true. I'd listened to so many women over the past months confessing to pathetic little affairs because they felt so lonely, so abandoned, so jealous of their husbands' mistresses, so unwanted: I'd imagined them weeping into their adulterous pillows in agonies of guilt and remorse, not caring overmuch about the men they'd just slept with, and certainly not having enjoyed it much. If one was going to commit a sin, I decided, then let it be a deadly one.

Meanwhile I was missing Josh terribly. I felt bereaved. I wanted his body and his laughter, his loving and his caring. I wanted him here to touch and hold, and the wonder and surprise of being with him. I did *not* want him to be on the bloody Great Wall of China!

I was still deeply anxious about Rachel. What would I say to her, and what would she say? The thought of her tears released my own. That little sweet face torn with pain. Yet it had to be: I was certain of that now. Again I remembered the women who came to seek help from us, grey with resignation, explaining so sadly how they would have left their husbands years ago but for the children, and how those same children, finally quitting the family home with relief, would offer by way of a parting shot – 'Why on earth did you ever stay with him, Mum?' That was never going to be me.

But still there was no letter.

Again work numbed the anxiety and the longing. Spring fever seemed to be quickening women's urge to seek Pastures New. My spirited little tag – '*Why wait till death? Part now!*' – even appeared as 'Quote of the week' in the *Evening Standard* Londoners' Diary, and was immediately adopted as the text for an outraged article in the *Daily Telegraph*. The author allied himself with traditional marital values, deploring what he described as the 'diseased cynicism' implicit in our 'disgraceful little quip'. There followed a fruity diatribe against 'so-called liberated women making mischief on the wilder shores of feminism', and the piece concluded with a reported rumour that these diabolical sentiments could be traced to a certain scandalous agency in Pimlico Square which, the author hoped, would soon be closed by public demand.

The article did wonders for our business; and after one particularly hectic afternoon we got together seriously to consider taking on further staff. But who? Who could we trust? We got nowhere. Finally we shook our heads and decided to be more selective. We would have to start turning clients away.

But which clients? This proved to be the real headache. Gail basically loathed the idea of turning anyone away. Business was business after all, and you should never rock the boat 'or you kill the goose that lays the golden eggs', she proclaimed, confidently mixing her metaphors.

I tried to point out that quite a number of our geese were unlikely to lay any eggs at all, golden or not, and we'd do much better without them.

Caroline didn't help resolve the problem. She was by now far too deeply involved in Adultery Tours to see beyond the need to fill cabins on Mediterranean cruises and hotel rooms overlooking elephants' watering holes. I began to fear that for her the delicate matter of pairing off faithless husbands was becoming merely a tiresome preliminary to the main business of life, which was knocking back sundowners while watching rhinos wallow in mud. In short, for Caroline upper-class boredom seemed to be setting in. Her enthusiasms could move the world, but they had a short life.

The three of us were having lunch in Renato's and still getting nowhere when the mini-skirted Karen came fluttering across the square towards the restaurant. She looked so agitated that I feared she might be fleeing from Eamonn's attempted rape. The door burst open and the girl rushed up to us. There was a gentleman to see us, she said breathlessly. It was of the utmost importance, he wished to assure us. He wouldn't say who he was, but in Karen's opinion he wasn't someone to be kept waiting. She looked uneasy.

We called Renato for the bill while Karen scurried back towards the shop.

'What d'you imagine, darlin'?' said Gail, glancing nervously out of the window. 'Police?'

I could see she was thinking they must have caught up with Rick at last.

'Tax inspector,' I suggested.

Caroline was shaking her head.

'No! Detergent salesman obviously: they always dress up to look important. No hurry.'

She sipped her champagne thoughtfully, then casually handed Renato her American Express Gold Card.

'It's my party today,' she said. 'And by the way, after the detergent salesman's gone I'm reprogramming Patrick, let me tell you. I'm going to get him right this time.'

Gail was looking anxious to leave, and so was

I. We got up, leaving Caroline to follow in her own time.

The mysterious gentleman was standing in the Enterprises office making a point of not talking to Eamonn, who was peering at the man's back with a twisted expression of dislike on his face. As he saw Gail and me enter he squashed his nose upwards with his forefinger. The man turned round in time to see it. Eamonn lowered his head over the computer. Out of the window I could see Caroline making her easygoing way across the square.

'Good afternoon!' Gail said, offering her hand. 'And how can we help you?'

The man ignored the extended hand. He glanced at Eamonn and Karen, and sniffed. He was dressed in an immaculately tailored dark-blue suit, with a regimental-looking tie and a pale-blue handkerchief protruding from his breast pocket. His shoes were so sparklingly polished I wondered if the entire regiment had been spitting on them. His hair suggested that he kept a pair of monogrammed brushes on his dressing-table. His face was pinkish. He was perhaps fifty.

We introduced ourselves. He didn't.

'You have a room in private?' were the first words he uttered, again glancing disapprovingly at Eamonn's hair and Karen's mini-skirt. Gail's own hair looked more than usually free-floating after her haste across the square. Mine was straight and gypsy-like, and I was wearing jeans.

Gail coughed. She asked Eamonn and Karen if they'd mind opening up the shop and telling any customers could

384

they kindly wait a short while. As the two of them left, the man carefully flicked the back of an armchair with the back of his hand, and was about to sit down when Caroline entered. She was smiling, well content after her several glasses of champagne. She threw a glance at the tailored gentleman and lit a cigarette.

'So, what are you selling?' she announced, not exactly impolitely.

The man didn't answer, and neither did he sit down. Gail introduced Caroline. It was the first time she'd ever referred to her as 'The Hon Mrs Caroline Uppingham'. It sounded absurd, and Caroline winced.

'Oh shit! Don't be so fucking ridiculous, Gail,' she said crossly. 'What's the matter with you?' And she turned back to the well-tailored gentleman. 'So, what *are* you selling? We're frightfully busy, you know.'

His expression didn't change. But this time he did sit down, adjusting the handkerchief in his breast pocket as he did so. Then he looked up at Caroline who was blowing clouds of cigarette smoke in his direction. He folded his hands, cleared his throat, and for the first time a wafer of a smile appeared on his lips.

'Actually, I'm from the Palace,' he said.

12

Royal Game

————————o————————

'Jaysus!' Gail lowered her face into her hands and let out a long moan. 'Jaysus!' she repeated. 'And I'm a fockin' republican.'

I said nothing. Even Caroline said nothing. I looked at her, and then at Gail. Then I looked across the empty office towards the window and the pavement outside in case the man from the Palace was still lurking, perhaps gazing up at our signboard of me unzipped and no doubt preparing in his head what he was to report back to his royal mistress. I winced at the thought. We didn't even know his name. My only relief was the absolute certainty that we would never see or hear from him again.

But he wasn't there. I looked back at Gail and Caroline. It was as if both of them had been mugged. For a few moments we went on saying nothing. Gail discovered a powerful need to scratch. Caroline lit another cigarette. Through the wall I could make out the voices of

Eamonn and Karen in the shop, and wondered what they were selling to whom. Why, oh why, hadn't we stuck to dealing in second-hand clothes? Whose bloody awful idea was it to meddle in marriages anyway? Then I remembered it was mine.

I made an effort to pull myself together.

'Look, I can't actually believe this,' I said vigorously, gazing first at Gail, then at Caroline. 'I mean, it's obviously a joke, isn't it? It must be. Of course it is.' I paused, waiting for a response which didn't come. I made another effort, and began to laugh. 'And it's really a rather brilliant joke when you come to think of it. The very idea of it. Christ, to think we were taken in for a while. And don't say you weren't, Caroline.'

Caroline still wasn't saying anything.

'Just imagine it,' I went on, ignoring the heavy silence around me. 'What d'you suppose he's telling his friends right now? They're probably in a café round the corner, splitting their sides. They'd have had a bet, don't you think? "Which of us dares walk into that marital advice agency we read about in the papers and announce he's from the Palace, and that the Duchess needs help with her disastrous marriage to the Queen's younger son?" As if the royals would ever do such a thing – it's utterly absurd. But God, he did it well though, didn't he? Smooth operator. A picture of discretion. No names actually mentioned, you notice. Just sounding the ground. He'd have had a tape-recorder on him, wouldn't he, so he could prove we were taken in. So what do you imagine he really is? An estate agent? A journalist? He's probably from *Private Eye*.'

Caroline was looking at me balefully.

'Why don't you just stop waffling, Angela? He's from the Palace.'

I bridled.

'Caroline, *you* were the one who thought he was a detergent salesman.'

She didn't answer. Gail was gazing at her, frowning.

'How do you fockin' well know he's from the Palace?' she said, venting her irritation on her hair.

Caroline was looking evasive.

'Oh, just one or two things he let slip. Things he wouldn't have known otherwise.'

'Such as?'

There was a moment's pause. Caroline looked away and drew heavily on her cigarette. She never liked being questioned.

'Nothing that would mean anything to you,' she said quietly.

Probably Caroline didn't intend it as a put-down: she was just telling the truth in her inimitable fashion. Now it was Gail's turn to bridle.

'Shit! What a load of shit! So, how is it *you* know? How is it you pretend to know everything?' Gail took up her washerwoman's stance, hands on hips, and glared at Caroline. Then her mouth curled into a sneer. 'I suppose it's because you know the insides of the Palace so intimately?'

Caroline was still gazing away towards the window. 'Yes, I do . . . fairly,' she said.

With that she picked up her shoulder-bag and sauntered back to the shop with that swinging gait of hers, as if all the world could wait. Gail and I exchanged fierce looks, and followed her, Gail's feet thumping on the floor with irritation.

'Upper-class bitch!' she mumbled.

We were busy all that afternoon. Caroline flitted in and out. Customers who were taking unduly long peering among the racks she would leave peremptorily to Gail or me, announcing that she had an interview to conduct next-door, or that there was business to arrange with Adultery Tours – she said 'Adultery Tours' particularly loudly, to the surprise of several ladies who had been quietly searching for head-scarves.

In spite of Caroline's inside knowledge that the man really had been sent by the Palace, at least I could comfort myself with the conviction that after one look at the three of us he would never come back. Quite apart from our unprofessional appearance, it must have become perfectly obvious to him within minutes that we weren't exactly the marriage-mending establishment Her Royal Highness imagined us to be, but precisely the reverse. Christ, the man had even picked up one of our little cards advertising *Pastures New – Why wait till death? Part now!* I could imagine him standing in front of the Duchess in his Savile Row suit, giving a pompous little cough, then, 'Excuse me, ma'am, but . . . er . . . perhaps not quite appropriate for Your Highness's needs . . . er . . . not exactly a professional establishment . . . er . . . more a clothes shop, ma'am. Second-hand clothes. Perhaps Your Highness has been poorly advised . . . If I might suggest that most discreet psychiatrist in Devonshire Place whom Her Majesty the Queen became acquainted with over her other daughter-in-law and her digestive problems.'

I had a smile on my face as I thought about it. From the scowl on Gail's face I imagined she was thinking about it too. Caroline however, after the initial shock, seemed to have taken the whole affair in her usual confident stride. She continued to breeze in and out of the shop, occasionally humming to herself. Knowing Caroline, I was sure she was already getting into training for the interview with Her Royal Highness, preparing the Exocet-like questions she would have absolutely no inhibitions about asking. I almost wanted our 'royal commission' to go ahead after all, simply for the joy of hearing Caroline dish the regal dirt on her third vodka-and-tonic.

'What are you fockin' smilin' about, Angela?' growled Gail, scrawling out an invoice so ferociously that the biro tore through the paper.

'I was just wondering if we'd be entitled to a "By Royal Appointment" crest over the door,' I said.

At last there was a break in the cloud cover which had hung over Gail the entire afternoon.

'And where would we hang the fockin' thing, d'you suppose?' Then she managed a smile. 'Underneath that sign of you half naked outside the shop: that would be about right, wouldn't it? Or maybe Rick could run up something tasteful using it as a fig-leaf. About the right shape, isn't it?'

Thankfully Gail had cheered up. Just occasionally, when customers were out of earshot, the scowl returned as she reminded me of some of the questions the man from the Palace had thought fit to put to us.

'Fockin' cheek, asking what qualifications I had – what universities I'd attended. Jaysus! There's me who used to sell Beatles T-shirts in Liverpool. You who got groped in a bank. And Caroline with her one-and-a-half o'levels. Qualifications! I wanted to ask him what qualifications he'd acquired to lick a royal arse.'

Customers regularly curtailed these little homilies until thankfully it was time to close the shop. Caroline had left already, preparing to create mayhem at Coutts Bank for refusing her permission to open an account in the name of Adultery Tours. Eamonn, who'd overheard the phone call, swore he'd never heard anyone speak to a bank manager like that. Karen was still looking shell-shocked, though it occurred to me this might have been due to Eamonn's intimate attentions behind the computer.

I drove home on a soft spring evening, making a slow detour along the river to try to drown the absurdities of the day in the sight of the gentle tide. A heron was standing sentinel on the mud, and a flotilla of ducks was moving purposefully nowhere in particular. The river curled away westwards, turning silver in the sharp light of early dusk. A few scullers skimmed over it like black water-insects. Here and there fishermen were crouched motionless on the towpath.

How did so many accidental things come together to produce a scene of such eternal peace? I realised that I could feel the balm of it all precisely because almost nothing in my own life was at peace at all. It was the strangest sensation. Had everything within me been resolved I might have taken in nothing of what lay before me except its tranquil ordinariness, while my mind played with simple and equally ordinary thoughts – what supper to cook, what clothes Rachel needed for the summer, what holidays to plan, what spring flowers to plant in the garden. The banality of daily contentment. As it was I felt swamped by the sheer loveliness of the evening: I wanted to embrace it, make it mine, hold it as a guiding light to all those new paths in my life I would very soon have to take. The exhilaration of this moment made the prospect of taking them appear exciting – so many golden opportunities to be seized, so many risks not to be shunned. This was a time when too many women's lives dimmed, I realised, when hope lost its gloss, happiness its flavour. Don't waste it, I told myself. Make this your thirtieth year to heaven, not to housework.

Joggers on the towpath might have been surprised to know the reason for my smile – that my husband was probably at this precise moment screwing his fluffy blonde mistress, while my own lover was plodding somewhere along the Great Wall of China. They might not have thought these were good reasons to smile; but then, what I knew was that my lover would soon return to share my life, while my husband would soon be leaving it for ever.

Caroline was next-door reprogramming Patrick when the phone call came. At first I assumed it was either a wrong number or a crossed line because there were clicks, acres of silence, then distant voices apparently talking to one another. I was on the point of replacing the receiver when a clipped male voice asked suddenly, 'Is that Lady Uppingham?' I laughed and said I didn't know she'd been elevated to the peerage quite yet, and no, it wasn't *Mrs* Uppingham, this was Angela Merton, and could I help?

There was no response. Gail, who had been in the middle of going through accounts with me, looked exasperated and said loudly, 'Who the fock is it?' at just the moment when the same clipped voice came back with, 'Mrs Merton, I have a call for you.'

This time it was a woman who spoke.

'Mrs Merton?'

The breathless way she pronounced my name made me disinclined to take this call very seriously.

'Yes, it is – for the time being anyway,' I answered flippantly.

There was a sound of some awkwardness on the other end of the phone. Then the breathless voice continued.

'Mrs Merton, I'm phoning as lady-in-waiting . . .' at which point I went into a mind-spin. Suddenly this was no longer a joke, and I began to feel deeply perturbed. Could it possibly be that this wasn't a misunderstanding after all, and the reputation of Outfit Enterprises was such that we were actually about to be consulted on how to break up a royal marriage? Jesus, we were never going to get out of this alive. Oh, why wasn't I at home preparing a nice chicken casserole for Ralph and Rachel and taking gentle walks on the common? I could have found a part-time job typing letters for the vicar. I could be taking pottery lessons at the local art school. Instead, here I was about to be invited to help bring down the noble House of Windsor, for which my name would ever after be engraved on the roll of traitors along with Pontius Pilate, Guy Fawkes and Lord Haw-Haw. I shuddered even as I listened to that breathless voice explaining how Her Royal Highness had been informed of our establishment and was expressing a wish to see our selection of designer clothes if a visit might be arranged after hours when the shop was closed to the public. '. . . Perhaps this could be made possible, Mrs Merton,' the voice went on.

'Whenever it would be convenient,' I heard myself say. 'We have a wide variety of clothes, of course.' *Clothes*! The word 'clothes' buzzed in my head as I put the phone down. For Christ's sake, so that was all she wanted! A tremendous gust of relief swept through me. Of course! It made sense. After all those snide comments in the media about the Duchess's extravagant lifestyle and addiction to glamorous holidays, naturally she'd be anxious to demonstrate that she had humble tastes at heart and that wearing second-hand clothes wasn't at all beneath her – in other words, she wanted an image more fitting to a woman who slogged her way up Everest for charity and paid tender visits to starving Ethiopia or wherever it was she was always being photographed.

So – naturally – second-hand clothes!

'Yes, that *was* the Palace, Gail,' I said, grateful that the shop was empty for a moment. 'Caroline was quite right, it wasn't a hoax. It was real enough. But it's nothing whatever to do with royal marriages. All the Duchess wants is to look at' – and I laughed as I said it – 'is clothes!'

Gail seemed half relieved, half puzzled. She turned questioningly to Caroline, who had come up the back stairs without my noticing, and was standing with one hand on the rail and a quizzical look on her face, gazing at me. I knew that expression of old.

'Clothes!' she echoed. And then she laughed. 'Second-hand clothes! Angela, darling, when were you born? Where have you been?' She smoothed her fair hair back from her forehead and perched herself on the edge of the table, her legs swinging. She continued to gaze at me with an expression of incredulity. 'What a complete load of balls!' she said loudly. 'The idea that HRH is seriously interested in buying second-hand designer clothes – for Christ's sake, girl, the woman gets three hundred grand plus from the Privy Purse; she lives in palaces and castles; she jet-sets the world; she meets kings and presidents. And you're seriously telling me she wants to be received at the Elysée Palace by Madame Mitterrand wearing an outfit last seen on some old slag at the Epsom Derby? What sort of press is that going to get her? Angela, don't be so fucking ridiculous!'

Gail seemed to be nodding in agreement.

'Mmm!' was the best I could offer. Put like that, it did seem unanswerable.

Caroline swung herself off the edge of the table and poured out a large vodka-and-tonic. Now she was getting down to business.

'Do you really imagine,' she went on, 'that all those questions we were asked by that fart from the Palace were aimed at discovering whether we knew about Chrissie Clyne and Janet Reger knickers? It's perfectly bloody obvious: she has to pretend it's about clothes. Of course she does. She's probably even told the Queen it's about clothes. But that's just a front. The Palace lives on secrets: it always has. It's the only way royalty survives. No, the woman doesn't want us to dress her, for God's sake; she wants us to dump her husband.' She gave a laugh. 'Or, more to the point, find him someone he can hump.'

All I could tell myself was – 'For God's sake, I hope Caroline can handle this.'

The shop began to fill with customers, and there was no chance to talk any further until after we'd locked up. We waited until Eamonn and Karen had left and then held a hurried conference in the Enterprises office. Gail was deeply gloomy, muttering about wanting to go straight back to County Wicklow and keep hens. I was apprehensive, choking back fantasies of royal retribution, charges of high treason, banishment to the Bloody Tower where we'd end up one of those historic mysteries like the little princes. Jesus, there was probably a law against what we were doing, passed in the twelfth century and never repealed. Caroline on the other hand was by now entirely cheerful. She was much more involved in reprogramming Patrick, determined, she said, to get it right this time, and had to be prised away from the computer before she'd focus her mind on the question of our royal client.

'Oh, she's just another unhappy woman with a silly bastard of a husband,' she announced vaguely. 'She kissed her prince and he turned into a frog. Now, about Patrick, d'you think I should put in about him trying Growmore on his prick?'

Gail became exasperated, and began to throw her hair around. I suggested Caroline might start taking this a bit seriously.

'Oh, I am!' she said lightly.

'Well then!' Gail took up her washerwoman stance. 'First of all, what are we going to do about these two youngsters here, Karen and Eamonn? We can't have them blatherin' and chatterin' away all over the fockin' town. Here we are, a respectable divorce agency; we've got our reputation to keep up for Jaysus Christ's sake. And now we're mixin' with the proper royalty we can't be takin' any chances with the likes of my nephew and that little tart with a G-string for a skirt.'

As always the Irish in Gail's voice grew richer as she began to savour her own eloquence. The gloom had lifted, and thoughts of keeping hens in County Wicklow seemed to have evaporated.

'I think we just don't tell them,' I suggested. 'Everything's going to happen after shop hours anyway.'

For once there seemed to be some agreement, until Caroline pointed out that we'd need Eamonn to program the computer, so how could we possibly keep the identity of an English royal couple secret when every intimate detail of their life together needed to be fed into this bloody thing?

And she gave Cupid a firm tap with her fingers.

'Simple!' I said confidently. 'We give them false names. Ordinary names.'

Caroline's eyes widened, and she gave out a little snort.

'You mean, names like Gary and Debbie? Oh yes, I can see that would be really foolproof. Let's imagine it – "Now tell me, Debbie, why did you agree to marry someone in line to the throne?" Or – "When Gary first made love to you, Debbie, was it at Balmoral or Buckingham Palace?" Naturally Eamonn wouldn't rumble that in a million years, would he?' Caroline glanced at me and clicked her tongue. 'For God's sake, Angela!'

I could feel my irritation rising.

'Maybe you could try employing a little subtlety, Caroline,' I said sharply. 'If you know what that means.'

Caroline was about to explode when Gail slammed her fist on the table.

'For fock's sake, you two. Cut it!'

It was the voice of Mother Superior. Caroline took a deep breath and turned back to the computer. I imagined Patrick might be in for a very bad time.

And then the phone went. I grabbed it.

'Mrs Merton! Six-thirty next Thursday would suit Her Royal Highness,' said the familiar female voice.

The letter from Josh was postmarked Singapore. I'd used my key to his flat almost every day in the hope of finding one. Now after so many weeks I'd almost given up hope, and the emptiness of the flat felt like the emptiness of my life: I had to struggle hard to go on believing he still wanted me, that he would come back and everything would be the same. I remembered the bra I'd once found by his bed, and wondered how many bras had lain strewn across the hotel bedrooms of the Far East in all those weeks he'd been away. Jesus, I thought, China has a population of one thousand million, one half of whom must be women: even allowing for all the ones who look like little wrinkly puddings dressed in boiler-suits, that still left an awful lot of sloe-eyed waifs who couldn't wait to offer a favour to some lone Westerner who might sweep them off to where they'd be allowed to wear decent clothes and have as many children as they wanted. And I was jealous of them all, even while laughing at myself for being so.

I wanted him back so much. I wanted him back so that our life could begin.

Nearly always there was nobody in the flat when I called, though his mail would be carefully piled on his desk, some of it opened; so I knew that Stella, his agent, came there regularly. I told myself not to snoop, and invariably did. There were notes from Stella saying this or that had been dealt with, cheques paid in, bills paid, jobs turned down, jobs deferred with a question-mark. One of these, Stella had scrawled, was for swimwear: the note mentioned a well-known model's name and the suggested location – Tahiti! Christ, I'd see to it he turned that one down. First half the women in China and now the most beautiful model in England: oh, why did I have to fall in love with a photographer?

I found myself wondering if Stella still loved him. I read every word of those little scrawled notes to see if I could detect a hint of intimacy – some reference to what they used to have between them. After all, it had been not just one affair, but *two*. I felt almost cheated to find nothing.

Then one morning I got in early and Stella was there. She turned round, not at all surprised, and half smiled. She was holding a pile of letters, one of which she'd been reading. I said, 'Hello!' a little awkwardly, then asked if maybe she'd heard anything from him.

She laughed.

'No, of course not!' she said, placing the letters on the desk. Again – just like the last time I'd met her –

there was this clear suggestion that she knew him so much better than I did. 'Nobody hears from Josh when he's away,' she added. 'Would you like some coffee?'

Without waiting for an answer, she walked towards the kitchen as though it were her own. I wondered if one of their affairs had been conducted here in this flat – perhaps both of them! Stella had her back to me, casually preparing the coffee, and I thought how often Josh must have gazed at her like this, admiring her poise, her figure, the lovely hair with a sheen of red in it. She had such self-assurance, not feeling the need to say anything, knowing I was standing there behind her burning to ask all kinds of questions, and knowing that she had all the answers.

'I'm afraid there's no milk,' she said, still not turning round.

I plucked up courage.

'Did you used to live here?'

She handed me the coffee, and her face had a slightly amused look.

'No!' Then she added in a slightly barbed way – 'Don't worry, the place isn't polluted.'

For a few moments there was only the sound of coffee-cups. I was feeling deeply uncomfortable. There was something less friendly about her than there had been a few months ago. I couldn't make out if she was jealous, or critical, or perhaps just disapproving now that Josh was no longer around and she didn't have to be Mrs Goody Two Shoes. She made me feel young and a little foolish. Again I plucked up courage.

'Stella, can I ask you something? Do you think I'm doing the right thing?'

She looked at me for a second or two. Then she raised her eyebrows.

'I'm not sure I know what you *are* doing,' she answered, seating herself easily on the arm of a chair and crossing her legs to show me they were every bit as good as mine. Then, still looking at me with no particular expression, she added – 'Your husband seems to be doing extremely well. That must make life a lot easier for you.'

I could feel the flush on my face. Suddenly it all became clear to me. I knew exactly what she was thinking.

'Easier for *him* perhaps,' I said firmly.

'And not for you?'

This time I just looked at her. I waited for her to go on. She hadn't quite known what I meant. I was beginning to feel I had the upper hand, and she obviously didn't like that.

'But I suppose there are always worries with a successful and handsome husband, aren't there,' she continued, rather less coolly than before. She was being forced to say the things she would have preferred me to say. 'All those little temptations. Men aren't very good at resisting them, are they.' You bitch, I thought. 'But still, you've been having your own fun.'

It was time to draw a weapon.

'I'm leaving him,' I said.

I could see she wasn't sure whether to believe me. She uncrossed and recrossed her legs.

'You are?'

I just looked at her for a moment. Then I smiled.

'Why do you think I asked you if you thought I was doing the right thing?'

Now Stella seemed confused, then almost abashed. And when she turned her head to look at me again her face was altogether softer.

'And your daughter?' she said.

This was clearly the second line of attack.

'She'll come with me,' I answered.

I was astonished by my own confidence. Stella got up from the arm of her chair and crossed the room towards the desk with all Josh's mail neatly stacked.

'Well!' she said, flicking the pile of letters with her fingers like a pack of cards. Then she glanced at me out of the corner of her eye. 'D'you really want to know what I think?'

'Of course!'

Stella rested her hands on the back of a chair and leant forwards towards me.

'It's not at all what I thought five minutes ago, I can tell you,' she said. 'What I think now is that you'd better get a move on.' She paused for a moment, then turned and walked towards the window. 'Josh went away partly to try and forget you,' she went on.

'And I told him I thought that was exactly what he ought to do.'

I was horrified. I felt sick. I stuttered something like, 'Why? What d'you mean?'

Stella suddenly turned round, then came and sat next to me.

'Because I thought you were playing games. Things were bad at home – a tired marriage and all that. You found a job. You found a lover. Josh is good at that: he's sexy, and romantic. And he was available – which was more than you were. So, you could get fucked stupid when you wanted, then, when it suited you, you could go back to Ralph and play happy families again. With just a little regret perhaps – Josh'd always be the best fuck you ever had, and all that; but it wouldn't have worked, would it, you had to wake up to reality one day. And your daughter, you obviously couldn't sacrifice her, could you. And then Ralph became successful again – amazing what success does to a man; and he was kind, and he was never that bad in bed, was he. Anyway, much better to have your life all in one piece. No more mess. No more silly dreams. When men do it, it's called sowing their wild oats. You just left yours a bit late . . . That's what I thought. You did ask me.'

I sat back heavily in the armchair.

'Jesus!' I said. 'I need a drink.'

Stella gave a laugh and got up.

'Why not? It's nine-thirty in the morning, after all.'

And she went over to the drinks cupboard and took out a bottle of vodka.

'Tonic?'

'Anything! Lots!'

Handing it to me she then reached down for the briefcase she'd left beside the chair, opened it and drew out a slip of paper.

'You'd better have this,' she said, holding it out. A number was scrawled across it. 'That's where Josh'll be on Friday. It's a hotel in Bombay. He's in Singapore at the moment but I don't know where.' She went over to the door and took down her coat. 'And now I have to go.' She turned to look at me. 'Forgive me for lying to you, Angela. Josh phones quite often, and he *always* talks about you — which you don't bloody well deserve.'

'Is he all right?' I said, feeling rather weak.

'Of course, he's perfectly all right. When is he not? You know Josh.'

I sat there grasping my vodka in both hands while Stella wrapped her coat round herself and thrust some papers briskly into her briefcase. I watched her. I had an almost craven feeling of gratitude to this woman I couldn't bring myself to like.

Stella was standing looking at me, one hand on the door handle. She had a half-smile on her face.

'Well,' she said, 'at least you'll have no trouble finding someone suitable for Ralph, will you. You've always been an *enterprising* woman.'

Touché, I thought. I wondered whether at heart she

hated me. Maybe she did. I knew I had to ask her one thing more.

'Will you tell me something?' I asked. 'Were you in love with Josh?'

The question made her laugh.

'Of course!' she said.

'Twice?'

It was a stupid question. Perhaps it was a mean question. She didn't answer it.

'I suppose what you really want to know is why I married somebody else instead.'

'Of course!' I echoed.

'Because I was frightened. I rushed off and married someone I felt safe with. A terrible mistake. Not that you'll ever have that sort of trouble if you live with Josh.'

'And second time round?' I said, ignoring the jibe.

She laughed again.

'Because after three years of marriage I had a great longing to feel *unsafe*.'

'And then?'

'Well, I was right to feel unsafe. Josh met someone else. Fortunately, so did I. And after that it suddenly became easy to be friends.'

'And who was the somebody else he met?'

Stella gave me a sideways look, half out of the door.

'You!'

The door closed, and I was left with a large vodka and the sensation of having just spent one of the most uncomfortable half-hours of my life. I felt relieved and battered. I desperately needed to talk to Josh. I wanted to hold out my life to him. I wanted to tell him everything I hadn't been able to tell him.

But he wouldn't be in Bombay until Friday. And today was only Tuesday. It terrified me that everything might just disappear.

And then on Wednesday the letter came. It was lying on the mat downstairs. I tore it open. It was very short – just a few lines.

> My darling, I've written you letters longer than the Great Wall of China and torn them all up. I thought I'd get away from you, and can't. I suppose that means I love you, doesn't it? So, come live with me and be my love. OK?
>
> Back on the 19th,
> Josh
>
> PS: Where shall we live?

Gail had spent the morning betraying her republican soul by having her hair done for the royal occasion. Caroline was less than flattering about the result, not without some justification: it did look as though Gail's hair was already fighting back, and within a short time would certainly spring up again even more fiercely than before, no doubt at just the moment HRH chose to arrive. Caroline herself had made no concessions at all, but then she never needed to: Caroline would have looked 'class' if she'd dressed at an Oxfam shop. I hadn't done anything special either — except just before leaving the house I'd remembered that one of my Butler and Wilson geegaws was a mock Order of the Garter medallion, and I'd pinned it to the lapel of my jacket. Rachel went to school wide-eyed that I was wearing real diamonds. Then Caroline took one look at it and ordered me to remove the thing: it was in appallingly bad taste, she said — 'really naff!'

'Fock the whole business,' was Gail's verdict.

'We're just here to show the woman some clothes, remember!' I said, trying to calm matters. 'That's all!'

Caroline laughed. Gail looked morose.

'Privileged bitch,' she added sourly. 'I suppose you're going to tell me you were at school with her.'

'No!' said Caroline vaguely. 'Not exactly. She came after I left.'

Gail tried not to look astonished, but couldn't suppress a smile.

'Jaysus!' she muttered, shaking her head violently, which did no favours to the brand-new hairdo.

Between customers we managed to agree on one thing at least: that our royal client absolutely needed a pseudonym. We couldn't go on whispering her name furtively out of fear of being overheard in the shop; and if Caroline was right and this visit was about more than designer clothes, then His Nibs the Prince would need a pseudonym too. Besides, at all costs the truth had to be kept from Eamonn, who would be undertaking the royal data profiling. We tossed a few possible names around before Caroline reminded us that she'd already suggested we call them Debbie and Gary, and what was wrong with that?

So Debbie and Gary they became. Now it was just a matter of waiting. We closed the shop and the office at half-past five, saw Eamonn and Karen safely off the premises, then set about making a selection of clothes that Debbie might conceivably think of wearing. I also gave Torquemada a spit and polish, guessing that our resident confessor might have quite an evening's work to do. I decided that Harrods Founder's Blend would be the most suitable coffee to offer the lady, though Caroline suggested Blue Mountain might be more appropriate, judging by recent photographs which had appeared in the tabloids. Gail was long past thinking that was funny.

By now it was six-fifteen. Again we waited.

'Who's for a drink?' announced Caroline.

I said I thought perhaps one oughtn't to receive royalty half pissed.

'Rubbish!' Caroline retorted. 'They all drink like fishes. What d'you think the Queen keeps in that little handbag she always carries around with her?'

She poured herself a jumbo vodka-and-tonic and relaxed into a chair with her feet up on the desk. A thoughtful expression wafted over her face.

'I wonder which of the ladies on our books will turn out to be ideal for Gary?' she mused. 'It had better not be the same one as Patrick's.'

Gail clicked her tongue.

'We don't have any fockin' princesses on our books, for Jaysus Christ's sake.'

Caroline waved her vodka-and-tonic cheerfully in the air.

'Oh, that doesn't matter two hoots. She becomes royalty by marrying him, doesn't she? We're not talking about the heir to the throne: she doesn't need to have fifty generations of blue blood, otherwise I might offer myself. That's not so bad an idea, come to think of it, except I don't think I'd fancy mother-in-law.'

Gail merely looked even more exasperated. But Caroline was enjoying herself.

'Whoever it turns out to be, d'you think I might recruit them for Adultery Tours? A nice Caribbean cruise perhaps? He is a sailor after all. And they could visit his aunt, couldn't they?'

I decided to go over to the window to see if there was any sign of a royal car. It was six-thirty. Were royals always punctual, or never? I thought of Rachel looking forward to yet another '*teckvai*'. Then I wondered if Ralph might be leaping on Mrs Claridge at this very moment. When was I going to spring the trap by handing him his little note to her – '*Darling, sleep well!*' More important – far more important – there was Josh. Tomorrow I could phone him. Christ, what was I doing about to offer Harrods Founder's Blend to some errant Duchess when all I wanted was to offer my life to someone even more errant, damn him?

'I wonder if he *would* fancy me?' From the back of the shop Caroline was still pursuing her cheerful fantasy. Gail was looking disgusted, and pacing up and down. 'I know I'm a bit older than he is,' Caroline went on reflectively, 'but he might appreciate a touch of maturity after Debbie, mightn't he? And I've got much better legs, better tits, and lots of money. We could even make it a double divorce. Jesus, what a great idea! Patrick would go along with that, I'm sure: he's a decent chap after all, even if he has only got four inches.'

The vodka was clearly doing its work. I prayed that the royal car would arrive before Caroline spun off into orbit.

And suddenly there it was.

Royal cars, I realised, always look like royal cars even when they're doing their very best not to. It's partly the gleaming depth of polish, suggesting platoons of little minions with nothing else to do but apply the wax and shammy. But mostly it's the way they're driven – the exact opposite of the way Caroline drives – as though some anti-magnetic force were compelling all inferior vehicles to keep their distance; though it was obvious from what was happening outside that the same law of physics didn't apply to people.

'Mary, mother of Jaysus, the whole fockin' square's out there gawpin',' said Gail in an agitated voice. 'I thought this was supposed to be a secret.'

Caroline shrugged her shoulders.

'Oh, come on Gail, you know about royal secrets,'

she said laconically. 'They're what you read about every day in the papers.'

Gail turned her face sharply away from the window and looked offended.

'Not me. Certainly not!' she retorted indignantly. 'I don't give a fockin' toss for your Royal Family. They're nothing to do with me whatsoever, thank the Lord. I come from a sensible republic that doesn't go in for all that crap. Pack of snooty layabouts.' She pressed her nose back against the window. 'Oh Jaysus, here she is!' she exclaimed excitedly. 'Here's Debbie!'

'Gail,' I said nervously as I hurried to the door. 'For Christ's sake do please remember not to call her Debbie.'

'What the fock do I call her?' she whispered urgently as I prepared to open the door.

'Ma'am!' I muttered — and switched on my most welcoming smile.

Our royal visitor stepped inside, leaving two men in double-breasted suits waiting heavily on the pavement. I was still thinking I should probably have curtsied when to my astonishment I saw Gail take three firm paces in front of Caroline and proceed to swoop almost to her knees.

'Ah, to be sure, your worship, 'tis an honour and a pleasure to be receiving you, and bless you if you don't have eyes just like mine – it must be Irish that you are,' she began breathlessly. 'I'm Abigail O'Connor at your service, your grace, and if your holiness would allow me to take your coat I'd be most happy to oblige you with anything that might take your royal fancy. For example . . .' And Gail dived between Caroline and me to reach for a suit on one of the racks. 'With your lovely complexion, your honour, this delicate little *ensemble* . . .'

But Caroline had already laid a hand firmly on Gail's shoulder. She was smiling in an entirely relaxed way at our visitor, and extending a friendly hand.

'I'm Caroline Uppingham and this is Angela Merton,' she said warmly. 'Perhaps something to refresh you first?'

What Caroline had noticed was that the royal eyes were fixed, not on the racks of clothes on either side, or on us, but on something that seemed to shine unusually brightly and beckoningly at the far end of the room, like a shrine in glistening chrome and brass.

'You know, what I'd like most of all,' she replied eagerly, smiling at the three of us, 'is a cup of your coffee.'

We exchanged glances. We were on our way.

13

Black Mischief

————— ○ —————

With tremendous relief we appointed Caroline to conduct the royal interview – or several interviews. This was mainly a tribute to her skill at wringing frightful truths out of the most unlikely clients. But it was also an acknowledgement of social rank, Caroline being a million miles closer to royalty than Gail or myself. To my surprise, Caroline took offence at this seemingly obvious fact; she awarded me an icy glare before pointing out that her own ancestors had worn all the crowns of Europe that were worth taking seriously, whereas Debbie was just an upstart whose father happened to have groomed a few royal polo ponies. I muttered an apology and reminded myself that the key to Caroline's cavalier treatment of the world at large was her conviction that she was far more magnificently bred than anyone else who was privileged to inhabit it. Her dismissive treatment of Patrick, I'd come to realise, was related more to his being heir to the *smallest* county in England than to the comparable size of his prick.

It was having the two together, so to speak, that she found doubly insulting: hence the murderous frown whenever his name was mentioned.

In other words, if pressed, she was prepared to do HRH a favour.

'All right, I'll do it,' she said, leaning wearily on Torquemada after Debbie had finally departed in the royal limousine on that first evening. 'But I warn you, if she's terribly boring I shall send her packing.'

Neither Gail nor I had the slightest doubt about that.

The week following soon developed a distinctly surreal air, chiefly because it now required a considerable mental effort to remember who was supposed to know what. The Duchess paid us three consecutive visits, always in the evenings: 'consultations', as Gail solemnly referred to them, her republicanism having melted away at the first touch of a royal glove, though at least she no longer addressed the lady as 'your holiness'.

The press, who I'd assumed would rumble the truth within minutes, proved strangely gullible. At first we were besieged: whey-faced reporters bombarded us much of the day, begging us – bribing us – to tell them what outfits HRH had purchased the previous evening, for how much, when did she intend to wear them, whose clothes had they been originally, what had made her decide to come to our shop, and various other equally boring questions to which we replied smilingly that the royal visits were strictly confidential, as indeed they most certainly were. If only those sallow little jerks really knew!

As a result, the idea of HRH paying visits to a second-hand clothes shop created a certain media buzz, prompting small news items and a sneering page or two in most of the tabloids. But then, once it became apparent that no scandal could be extracted from the story – or so they imagined – it soon died a death: more exciting royal game was to be had elsewhere, and the whey-faced reporters turned their attentions back to the other royal marriages on the rocks.

More tedious than the press were the royal 'heavies' who had to be fed small talk in the shop while ma'am was taking an amazingly long time with Mrs Uppingham next door trying on clothes. They refused anything to drink, glanced frequently at their watches, almost as frequently at my breasts, and between times gazed blankly at the racks of clothes. Only once or twice did they exhibit a little curiosity: this was when Caroline's voice could be heard through the wall berating her royal customer with questions like, '*What* size did you say?' and, 'Really? You mean nothing on at all – on the royal yacht?' Gail and I smiled sweetly at their puzzled faces, and commented on the weather.

Then there was the problem of Eamonn. As far as he was concerned the personal notes he was required to feed into the computer next day were merely the distressful outpourings of a young woman called Debbie concerning a husband by the name of Gary who seemed permanently to be at sea or else on the golf-course.

'Hardly a thrill a minute, this prat: why the hell did she marry him in the first place?' he muttered, gazing through his curtain of hair at the computer screen. 'Some odd things about him, though, aren't there? I wonder who Cupid'll come up with.'

We all wondered that.

'My boyfriend's called Gary,' Karen chipped in cheerfully. 'And if he got up to some of the things this one does, I'd kill 'im.'

Eamonn looked as though he'd like to kill him anyway. Our young Irish Adonis, who consistently gobbled up every twiglet of a model who arrived at the shop, had evidently got nowhere with the shapely Karen. Her mini-skirts had been getting briefer by the month, and if she teased him much more I feared his jeans might actually explode, taking Cupid and all our royal notes with them.

'Who is this Debbie, then?' he enquired grumpily.

'Just a woman who works during the day and is only free in the evenings,' I said.

'Works! Seems to spend most of her time on holiday, from what I can see.'

'Her work often involves travel,' I said guardedly.

Eamonn gave me a scornful look.

'Yes, from one end of a swimming-pool to the other, topless. That's the kind of travel I'd like.'

None of us said anything.

417

'Sounds a bit of a tart to me,' Eamonn added, gazing wistfully at Karen's legs.

Gail and I exchanged glances.

'You might say that,' I agreed.

Gail looked at me severely.

So all day we'd wait patiently serving in the shop or interviewing clients until Eamonn and Karen had left; then we'd quickly lock up and pore over the notes he'd been programming.

'Does Debbie actually want a divorce?' I asked Caroline one evening towards the end of the week. 'Or does she just want us to find him someone he'll fall for, so she can appear to be the injured party?'

'The second, I think,' said Caroline wearily. She was already slumped in a chair with a vodka-and-tonic. The third royal visit had just ended, and in the twilight of Pimlico Square the royal Daimler could be seen smoothing its way through the traffic in the direction of Sloane Square. 'Yes, the second,' she said again, more emphatically. 'But perhaps a divorce after that, once she's looking squeaky-clean and Gary's made a complete ass of himself.' She knocked back the rest of her drink and got up. 'Oh, for God's sake let's all go home.'

I was beginning to wish we could all go home for good. Caroline's nonchalant treatment of this whole business, and Gail's sudden wide-eyed conversion to royalism, had the effect of camouflaging what I felt sure was likely to be an apocalyptic disaster. I could see no way we could avoid being engulfed. It was one thing to spread a discreet message among our unhappily married customers – *'Why wait till death? Part now!'* But it was quite another matter when the client who came to us for marital salvation happened to be the wife of the Queen's son. If only I could convince myself that the whole thing was a foolish game, and that nothing whatsoever would come of it. But try as I might, I couldn't: our track record for finding suitable substitutes for miserable wives was frighteningly impressive – our Roll of Dishonour might under different circumstances have entitled us to a Queen's Award for Industry. I smiled at the thought, but the smile didn't last very long. I had an uneasy feeling that Cupid might actually pull it off, just as Torquemada had miraculously compelled our royal visitor to unburden her soul with the merest whiff of Harrods Founder's Blend. Whatever the magic was that we'd somehow acquired, there was no denying that it was potent.

What made it worse was that all these ideas had originally been mine – ideas which at the outset had seemed so entirely innocent. Well, perhaps not entirely innocent, but certainly no more than mischievous, in the spirit of my new-found freedom. Yet now I kept finding myself lying sleepless in the silence of the night wondering if some divine joker had taken charge of my fortunes and was propelling me willy-nilly towards some hideous chasm. At these moments I'd tell myself that all I'd ever wanted in this job was a modest occupation that would fill out my life, colouring the greyer areas of it and exercising those regions of the brain left unused by being a wife and mother. And look where it had landed me! With a husband I was about to leave. A daughter I scarcely saw. A lover so far away that the telephone was about as effective as a conch-shell. And now the imminent collapse about my ears of a sizeable chunk of the House of Windsor. No wonder I couldn't sleep.

I wanted Josh. Oh God, how I wanted Josh! I wanted his body, his love, his laughter, his common-sense: I wanted him to come riding towards me in shining armour to carry me away from all this – and if he wasn't actually on a white stallion then let it be that little yellow plane tied up with string and sealing-wax, and I would have orgasm after orgasm while he looped the loop on the giant bed of the clouds.

That was the life I wanted, not this one. Christ, I hadn't made love for two months!

It was the first of May. Dawn was creeping into the bedroom in what I could have sworn was the middle of the night. Again I'd hardly slept. It was five o'clock: what an appalling hour to be awake. I lay there and cursed it. Finally, as if my curses had broken some kind of barrier, I determined that today I would act. I would stop dreaming and plotting my future: I would set it in motion; give it a kick-start. The first of May – a good day to begin.

I rolled over, and in the half-light gazed at the lump in the double bed that was Ralph. I felt indignant. What on earth was I doing sharing a bed with a man I no longer loved, no longer fancied? Here we were, month after month, performing the same bedtime pantomime of a polite 'Goodnight', after which we'd turn our backs like distant book-ends and dream of other partners we longed to be with. It was insulting and absurd. It must stop.

After months of dithering I acted quickly. Magdalena was visiting her sick mother in Portugal, so I gathered up my dressing-gown and some clothes and moved into her bedroom. What would happen when Magdalena returned I couldn't begin to think about; for a couple of weeks or more this little cubby-hole would be mine. At least the size of it might stifle my dreams of erotic nights: any lover would need to wedge himself against the wall or run the risk of bouncing lustily into the corridor. Twisting round in the minute space, I dumped my stuff on a chair, then fished in my handbag for Ralph's note to Heather Claridge which Rick had stolen from the woman's flat. The words, *'Darling, sleep well!'* were just visible in the dawn light. Creeping back to the bedroom next door, I carefully smoothed my pillow and placed the note on top of it. As an afterthought I weighted it down with a packet of condoms which Ralph always kept in the top drawer of the dressing-table.

I thought I might feel pleased with myself; but I didn't. I felt scared. Ralph and I had always been so scrupulously well-mannered towards one another that I wasn't sure what it would be like to have a row with him. What would I say? How would he react? And how would I confront him with my own confession about Josh? I tiptoed downstairs, made myself a cup of coffee, and tried to imagine how the encounter might go.

The first scenario was theatrical. 'Ralph, you bastard, you've betrayed me. How could you? After all these years, all the things we've fought for, all the trust we've built up. I hate you and I hate you. And by the way I've been having it off above the shop two or three times a week for the past eight months. Sorry about that.'

None too convincing. So I tried again – the version I might perhaps have arrived at after years of wise professional counselling. 'Ralph, let us be honest and admit that we've grown apart. We have other needs, other dreams, other destinies; we need to release one another. Let us part in harmony and with mutual respect. I'm happy to respect you for bonking that blonde stick-insect who everyone says is a pain in the arse; and I want you to respect me for being screwed rotten every lunchtime, on the floor, in bed, on the dinner table, and upside down in an aeroplane at five thousand feet.'

My language seemed to be letting me down there. I tried once more – the vale-of-tears version. 'Oh Ralph, this is the unhappiest day of my whole life. I've fought against it, as I know you have. But there comes a time when one has to admit defeat, and that is the moment to be brave and say goodbye. I shall always love you, always treasure the memories we share; it's just that right now my most vivid memories are of that blonde bitch leaving you love-notes by her bed, and of my lover with a huge erection licking peach-juice off my breasts.'

That clearly wouldn't do either. Was it honesty

getting in the way, or perhaps just my usual retreat into absurdity?

I never knew the answer because I fell asleep in the kitchen chair. It was eight o'clock when Rachel woke me.

'You all right, Mum?'

I mumbled something inadequate before guiltily preparing her a breakfast she didn't want. Then I gave her a huge hug which she didn't want much either.

'Are you sure you're all right, Mum?'

There was the sound of a car-horn outside. Rachel scrambled her school things together and flung herself out of the front door with a 'See you later, alligator.'

The house was silent again. I made myself some more coffee and steeled myself for Ralph to wake up. I longed to have a bath, but the thought of Ralph striding in clutching Heather Claridge's note while I sought refuge under the soapsuds made me shudder. I longed to get dressed, but to be caught in panties and bra seemed too hideously appropriate for adulterous confessions. So I just sat in the kitchen and waited. I clung to the thought that I simply had to get through this – that I *would* get through it, I *would* survive – and that in three days' time Josh would be back, and then the business of sorting out our new life would begin. Oh God, how I wanted him! The waiting was intolerable. Ralph, for heaven's sake WAKE UP!

He came into the kitchen like the fine actor that he is, on cue – just as the phone went. I seized it and barked, 'Yes!' It was Caroline. And she launched.

'Angela, I have to tell you – ' I tried to say she didn't have to tell me at all, but my words were already drowned by an outraged flow. 'I *have* to tell you before I scream,' she went on. 'You won't believe this, Angela: if you're my friend you certainly won't believe it. It's the worst thing that's ever happened to me. Ever!' There was the briefest pause while I could hear Caroline draw deeply on a cigarette. 'Well, I decided to work late last night, programming Patrick. I thought it was about time I knew who his ideal woman was. And who do you think Cupid came up with? Go on, guess! Try! Go on! Oh, for Christ's sake, all right, I'll tell you. But you won't believe this: it's shameful, humiliating – absolutely disgusting! It's *me*.'

I shouldn't have laughed. I could hear Caroline swear she'd never speak to me again. How could I be such a heartless cow? It was my bloody stupid idea to install this fucking machine in the first place, and the least I could do was commiserate. Didn't I see that I'd ruined her life?

In the silence that followed the angry click of the telephone I just stood there sobbing with laughter, the phone still in my hand. Nothing around me felt real. Here I was, sleepless and dishevelled in my dressing-gown. And there was Ralph, bare feet planted on the kitchen floor, clutching a towel he'd thrown round his loins and holding Heather Claridge's note in the other hand. So this was it, our moment of truth, our time of the gladiators, our grand finale, the end of our marriage. And what was I doing? Laughing! Oh, God bless you, Caroline: this deserves the largest

424

vodka-and-tonic of your life even if you decide never to speak to me again.

Ralph and I looked at one another. The longer nothing was said, the more I was overcome by the feeling that nothing really needed to be said. Caroline's phone call had driven away all speeches, all recriminations and all secrets. I knew, and Ralph knew. It was like finding ourselves at the farther shore without having made the long journey to get there; and without the storm.

'Well, do you love her?' I managed to ask eventually.

At first Ralph looked surprised. Then he smiled. And as he smiled he looked handsome, self-assured, just as I remembered him the day he first walked into the Chelsea boutique and gazed at me – before I sneezed all over him, before he asked me out, before I knew I would devote myself to this man. It was a replay lasting a few seconds only: precisely the same look on his face, except that the face was older – and this time the look wasn't for me.

'Yes!' he said. 'I do love her.'

For a moment there was a twinge of guilt in me that I should feel so relieved. Then I wondered what I'd have done had he said no.

'And how long have you known her?' I asked coolly.

Ralph seated himself on the edge of the kitchen table, and went on gazing at me.

'About as long as you've known Josh.'

I felt myself give a sudden jolt, and instinctively I

began to splutter out a denial. But I'd hardly got beyond the splutter before another wave of relief passed over me. A curtain of secrecy had just been whipped away before my eyes; now I wouldn't have to go through the humiliating business of confession. But who could possibly have told him?

'How did you know?' I said cautiously.

Ralph laughed, and stood up. He walked over to the stove and began to make himself some coffee.

'Why is it we all believe we can keep secrets when we're in love?'

I waited for him to go on, wondering what was coming next.

'Remember that party? Your shop-warming party a bit more than a year ago? I saw you – the two of you. It was laser-beams, my darling. Laser-beams. You were burning each other's clothes off. And you changed from that day onwards.'

I felt sheepish. All those months when I thought I was successfully leading a double life.

'And you?' I asked. 'When did *you* meet her?'

Ralph gave me a knowing look.

'Heather was at that party too. You don't remember. You wouldn't: you were far too preoccupied.'

I tugged my dressing-gown indignantly around me, and took a deep breath.

'You mean, that woman whose tits you were groping in the dark, and you told me next morning you were too pissed to remember?'

Ralph nodded.

'I was lying.'

He still had the same calm expression on his face. I gave a snort of indignation.

'Jesus Christ! And when did you fuck her?'

'The next day.'

Now I was beginning to feel quite outraged.

'Ralph, you're dreadful! I waited for *months*!'

I wanted to say, 'I bet you've never fucked her in an aeroplane doing a loop the loop.' Instead I became serious.

'Ralph,' I said, steadying my voice. 'This is in danger of becoming the most civilised marriage break-up in the history of divorce. Now tell me, please, I want to know – before we talk about who's going to live where and who's going to have your mother's birdbath – what is it that this Claridge woman gives you that I didn't? Does she stimulate your mind? Does she cook better? Is she incredibly attentive? Is she better in bed?'

He said nothing for a moment, just sipping his coffee.

'The truth is,' he said eventually, 'she's not as nice as you.'

Now I was confused.

'And what's that supposed to mean?'

Ralph gave a shrug.

'Just that. She's nowhere near as nice as you.'

I looked at him hard.

'What you're telling me is, she's a real bitch, and

you love it. Is that it? You mean, what I should have done all this time is beaten you up, created mayhem, made your life hell, had dozen of affairs?'

Now Ralph was looking puzzled.

'Not exactly,' he said. 'Heather's not that kind of a bitch. What she is is a fighter. We argue a lot. We row.'

'And you like that? You really like that?'

He didn't answer. But I understood. I was stunned. So I'd got it wrong all along. Why had I always thought marriages were supposed to be about peace and harmony? Smoothing things over? Creating a loving atmosphere? Supporting your man and all that? Making life easy? God Almighty, all those years I was being a considerate and thoughtful wife, doing what all the good books say, and what was it my husband really wanted? He was longing to live in a bloody minefield. Suddenly it made me feel tame, demure, soggy, boring; and I wasn't any of those things. Josh wouldn't think I was – at least I sincerely hoped he wouldn't. Josh thought of me as dangerous, provocative, randy, unpredictable. Someone on fire. Someone a man could get burnt on. 'And I am! I am!' I said to myself.

'So you mean I'm too *nice*, Ralph. Is that it?' I gave him a furious glance as I swept out of the kitchen. 'Well, I can tell you – I'm not at all nice,' I said, looking down on him from the staircase. 'Not one bit. I want a divorce NOW! And I want you out of this house NOW!'

It was a bad day to be late at work. Gail was steaming with fury because neither Caroline nor I turned up at the shop until midday. It was no use explaining that we both had good reasons – I was distressed because I'd just kicked out my husband, while Caroline was distressed because she was going to have to welcome her husband back. Gail saw nothing amusing in this whatsoever, and invoked powerful Gaelic saints to destroy us.

Caroline wasn't listening. The only person she was interested in communicating with was Eamonn, whom she was subjecting to fierce monologues about 'computer error'. But Eamonn wasn't listening either. He was more concerned by the fact that someone had broken into the Enterprises offices during the night and had tried to tamper with Cupid. He was sitting there shaking his head, patting the computer affectionately.

'Christ, when you think they could have exposed the love life of half the government,' he was saying.

Mercifully, he'd already taken the precaution of booby-trapping the thing, he explained; so there was no way any vital information could possibly have been stolen.

'The fockin' press – it must be,' Gail stormed.

At first she blamed Caroline for not having set the burglar alarm the previous evening. After that she blamed me for being more concerned about my own marriage than the royal one. Then she remembered that Eamonn wasn't supposed to know anything about our royal connection, and in her confusion decided to blame the entire nation for being a bunch of 'fockin' Protestant hypocrites' who deserved everything the IRA threw at them; whereupon Caroline accused her of being a menopausal Irish peasant, and Gail swept out.

Only after the storm had blown over that afternoon did I begin to panic. Was this our Watergate? Or at the very least our Waterloo? In any case, if someone was that concerned to get at our computer it must surely be because the true reason for our royal visits had leaked out. Somebody had put two and two together.

'Does it have to be the press?' I said. 'Who else is there who'd want to hack into a computer?'

'Oh, a lot of other people,' Caroline suggested. 'It could be one of our victims wanting to know more about his ideal partner. We've had some pretty rough diamonds on our books, remember.' She laughed. 'Or it could be Patrick. Christ, he'd have a shock! It could even be the Palace.'

The more we thought about it the more we decided it couldn't possibly be the press after all, because the press wouldn't be leaving us alone. They'd be round here constantly. We'd be doorstopped. The Duchess would be being pestered wherever she went. The tabloids would be full of it already. A story like that was dynamite. Princess Di's little whingeings were nothing compared to this.

So it had to be somebody else.

'For Christ's sake, what does it matter?' Caroline declared. 'It's only royalty after all.'

And that, as far as she was concerned, was that. Caroline went back to muttering about Patrick, and how insulted she felt at being his perfect woman.

None the less I hated the feeling that we were being watched, and not knowing who was doing the watching. It was like being haunted by ghosts you could never see. Every time the phone went I gave a start, imagining I would hear a deep, threatening voice. Then it would turn out to be some Sloane asking if she could bring in a Saint-Laurent dress. Life insisted on pretending to be normal.

The worst of it was that Caroline had almost finished the royal data profiling, and in a few days we'd know who the Duchess's substitute was to be – or at least we'd have a clear profile of what kind of woman was supposed to be ideal for the Prince. The countdown had already begun. I shuddered and wondered how quickly I could emigrate.

I did only one sensible thing that afternoon. I phoned Ralph at the TV station, apologised for my tantrum, and suggested he stay in the house at least until we'd had a chance to work out how and where we were going to live, all of us. That made me feel a lot better, especially when Ralph said he was sorry he'd been provocative, and it was terribly important – wasn't it? – that we should sort all this out cleanly, particularly for Rachel's sake. That was when I decided it was Ralph, not me, who had always been 'nice', and this was why I'd fallen in love with Josh, who wasn't 'nice' at all. And having put down the phone I thought of nothing but Josh for the remainder of the day. I daydreamed about where we might live, about waking up next to him each morning, curling up with him each night, making love whenever we fancied – until Rachel broke into my hot reveries by waving a piece of paper in my face and demanding who was leaving messages around the house saying, '*Sleep well, darling!*' when the handwriting wasn't either Daddy's or mine?

A used condom would at least have been possible to explain.

I was dealing with a particularly tiresome customer when Josh just walked into the shop. I froze. Then I thrust the Lanvin suit at the woman and threw myself into Josh's arms. The customer looked aggrieved. Caroline called out, 'Jesus Christ, Angela!' and Gail growled at her to shut up.

It was typical of Josh to insist on giving me surprises: I hadn't expected him back in England for two more days. He was thin and deeply sunburnt, and he looked older, as people do when they are thin. To hell with customers and Caroline – I buried my face in his neck, and his arms around me felt like the first touch of my new life. I have no idea what I said, no idea what he said. He was here: that was all. He smelt of warmth and travel.

In his flat Josh's baggage was strewn around the floor and across the furniture. Suitcases. Packages. Camera cases. Shoulder-bags. A coat. A travel wallet. He'd just dumped the lot, he explained, and hurried downstairs.

'To make sure you were still there.'

My fingers stroked his face. It felt rough and unshaven.

'*You* were the one who went away. Remember?'

I took his hands and held them against my breasts. Then I touched the long scar at the base of his neck; ran my hands under his shirt and held him to me. I wanted to laugh. I wanted to talk. I wanted to make love.

'I've got something for you,' he said with a half-smile, pushing me gently away from him. 'Something for you to wear.' He put on a serious expression. 'But I'm afraid there's a condition. You have to wear nothing else.'

He reached out and very gently began to unbutton my blouse, unhook my bra, my skirt, peel away my tights and pants, remove my shoes. He'd been back five minutes, and I was naked. Ah well! Then he unfastened my hair so that it fell over my shoulders and breasts. I was shaking. All kinds of creatures were doing a dance inside me.

Josh gazed at me for a moment before slipping one hand into his pocket and bringing out a tiny leather box. He opened it; then with his thumb and forefinger he took out a ring. He looked at me again gravely as he reached out and pulled my left hand towards him.

He slipped the ring on my wedding finger.

'Will that do?' he said quietly.

The ring was gold, set with three dark opals.

'Fire opals,' he added. 'For your fire. And mine for you.'

I looked down at the ring. Then at Josh's face. It became blurred with my tears.

'I want your fire,' I said, reaching out to touch his face. 'Now!'

I hindered him with my fingers and my lips as he undressed. Then he pulled me with him to the floor and we made love among the litter of his room.

I'd quite forgotten there was a language of silence for lovers. It filled the intimate spaces between us: such a simple language – of eyes and touch, with just occasionally a little word that broke through. Murmurs in the ear, hardly more than the sounds of breathing. 'Yes!' 'Quite sure?' 'Yes!' 'Soon?' 'Yes!' 'Good!'

Finally I raised myself on to one elbow, and ran my fingers down his stomach.

'Tell me, Josh.'

'Tell you what?'

'Anything.'

'Anything?'

'Anything!'

'It's bloody uncomfortable here on the floor.'

I laughed.

'I love you, Josh!'

'Good!'

I leant over him, and touched his lips with my fingers.

'And the only reason it's bloody uncomfortable is because you were too impatient to make for the bedroom.'

He reached up and held the weight of my breasts in his hands.

'I was hungry. Two months! ... More than two months!'

434

I searched his face.

'Promise?'

He nodded.

'And you?'

'The same. I promise.'

He put his arms round me and we lay there in silence until some distant clock struck three. The habit of being a lunchtime lover roused me, and at the same time I imagined what it would be like to be naked at night with him, always. Dipping into sleep and waking, two bodies together. Christ, I thought, I'm in love and in lust. How vulnerable, and how wonderful!

'I must go,' I said.

Josh watched me dress as he lay there among the clutter of his baggage.

'Two months, and she's leaving me already,' he said, smiling. 'Short rations.'

I bent down and kissed him.

'You shall have it all. And I need to tell you all.'

He grasped my arm as I stood up.

'How about a brief summary to be going on with?'

'OK,' I said. 'A précis of two months. Ready? Item One – Ralph and I are splitting up. Item Two – yes, please, I *do* want to live with you; as soon as possible. Item Three – I want Rachel to meet you, and I'm absolutely terrified. Item Four – all hell's about to break loose downstairs: when I tell you who our latest client is, you'll understand. Item Five – I am totally and ridiculously in love with you, and you'd better feel the same or I promise I'll kill you.

Oh! and Item Six – you'd better get some clothes on or bloody Stella Neale will walk in and decide that two affairs with you weren't enough; and then I'd kill myself as well as you.'

That afternoon and the next day Caroline divided her time between fine-tuning Cupid by royal command and castigating me for never having told her about Josh.

'Jesus, you're a snake in the grass, Angela!' she snapped. 'All these months. And you a married woman!' (That made me laugh.) 'Why didn't you say anything?'

'Because I didn't want you telling me how Josh has already had all your other girlfriends, and that I was a fool to imagine it could possibly last.'

'Well, he has!'

'Thank you, Caroline. So, now you understand.'

It was always hard to know what Caroline did understand. Like many people who put on a show of being unconventional, she was herself deeply vulnerable to convention. The revelation that she was Patrick's ideal woman had pierced right through her armour of contempt for him. I could tell this just by the sulky look of submission on her face whenever I teased her by mentioning the subject. She'd even stopped sneering about his only having four inches, which I suspected was quite untrue anyway – just as untrue as her Roman racing driver having three balls. Caroline liked to be outrageous from a position of privilege and safety. What so upset her about Josh and me was that it was for real: I was actually ending my marriage for him, uprooting myself, taking a huge risk. Caroline's risks tended to be theatrical rather than actual: there would always be someone ready to bail her out if things went badly wrong. And being quite as well-connected as Caroline meant that whatever wild enterprise she embarked on there would always be some member of her extended clan to man the lifeboat and assist her safely ashore with a vodka-and-tonic in the other hand.

'Josh *is* terribly sexy,' she acknowledged grumpily. 'Would you let me borrow him – just for one night? You'd do that for a friend, wouldn't you, Angela? After all, you can have Patrick whenever you like.' Then she laughed. 'But perhaps you wouldn't like that at all.' And she gave a sigh. 'Oh well!'

We were sitting in her garden. She was smoking cannabis, which she didn't enjoy particularly, she said. But you had to do it sometimes, didn't you? After all, it *was* illegal.

'And what about Rachel?' she went on languidly.

I said I was taking her to meet Josh tomorrow, and that I was terrified. Why was it, I added, that all the manuals on divorce told you everything you could possibly want to know except how to introduce your daughter to your new lover?

Caroline laughed.

'I've never had to do it, thank God! Except once when Samantha came back from school early and caught me in bed with my doctor. I said rather breathlessly that he was taking my pulse. I don't think she believed me.' She gazed at me thoughtfully through a haze of cannabis smoke. 'But kids are far tougher than we are,' she went on. 'We break. They bounce.'

I imagined it would take quite a lot to break Caroline.

When tomorrow came I prepared myself early for this fearful confrontation. What would I do if Rachel hated him? There was nothing in the divorce manuals on that either. Magdalena was still away, so I did the morning school run, and buttonholed Rachel's teacher to say that my daughter would have to leave at lunchtime because I was taking her to a matinée. I hoped this sounded a suitably improving reason, and at first the woman looked at me with less than her usual disapproval. But then I explained that I'd be sending a taxi for her, and the anti-middle-class face switched on immediately. The expression said, 'If you can afford that sort of thing why are you sending your daughter to a state primary school?'

I was in no mood for this kind of inverse snobbery, and said rather archly that I was a working woman, not a slave. What I didn't say was that the object of this little cultural outing was for Rachel to meet my lover and his daughter Jessica. I left the school dreading it, and practised saying, 'Rachel, this is Uncle Josh.'

Then I drove to work. It was ten-thirty by the time I got to the shop, and I found Gail frantic. Her hair was wild even by her standards, and her clothes looked as though her dream of a chicken farm in Wicklow had come true.

'Jaysus Christ, thank God you're here,' she said breathlessly.

There were only a couple of customers in the shop, quietly minding their own business, and I couldn't see why Gail should be in quite such a state.

'Just go next-door, for pity's sake,' she went on. 'It's Caroline.'

I had terrible visions. Caroline had OD'd on something and was hallucinating. She had decided to murder Patrick rather than be his ideal woman. She was being held responsible for the entire debts of Adultery Tours and was now destitute.

I dashed in through the rear entrance and up the stairs to the Enterprises office. And there was Caroline, seated perfectly calmly in front of Cupid, a cigarette in one hand and the telephone in the other. There was no sign of either Eamonn or Karen.

She glanced up when she saw me and smiled brightly, while continuing with her phone conversation between earnest drags at her cigarette.

'Cancel it, then!' I heard her say. 'You must be here! You absolutely must! No, it has to be this morning because the reception's tomorrow evening and we've got to have you looking absolutely stunning. Around midday and I'll show you everything. Then we can have lunch and I'll brief you. Tell you what to wear and all that. Masses to do. Fix a hair appointment with Nicky Clarke. Find the right outfit

. . . Yes, all right; I'll teach you to curtsy if you really feel you must . . . Good! See you then, and don't be late.'

She put the phone down and took another long drag on her cigarette before turning to me.

'Whew! Quite a morning, and it's not even eleven o'clock.'

'What on earth's happening, Caroline?' I said. 'Gail's going mad in there. And where are Eamonn and Karen?'

Caroline gave a dismissive flick of the hand.

'I've sent them off for the day. Now listen, and hold tight. Christ, I suppose it's a bit early for a drink, but I do feel like one.' She reached for the drinks cupboard, then thought better of it. 'No, I'd better be sober today.'

I sat down and looked at Caroline. She seemed extraordinarily pleased with herself, tapping her fingers on the computer, humming a little tune, enjoying keeping me on tenterhooks.

'Well!' she said, gazing about her imperiously. 'Now, tell me what you make of this. Cupid's finally done his work and come up with the Prince's ideal woman. And guess who she is.' Caroline looked at me with an impish smile on her face. 'She's a six-foot black Rastafarian!'

And she roared with laughter. I just blinked.

'And you're taking this seriously?' I said incredulously.

Caroline merely looked perplexed.

'Of course I am. How often has Cupid been wrong? Except for me, that is.'

'But . . .'

Suddenly I felt all my energies drain away. I could see no point in arguing with Caroline. If she was determined to go ahead with this wild escapade, then let it be.

But she already had gone ahead with it, she explained. She'd immediately phoned the Palace on the Duchess's private line. This was nine-thirty in the morning, and she'd got straight through. She'd put the position to her direct, and no, there'd been no problems there whatsoever, Caroline assured me. In fact the idea had gone down extremely well, especially when Caroline mentioned that a young woman who'd brought some clothes into the shop the other day, when both Gail and I were out, fitted to perfection the 'data profile' Cupid had given us. She was Jamaican, in her early twenties. Extraordinarily beautiful. A black goddess. Six foot tall at the very least. Wildly Rastafarian. The girl had come to this country to further her career as a model, but royalty would probably do instead, Caroline had said to the Duchess, rather tactlessly, she admitted with a laugh.

She paused, stretched herself out like a contented cat, and lit another cigarette.

'And, oh Angela!' Caroline went on. 'She's got such a great name. Delilah! Isn't that terrific! Can't you see it? – HRH Delilah, Duchess of . . . It really ought to be something more exotic than an English county, shouldn't it? Duchess of the Indies perhaps. She'd do wonders for the Royal Family, don't you think? Liven them up no end. Just imagine it. Break-dancing at Balmoral instead of those ghastly Scottish reels. Steel bands in Windsor Great Park. Carnivals at Sandringham. Reggae blaring out of Buck House. Marijuana everywhere. Then think of the breeding. She'd certainly warm up that thin Hanoverian blood. My God, Angela, we might even have a new Edward the Black Prince!'

The idea so delighted Caroline that the drinks cupboard now proved irresistible, and she bounded over to it to pour herself a generous vodka-and-tonic.

'Should really be Jamaican rum, shouldn't it?' she mused. 'But we haven't got any.'

Then, with her glass in her hand, she returned to her chair and sat back with an expression of the purest pleasure on her face, savouring her morning's work.

'Anyway,' she added, getting back to her story, 'I then asked the Duchess how she thought the Prince could be persuaded to meet this divine creature. Did she have any bright ideas? Well, she did! It turns out she's patron of some international basketball thing – don't ask me what. But here's the stroke of luck! A team from the West Indies is over here right now apparently, and there's a reception for them at the Savoy tomorrow night, which she was going to attend anyway. So what could be better? The Prince is a sporting sort of chap – well, he plays golf: is that very different from basketball? I suppose it is. Never mind, she'll drag him along: he'll like the free booze, she says. And who will be there flying the Jamaican flag as it were? The gorgeous Delilah, dressed to kill. With me in attendance to make the introduction.

HRH can then pick her moment to introduce the girl to her husband. You know: hands across the ocean, spirit of the Commonwealth and all that. And bingo! To hell with basketball. Cupid will have done it again – with any luck.'

Caroline was looking exceptionally pleased with herself. There was no hint in her manner that this might be something far too hot to handle. Caroline was a woman who felt she could handle anything once she put her mind to it, and in my experience of her she had yet to be proved wrong. I imagined that some of the French royal mistresses before the Revolution must have possessed the same unwavering self-assurance – Diane de Poitiers perhaps, or Madame de Pompadour: women who controlled the crown without ever wearing one. I went back into the shop thinking that my own problem of Rachel being about to meet Josh was extremely small beer by comparison, though it still felt menacingly large to me.

To my surprise Gail was now in a state of calm after the storm, and looking reflective. An unreal air of peace prevailed as the two of us dealt quietly with customers as they brought in clothes, or searched for them among the racks.

'You know, 'tis a terrible thing,' she announced when the shop was empty for a moment. 'Here am I married to a shoplifter, and me last husband was a fockin' burglar. All the same, I can't get it out of me head that there's such a thing as respect for the state of marriage, Angela; and you know, I don't think the Good Lord can be altogether happy with what we've been doing here these past months. Not happy at all!'

I must have looked astonished by this sudden confession because Gail suddenly came over and laid a reassuring hand on my shoulder.

'It's not that I blame you, darlin'. Not one bit, I promise you. We all know these things just happen, don't they? It's the way life takes you; the trouble is, it sometimes takes you where you fockin' well oughtn't to go, that's all.'

I looked at her, by now entirely puzzled.

'Why this all of a sudden, Gail?' I said.

She shrugged her shoulders and said nothing for a moment. Then she wandered over to the window and gazed pensively out into the square.

'Well, you see, I've been doing a bit of thinking – and that's a rare and precious thing to happen, I can tell you. And this is how I see it. Here we are: you're busting up with Ralph, and our Lady Caroline is doing her best to bust up with her Patrick. And all the time we're busting up everyone else's marriages as fast as we can pop the champagne corks. And yet out there in the world it's a beautiful spring day with all the leaves bursting, and the blossom and bird-song and everything.' She paused, then turned to look at me. 'And I think I may be fockin' pregnant!'

I scarcely had time to gulp before the door opened and a vision of the Queen of Sheba floated into the shop, sheathed in gold. The girl's legs, I swore, began where her navel ought to have been, and after a long journey they ended somewhere far below in a pair of platform shoes. Her hair was tugged back in a crinkled sheen into a knot through which she'd thrust a large tortoiseshell pin. The bones of her face looked as though they'd been carved round a pair of enormous dark eyes which appeared to drink in the entire room around us. You could have stood a pair of coffee-cups on her cheek-bones, and run a scaling-ladder up the column of her neck. The leggings which showed through the slits in her golden tunic were printed from toe to crutch with rampant leopards snarling upwards. She was, in short, entirely magnificent.

'Mrs Uppingham?' she asked in a voice that seemed to have been dipped in molasses.

'You must be Delilah,' I said, feeling like a fat dwarf. 'Mrs Uppingham is expecting you. You'll find her next door. Just walk in.'

I watched her. I'd seen a heron walk like that once, stalking at low tide.

'And who in God's holy name might that be?' said Gail once the girl had made her way next-door. Even thoughts of her own pregnancy seemed to have receded behind this vision of black beauty. And then suddenly her eyes widened and her mouth fell open. 'Not . . . You don't mean . . . You couldn't . . . You *could*? Oh Mary, mother of Jaysus!' And Gail raised both hands and began to run her fingers through her storm of red hair, raising her eyes towards the ceiling as if to heaven. 'Holy Mary!'

she said once more, shaking her head and lowering her hands slowly to her breast in what for a moment I took to be an attitude of prayer. But the hands continued down to her belly, folding themselves across it as if in protection of the foetus wriggling there. Then she looked at me for a moment before announcing – solemnly and appropriately – 'Well, I'll be focked!' And burst out laughing.

It was an enormous relief to do the same. And then customers began to drift into the shop again, and I still had no chance to ask her if she really was pregnant, or was just saying it because she was a couple of weeks overdue. As I brought out clothes, and went through the familiar rigmarole of chat and encouragement, I found myself thinking of the three of us – partners in what was to have been merely an up-market branch of the rag trade – and wondering which of us was in the position she would *least* have expected when we first began. There was Gail, a middle-aged professional woman, apparently finding herself about to become a mother at the age of God-knows-what. There was Caroline, who'd decided to dabble in the clothes business only because she was bored, at this very moment preparing to launch an Exocet missile into the House of Windsor. And then there was me, ex-bank clerk, ex-boutique girl, ex-celebrity's bimbo turned dutiful wife and mum, any minute now about to introduce her beloved daughter to her mother's lover.

As Gail had said – 'It's the way life takes you, and sometimes it takes you where you fockin' well oughtn't to go.'

A taxi was slowing down across the square, looking for the right address. Then I could make out Rachel in the back of it, pointing. The driver edged cautiously across the traffic, indicator flashing. I was shaking.

'It'll be all right, darlin',' Gail was saying quietly. And she put an arm round my shoulder. 'You're a great girl. You deserve to be happy. And if you're happy, so will Rachel be.'

I hugged her. I'd never realised quite how much I loved Gail.

'Christ, I hope you're right,' I mumbled, and made for the door.

I'd left Josh to buy the theatre tickets. We were going to the latest Lloyd Webber musical, which I hoped would at least smother the worst of Rachel's intimations of disaster. Josh was bringing Jessica, thank heavens: the girl was here from boarding school for the weekend, he'd explained; a final outing before GCSEs, if she could be persuaded to turn up for them. Well, at least her presence would inject a note of domestic normality into the afternoon. There we'd be – mother and daughter, father and daughter: just a cosy family outing. Would Rachel suspect it was more than that? Yes, of course she would: kids have radar for things like that. So, afterwards I would have to tell her. Oh God, if only someone could tell me how to do it.

I led Rachel into the shop. She'd only been here once before, and was looking hunched and shy. Gail led her away to show her the bins full of scarves and belts while I phoned Josh. I felt embarrassed trying to be formal. Yes, Jessica was here, he said, matching my formality; and they were coming right down. I was glad he didn't ask us up: it was bad enough Rachel meeting Josh at all, without her seeing the place where we made love.

'Are you ready, darling?' I said as calmly as I could. 'They'll be here in a second.'

I realised Rachel had never asked a single question about Josh. Did this mean she suspected nothing, or that she knew everything already? I glanced at the pretty, dark-haired miniature of me waiting by the door, and was filled with love and dread.

'Here they are,' I said.

'Enjoy yourselves!' Gail called out as I ushered Rachel outside.

Josh was beaming. Jessica was looking shabbily glamorous. I introduced them. Rachel lowered her eyes and said nothing. Oh God, did she hate them already? I gave Josh a pleading glance.

He was looking at his watch. Then his eyes met mine, and he winked.

'Now,' he said. 'How about a change of plan?'

I felt startled, and said nothing. Rachel was looking down at her feet. Jessica was tossing her hair back, and laughing – oh God, could I really cope with having a step-daughter that pretty? Josh had a teasing smile on his lips.

'Well, here's the proposition,' he said. 'It's spring. It's going to be a beautiful weekend. I have a cottage in Cornwall. Why don't we go there?' He looked down and very lightly touched Rachel's hair. 'Have you ever flown, Rachel?'

She looked bewildered, and nodded.

'Twice!' she said in a half-whisper.

'But I bet you never sat next to the pilot.'

I was feeling numb. Jessica was saying, 'It'll be great! You'll love it, Rachel.'

Suddenly I thought – what an absolutely terrific idea! I didn't even have to phone anyone. Ralph was away for the weekend, and I'd left plenty of food for Fatwa. There was nothing that need stop us. Rachel was looking at me questioningly.

'Josh has a little plane,' I explained. 'Or one he uses sometimes,' I corrected. 'He can fly us there. Would you like that?'

Rachel said nothing, and looked down at her feet again. There was an awkward silence. I didn't like to look at Josh. Then Rachel reached up and rather awkwardly pulled my head down to her level.

'Mummy,' she whispered. 'I haven't brought a toothbrush.'

I laughed with a huge sense of relief.

'Rachel's worried that she hasn't brought her tooth-brush,' I said.

Jessica bent down and tapped a small bag which I hadn't noticed by her feet.

'We thought of that,' she said. '*Two* toothbrushes. And *two* nighties!'

Rachel looked up gratefully. I could see her wondering who this guardian angel was who'd suddenly floated into her life.

'But what about all this?' she said more confidently, tugging at her uniform. 'I can't wear this horrible school stuff all weekend.'

Jessica laughed, and put an arm round the girl's shoulder.

'Look, Rachel, there's a Kids Gap near where we're going. At Newquay. It'll be open late Friday. Why don't we get you some great T-shirts and jeans? Like these!'

Jessica's own jeans were dark-blue and skin-tight, slashed at both knees and heavily frayed over her Doc Martens boots.

Rachel gazed at her, goggle-eyed. Then she looked wonderingly at me. I nodded.

'Absolutely! Why not?'

I glanced at Josh, and he winked again.

'Shall we go, then?' he said calmly. 'We should take two cars, don't you think? Then you won't have to come back here afterwards.'

I wished I could have hugged him. I hugged Jessica instead, and then Rachel. God, I felt happy! This was the way it was going to work. Oh Josh, my man of so many surprises, how I love you!

Rachel was squeezing my hand, pulling me down so she could whisper again.

'Does he really fly a plane?'

I nodded. Josh was smiling at her.

'And I'll show you how to fly it,' he said.

It was at that moment that Rachel discovered hero-worship. Well, I thought, looking at the radiant expression on my daughter's face, this has to be as good a way to begin as any.

'We'll follow you,' I said. Then, as I pointed to where our car was parked, I muttered to Josh – 'Separate bedrooms! And no loop the loop! Promise?'

He chuckled.

As we drove away into the spring afternoon I felt as though I was already being catapulted into a new life. I had no idea what would be said this weekend. Maybe nothing. Just let it be. But it was a beginning.

And perhaps it was also an end. I thought of Caroline, and the events of tomorrow evening. The West Indian reception. The plot she'd hatched with 'Debbie'. And the further London fell behind us as I drove westwards towards the little airfield, the more totally unlikely it seemed that it would have the slightest chance of working. I realised how much I'd allowed myself to become deluded by the sheer force of Caroline's self-confidence. She was like that: you went along with her, or you walked away. But this time it was clear that she had ludicrously overstretched her talents. Caroline could work wonders, but not miracles. All around me spread the timelessness of English woods and fields; and there was no more likelihood that Caroline's plot would work than that all this should turn overnight

451

into swaying palm trees rising out of a mirage of camel caravans.

No! The world – even Caroline's world – was about to return to normal. I wondered how she would accept her defeat.

14

Check Mates

———————— o ————————

The first hint that something was wrong came when I phoned Caroline. It was eight o'clock on the Sunday evening. Rachel had just passed her final judgement on our weekend – 'We *are* going to take Fatwa with us, aren't we, Mum?' – and was now snuggled in front of the TV set which I'd succumbed to installing in her bedroom. She was still refusing to part with the skin-tight jeans Jessica had so carefully slashed for her. 'Of course, darling!' I said. 'If you really want to sleep in them that's perfectly OK with me.' Anything was OK with me: after the way she'd handled the weekend I'd have allowed her to watch video films all night, play her Madonna tapes at full belt, smoke pot, or whatever else took the little angel's fancy.

'And of course we'll be taking Fatwa,' I assured her, wondering what fresh killing-fields we'd soon be providing for our vicious feline.

Then I picked up the phone and tapped out Caroline's number.

Had it been a call I didn't make very often I mightn't have noticed anything unusual. But I'd been phoning Caroline at least a couple of times a week for the past year or more, and that was why the barely audible little click puzzled me. Then there was the slightly hollow sound on the line while we spoke, as if somewhere a door had been silently opened.

At first I didn't think about it: I was far too anxious to know how the famous West Indian reception had gone on Saturday evening, and then of course to tell her all about my own triumphant weekend.

I never got that far. Caroline was high as a kite on something.

'Did it work?' she answered, shrieking down the phone. 'Of course it worked! You mean, you don't know? Don't they have Sunday papers in Cornwall, for Christ's sake?'

Then she told me. Delilah had looked absolutely devastating. Caroline had spent most of Saturday honing her skills on the girl's outfit. In the end she'd settled for a tube of a dress that hugged everything that mattered down the entire six-foot-plus of her, braiding her plaits of frizzy hair with brightly coloured ribbons and beads, and finally giving her a single huge chunk of gold bracelet such as a Roman emperor would have coveted. The dress itself was brilliant red — like a flame, Caroline assured me. A tall flame that flickered as she moved. And God, how she did move, and how it did flicker!

'And so did everyone's eyes,' Caroline added with

454

a chuckle. 'Not a man in the place gazed at anyone else, I promise you. Certainly HRH didn't. The poor bastard didn't stand a chance.'

'So what happened?' I asked, a little bewildered. 'He talked to her?'

There was a whoop on the far end of the phone.

'*Talked* to her? Darling, you must be joking. He swept her off! To hell with royal protocol: he just went – in the middle of the bloody reception. Even the Duchess seemed a bit miffed; I think she'd expected at least some display of royal reserve. Some sort of restraint. You know, hands clasped behind the back, naval style; a bit of, "How very interesting, yes, I am a little acquainted with Jamaica, what part do you come from?" Then perhaps the discreet scribbling of a phone number and on to the next royal handshake. Not a bit of it. It was paint-stripper eye-meet, and the next minute it was – off! He drove her away into the night. God knows where. Not even his bodyguard was quick enough. It was unbelievable. It all happened so fast they even managed to give the press the slip, though there wasn't a single paper this morning that didn't carry a shot of them leaving. Even the *Independent*, though of course it was on the sports page under "Basketball".' Caroline gave a raucous laugh. 'I told Debbie before I left that if he should chance to phone in she should tell him about Adultery Tours, but I'm afraid she wasn't amused.'

'You mean, they've just *gone*?' I said.

'Yup!'

'But . . .'

'There's no "but" about it. They've taken off. Vanished! Isn't it wonderful! Cupid's finest hour! Love at first sight. On both sides, what's more. You mightn't have thought a girl like Delilah would have had difficulty finding the right man up to now, would you? But it's true: she told me. Nor would you have thought she'd fall for some fart of an English royal. But she did: I could see it in her face. Instant! . . . Now, how was your weekend? Tell me.'

I didn't tell her. It had come to me suddenly what that little click on the line might have meant.

'Caroline,' I said. 'I have a feeling this phone's tapped.'

There was another snort.

'Don't be absurd, Angela! We're not in Russia. Come over and have a drink, for God's sake. I'm dying to hear about your weekend.'

I explained that I couldn't just leave Rachel, and in any case Ralph was due back very soon, and we had a ton of things to sort out.

'But it *is* all settled,' I said. I was about to add that Rachel and I were going to move in with Josh just as soon as we could find another place to live: then I thought that if the phone really was being tapped, the less said the better.

'What d'you mean, "it's all settled"?' I could hear the exasperation in Caroline's voice. 'Christ, Angela, you're such a shit not having said a thing about this. Springing it on me like that. You're a real snake in the grass. How dare you? Just like that! And now you're probably going to move to some ghastly village in Gloucestershire and leave me to rot here among all these stockbrokers and merchant bankers – like Patrick. I hate you!'

I left her to hate me, and put the phone down with a 'See you in the morning, Caroline.'

It wasn't until I'd said goodnight to Rachel and sat down with a glass of wine waiting for Ralph that I began to take in everything Caroline had said. This extraordinary story. The Queen's son just vanished into the night with a Jamaican model. The papers full of it. And now my phone being tapped – if that's what it was. But why *my* phone? In that case, Gail's and Caroline's telephones must be tapped as well. I began to feel horribly uncomfortable. It was so easy to see how paranoia overcame people – that feeling of being got at by invisible forces. And who might these invisible forces be? Then the phone went, and I jumped. It was Ralph, saying he'd be back late. That was all – just that he'd be late. We didn't owe one another explanations any longer, I realised. I didn't even ask him where he was. I didn't actually care where he was. Presumably he was with his fluffy blonde he intended to live with, so he'd announced. The one with no tits. Funny! He'd always liked mine. Oh well, so he was settling for the lesser things in life. My thoughts drifted away from Ralph. I felt lonely and exposed again. I longed to phone Josh, but if the phone was tapped . . . ! No! I musn't drag Josh in.

So I just sat there alone with my glass of wine. And

then a second glass of wine. Oh, why not? It was the right sort of evening to get pissed.

I went on thinking about the telephone. Tapped! What did that mean? Whenever I'd read about phone-tapping in the paper, it had always sounded such a childish game. All that nonsense about security risks: who could really take that kind of stuff seriously, as if we were still in a state of war, as if there were still an Iron Curtain? Why didn't men stop pretending life was like a John Le Carré novel, and grow up?

But now it was actually happening to me it didn't feel at all like a childish game. It felt threatening and extremely dangerous. Caroline may have declared this wasn't Russia, but right now it felt as though it definitely was. Russia under Brezhnev, what was more. With the Gulag Archipelago looming not far away. I felt very isolated in this house – in the dark, alone apart from Rachel upstairs. I couldn't even go and see anybody, phone anybody.

And who would be doing the tapping? Not the press, surely: they didn't have that kind of power. Or did they? But anyway it wasn't their style; they'd be milling round the house, doorstopping me every time I went out to buy a loaf of bread, thrusting microphones in my face. That was how the ratpack behaved, wasn't it? And here there wasn't a sound. Suburban slumber. The silence of gin-and-tonics.

So, who then? The Palace? No, it couldn't be! The British Royal Family wouldn't stoop to that sort of thing, however outraged they might be by Caroline's little *coup de théâtre*. No, no, no! Our royalty were upholders of decent values, even if they did make a dreadful cock-up of their marriages just like everybody else.

So . . . ? It was all most disquieting. I decided to settle my nerves with another glass of wine, then do something ordinary like put an omelette together. Yes, that was a good idea – something undemanding. It had been a long day, after all. Morning on the beach with Josh, Jessica and Rachel. Afternoon flight back from Newquay – England a carpet of spring spread out beneath the cotton-wool clouds. Then the drive back from that little airfield somewhere beyond Basingstoke.

Finally the confrontation with Rachel.

This was what I'd dreaded for so long – that worst guilt of all, betraying one's child. I'd thought of a dozen ways of avoiding it, from calling the whole thing off to breaking down in front of her in the hope that my craven tears might wash away her pain. In the end my own distress was so unbearable that I just came out with it. The relief was enormous. I knew I was telling the truth, and that I trusted Rachel to understand this, and to understand me; that it was my life as well as hers that mattered; that my happiness could embrace her; that my love was undiminished; that Ralph would always love her too.

She cried, but only a little. She'd known so much more than I could ever have guessed, the little minx. She'd observed. She'd listened. She'd drawn her own conclusions. She'd even talked about it at school, she said. Well, she announced, now she'd have two homes and two daddies, wouldn't she. *And* the elder sister she'd always longed to have had. She adored Jessica: I could see that from the start. As for Josh, she'd actually flirted with him. Jesus, I thought, rivalry begins at nine!

Thinking back on the day, I felt exhausted. How could so much have happened? Then I remembered the omelette! Yes! What should I have? Cheese? Mushrooms? Ham? I settled for cheese – which I couldn't find until I realised for some reason I'd left the dish with the farmhouse cheddar on the window sill. I reached over for it . . . and there was a face peering in the window.

I dropped the cheese and stifled a scream.

I slept appallingly. God knows what time Ralph came back. Rachel went off to school, her eyes full of dire and vivid stories to tell: she'd be the heroine today. Leaving Ralph to sleep, I took the bus in to work. I wanted most of all to be with people – ordinary people. I wanted to feel I was one of them. I even wished someone would talk to me, chatter away about banal and boring things – their dogs, their grandchildren, anything at all. Even their illnesses would have been a comfort this morning. But no one did. I couldn't help wondering if someone on the bus was perhaps there to watch me, and I carefully looked around to see who it might possibly be. There was one pasty young executive in an Armani suit who I convinced myself was the most likely candidate. But then he got out near Chelsea Town Hall and walked briskly away.

I reminded myself that in any case private eyes never looked like private eyes, so it might be anybody – even the slob up in front who was picking his nose behind the *Daily Mail*. Even so, I felt a lot calmer by the time I got off the bus at Sloane Square. I began to tell myself that yesterday evening I'd been thoroughly overwrought. Christ, how often does a woman fly off to Cornwall in a private plane with her daughter, her lover, his daughter and a colossal secret that's about to be revealed possibly with cataclysmic results? And then half a bottle of wine. No wonder I'd started to imagine things. Perhaps the man in the window just happened to be passing along the pavement and glanced in at that moment. As for this whole business of Delilah and HRH, it was entirely Caroline's business, I reminded myself. If the Queen's son really had gone into hiding with a Rastafarian model, it was nothing whatsoever to do with me. Caroline had set it up: let Caroline deal with it.

I felt better. It was a glorious morning scented with early summer. I thought of Josh, and felt a wave of relief that in Cornwall I'd been able to tell him everything that had been happening with Pastures New in the months he'd been away. We'd shed the children for an hour and were walking along the headland, just the two of us. Josh had listened without saying a thing until I got to the story of HRH and Delilah; then a look of amused disbelief began to spread across his face. 'Why did I ever think you were just a nice girl who sold second-hand clothes?' he said. And he chuckled. 'Pastures New, eh! And was that how you managed to shed Ralph too?' I shook my head and explained that Ralph had leapt the fence all on his own. Josh gazed at me, and his expression changed. I wondered what thoughts were going through his head. Then he placed his hands on my shoulders. 'Rachel's going to be all right, you know,' he said very seriously.

I loved him for saying that.

And right now he'd be driving Jessica back to boarding school. He wouldn't be returning till tomorrow, he said: there were a number of things he needed to do out of town. How I could have done with seeing him today, to tell him how much I loved him, tell him about my conversation with Rachel, tell him that everything was going to be all right just as he'd predicted.

As I turned into Pimlico Square I glanced across to see if his car might still be there. But it wasn't. I looked at my watch. It was half past nine. How did I manage to be so punctual in the midst of all this?

I stepped on to the zebra crossing – and as I did so the blare of a car-horn made me leap back, and a car shot by within a foot of me. I caught the briefest glimpse of the driver – a woman – who was waving her arms about like a tic-tac man at a racecourse. I yelled out, 'Bloody idiot!' but my words were drowned by two, three, four other cars screeching past in pursuit. I felt quite shaken: I could have been dead. To my astonishment, the first car swung violently to the left, mounted the pavement, and drove straight across the island in the middle of the square, taking with it a traffic bollard, several pots of geraniums and the lower portion of a men's lavatory. Then it spun to a halt more or less outside the shop. It wasn't until then that I recognised Caroline's dark-blue Mercedes. Suddenly the pursuing cars, which had taken a more conventional route round the square, were surrounding it – on the pavement, on double yellow lines, double-parked, wedged between other cars. Men were leaping out with notebooks, microphones, cameras, dragging cables, running, shouting – 'Mrs Uppingham! Mrs Uppingham!'

Caroline was too quick for them. I saw her vault out of her car and in three paces she'd barged into the shop, flinging, 'Fuck off!' over her shoulder. She bolted the door, and the ratpack was left baying outside, banging on the window – 'Mrs Uppingham! Mrs Uppingham!'

Perplexed and still somewhat shocked, I made a cautious detour round the square to keep well clear of the pandemonium, then slipped unobtrusively down the side passage and let myself in via the rear entrance to the shop. Gail was standing by the coffee machine looking bewildered, one hand on her belly. There was no sign of Caroline.

'Mary, mother of Jaysus!' she said when she saw me. 'What a day to be having a pregnancy test. To be sure it'll be a miscarriage or triplets after this, darlin'.' She smiled grimly. '*And* I've had a fockin' phone call from Conor. He knows the full story, he says. Knows perfectly well Debbie didn't come here for second-hand clothes. Knows we helped fix the whole thing with that Rastafarian lamp-post. But he won't publish it, he says, on one condition – that we let him have access to all the other stuff we've got stored away in Cupid. The dirt on just about everybody who matters. Oh Jaysus, can you imagine? What are we going to do? We're done for either way. Angela, this was *not* what I came to work with you for. I'm off back to Ireland, I tell you.'

As she said this there was a violent banging on the door. I looked round and saw the diminutive figure of Rick standing on the pavement with his back to the shop. He was half crouched in a boxer's stance, legs apart, and fending off the encroaching ratpack with an iron bar as if he were Horatius guarding the bridge; and every now and then swinging round to batter on the door for us to let him in.

'He's come to take me to the fockin' hospital,' said Gail helplessly. 'Jaysus, here I am, pregnant for the first time at forty-three, and look what happens. I don't think the good Lord can be intending me to be a mother. Perhaps I should just take the gin and forget it.'

I let Rick in and swiftly relocked the door. Photographers flashed their cameras at me as I did so, and voices yelled out, 'Where's Mrs Uppingham? Mrs Uppingham? What about a statement?'

There was still no sign of Caroline. Beyond the jostle of reporters two policemen were gazing with curiosity at the geraniums, the shattered bollard and the portion of men's lavatory still draped across her car.

I found her seated comfortably in an armchair in the Enterprises office looking extraordinarily pleased with herself, an assortment of newspapers spread around her. A couple of headlines caught my eye – 'HRH AWOL!', 'Black Magic! Prince vanishes!' Caroline herself was gazing at one of the tabloids which showed the Prince shouldering his way out of the Savoy reception with the gorgeous Delilah on his arm. And there just behind the girl was Caroline, smiling triumphantly. Even if no one had seen her step out of a taxi with this flame-coloured vision, which a great many had, that expression of triumph alone would have told the world that the Hon Mrs Caroline Uppingham held the key to this latest and biggest royal scandal. No wonder the press had leapt on her.

'Yes, they were on my doorstep this morning,' she announced airily, 'making a ridiculous amount of fuss. I merely told them the Duchess was a sort of friend, and that I'd gone to this West Indian reception at her request, not being particularly interested in basketball myself. And that I'd taken this girl Delilah, who's West Indian after all, and tall as any basketball player what's more, and that she'd been introduced to the Prince. That's all. But the press seem to think that *isn't* all; that somehow I must know where they've gone – which I don't. How could I? It's all very silly really. Haven't they got anything better to do?'

She looked entirely unperturbed, as though this were

some small misunderstanding which a little common-sense would very soon sort out. Or perhaps a quiet word with some well-placed member of the Uppingham clan might do the trick.

'It's all thoroughly tiresome,' she added. 'Not what one expects. Pursuing me like this. No manners.'

I said I thought it was a great deal more than just tiresome. I reminded her that she had after all just helped create the biggest royal scandal since the abdication of Edward VIII: the Queen's son, third or fourth or whatever-he-was in line to the throne, doing a bunk and certainly a bonk with some beautiful Jamaican model he'd only met five minutes before.

'Caroline,' I said. 'This is serious! This is not a game! Don't you understand? This could rock the Commonwealth, it could bring down the monarchy.'

Caroline seemed unimpressed.

'Oh, I expect we could find another one,' she said languidly. 'There are plenty around. I could ask Juan Carlos. I rather like him, and he's probably got a spare son tucked away somewhere.'

Now she was becoming thoroughly exasperating. Meanwhile, I pointed out, all these pressmen were battering at our door.

'Look, Caroline,' I said. 'I think maybe you should issue a statement. That's what they want. Then maybe they'll go away.'

Her eyes brightened.

'A statement! Oh yes! You always did have such

466

good ideas, Angela. But I think I need a drink first.' She reached over to the cabinet and without even needing to look grasped a bottle of vodka. 'For the nerves, you know,' she added, laughing as she poured out a half-tumblerful and topped it up with tonic and a lump of ice. 'Oh, by the way, I sent Eamonn and Karen away till this afternoon. Could do without them on a morning like this. Now! My statement! What shall I say?'

She looked thoughtful for a moment. Then – 'Well!' she said buoyantly. 'I could give them a bit of my philosophy of life, couldn't I. What I really think. They might like that. I could tell them that all this royal marriage thing is a load of garbage really. That the royals are no different from us once they've got their clothes off: they all want a good fuck, don't they, just like me, which is why I should never have married Patrick, and no doubt our Duchess Debbie should never have married HRH for the same reason; so it's no wonder she's only too happy to unload him on to someone else, and no wonder he couldn't wait to get the knickers off that gorgeous Jamaican girl. What man with balls wouldn't? I don't see anything wrong in that at all: it's perfectly healthy male rutting and we all ought to thank God the royals are still capable of getting it up, unlike quite a lot of men one meets socially nowadays. Shrivelled little things! Don't even know what sex they are, half of them.'

Caroline looked pleased with herself, and with her vodka.

'D'you think that's the sort of thing the press would like to hear, Angela? Tell me honestly.'

I said it might be best after all if she said nothing to the press whatever. Caroline looked disappointed.

'Well,' she went on, 'I suppose the only thing that really matters is that no one should know we fixed the whole thing up with the help of our little friend here.'

And she gave Cupid a friendly tap with her vodka glass. I gave Caroline a serious look.

'One of them does know,' I explained. 'Our friend Conor. And he's offering a none-too-gentle form of blackmail not to publish.'

For the first time Caroline looked genuinely alarmed.

'Shit!' she said. 'What kind of blackmail?'

I told her about Conor's phone call to Gail, and the condition that he have access to everything stored away in Cupid. Caroline fell silent. Then her face became set, and her eyes fierce.

'He shall not have it,' she said vehemently. And she let out one of her snorts. 'Christ Almighty!' she went on. 'Just think what's hidden away inside this little fellow.' And she gave Cupid a more vigorous tap with her glass. 'The private sex lives of three government ministers, at least twenty other MPs, eight judges, most of the top brass of the BBC, half the City, two bishops, one archbishop. Not to mention all those intimate revelations about HRH and the Duchess.' she paused. Suddenly she looked horrified. 'And what about all that stuff about

Patrick not enjoying fellatio and only having four inches. And *me*! All those terribly confidential things about *me*! Oh God, no! No! No! No! Over my dead body will that dreadful little fart get his hands on any of this lot!' Her eyes narrowed, and her mouth became set. 'I'll fix that little shit. I don't know how, Angela, but I will.'

I left Caroline to her storm of indignation and went back into the shop to see how Gail and Rick were surviving the siege. The hospital visit had been postponed until there was a chance of getting out undetected, she explained gloomily. Meanwhile she'd placed a *'Closed'* notice in the window. Many of the reporters had taken themselves off, I noticed, though a few of them still lingered, wandering up and down the pavement smoking and looking bored. The phone had been ringing continually, Gail said, until she just left it off the hook.

'To hell with everybody. What a way to run a fockin' business,' she grumbled. 'And what a day to be pregnant.'

Then we sat down and tried to think what to do next.

Out of curiosity we turned on the radio from time to time. Each news report began with the alarming disappearance of the Prince, though BBC News soft-pedalled the fact that he'd disappeared in the company of a certain mysterious lady. She was variously described as a personal friend of the British High Commissioner in Jamaica, a delegate to the International Council of Churches, and a celebrated basketball coach – as if any of these labels explained perfectly satisfactorily her disappearance with the Queen's son for what was now thirty-six hours, or more significantly, as Rick pointed out, two whole nights. The commercial radio stations entered into the spirit of the royal drama with far greater imagination and gusto: they dwelt glowingly on the woman's beauty and exotic allure, pointing out that the Prince wasn't the only member of the Royal Family to feel the call of the Caribbean, and suggesting that even as we spoke the eloping couple were likely to be wallowing in the emerald waters of Mustique, dressed happily as nature intended.

But the prize went to French radio, which we picked up by pure chance around midday. They had evidence, they claimed, that the girl was not Jamaican at all, but from Haiti, and that the disappearance of the Queen's son could easily be explained by anyone with first-hand experience of voodoo. It was well known that people were always disappearing in Haiti. Furthermore, it was no coincidence that the girl's name was Delilah. The British would do well to learn a lesson or two from the Old Testament, and in particular Her Majesty should brace herself for the likelihood that her son would return with considerably less of a head of hair than before. Not that this should be any cause for alarm, the reporter emphasised, since the Prince would then be on equal terms with other male members of the British Royal Family.

'Disgraceful!' Gail muttered angrily. 'No sense of respect at all, the fockin' frogs.'

If Gail's republicanism was vulnerable to a royal handshake, it was doubly vulnerable to any adverse comment by the French, whom she loathed and despised with a passion, having once taken the hovercraft to Boulogne.

It felt peculiarly unreal being on the launching-pad of such a global missile when absolutely nothing was happening here at all. By one o'clock the last pressmen had melted away and we cautiously put the phone back on the hook. And still nothing happened. I decided I would venture out to get some pasta salad from Renato. Gail declared she was tired of waiting to be told whether she was pregnant or not, and 'to hell with the fockin' hospital'. Rick, who'd been fluttering around her with great solicitude all morning, announced that in that case he was going off to the chemist to buy a pregnancy self-testing pack which Gail could put to use here in our loo. He returned a quarter of an hour later clutching a paper-bag from Boots, and accompanied by Eamonn and Karen whom he'd found disconsolately sitting in a coffee-bar much mystified by the goings-on they'd been witnessing from across the square. They looked around them suspiciously, then took themselves off to the Enterprises office, from which Caroline still hadn't emerged.

Soon customers began to drift into the shop, and the afternoon took on an uneasy air of normality.

Then around three o'clock the phone rang. I answered it and heard the receiver on the other end being put down immediately. The same thing happened twenty minutes later. Dead phone calls always rattle me: suddenly I was reminded of all my fears of yesterday evening, which the chaotic events of the morning had pushed to the back of my mind.

I decided I must tell Rick about my suspicions of phone tapping. It was hardly the ideal moment since he was busy poring over the instructions on the pregnancy testing pack and trying to persuade Gail to take herself off to the loo. But instead of dismissing my fears as paranoia, as I assumed he would, Rick put down the pack and gave me a sharp weasel look.

'You could be right, sweetheart – considering what's 'appened,' he said. 'You could very well be right.' He glanced at the telephone; then it was as though an inner light began to shine in his eyes as they flickered round the shop. 'And let's suppose you are. After all, we know someone broke in and tried to 'ack into the computer the other night, don't we? And it wasn't the bloody milkman, was it?' Rick's eyes were still roving like little gimlets, fixing on the racks, on the clothes displayed in the window, on the wall-lights, the till, the chairs, on Torquemada. The solitary customer in the shop began to look agitated, and left without a word, glancing back nervously as she closed the door. 'And if you *are* right, sweetheart,' he went on, 'whoever the fucker is may not 'ave stopped at phone-tapping.'

With that he began to bound about the place, disappearing among the gowns and dresses, running his hands along the skirting-board and round the light-fittings, standing on chairs, getting down on all fours. I had absolutely no idea what was going on and looked uneasily at Gail, who had been left standing in the middle of the shop clutching the pregnancy pack.

'What the fock are you doing, Rick?' she called out. 'D'you want me to take this thing or not? Jaysus, it says I've got to pee into something. Into what? Tell me! You're the fockin' father after all.'

But Rick wasn't listening. He was continuing to act like a caged wolf, and all the time making soft whistling noises between his teeth.

Suddenly the whistling stopped, to be replaced by a loud 'Huh!' There was a rustle of dresses on one of the racks and Rick emerged with a triumphant expression on his face and holding out a tiny object in the palm of his hand.

'You *were* right, Angela! Bloody right!' And he slapped the object down on the desk in front of us. 'Tapped and bugged!' He gazed furtively about him again. 'And now the question is – 'ow many more of the little bastards are there?'

For a moment I thought – can this be real? Is this actually happening to me? And then Rick found another, and another, and another. He kept returning like a retriever and laying them before us. I looked at them – tiny microphones with the wires ripped out of them. Who could have put them here, and when?

What was particularly chilling was that none of us

had suspected a thing. Nothing in the shop appeared to have been touched or moved.

'Yeah, that's exactly it,' Rick said. 'A professional job. That's 'ow they work.' Then he added with a note of pride – 'I've installed a few of them meself in me time.'

'Yes, and you *did* time as a result,' Gail muttered, peering with distaste at one of the tiny microphones.

Rick ignored her.

'Look, sweetheart,' he said turning to me. 'Yer in deep trouble 'ere.'

'Well, tell me!' I said, feeling my stomach contract violently. I realised I was looking pleadingly at Rick, begging him to tell me how the hell to get out of this mess. 'Who is it?' I stuttered. 'Who's doing this? The Palace? It can't be, can it? Just because of . . . because of . . . that girl and . . .'

Rick gave an unpleasant laugh.

'Because of what's in that cosy little machine of yours next door. That's why. It's a bloody H-bomb, ain't it! Listen, sweetheart' – and Rick leaned forward and jabbed his sharp face to within a foot of mine – 'You may think that just because the royals smile a lot and wave their 'ands about they can't play it dirty. Well, let me put you wise, darlin'. They can be utterly fuckin' ruthless if it suits 'em, and I reckon it suits 'em right now. Oh, it'll all 'ave been done decent and proper. Just a wink and a nod to one of the private detectives. Next thing yer know it's Special Branch on the blower to a few mates, all unofficial like – "fifty grand for you in this – OK?" Well, of course it's OK. There's agencies just waiting for this sort o' black-bag job. All ex-M15, ex-MI6, ex-CIA, ex-SAS, ex-KGB as well nowadays.' Rick tapped his forehead knowingly. 'I've been around all that, I can tell yer. Thieves in the night, they are. Real pros. Mind you, if they're caught – well, the Palace know nothin' about it, do they? Course not!'

I had a deeply unpleasant feeling of helplessness. It was as though someone had jumped aboard my life and hijacked it.

It was Gail who came to the rescue. I don't believe she'd been more than half listening: she was still fingering one of the little microphones, and holding the pregnancy pack distastefully in the other hand.

'Rick,' she announced ferociously. 'If you think I'm going to pee into some wine-glass in our loo when it's certainly been bugged so the whole of Buckingham Palace can hear the sound of me pissing, you've got another fockin' thought coming.'

Caroline, who'd emerged from the Enterprises office and had been standing quietly at the back of the shop all this time, vodka glass in one hand, looked across at Gail and smiled.

'Oh, that's no problem,' she said calmly. 'Patrick told me how when the Queen goes to a City function someone's always detailed to line the loo with tissue paper so no one can hear the royal tinkle. You could do the same.'

Gail looked cross, then suddenly grateful. She

grabbed a box of Kleenex and strode purposefully towards the stairs. Caroline nonchalantly handed her the vodka glass as she passed.

'Here! You'd better take this.'

Gail looked at it bleakly.

'Right!' she exclaimed. 'The moment of fockin' truth. How'll I know if it's twins?'

But Rick was paying no attention. His brow was creased into a deep frown, and the weasel eyes were still flickering round the shop.

'Sweetheart!' he said, turning to me. 'The first thing we gotta do is get that bleedin' computer out of 'ere before whoever it is breaks in again and this time nicks it good an' proper.'

And before Caroline or I had a chance to say a word he was down the back stairs making for the Enterprises office. We heard the door slam and the sound of hurried footsteps next door.

'You mean he's making off with Cupid?' said Caroline, looking horrified. 'Just like that? With the true confessions of half the ruling establishment of this country on board, not to mention the tender secrets of my life? For Christ's sake, Angela – where to?'

'Pastures new!' I suggested, managing a smile. 'That's what we advertised after all.'

I added that if anyone knew where to find a safe house, I was quite sure Rick did. Caroline began to look a little placated. Then we both of us heard faint sounds from below stairs: soft moans, followed by – 'Holy Mary, how the devil am I supposed to pee to order? I'm bursting a fockin' blood-vessel down here.'

I glanced out of the shop window in time to see Rick and Eamonn sliding our computer into the back of Rick's van. Then he drove off round the square and past the church until the van become swallowed up in the afternoon traffic. I heaved a sigh of relief. Now at least if the heavies broke in tonight they'd find nothing except racks of clothes and a machine to make themselves coffee if they wished. Perhaps our nightmare was over. I blessed Rick, thought of all the things I'd be telling Josh tomorrow, and wondered how Gail was getting on with the pregnancy test downstairs. She must have been there ages. Was it really that difficult to pee?

It seemed no more than a minute or two before the door burst open and Rick almost fell into the shop. His jacket was torn, and a trickle of blood oozed from his left eyebrow. Caroline and I both hurried over to help him. He was gasping.

'Bastards!' was all he could say. 'Bastards!' He was shaking his head and dabbing his eyebrow with an already bloodstained handkerchief. Then he slammed his foot violently on the floor and shot a furious glance in the direction of the street outside. 'Christ, *I'm* supposed to be the one that lifts things. I'm disgraced! Dishonoured! Fuck them! It's gone! The computer's gone! They rammed the van. Drove off. Bastards! Fucking bastards!'

We sat Rick down and washed the blood off his face. He was breathing heavily like a boxer in his corner, clenching and unclenching his fists. Neither Caroline nor I said anything for a while. So this was the end of the road. Outfit Enterprises had gone. Everything. And to my surprise I didn't care any more. It was almost with relief that I said to Caroline – 'Well! So they've got what they want.'

Caroline gazed at me for a moment and began to laugh. She went on laughing, turning away from us and doing a little dance across the floor until she reached the racks of clothes and threw her arms round them, still laughing.

'No!' she gasped. 'No! They haven't! They haven't at all.' She shook her head until the blonde hair fell all over her face. Then she tossed her hair back and gazed at Rick and me with a look of absolute triumph. 'You see,' she went on, her voice still trembling with laughter, 'when you told me about Conor this morning I knew I had to do something. I wasn't bloody well going to let him have Cupid. And then Eamonn came in and I told him he simply had to do something. Well, he did! Brilliant!' She just looked at first one of us, then the other, her eyes gleaming. 'Angela, we booby-trapped it!' And she raised both hands as if acknowledging the applause of the crowd. 'Without the password, my darlings, anyone trying to hack into it will find everything on the screen suddenly turns to complete gobbledegook. And then it all vanishes. Every single thing! Cupid's wiped. Empty. All our records gone.' She paused, and a look of childlike joy came over her face. 'Except one little phrase I got Eamonn to put

in. It'll come up on a blank screen in big bold letters —
"Heir today. Gone tomorrow?"'

'Let's face it,' she added with a mischievous laugh,
'after one triumph you never know who at the Palace
may wish to consult us next, do you?'

Oh, Caroline! was all I could think. Then, in the
stunned silence of the empty shop, Gail timed her
entrance well. She emerged at the top of the stairs
holding a glass in front of her as if it were a chalice.
Floating in the liquid was a reddish-orange blob.

'Well!' she announced. 'Either I'm bleedin' to death.
Or it's Caroline's vodka. Or I'm fockin' pregnant.'

'Can we really afford it, Josh?' I asked.

We were standing in the empty space that would
become our bedroom. Josh was looking dubious, hands
thrust into his trouser pockets.

'Probably not . . . But I don't imagine that'll stop
us. I'll just have to take on lots more jobs photographing
naked models while you go out to work in Marks &
Spencer's.'

'But it *is* beautiful,' I insisted. 'I always dreamed of
having a house on the river. And it *is* incredibly convenient
for Rachel's school. Are you listening, Josh, or are you just
panicking? And by the way' — I put my arm through his
and pulled him towards me — 'the only woman you're
going to be allowed to photograph naked from now on
is *me*. And also by the way, whatever happened to that
book you wanted to photograph me for?'

'Oh, did I?' he said, still not looking at me. 'That was only to get you into bed.'

'Swine!'

'I know. But it worked.'

We did our rough calculations, seated on the bare floorboards with a scrap of paper between us. We wrote down so much for Josh's flat – with any luck. So much for a half-share of my house – though I was tempted to ask for more since Ralph was moving into Heather Claridge's mansion; at least it sounded like a mansion, the jammy bugger. That left a short-fall of – Jesus, could we possibly afford a mortgage that big?

'Probably not,' Josh said again. And this time he laughed.

We always had two fail-safes. There was the cottage in Cornwall, which Josh loved, and I knew I very soon could. Then there was what I might be able to get for The Outfit, which was my nest-egg back again, and which I wanted to keep for whatever I decided to do next with my life. *Not* the rag trade ever again: that was certain. And nothing whatever to do with computers, or coffee-machines, or anything that might encourage wives to weep about their dreadful husbands. And nothing – though I would always love her – ever to do with Caroline.

Her announcement had been as spontaneous and casual as all the other decisions I'd known her make. She was bored, she said. Life after Cupid didn't seem interesting any more. She thought she might take a holiday.

A cruise perhaps. Adultery Tours could always fit her in. The only problem was whether to take Patrick. Now she was his perfect woman it seemed only fair. On the other hand, how could one go on an Adultery Tour with one's husband? Perhaps they should get divorced quickly and start again. Meanwhile she felt overwrought. It wasn't so much the harassment from the press and the Palace heavies; it was more the public adulation that had come her way now that the Prince and Delilah were happily ensconced in Buckingham Palace, and the archbishop (not the one Cupid had helped so satisfactorily) was being most co-operative about the divorce. It had all been a bit much for her, Caroline complained: now she couldn't sleep without tranquillisers; in fact she couldn't get up without tranquillisers. So she wouldn't be coming to the shop any more, she announced. Then she embraced Gail warmly, said please could she be godmother, and wandered away towards the door chanting gently to herself to the tune of a well-known hymn – 'She who would valium'd be, 'gainst all disaster.'

And that was it. She invited us to a farewell lunch with white truffles at Renato's; then, after dropping a pile of parking tickets into the waste-bin, drove away.

Gail and I managed the shop together for the remainder of the week. Karen had already departed, taking Eamonn's eyes with her. Eamonn himself remained for several days, in deep mourning for her mini-skirts, but more particularly for Cupid, whose empty space he would gaze at with the sadness of a lost lover. But by Wednesday his computerless life proved intolerable, and he ambled into the shop at mid-morning to announce that, after having programmed other people's Pastures New for so many months, he must now find his own.

That same afternoon Rick parked his van at the rear of the shop and began to unload half-a-dozen crates of Pampers, several cases of baby lotion and three Moses baskets. 'Just for an hour or so, sweetheart,' he explained, 'while I go and do over Mothercare.'

The following morning Gail arrived late to explain that the doctor at the pre-natal clinic had advised her to give up work, otherwise the baby would be at risk. It was sad, she said. She would miss me. She would even miss Caroline. It had been a wonderful time. How would I manage? I side-stepped the question and asked her how *she* would manage without the income from the shop. She shrugged and said that Rick was a wonderfully loving husband who would never let her down. He was so much better at his job than her previous husband, who had only managed to end up in jail. There was always work for a good shoplifter. I mustn't worry: she'd be all right.

That was Thursday. On Friday morning – the day before Josh and I went to look at the house on the river – I collected up our account books and called in on Messrs Anstruther and Pratt. Mr Anstruther, whom the recession had thinned down a little, was polite enough to have forgotten our previous encounter when Caroline had presented him with the used condom she'd found in our basement. He smiled cheerfully at me. Property prices had picked up, he said; I should make a fairly decent profit, especially since I was offering a flourishing business – and he could see from our books that ours had indeed flourished. And two adjacent premises was always an attraction. He had one client in particular who he was certain would be most interested. He would ring me to fix an appointment.

And if he's right, I told myself, then some of that profit will go to Gail. I could have done nothing without her – nothing at all.

'I'm going to give up the shop,' I said to Rachel that evening. 'And tomorrow I'm going to look at a new place for us to live.'

She gazed at me with large eyes, blinking away the tears. I fought off a longing to bribe her – 'You'll have an even nicer room; you can see Daddy as often as you like; you'll be just as near all your friends; you'll see a lot more of Jessica – you'd like that, wouldn't you? We could have a puppy if you want.' I just hugged her instead. She sniffed.

'Will Josh take us up in his plane again soon?'

I nodded gratefully. At least the bribe was her choice.

I told Josh what she'd said, and he smiled.

'*You* were scared about Rachel. What about me?'

I realised I'd never thought about that. And I kissed him. He put his arm round me and we made a final tour of the empty house. Our bedroom. Jessica's. Rachel's. Josh's studio. A snuggery for me. Sitting room opening on to the garden. Kitchen – Jesus! Whoever lived here must have hated food.

'According to the estate agent they hated each other,' Josh added. 'You don't suppose their names were Gary and Debbie?'

The client would be at the shop at eleven, Mr Anstruther explained portentously. It was a woman, he added, his tone of voice making it clear this meant she'd certainly be late – unlike me, of course; I was an honorary man, being successful. Patronising bastard!

I was on my own. It felt like the day after a long party, the shop suddenly empty, hollow. Even the racks were half bare. I hadn't been taking in any new clothes, and gradually our stock was diminishing. My eye fell on one of Dante Horowitz's cobwebs, and I thought of the evening I'd put it on for Josh. Perhaps I should take it with me after all, just in case Josh got too excited photographing some little stick-insect with Bambi eyes.

It was ten-thirty. I wandered into the Enterprises office, now even emptier than the shop. It was hard to imagine the place as the scene of so many marital dramas and fruitful rematches: hard to believe that a palace revolution within the House of Windsor had been hatched here – as hard as it would be, I imagined, to sit in a Zurich café and tell oneself that at these tables Lenin had plotted the Bolshevik Revolution. And even though we'd boasted no Lenin in Pimlico Square, we did have one feckless lady of ruthless common-sense who even now was floating across the eastern Mediterranean in the company of a husband equipped with four inches or possibly a racing driver equipped with three balls – Caroline hadn't been prepared to say which.

I was still musing on these far-off themes when there was a loud thump on the door, and I looked up to see two well-dressed young men gesturing through the window, one of them carrying before him a large box. Puzzled, I went over and unlocked the door.

'For Mrs Uppingham!' said the one carrying the package.

I explained that I was Mrs Uppingham's partner, whereupon the second man simply thrust me a piece of paper and a biro.

'Just sign here, madam, if you will – where it says "Received".'

Still mystified, I did as I was told.

'Would you like us to carry it in for you?' said the first man.

I indicated that he could put it anywhere he liked on the empty floor, and thanked him. Then without a further word, the two of them left.

I gazed at the box. There was no label on it. Nothing at all. Could it be a gift of wine, perhaps? Some admirer of Caroline's? A grateful client back from his Adultery Tour? No, it was far too bulky. And why no label? But there didn't seem to be any point just leaving it here; and since Caroline was several thousand miles away, and gone for heaven knew how long, I began to prise open the box.

Just one thing was inside. It was Cupid!

There was no sign of the two men. And no message. I just stood there, too bewildered to think. I walked round it, wondering if this might be some sort of trick. Perhaps it was timed to explode, or a live python might be concealed inside it. I wished Eamonn were here. Or Rick. In the end I plucked up courage, removed the computer from its box and placed it where it had always been, on the small table over by the wall.

As I gazed at the familiar little machine there was a ring on the doorbell next door. I hurried down the back staircase and up into the shop, and saw a young woman peering through the window. It was almost eleven o'clock; presumably this must be my client – my potential buyer. I smiled as I opened the door. We shook hands. She seemed about my age, perhaps a little older: smartly dressed, with long dark hair and large éyes set rather widely apart, and more or less exactly my height. In fact, she looked disturbingly like me altogether.

She introduced herself. She was nervous, eager, full of questions. How did we obtain the clothes? How did we price them? How did we find customers? Would I be prepared to pass on my lists of names and addresses? Any other help and advice would be enormously welcome. This was exactly the kind of business she'd been dreaming of, she said excitedly. Her children were at school now, she explained; she had a little nest-egg of her own, an inheritance from her parents, and she felt it was time to do something positive with it. Being just a housewife and mother wasn't enough; didn't I agree? And in a place like this she'd feel independent, be her own boss, meet so many people, learn so much.

'It's where you learn about life, I can tell you,' I said, only realising after I'd uttered them that these were the very words Gail had used on our very first meeting at Caroline's garage sale.

I smiled, and pointed at Torquemada.

'That espresso machine may look old, but I promise you it makes the best coffee in London. You'll find customers like to chat a bit over a cup of coffee. It's not like an ordinary shop; they don't just come in to buy clothes and walk out again.'

She said she liked the sound of that. And the smell of good coffee added something to a place, didn't it? I agreed, and led her next door.

'We used this as an office,' I explained. 'Where one can be comfortable, and private. Sometimes one gets to know one's customers very well. The drinks cupboard can be useful too. And of course,' I added, pointing to the computer, 'we kept all our records here.'

'Oh, a computer!' she exclaimed. 'I've never used one.'

'Well, it's yours if you want it,' I said.

She looked bewildered with gratitude.

'How wonderful! How very kind! D'you think I'd ever learn how to work it?'

'Of course!' I said. 'It's straightforward once you get the hang of it.'

And with a sudden pang of nostalgia I plugged Cupid into the power socket and turned it on for what I knew would be the last time. I felt sad: it was like saying goodbye to an old friend with whom I'd shared so much. It was hard to think of Cupid now as just another computer, filled with nothing.

'I'll show you! You start with simply a blank screen,' I said. 'See!'

But the screen wasn't blank. Bold letters began to form themselves before our eyes, curling elegantly across the screen as if an invisible hand were inscribing them there.

'Up Yours, Uppingham! Windsor.'